D1825087

# The Wind Guardian

# The Wind Guardian

*Frank Scozzari*

Published 2015 by Creativia

Book design by Creativia (www.creativia.org)

Cover art by http://www.thecovercollection.com/

fgscozzari@yahoo.com

# Prologue

The shadows of the two lovers danced awkwardly on the bedroom wall. Their images projected like giants, stretching halfway across the ceiling. On the nightstand by the bed was a clock radio blaring out the classic Rolling Stones tune, *Sympathy for the Devil*. And there, on the bed, beneath a woman ten years younger, lay Jack Garner. The woman, straddling above him with palms pressed against his chest, rolled her hips in rhythm with the music.

Jack turned and looked over at the clock.

The blue digital numbers read: 8:30 p.m. He smiled.

*Plenty of time*, he thought.

The young woman was not pleased by his distraction. She reached down with her hands, turned his head back toward hers, and stared down at him wrathfully. In a single motion, she rolled and pulled Jack on top of her, and with her arms snaking up behind his neck, she pulled him down against her bare body. Rolling again, she came back on top, straddling once more, and she kissed him deeply.

Outside the bedroom window, dusk settled over the small coastal community of San Roque. Like every other California beach town, it had the typical storefronts which lined its beach promenade, known as *Front Street*. The cafés, which were most active during the summer months, were idle now. Beyond the promenade were the roof-tops of many apartment complexes, and further out were the vibrant green coastal hills, soon to be singed brown by the coming summer sun.

The Coast Road, which dissected the town, approached from the south winding through small coastal hills along a creek filled with sycamore trees.

To the north the road followed the coast for two more miles to a great promontory where mountain cliffs dropped precipitously to the sea. Near the end of the promontory a huge rock jetty fingered out into the Pacific, which served as a breaker for both the beach at San Roque and for the small port of San Miguel. At land's end was a still functioning, nineteenth century lighthouse, one of the original California light stations. As it had for over one hundred and fifteen years, its perennial light flashed every six seconds sending its beam across the ocean to ships up to twelve miles out.

Beyond the promontory lay an isolated strip of rugged coastline, one of the few undeveloped pieces of property left on the central coast of California not owned by the military or State Park system. Here, twenty miles of green hills and windswept marine terraces had remained virtually unblemished since the time of the Chumash Indians. Though development had spread rampantly in the southland, especially over the past ten years, it had not yet stretched its covetous paw into this place. The P.A.P.C.—Pacific Alliance Power Company—made sure of that. They had leased the land in a tricky transaction from a cattle rancher to build a nuclear power plant, and had since gained ownership through an eminent domain suit. In doing so, the nuclear power plant served, in an ironic way, to ward off resort development along the coast. Now by virtue of federal trespassing laws meant to protect nuclear facilities, the area had become a virtual wildlife reserve. Aside from a few cattle ranchers grazing herds on the western slopes, the Plant's operational crew and security personnel were the only ones to step foot within the

*Protected Zone.* It remained now as a sanctuary only to coyotes, seals, dolphins, and whatever other natural wildlife had always thrived there.

From a couple miles south, a pair of headlights snaked along the road, following the twisting inlets of the creek. The vehicle came around the last long bend, lined with poplar trees, turned on Front Street and turned again on Second Street before settling into the parking lot of the *Sea Gypsy* apartment complex. The driver stepped from the vehicle to the faint sound of music coming from the small house across the street.

Inside, the shadows of the two lovers still danced awkwardly on the bedroom wall. Jack and his young companion were deep in their love throes, indulging in the intimacies of physical love. It is why they did not hear it when the Visitor first knocked, until the knock came again.

"Did you hear that?" Jack then asked.

The young woman did not answer, but the expression on her face said that she did. Jack turned and looked over at the clock radio. The blue digital numbers now read: 8:45 p.m.

*It's early*, he thought. He was expecting no one. His ride wasn't due for another hour.

Again came the knock.

He reached over and lowered the volume on the radio.

"Someone's here," he said, flatly.

He pushed the young woman off of him, dragged himself from the bed, slipped into a pair of trousers, and grabbed a light-blue shirt from the chair. As he staggered down the hallway, slipping into the shirt, the knocking became more persistent.

"Okay! Okay!"

On the porch the Visitor stood waiting, patiently, neatly dressed in a regal-blue uniform with shiny black dress shoes. His hair was meticulously slicked back and on his chest was a gold badge which glistened from the street light.

Jack flipped on the porch light and swung open the door, surprised to see a familiar face, but not the face he was expecting.

"What's up?" he asked.

He turned and glanced at the mantel clock on top of the desk in the front room. As he did so, he pulled the corner of his shirt over his shoulders. And in that same millisecond, the Visitor pulled a gun from behind his back. Its barrel came up quickly, up against Jack's chest, and before Jack's head swung back around, two shots fired out, muffled by a silencer.

*Pooff! Pooff!*

Jack fell back into the front room, dead before he reached the floor. Stepping forward, quickly, the Visitor advanced into the room, closed the door behind him, walked over to an end-table, and turned a lamp on. He removed the silencer from the tip of his firearm, tucked it in his back pocket, and holstered the gun. Scanning the room, he grabbed a towel from a pile of laundry on a couch and tossed it over Jack's face. Then, kneeling beside Jack's dead body, he cast a careless glance over him. The two bullets had struck just below the sternum, less than a centimeter apart. The holes were bloodless and seemed to be already closing, though blood was already streaming from Jack's back, and the Visitor could see it streaming out onto the hard-wood floor.

The Visitor searched Jack's shirt pocket and found nothing. Then he rolled him over and checked the pants pockets as well. He glanced around the room, searching everywhere; the end-table, bookshelf, cabinet and couch. Near the door was a bookcase cluttered with encyclopedias, novels, and magazines—there was nothing of interest. On the television was the usual collection of junk, a TV controller and some DVD cases. The sofa chair was likewise piled high with miscellaneous items, laundry, some magazines, and a couple pairs of jogging shoes. Finally his eyes came upon a small roll-top desk against the far wall. On top was a small, ornamental palm tree, a key-stand from which hung an assortment of trinkets and keys.

He leaped to the desk, glanced through the items, and quickly pulled from the tree stand a photo I.D. badge, to which was clipped a plastic card.

He held the card to the light. It was about the size of an ordinary credit card. Upon it was the familiar symbol of three spinning atoms along side the name: *Jack Garner.* Angling the card to the light revealed several metallic, anti-counterfeit strips inside. Placing it flush against the desk-lamp so that it was fully back-lit, revealed a tiny rectangular chip inlaid in the bottom right corner.

The Visitor clasped the card tightly in his hand, and for a moment just stood there, holding it. He seemed content just to stay there, holding the card all night.

Then an unexpected noise drew his attention to the hallway.

A voice called; that of the young woman.

"Jack?"

With the same predatory instincts he had displayed earlier, the Visitor drew his gun, the barrel flashed up, pointing at the hallway, and he waited, quietly.

"Jack?" the voice repeated, closer now.

With his free hand, the Visitor slipped the card into his shirt pocket, gripped the pistol with both hands, and stepped slowly forward toward the hallway opening.

From the bedroom, the young woman entered the hallway, slipping into a bathrobe. She stopped midway to tie the band around her waist. Now, raising her head, she glanced up and saw a dark figure standing at the end of the hallway.

"Jack, who is it?"

The front room was dimly lit so she could not tell who it was, nor see the gun leveled at her chest.

"Jack?"

There was no answer at first. Then the pistol spoke loudly, without the benefit of the silencer.

*BAM! BAM!*

A bright double power-flash spit from its barrel. The woman staggered backward as if clubbed in the chest, and fell to the floor.

The Visitor advanced down the hallway, keeping aim on the woman. He could hear sound coming from the bedroom. He carefully stepped over the woman, straddling her for a second, glancing down at her dead face, then, swinging his gun barrel around, he entered the bedroom. His aim locked in the direction of the clock-radio, as if ready to shoot it. Realizing it was only a radio, he quickly swung the barrel to the other side of the room. It was clear. Then he eased back calmly, holstered the handgun, walked over to the radio, and turned it off.

At the window, he looked out for a moment. It was now completely dark outside. There were only two street lamps, a vacant lot next door, and across the street, not many lights were on at the Sea Gypsy Apartments. Except for the flashing neon that featured a gypsy woman holding a starfish, and the 'vacant' sign which blinked on and off, there were little signs of life. He looked down the street. The street was essentially barren. He drew the curtains shut.

He pulled the card from his pocket and gazed upon it once again. It looked no different than a hotel keycard, but, in truth, was quite different, he knew. It held all the information he needed. Of that he was certain.

He placed the card safely in his wallet, in a side compartment. Then he stepped out of the bedroom, over the dead woman, and returned to the front room. He clicked off the lamplight, and the porch light as well, and exited the small house, locking the door behind him.

# Chapter 1

Cameron Taylor gazed quietly at the image in the broken mirror.

*Only twenty-eight years old and already burnt to dust!*

For him, waking up to an 8:30 p.m. alarm clock was just the start of another night's work. Stuck on the midnight shift at Mal Loma Nuclear Power Plant for the past eight months, he was still trying to adjust to his capsized schedule. Having answered a newspaper ad hiring *'Armed Responders'* to protect a nuclear power plant *'from acts of terrorism and industrial sabotage,'* he was initially enthused by the prospects of his new job. But the position turned out to be a boring routine of mundane security procedures and endless hours marching with a rifle on blacktop. Truth was, guarding a nuclear power plant from "acts of industrial sabotage" was simply not what it was cracked up to be, nor what he expected.

He stared into the mirror, naked except for a pair of white boxers.

*Nothing had changed,* he thought.

The time on the small, fold-out digital clock sitting on the shelf beneath the medicine cabinet was 9:20 p.m. Beside it, the tube of tooth paste, still with cap off, remained lying exactly as he had left it the night before. On the shelf beside that, carelessly discarded facedown was his badge.

*Here I begin my upside-down world,* he thought. *While the 'real' world sleeps, I drape on my armor.*

From the very start, his body had rejected the time change. He tried giving up caffeine, took *Ambien* to no avail. He had even purchased a yoga CD thinking the gentle sound of waves might help lull him to sleep. For some it came easy. For Cameron it seemed, adjusting to night work was next to impossible.

He reached in, turned on the shower, and climbed in with a million thoughts rushing through his head, none of which were any good. In less than five minutes, he stood fully clothed before the mirror with his hair slicked straight back. He donned a regal blue uniform. On the shoulder was a telling patch—the insignia of three spinning atoms in counter-orbits. Bordered across the top by the word "*Nuclear,*" and arched across the bottom with the words, "*Security Service.*"

He picked up his badge and held it to the light. He never imagined the treadmill it would eventually become.

It had all started out ambitious enough just eight months before. Cheerful at the prospects of his new job, Cameron was thrilled to have passed the initial interview. He took on the challenge of the physical agility tests like a school boy at a track meet.

The requirements included a four-hundred-meter dash in less than seventy-five seconds, a one-hundred-and-fifty-pound-sack-of-sand-drag across fifty-yards of blacktop, and a ten-foot-wall scale with a dummy rifle strapped to his shoulder, all of which he passed easily enough. Next came the security clearance and background investigation, which put some light on the enormity of the position. They wanted to know every detail of his past life, even what grammar school he attended.

*They're absolutely serious about this stuff,* Cameron remembered thinking.

First there was the fingerprinting—a *LiveScan* digital-ten-print which fed directly into the FBI's mainframe in Washington DC, and into the Department of Justice Office in Sacramento, revealing Cameron to be clean except for a few speeding violations. This was followed by an eighteen-page background questionnaire, confirmed by a polygraph test and scanned into N.O.R.A.—*Non-Obvious-Relationship-Awareness*, a 'next-generation' cross-referencing software capable of linking members of terrorist cells and crime groups in more than seventy-five countries. Lastly was the MMPI—the Minnesota Multiphasic Personality Inventory, which was evaluated, analyzed, and followed-up via an interview with a Pre-employment Consult Psychologist.

He was an odd-looking guy, Cameron had thought, bald with glasses, the picture perfect scientific type. Cameron anticipated trouble coming when he was handed the read-out of his MMPI. The first sentence read:

*You lied when taking this test to make yourself look better to your prospective employer.*

"Is it true?" The Psychologist asked pointedly.

Cameron hesitated. He knew enough about the MMPI to think twice about faking it. He had researched it ahead of time. The test was said to be capable of identifying an alcoholic with ninety-seven percent accuracy and to fish-out the major symptoms of social and personal maladjustment with prophetic-like accuracy, and was the primary screening tool used by employers for candidates for high-risk public safety positions.

"Sure it's true," he replied, staring at the computerized printout. "I need a job."

The psychologist nodded his head and scribbled in his notepad.

"Okay then," the psychologist said. "Next question: If you could be anyone in the world other than yourself, who would it be?"

Cameron had to think about it for a moment. Frankly, it was a bit weird being asked this question by a psychologist. The first thing that came to his mind was how therapists are crazier than their clients. And besides, what does it have to do with employment at a nuclear power plant?

But after a little thought, he thought he'd better answer. It might have some underling value after all.

"Bugs Bunny," he replied.

"Bugs Bunny?" the psychologist questioned, mulling it over like a scientist pondering a new mathematical equation. "That's interesting. I never had that answer before." He scribbled sentences on to his notepad.

Cameron looked worried. He was not trying to be funny. It was an honest answer.

"And why Bugs Bunny?" the psychologist asked.

Cameron glanced at the ceiling panels, thoughtfully. "Well, I really admire the crafty little rabbit. It seems no matter how dreadful things get, how bad the situation could be, I mean, you know how deep they'd pile it on him, and he'd still find a way out looking good and unruffled."

The psychologist gazed back with fascination and scribbled furiously in his notepad.

Cameron thought he was doomed.

Despite the seemingly failed psychological interview, two weeks later he received a slim envelope in the mail, on which the return address was the San Roque PO Box for Mal Loma Nuclear Power Plant. Inside was a five-paragraph letter welcoming him to an "Elite Security Force," a congratulatory statement on being selected, a line requesting that he report for training promptly at 8:00 a.m. the following Tuesday morning, and to arrive in what was described as "appropriate civilian attire."

Cameron was elated. After six months of unemployment, searching for jobs with a less than impressive resume gapped with lengthy periods of unemployment, and with a savings account nearly depleted, he was happy to find work again.

Now he gazed back at his reflection in the mirror, feeling it was all for naught. There is an ecstasy that marks the summit of life, beyond which life cannot rise. It seems Cameron's ecstasy had come and gone at the tender age of twenty-eight. Aside from the occasional raccoon that wandered into the perimeter fence tripping the alarm system, truth was there was little action to speak of. He found neither the intrigue nor sophistication promised by the recruitment ad. Night after night, he toiled to the same boredom. The job was without future, full of bureaucratic rules and regulations that seemed absurd at best, and governed by a bunch of corporate executives sitting in a high-rise office building in San Francisco. A born optimist, charmed by nature and amused by humanity, he was indeed stricken with the ills of monotony.

*Standing in the rain for hours on end with a rifle in one's hand; staring into a surveillance screen at the same motionless images; performing repetitive drills which neither made sense nor would ever be put to test; watching a clock hoping time will pass. Is that what life's all about?*

His reflective image raised a doubting brow.

*A security guard on the midnight shift*, he thought, straightening his tie. *Let's face it, that's what I am.*

The one bright spot in his otherwise dismal existence was Grace Baker, a twenty-six-year-old new hire at the power plant, with whom Cameron had commenced an accelerated romance. The attraction had been immediate and mutual. In three short weeks, the two had found a fondness for one another likened to the romances of old Hollywood. In Grace, Cameron found a wild, defiant beauty; the type men cross oceans for. And now Cameron found himself thinking more about Grace than the prospects of looking for another job, which he had considered until Grace came into the picture.

*Grace! Grace! Grace!*

He took a deep breath. *Time to defend the masses.*

With one last look in the mirror, he pinned his badge to his chest, turned, and walked to the kitchen to make a sandwich, fill his thermos with hot coffee, place both in his lunch pail, and pile in a heap of potato chips. Then he grabbed his car keys, and headed for the door.

# Chapter 2

Cameron raced down the narrow streets of San Roque heading for Jack's house, knowing full well he was late. Having stopped to fill his gas tank and engaging in a conversation about crossbows with the station attendant, he had lost another twenty minutes. Glancing at his wristwatch now, he noted it was nearly 9:40 p.m.—later than usual.

He stared blankly out the windshield.

*Damn it! Why am I always doing this to myself?*

Nearly passing Second Street, he slammed on the brakes, slid halfway through the intersection, revved the engine, threw it in reverse, and sped down Second Street, passing the flashing neon sign: *Sea Gypsy Apartments.*

As he pulled along the curb at Jack's little beach house, he saw that the porch-light was off.

*Not a good sign,* he thought

He leaped from his car, walked briskly to the porch, and knocked. When there was no answer he tried the buzzer, ringing it incessantly, and then tried pounding on the door—still nothing. He leaned far over to the side of the porch and tried peering through the front window, but the curtains were completely drawn. He tried the door knob but it was locked.

There was that inevitable sinking sensation.

*He left without me!*

Cameron left the porch in a hurry, not thinking to check the carport. Back in his little Honda, he raced down the small streets of San Roque. He made a couple quick turns and got on to the Coast Road, heading out toward San Roque Gate, the main gate of the power plant, a couple miles away.

*Think of what you're going to say,* he thought, nervously thumbing the steering wheel. *It's best to have a plan.*

John Harkin, his hard-driving, by-the-book Supervisor, had already placed him on notice for excessive tardiness, absenteeism, and various other work-related misconducts. Cameron's only saving grace was that when he wanted to work, and took it serious, he was damn good at it. And Harkin knew it.

Still, he was near the end of his rope, Cameron knew, and despite the fact that he hated his job, he needed it. And there was Grace too. The job provided him time with her, although it was strictly monitored time; monitored by surveillance cameras and motion detectors, and if there was to be any future between them, he was going to need a job.

*Indebtedness is a good thing,* Cameron thought, as he motored along.

He recalled several instances where he had come to Supervisor Harkin's aid, and hoped, now, that Harkin would remember them.

*Harkin owes me,* he thought. *No matter what he has to say about me being late, he owes me!*

There was that time with Kelly Murphy. *Yes! How could he forget that?*

The supervisors had commenced a competition between themselves on who could get their crews firearm qualified quickest, and with the highest average score. It was an annual event; a requirement of the State. As usual, Supervisor Harkin's crew had fired top-notch, and swiftly. Three of the five of the Security Force's top sharpshooters were among his shift, including Cameron. But the exception was Kelly Murphy. She just lacked the natural agility to fire a handgun. And, with the specific wish of the higher-ups to have women in armed positions, and for them to qualify first—a wish inline with affirmative action and political correctness—it was imperative that Kelly succeed. Upon Harkin's request, Cameron took Kelly under his wing, and trained her, in a different way than Harkin, in his own direct but non-threatening style. In the end, not only had she qualified, but she qualified highest among all female officers. It was a huge feather in Harkin's hat.

Also, Cameron now recalled, there was the incident of the NRC quarterly meeting. The 'NRC' or Nuclear Regulatory Commission, the federal watchdog agency charged with the task of controlling, regulating, and monitoring everything nuclear, scheduled quarterly meetings, and this particular one, to be held at the power plant, was to include the local congressman.

"Some clown," as Harkin described, had called in a bomb threat to a local hospital, advising them to get "one hundred cots ready."

Cameron was consequently asked to double-back from his midnight shift and stand post on a mountaintop with a pair of binoculars and a high-caliber rifle. His orders were simply to observe and report any unusual activity in the back country.

Despite the short notice and lack of sleep, Cameron accepted cheerfully, without complaint. In fact, he didn't mind it at all. He got paid time-and-a-half and spent most of the day watching migrating grey whales through the high-powered scope.

As Cameron sped along the Coast Road, he could see the white crashing waves of the Pacific flashing beneath him. In the distance the lighthouse flashed, there at the very tip of the promontory. As he neared the power plant's main entrance, he saw some activity at Port San Miguel, which lay just beyond. A group of fishermen had come in late and were hoisting their small boat from the water onto the landing platform.

Cameron zoomed around the corner into the short approach road. A solitary figure sat in the guard booth—a small, eight-by-six, four-windowed box just large enough to fit one guard on a high stool, some gear, and a shelf for coffee and log books.

Ahead was the brightly illuminated access to Mal Loma Nuclear Power Plant. There was a kiosk along side the guard booth with two toll-barriers resembling a railroad crossing. Flood-lamps perched atop high-rise poles, similar to the lighting provided at a ball park, flooded the area in a thirty-yard radius. On either side of the entrance were ten-foot high cyclone fences, topped with overturned rolls of razor-wire. A large, illuminated sign posted on the right roadside left no doubt of the property's ownership and restricted access:

MAL LOMA NUCLEAR POWER PLANT
Pacific Alliance Power Company
TRESPASSING STRICTLY PROHIBITED

Marvin Spencer, the security officer assigned gate duty tonight, wore the same finely-pressed, regal blue uniform, with the flying atoms and words *'Nuclear Security'* bold across the shoulder. He stepped from the guard booth with a Mini-14 magazine-fed, combat rifle strapped to his shoulder. A field utility belt, strapped around his waist, contained a holstered handgun, a radio, a flashlight, and several ammo clips.

As Cameron pulled up to the toll-bar, he checked his wristwatch.

*Twenty minutes late!*

"Hey there, Marv," Cameron greeted, as he rolled down the window.

"Harkin wants me to log your 'in-time'," Marvin said bluntly.

"What?"

"Yeah, sorry to say, but he called me and asked me to log in your time."

Cameron frowned. "Did he say anything else?"

"No, just that; 'log in your time.'"

*Shit!*

Marvin leaned in and looked over at the empty passenger seat. "Where's your side kick?"

"He didn't come by already?"

"No."

"He hasn't?"

"He hasn't. That's what I said."

Cameron looked puzzled. He had assumed, because he was running late, Jack had left without him, and was already en route to the power plant.

"Maybe someone's in deeper shit than you?" Marvin said. "That's always a good thing, ya know."

Cameron glanced at himself in the rearview mirror. He nervously swept his hand back through his already-combed hair. "Can you give me ten minutes, buddy?" he asked.

"Sorry, I can't do that. Harkin knows how long it takes from the gate."

"Come'on buddy."

Marvin gazed up the access road, thoughtfully. "Five minutes," he said. "That's the best I can do. Five minutes."

"Thanks," Cameron replied. "That's better than nothing." He stared straight up the road. "Have fun."

Marvin nodded an acknowledgement, went back inside the guard booth, and lifted the toll gate.

Cameron accelerated up the winding access road, feeling doomed. He was still several miles from the power plant, and he knew Harkin was in 'documentation' mode, building an employee disciplinary docket or worse yet, a termination case under the Fair Labor Standards Act.

*It was Harkin's way not to take it personally,* he thought, *just log the facts and drop the axe. I'm as good as fired. Thanks for all, boss!*

Adding insult to injury, two departing coworkers, driving home from their swing shift, passed him. And as they did so, they honked their horns, as if letting Cameron know what trouble he was in.

Cameron frowned. *Thanks pals!*

Within minutes Cameron's little Honda crested the small mountain divide that separated San Roque Gate from the ocean on the opposite side of the promontory. Dropping down to the coastal slopes beyond, he zoomed along the steep cliffs above the smashing waves. His headlamps illuminated the road before him. Through the windshield he could see the dark, brooding ocean, speckled white with white-caps rolling out to the horizon.

# Chapter 3

The coast here was as magnificent as the Amalfi. Where mountains met ocean at the edge of a continent was always the perfect formula for grandeur and wonderment. It made Cameron
recall the first time he saw it, in daylight, white waves crashing
in turquoise blue coves, deepening in color to the outer reefs;
sea lions lounging on rock inlets, and further out, the occasional
spouts of California Grey whales moving with their seasonal mi-
gration from Mexico to Alaska. Sloping upward from the ocean
were long, emerald-green terraces of tall shore grass, which
replicated rows of shimmering silk banisters, diminishing in size
until vanishing in the distant haze. Cameron especially liked
this time of year, when everything was in bloom. Although it
was dark now, he could imagine it vividly. Eastward, where the
slopes angled steeply up to the towering coastal mountaintops,
emerald green hillsides were brush-stroked with bright yellow
lines of mustard flowers.

It was the *Great Irony,* Cameron thought, entering the *Protected Zone.* By virtue of the Pacific Alliance Power Company
and the Nuclear Regulatory Commission, and all the entry pro-
hibitions that came along with it, the California pelicans, and
sea otters, and the red and black abalone, which clung in the
tide pools, and all the other wildlife, remained as bountiful as
they had been during the time of the Chumash Indians one-

hundred years before. It was here the Chumash had lived in harmony with nature for centuries, navigating Pacific currents in their reed-built *tomols*, building their bent-poled shelters along the coastal terraces, and burying their dead on windswept knolls above the sea. It was a place where the warm *Santa Anas* swept across the ocean, carving artistic formations in the sandstone cliffs and chattered through the leaves in the sycamore canyons—where wind still whispered through the tall shore grass—*oddly enough, all due in thanks to a nuclear power plant!*

And thinking of the power plant, Cameron recalled the first time he set eyes on it. He was humming along the access road on his first day to work when suddenly, ahead, there were two enormous white domes. To him it appeared as if Poseidon had misplaced two huge Trojan helmets on the Pacific shoreline. It reminded him of a time he had taken a helicopter ride to the Grand Canyon, flying low toward the South Rim, one-hundred-feet above the tree-tops; then suddenly breaching the rim, the view gave way to a five-thousand foot drop and an awe-inspiring view of the Canyon.

It was the exact same feeling, Cameron thought—*Jaw-dropping.*

The power plant was indeed a futuristic-looking complex, awkwardly perched at the ocean's edge. Stretching out before the two massive containment domes was the Turbine Building, a structure large enough to house a football field, and nestled in-between was the Auxiliary Building, a multi-terraced, skyscraper-looking structure which served as the 'brains' of the power plant.

*A marvel of Modern Technology,* Cameron mused.

And from the start, he was mystified by it. Everyone was mystified by it. Building a nuclear power plant on a pristine coast of velvet-waving shore grass seemed as idiotic as painting over a *Van Gogh* with motor oil. And yet, despite the absurdness of it, the reasoning was undeniably prudent. Ideal was a power plant strategically placed, out of eyesight and earshot of the masses, and isolated far enough from areas of population as to provide a cushion zone in the event of a radiation leak or nuclear disaster. From here there would be time to orchestrate a mass evacuation, should the unlikely necessity arise.

In truth, it was no easy task building a nuclear power plant on a coastal terrace in central California. For the Pacific Alliance Power Company, it had been a battle from the beginning. It rubbed so hard against conventional thought that it instantly confronted a firestorm of hostility. The permitting process was constantly thwarted by legal action brought on by the Sierra Club, Abalone Alliance, and Mothers for Peace. But eventually, with the backing of the federal government, whose new mantra was 'Independence from Middle Eastern oil,' the permits were granted and the power plant was built.

Contingency plans, evacuation plans, coordination plans, of every kind, with every vital agency, were made. Local, state and federal law enforcement agencies, the U.S. Coast Guard, and even local National Guard unit stationed forty-five minutes north, had committed to a quick-response plan to provide immediate assistance for any event, including terrorist threat. In the event of a mass evacuation, letters of agreement were signed with many local businesses and corporations to provide aid and assistance. Local municipalities, as well as Amtrak and Greyhound Bus Lines, signed-on for transportation purposes, and McDonalds Corporation agreed to provide emergency food to a weary population if a mass evacuation became necessary.

A problematic matter was in the winds. The area was known for its *Devil Winds*—unpredictable winds—sometimes blowing from offshore, sometimes from the land, often converging in flurries and funnels visible at sea. Several tests with balloons never netted the same wind direction. This caused great concern among the scientific authorities who tried to predict, with reasonable consistency, the wind currents for evacuation and planning purposes.

Yet an early warning system was developed based on a 'best guess' scenario of prevailing wind conditions, strategically dissecting the central coast into a twelve-ring "Protective Action Zone" which radiated out from the 'epicenter' of the power plant. Each ring varied in its level of response determined by wind and proximity to the Plant. Tall warning sirens were tactically placed in all neighborhoods, mountainsides, school yards, city streets, and along beaches and highways, throughout the region. Automated gamma ray detectors were positioned along Protective Action Zone *Two*, a six-mile radius from the Plant, which fed data into a centralized computer which would enact an automated alarm if dangerous levels of radiation were detected. Local media, radio and televisions stations all had prescripted instructions; how, where, and when to provide emergency airway information should a Level-One Emergency be enacted.

Orchestrating the efforts was the Nuclear Regulatory Commission through volumes of federal regulations designed to increase safety measures and prevent the possibility of a nuclear disaster. Millions of dollars were expended for earthquake upgrades after fault-lines were discovered just offshore. Back-up power supplies, to ensure the constant pumping of millions of gallons of ocean water to cool the reactors, consisted of no less than six huge diesel generators, a battery room the size of a tennis court, and four separate electric lines traversing the hilltops to a neighboring fossil-fuel plant thirty miles north. The reactor containment domes, standing two-hundred and fifteen feet high and constructed of three-foot thick concrete and steel, were capable of withstanding the impact of a commercial jetliner. A sea wall and huge support braces were built on the western front to handle a sixty-foot tidal wave. P.A.P.C. had even gone so far as to employ marine biologists to take samples from the ocean to monitor the effects of the discharge and ensure the protection of the marine life. In the end, despite many protests and demonstrations, the power plant was built, became operational, and began producing mega-watts of electricity for hungry cities throughout California.

Cameron's little Honda sped over the last hill and down toward the small city of lights, from which rose the two white containment domes of Mal Loma Nuclear Power Plant. He headed directly for the Security Building, which, illuminated brilliantly, hung like a jewel at the southern end of the perimeter fence. He could tell by the number of cars left in the parking lot that the shift change was well underway. It meant his post replacement was still waiting. Speeding into the lit parking lot, he slid in between two large cars. He grabbed his lunch pail, leaped out of the car, and headed for the entrance lobby.

# Chapter 4

Nine miles inland from the power plant, a streamlined Dodge Ram 1500 truck lumbered slowly up a steep canyon grade along the eastern flanks of the coastal mountains. The vehicle was *crystal black pearl* in color with four-wheel drive and a high-wheel clearance. It had a standard transmission and a pair of high-strength, polypropylene lamps which now lit the way up the dark, uneven road.

The Driver clutched and down-shifted, causing the truck to nearly roll backward, but its all-terrain tires quickly gripped the turf and the truck continued to climb until the road gradually leveled.

Ahead was a locked gate. The truck's brake lights came on and the door opened. The driver stepped out to a strong gust of wind blowing through the sycamore trees. He glanced up at them. To the south, the mountaintops glowed from the distant lights of San Roque. Directly west was the huge, dark shoulder of the mountain he climbed, still separating him from the sea.

The Driver retrieved a set of bolt cutters from the bed of the truck. Using the headlamps to illuminate the gate, he snapped the lock and swung the gate open. He dumped the bolt cutters back into the bed of the truck, returned to the cab, and preceded through the gate.

The road ahead was dark and narrow, and equally as steep. Leaning forward, the Driver strained for a better view.

Ahead was a familiar landmark—a huge, brooding oak tree in an opening in a sloping field. He knew this place, and knew the sycamores would soon thicken and the embankment to the south would steepen into a cliff. Having scouted the road two weeks earlier in daylight, on a warm day, he had etched landmarks in his mind. He had hiked all afternoon with a daypack until the road narrowed and steepened, finally reaching the top. The further up he got, he noticed, the less traveled the road was, evident by the increasingly taller grass and lack of fresh tire tracks. Judging by what he saw, the upper portion of the road hadn't been used in weeks.

He had found the road on a standard topographical map issued by the U.S. Geological Survey, which he had conveniently downloaded off the internet. It followed through a dense grove of oaks and up a narrowing canyon filled with sycamore trees. The snaking line on the map was marked; 'Miguelleto Canyon Road.' It was a remote passage at best, used sparingly by cattle ranchers to gain access to grazing lands on the northern coastal slopes. In the lower stretches, the map indicated three creek crossings, two over cement spillways and the last over bare boulders. The road started out on asphalt, and ended on dirt, and there were two places where earth slides had covered the road, but jeep-tracks had since blazed a path around them. The upper portion of the route was nothing more than a two-wheeled jeep path.

Now, in darkness, beneath tree-filtered starlight, the Driver followed the same path he had walked two weeks earlier. His Dodge truck's hemi engine powered smoothly uphill, its headlamps bearing down on the bumpy terrain. A couple of times, he encountered steers on the road, having to nudge the animals aside. Further up he came to a second locked gate where he repeated the earlier process with the bolt cutters. This time, when he stepped out of the truck, he heard a crackling noise. Looking up he saw the dark outline of a huge, power tower. It was a place where the high-voltage power lines stretched from the power plant at Mal Loma over the mountaintops to inland cities. Hunched over like colossal, high-shouldered Martians, the silhouetted, two-legged steel towers connected one hilltop to another, linking them all the way to California's Central Valley.

*Getting close,* he thought.

Nearing the top of the grade, the truck came out of the sycamore trees onto a sharp, slope of starlit chaparral. The road practically vanished, steepening into tall, waving grass. As the truck climbed, nearly vertical, its engine bore down. The Driver downshifted, and the truck's engine labored briefly, until easing as the grade gave way to sky.

The Driver reached over and switched off the headlamps. The darkness was sudden and complete, causing his eyes to dilate. When his vision returned, the stars filled the night sky, and before him emerged a vast, panoramic view of the Pacific coastline.

He had summited a barren, grass-covered peak, from which one could see as far north as Point Piedras and south to Point San Miguel. West, beyond the vague white outline of the jagged surf, loomed the dark ocean. It was a perfect crow's nest. The view was unobstructed by tree, pole line, or clouds. Above was only the brilliant white starlight.

For a moment the Driver just sat there, taking it in. Then he checked his position, left and right. The mountaintop was cone-shaped and the truck was resting slightly back on the eastern slope, positioned perfectly just below the rise. He was on the dark side of the mountain, he knew. The truck could not be seen from the West, even with the most sophisticated night vision equipment, and from the East, he was a good fifteen miles from the nearest human being.

He killed the engine, and stepping from the truck, he was greeted by a shoreward breeze. It blew briskly through his short-cropped brown hair and against his handsome face. He walked slowly to the precipitous, western edge. His deep, remarkably blue eyes gazed downward intently. There, straight below him, fifteen-hundred yards away, was a small city of lights; the layout of which was completely familiar to him. Encircled in a ring of lights was an elongated building with two magnificent domes protruding from the back end. He had seen it before in daylight, had studied aerial photographs and maps, including a detailed, satellite-image downloaded on *Google Earth*, and what he saw now was the perfect nighttime perspective.

He nodded his head contently. *There she blows.*

Kneeling down, he cupped his hands, lit a cigarette, and let the wind blow a straight line of smoke eastward behind him. With hawk-like attention, he studied the topography and layout before him. From this high vantage point, the two enormous, concrete containment domes seemed dwarfed in size, gleaming white beneath the blackened sky. The perimeter fence surrounding the Plant looked like a sparkling silver chain, illuminated by evenly spaced diamonds of high-intensity flood lights. Along the eastern fence-line, the side closest to him, two stick-figures marched slowly. To the south was the Security Building, separated from the power plant by one-hundred feet of asphalt, which, from this distance, appeared to be less than two centimeters. The bulk on the Turbine Building was concealed beyond the containment domes and the auxiliary building, but the rooftop was exposed at both ends.

The Driver turned his attention north beyond the blackness of the western slope. There, before the vague white outline of the surf, was a single pair of headlights traveling slowly along the terrace. It was one of the Plant's two security mobile units; a modified eight-cylinder, Jeep Cherokee. Having completed its patrol route along the northern property boundaries, it was en route back toward the power plant.

The Driver watched it, taking a long drag from his cigarette; his practiced, deep-blue eyes flickered contently.

Behind him, to the east, there was nothing but blackness, except for a few distant lights of distant cities.

It was an absolutely clear night. *Nearly perfect conditions.* The wind would be a factor, strong and steady from the west, but he had accounted for that. All the necessary equipment had accompanied him in the truck and the necessary adjustments could be made easily enough. The temperature was a cool fifty-eight degrees, nearly ideal for keeping a trajectory. His line of fire would be straight for the furthest possible distance, he knew. He was lucky, he thought, to have a clear night without fog. He flicked the cigarette butt into the grass.

A strong gust of wind came against him and he braced himself with a hand in the grass. He waited for the wind to subside, then leaned forward and rested his elbow back on his knee.

The wind will definitely be a factor, he thought, but not a problem. Just a couple turns of a screw. Nothing more.

Besides, he thought, they wanted wind.

# Chapter 5

Cameron burst through the front double-paned glass doors of the Security Building, scanning the large entrance lobby for any sign of Supervisor Harkin. Harkin was nowhere to be seen.

The wall clock read 10:20 p.m.

*Only twenty minutes late*, Cameron thought. *Not bad.*

Straight ahead was the search train, a long gauntlet of sophisticated security search-machines; x-ray machines, explosives detectors, and metal detectors. Among the devices was a Barringer *Sentinel* Contraband Detection Portal, capable of detecting traces of ammonium nitrate, semtex, RDX, PETN, TNT and other explosives; nerve and blister agents such as mustard gas, Agent VX, tabun, sarin, soman and cyclosarin; and a wide range of narcotics including marijuana, cocaine, methamphetamine, and heroin.

Beyond the search train, elevated and catty-cornered on the far side of the entrance lobby, were the bullet-proof, plexiglas windows of Security Computer Station Two—called simply 'Control Two' by the security staff. Inside was the silhouette of a solitary security officer seated before a console of blinking lights. Above him, virtually wrapping around the small cubical, were closed-circuit television monitors flashing different scenes from around the power plant.

Several security officers, male and female were scurrying about, preparing for the shift change. Two officers conversed loudly near the badge counter, and exchanged equipment. Two others, exhausted after a long shift, hustled quietly to their lockers, wanting nothing more than to unload their equipment and make a quick exit home.

At the head of the search train were Jimmy Becker and Rae Anderson. They had drawn the Security & Access post this night, and waited for Cameron with malicious smirks on their faces.

Cameron, looking up at them, frowned. *They're going to make my life miserable*, he thought.

The Security Building was the only portal by which a person could enter or leave the power plant. Everyone from top to bottom, along with all their accompanying baggage, was subjected to the airport-like security of the search train. In fact, it was much more rigorous than any airport security. Through these doors, one must pass; and through these machines, one must pass cleanly. Outside, a ten-foot tall cyclone *perimeter fence,* topped with overturned razor-wire and monitored by highly-sensitive microwave motion detectors, encircled the plant and ensured such was the case.

Cameron stepped ahead through the turnstile, shooting a discerning glance at a doorway along the north wall, through which a hallway led to Supervisor Harkin's office.

*For the moment, it's safe.*

He set his daypack on the conveyer belt, hurried on through the contraband detector portal, spinning simultaneously so that the detector would scan his body quickly, and nodded a friendly *hello* to the two waiting officers as he came out the other side.

"Hello Cameron," Rae Anderson said. She was a tall, slender redhead, quite beautiful.

"How's it going, Rae?" Cameron replied.

"It's going well. And you?" She held out a basket.

"Not bad."

Cameron dumped his keys into the basket, and trying to keep the conversation brisk, proceeded quickly through the metal detector. On the other side he lifted his arms in advance for Jimmy Becker, who approached with a metal detector wand. All the while, Cameron kept an eye on the open doorway which led to Supervisor Harkin's office.

Everyone in the lobby knew Cameron was late. Everyone knew Cameron was in a bad way with Supervisor Harkin. And for Becker, it was a moment of long-awaited retribution. Cameron, the unrelenting prankster, had pulled some good ones on Becker, most recently putting a dead fish in Becker's lunch pail. Becker was blamed for the foul smell in the briefing room for two weeks. Not that there were any hard feelings. Razzing was an acceptable form of entertainment in the boring world of security work, and turnabout was considered fair play.

Becker took his time.

"Come'on guys. Help me out," Cameron pleaded.

"Have to do our job," Becker maintained.

"Come'on, have a heart."

"We have procedures to follow…"

"Could ya hurry it up then, maybe?"

Cameron turned and Becker passed the wand slowly across his back, exceedingly slowly.

"Don't worry," Rae Anderson laughed. "Harkin's been hibernating in his office." Cameron glanced at the doorway that led to Harkin's office.

"He's been busy with paperwork since he arrived," she said.

Two rooms away, Supervisor Harkin was in fact sitting at his desk with his head buried in a huge pile of papers. He had arrived on shift finding an urgent memorandum from the Security Director sitting on his desk. It seems the brass wanted the monthly reports early, and Harkin, the type who never put off work, delved straight into it. Cameron's absences, tardies, and misconducts, were not far from his mind, but for the moment, not high on his priority list.

Cameron snapped up his keys, took his daypack, and broke off the chat undiplomatically. "Thank you kind friends for taking so much damn time." Then, beneath his breath, "dirty bastards!"

"Cameron!" Rae snapped.

"Not you," Cameron answered.

Becker laughed.

Sliding to the badge counter, Cameron collected his film badge. Before clipping it to his shirt pocket, he checked it for color, which was standard procedure. The card was colorless, as usual.

*No such luck,* Cameron thought, as he snapped it on.

Used to monitored harmful radiation exposure in increments of *millirems*, the film dosimeter badge gained color with radioactive exposure. Upon reaching a certain annual limit set forth by *CalOsha*—the California Occupational Safety and Health Agency tasked with the over-watch of industrial safety—employees got the remainder of the year off with full pay.

As he headed for the rear doorway he slipped past an exiting swing-shift officer and nodded a quick *hello.* Then, taking one last glance back through the entrance lobby, he ducked into the rear corridor en route to the briefing room.

He hurried past the Radiation Victim Carrier—another *CalOsha* requirement. It was an odd-looking contraption, a sort of stretcher engulfed in an oblong clear-plastic bubble with arm sockets. It was meant to be used for victims of radiation exposure. It had been aptly placed there in the rear corridor to serve as a steady reminder of the dangerous nature of the work. For most employees, coming on or off shift, it was simply the 'thing' parked in the rear corridor. No one really believed it would ever be used.

Cameron glanced back over his shoulder one last time. *No one.*

*Damn I'm good,* he thought.

He turned a corner, thinking he had made it to the Briefing Room unnoticed, when he ran into someone—someone big, and he could tell by the lizard-skinned cowboy boots, it was Harkin, all six-foot-two of him.

"Where's Jack?" Harkin's deep voice rumbled instantly.

Startled, Cameron looked up at him. Unlike the uniformed officers, Harkin was wearing a plain white, short-sleeved dress shirt, tan khaki *Dockers*, and almost as always, an unusually colorful tie. The privilege of plain cloths distinguished the shift supervisors from the security officers, both in rank and authority. Hanging beneath his arm on a shoulder sling was a sleek, 9mm *Glock*, Harkin's weapon of preference. That was another distinguishing privilege. The supervisors were not wedded to the Beretta 92G Elite II pistol, the standard-issue handgun for the line officers.

Cameron struggled for a response. "He didn't call?" He could see Harkin's gears were turning.

"No he didn't call. So you're saying he didn't ride with you?"

"I came alone."

"I thought you two ride together?"

"We do."

"But not tonight?"

"No."

"Did he call you?"

"No."

"Did you go by his place?"

"Yeah, I did. But he wasn't home."

Harkin pondered the information. "And he didn't call you?"

"No, he didn't call me."

Harkin grunted, stepped aside, and without another word, headed down the hallway toward his office. "You missed your Draw," he further groaned as he turned the corner back towards his office. "You've got Mobile One, Chris Peters' Shift. He's been driving around in circles waiting for you!"

Cameron was a bit surprised he had survived the encounter unscathed. He hurried down the hallway toward the briefing room. He did not want to linger and give Harkin time to reconsider and give him what was due.

# Chapter 6

Thirty miles north at Port Piedras, a fifty-four foot trawler taxied slowly out beneath the harbor lights. Onboard were Emil and Ramzan; an odd-looking pair whose facial features and size clearly distinguished them from one another. Ramzan was slight of frame, thin as a rail, with dark skin and sullen eyes. Though he was clean shaven now and wore a San Francisco *Giants* baseball cap, it was just part of their charade. He did not dress this way back home. Back home he wore traditional attire, modest in every respect, long flowing robes, a long, wiry beard, and when not wearing a turban, he donned a *Tarboosh*—an Arabic cap. Emil, on the other hand, a big, strong-jawed, rugged character with memorable steel-grey eyes, did not prefer the traditional dress, though he wore it once joining the brotherhood in accordance with Sharia law. Nor did he carry himself with such nobility as did Ramzan. With a bulky body, broad shoulders, and big hands, he lacked the finesse and dexterity that was evident in Ramzan's every movement. Emil's was more a deliberate motion. And though he was likewise dark complexioned, he had those fair eyes. They did not look alike, walk alike, nor even speak with the same dialect, but they came from the same part of the earth, and were bent by similar backgrounds. Between them, however, it was clearly understood. Of the two, Ramzan was the irreplaceable one.

No one really knew Ramzan's history, except Emil, and what Emil knew was mostly related to his special attributes—attributes, which in the under-circles of Islamic extremists and fanatics, had caused his rapid rise in an organization which despised Western thought, and sought in anyway to destroy it. But Ramzan had a history, one which had formed him as a man, or evil thing, depending on one's perspective. In a short time, he had become somewhat of a celebrity. Through his unpredictable tactics, creative ingenuity, and rapidly-compiling body count, Ramzan had gained notice by intelligence agencies worldwide; the crowning achievement of which was being named 'number eight' on the U.S. Department of State's most wanted list, and 'number six' on Interpol's.

*It was easy,* Ramzan had said. He simply followed the blood trail, the blood of his own, which always led him to his enemies, who in turn he punished, making them bleed as well, using the craft he had honed so well. For Ramzan, to ride now with Emil upon this ship on a foreign sea, on the shore of his most hated enemy, was spiritual fulfillment. Having been assigned this important mission, the greatest of *missions*; was a blessing sent from God, worthy of great praise. And he was ready to make good of it.

Emil's specialty was seamanship. Though he was likewise skilled in munitions and killing, and was committed to do so, it was his ability to sail, and to read ocean charts, that had brought him this coveted assignment. He had worked on fishing boats in the Mediterranean and Red Sea, and on oil freighters in the Persian Gulf. When he heard his calling to join the brotherhood, like a cog in the wheel of a big machine, his attributes were categorized and fitted in.

Now his grey eyes peered vigilantly out the pilothouse windshield as they passed, slowly, the many docks berthed with many fishing and pleasure boats. Ramzan stood nearby, also watching.

The mooring platform was an elongated structure built up from the water, stretching half a mile down the *embarcadero*. The docks followed the platform for its entirety, and with evening having come, most boats had returned from the sea. Above were restaurants, souvenir shops, and fishing supply out-fitters. And as they passed one restaurant with large glass windows, Emil looked up and saw several couples dining by candlelight.

"We have an audience," he said.

Ramzan did not speak. His dark, somber eyes flickered as he studied the activity. He was still thinking about an incident which occurred earlier.

"You once called me a fox among wolves," he said.

"Yes? It was meant to be a compliment. Simply that you use your mind instead of your strength."

"And that I can climb trees like a squirrel?"

"You can."

"Who is the squirrel now?"

Emil did not answer, nor did he say anymore. He just went further down on the throttle and concentrated on the water ahead. It was Ramzan's way, he thought, not to let things go. He was a perfectionist, even among the brotherhood.

An hour before, Emil had exchanged words with a young fisherman while loading gear from the dock. It was Ramzan's wise hand that had pulled Emil back just as he was about to leap from one boat to the next and pummel the young fisherman.

There was no need to speak of it further, Emil thought. He had already acknowledged the stupidity of it.

The harbor exit lay ahead to the left. Emil wrapped his big hands around the pilot-wheel and turned it down, and the trawler immediately began distancing itself from the docks and all the activity of the port. Keeping the wheel down, the boat headed out the mouth of the harbor.

The two men had entered the United States three months earlier, via a long, grueling route which began in Syria, from where they had flown to Greece, then to Mexico City, and then crossed the border into the United States near Nogales, affording a measure of anonymity. A flight would have incurred a *Passenger Name Record*—PNR—subject to scrutiny by the airline and the Transportation Security Administration. That would have been impossible, since both men were on the State Department's 'watch list'. Having crossed the border as they did, on foot, in theory they did not exist. They had simply blown in with the wind. And they had found help along the way from sleeper cells and sympathetic followers who shared in their faith. With money, passage came easy enough, and with a shared brotherhood, money was always waiting.

Once in the United States, however, they had to wait, endlessly it seemed, lying low in dingy hotel rooms trying to make themselves as inconspicuous as possible. They did their best to blend in with the locals. The shaving of the faces was particularly distasteful to Ramzan. It was not only an appearance issue, but one of faith and tradition. Having to feel the cold air against his cheeks was something he begrudged, but knew was necessary.

Their vessel, a well-weathered *steel monohull* commercial fisher, had been leased one week earlier under false names in a quick cash transaction. No documents had been drawn, nor credit checks conducted, nor was there any need for identity verification. A large wad of one-hundred dollar bills was simply followed by a handshake

Now, finally, the months of labor, and waiting, would find fruition.

The trawler exited the mouth of the harbor to a darkening sky. The Pacific unfolded before her, hurling huge waves against her bow. The western horizon was barely distinguishable now; marked only by an indiscrete line of purple and blue.

As they continued seaward, Emil checked the *Garmin GPS* screen. He had plotted a paralleling course that would keep them three and a half miles off the coast, and upon reaching that distance, he turned to the south on a parallel line with the shore.

"You can relax for now," he finally said. "We are a safe distance from the harbor, and from that one," he said, referring to the young fisherman. He glanced over at Ramzan to see his response, but there was none. "Thank you, Brother," he added, again referring to the incident.

There was silence in the pilothouse, and although Emil hoped for a reply, he knew there'd be none. He had grown accustomed to Ramzan's lack of verbiage. There was no need for words in Ramzan's world. Words only spoiled things, giving clues to one's enemies. If Ramzan needed to speak, it was for a reason. Ramzan spoke with actions.

Emil chuckled to himself, thinking he should have known that by now. "Go below and get some rest if you want," he finally said. "We have two hours."

Ramzan gazed back silently. His familiar disdainful expression said it all. They were on a mission. They were warriors of *God.* There was a *western* soul of hatred that despised them, the new *Crusaders,* and like the crusaders of old, they were full of religious contempt and ill-will, and Ramzan wished to kill and destroy them.

*No time to relax,* Ramzan thought. *Time to review and prepare.*

A great moment was forthcoming, atonement for centuries of butchery, he thought. There were tasks ahead, necessary to make such plans real. Too much time and money had been expended, and brothers across the globe anxiously awaited news of their success—an entire world waited. With what short time they had left, he needed to rethink and rehearse.

Ramzan had learned to trust in ritualistic practice. He had grown accustomed to the famous dry-runs he and his brothers had used to uncover flaws in security and surveillance systems.

It had worked well on 9-11 and a thousand times since. But in this case, a dry-run was impossible. They had to rely solely on scouting reports, mental assuredness, a firm plan, practice, and *faith.*

*Faith was the key,* Ramzan thought, *faith and devotion; devotion beyond the love of one's life. Something an American could never understand.* He grinned. *It is why the faithful will prevail.*

Behind them, the distancing lights of Port Piedras were now nothing more than glittering clusters on the shore. Ramzan looked back at them. Then he exited the pilothouse down the short ladder to the foredeck.

On the foredeck, he stopped to steady his legs before ducking into the Captain's cabin. Once inside, Ramzan went to a drawer and took from it a small black bag. The Captain's cabin, which was situated beneath the pilothouse, was barely ten-feet by ten-feet. It had a small dining table affixed to a stainless-steel pole with wooden benches on either side. Ramzan placed the bag on the table, opened it, and withdrew two smart phones. Clicking them both on, he waited for them to flash through their opening menu sequence. Then he took a small piece of paper from his shirt pocket with a number scribbled on it, and programmed the number into the speed-dial function of each.

Above Emil was still reflecting on the incident with the young fisherman. It was true, he had nearly allowed this one man to destroy months of labor. *How foolish would that have been?* As regrettable an incident as it was, he still wished to kill the young fisherman. He was a faithless, over-privileged American, arrogant as well, and for those reasons alone, deserved to die.

A glance at his wristwatch told Emil they were ahead of schedule. If all went as planned, with good faith, good timing, and some good winds, his wish to kill the young fisherman could still come true.

*Maybe I kill you later tonight?*

# Chapter 7

The Briefing Room was alive with activity, as was always the case during shift change. Though many officers had already taken post, there was still several awaiting dispatch. At the coffee pot was Pryce Johnson, a seasoned foot patrol officer assigned to Patrol Two tonight, the northwest quadrant of the power plant; Carl Harrington who drew the Patrol Three slot, which covered the northeast quadrant; and Grant, an off-going officer from the swing shift. Having finished his eight hours, he was hanging around only to see the results of his wager.

The three men spoke loudly, each holding five-dollar bills in their hands. On the far side of the room, Kelly Murphy, one of three females on the night shift, watched them as she slipped into a dark blue, company-issued jumpsuit, which closely resembled those worn by Air Force pilots. Her radio stood on its end on the wooden bench beside her, crackling with static.

Drake Fischer, the studious one, sat at the far end of the center table behind his odd-looking wire-rimmed spectacles. He was deep in thought, studying some kind of manual. It seemed Drake was always studying one manual or another.

At the front of the room, Sergeant Jacobs, the nightshift Sergeant, a short, stocky man, stood with a clipboard in hand. Before him was the Shift Assignment Board; a large whiteboard, mounted on the forward wall; where the night's assignments were posted. Essentially it was a visual grid of the post assignments, listing the twelve security posts in rows on the left and the three shifts in columns across the top; day, evening, and night. Using a dry-eraser, Sergeant Jacobs erased a name from it.

The Briefing Room was a twenty-by-forty foot gathering place where officers met at the beginning and end of each shift, got their assignments, and accessed their personnel lockers. It served concurrently as a break room, lunch room, coffee room, or just a place to hang out in between shifts. The large rectangular table in the middle of the room seated twelve, the exact number of field officers assigned to each shift. The biblical significance of this number was purely coincidental, although someone had once reference them as the twelve *Knights Templar* of the modern era. The lockers were on the east wall, one assigned to each officer, and there was a changing bench in front of them. At the back of the room was a countertop with a sink, a coffee pot, and a mini refrigerator-freezer.

The night-shift briefing had already taken place, assignments had already been drawn by lottery—a procedure which, in theory, was meant to keep officers from knowing their post assignment in advance—and the officers were awaiting dispatch. Sergeant Jacobs, having conducted the drawing, was now logging officer's names on the shift assignment board using an erasable watermark stylus.

He stood back for a moment and looked up at the board. Two blank spots still awaited the names of Cameron and Jack Garner. A glance at the wall clock told him the two were more than twenty minutes late. Crinkling his brow, he moved ahead and began copying the information from the board onto the '*Shift Assignment Record*,' a one sheet, eight-by-eleven form which served as the archival record of the night's assignments—a requirement of the Nuclear Regulatory Commission.

Just as Sergeant Jacobs lowered his head, Cameron poked his head into the room, sparking off commotion at the coffee pot. The three officers turned their heads in unison, looked at him, and then looked at the wall clock. Apparently in disgust, Pryce Johnston and Carl Harrington slapped their five-dollar bills down on the counter and Grant greedily snapped them up.

As the three men exited the briefing room, squeezing past, Pryce Johnston paused. "You cost me again buddy."

Cameron shrugged. "Sorry."

Cameron tried to avoid eye contact with Sergeant Jacobs as he made his way to the table. He swung his daypack down onto the table, pulled out a chair, but decided to remain standing and await the remarks he knew were forthcoming.

"You've got Mobile One," was all that Jacobs said. "Peters is out there waiting for you, running loops around the perimeter fence."

"All right," was Cameron's reply.

Jacobs turned to the shift assignment board, knelt down, and with the stylus, added Cameron's last name, *Taylor*, to one of the remaining blank spots. When he finished, he turned and looked around the briefing room.

"Where's your side kick?" he asked Cameron.

"Don't know," Cameron replied.

"You mean he's not here?"

"Not unless he came with you."

"Funny." Jacobs paused. "So you are saying he didn't ride with you tonight?"

"Nope."

"Did he mention anything to you about it?"

"Nope."

"You'd better let Harkin know."

"He already knows," Cameron said. Of course Cameron didn't want to chance another encounter with Harkin. "Frankly, I thought Jack was already here, drinking coffee, shooting the bull with you guys."

"Well, he's not," Jacobs mumbled. He gave Cameron a weary glance. "It must be contagious, hanging around with you and all."

"What?" Cameron asked.

"Hanging out with you..." Jacobs groaned. "You know what I mean."

"Not really," Cameron replied, though he knew exactly what he meant.

"He's saying people who hang out with you become screw-ups," said a voice at the end of the table. The three other people still in the briefing room, Sergeant Jacobs, Kelly Murphy, and Cameron, turned their heads and looked. Drake's pale eyes peered above the top of his wire-rimmed glasses, beckoning a reply. He used his index finger to push his glasses further up the bridge of his nose.

*Attack while the opposition is down,* Cameron thought. *Better not go there.*

"Thanks for clarification Drake," Cameron said.

Drake hesitated but kept his gaze on Cameron. Cameron could see the wheels turning in his head, formulating some kind of intellectual retort. Drake was baiting him, he knew. And as Cameron looked at Drake, he realized just how deceivingly nerdish-looking Drake was. Always with that neatly cropped red hair, pants impeccably creased and cuffed, and those golden, wire-rimmed glasses that gave him the look of a Rhodes Scholar. Drake was the stereotype model of the socially inept, but scientifically accomplished.

*Though nerdish he is not.* In fact, Drake was the elite among an elite security force. High strung but brilliant, he was as well known for his physical abilities as for his intellect. He had taken home the firearms trophy when Cameron, who also qualified in the top tier, declined the invitation to compete. This competition was among all the law enforcement agencies in central California, and yet Drake brought home the trophy. His bright mind, incredibly high personal standards, obsession with detail, and his in-depth knowledge of the security manuals, made him the top cadet in his class, and a darling among the administrators. But his arrogance and brown-nosing caused him to be disliked by his peers.

"No offense intended," said Drake.

"None taken," Cameron replied.

"Come on guys, let's get going," Jacobs said. "There are people out there wanting to go home." After saying that, he gave a mocking smile.

"That's our Sergeant," Kelly Murphy said. "Always smiling."

"It's because I know something is always up," Jacobs frowned.

The crackling of the radios brought everyone's attention back to the process at hand—the changing of the guard.

"Control One to Patrol One," the voice on the radio said. It was Lewis Smith, the Control One computer operator dispatching from his station deep in the heart of the power plant. "Control One to Patrol One. Please report to your post."

Lewis' familiar voice got Kelly Murphy moving. She snapped up her radio, keyed the transmitter, and replied, "Patrol One here. Ten-Four."

"Roger that," Lewis voice said, with that bright and classic tone of his.

His voice, which had a special phonetic hum to it—somewhat like that of a news reporter or radio talk-show host, had become the calming voice of the Night Shift.

Kelly tucked her radio into the sheath on her utility belt, made her way across the room to the door, turned back and looked back with a mischievous little grin. "Have fun boys."

Cameron smiled. Drake did not.

Shifting his eyes back to the shift assignment board, Cameron followed down the '*Night Shift*' column but couldn't find Grace's name anywhere. "Where's Gracie?" he asked.

Jacobs replied by tapping the corner of his clipboard against the very bottom corner of the board. There, in bold stylus, was Grace's last name: "BAKER."

"Lucky Grace, she got *Rover* again," Jacobs said.

The sight of Grace's name brought a smile to Cameron's face, and realizing it had done so, Cameron laughed to himself. *You really are smitten!*

Down the hallway, three offices away, Supervisor Harkin stood above his desk with a phone pressed to his ear. His brow furrowed as the phone rang, but no one answered.

Twelve miles away, in the small beach cottage across from the Sea Gypsy Apartments, the bodies of Jack Garner and the young woman lay motionless as the telephone rang on the dark nightstand. Beside it, the blue digital numbers on the clock radio flipped over another minute. Outside, in the shadows of the rear carport, Jack's BMW remained parked.

Harkin huffed, shook his head, and depressed his finger on the phone transceiver.

"Damn!"

Having an uncovered post was one thing, but Jack's post—Security Computer Operator Two—would not be an easy one to cover. By protocol, it was to be manned by a 'computer' certified officer, or at least a trainee, and since certification came only after months of training, testing, and many hours signed-off by an already certified operator, the pickings were slim, especially on the nightshift. Jack was one of three certified officers on the nightshift, and was generally reliable, but not tonight.

Harkin stared at the phone. Then he scrambled through the papers on his desk, looking for the employee phone log. He recalled that Sam Jenkins, a day shift alternate, had recently asked him for overtime. Specifically, Jenkins, a 'computer' trainee, wanted more hours so he could gain his certification and the stipend that came with it. Jenkins had even mention he'd pull a double-shift.

Harkin located the phone log, paged through it, dropped his finger to the name 'Sam Jenkins' which had a little asterisk beside it denoting '*Computer Authorized Officer*,' and dialed the number.

He waited. No one answered, and after a few rings, a standard recording came on asking the caller to leave a message at the tone.

"This is Larry Harkin," Harkin said into the phone. "If you get this message by eleven o'clock and want to work tonight, in Station Two, please give me a call at the Plant. I'd really appreciate it."

He hung up the phone.

In the Briefing Room, Jacobs pulled a sheet of paper from his clipboard and handed it to Cameron. "You didn't miss much," he said, speaking rapidly. "They'll be a training session on the sixteenth and seventeenth, a refresher course on CPR...you're scheduled for the sixteenth." Cameron grimaced—*terrific!* "And vacation requests for next quarter must be in by Tuesday." Jacobs paused. "And, oh, yeah, another bomb threat. That's it."

Cameron lifted his head and looked at Jacobs, his eyes full of anticipation. So rare were bomb threats, or intelligence reports of any consequence, that when they did come in, they were almost welcomed news.

"There was nothing to it," Jacobs said. "The Day Shift took the dogs out, searched all afternoon, and found nothing. Probably just some frustrated protester, as usual. Still we need to take the usual precautions."

Cameron nodded.

"The only bomb threat you really have to worry about is the one that isn't called in," Drake said from the end of the table.

Cameron and Jacobs looked down at him.

Drake shrugged. "The world is in a heightened state of paranoia."

"It's never hurts to be in a heightened state of paranoia when working at a nuclear power plant, especially in an age of terrorism," Jacobs said. "It keeps you in a heightened state of alert."

Jacobs checked Cameron's name off the list on his clipboard, and added a reminder note about Jack's absence.

Just then, Harkin burst into the room. The room went silent. He had that way—of entering a room and getting everyone's immediate attention. He glanced around quickly, and just as quickly, his eyes settled on Drake.

"Drake, what post do you have?" he asked.

"Patrol Four," Drake replied.

"Not any more." Harkin turned to Sergeant Jacobs, speaking quickly. "Put Drake in Control Two. Take Garner off the computer list, I don't mean permanently, I mean put him on the substitute list for the next week. Have him pull some foot patrols. Make the necessary adjustments to next week's schedule."

"Who covers Patrol Four?" Jacobs asked.

Harkin looked up at the shift assignment board, studying it briefly. "Who's still out there?"

"Peters," Jacobs replied.

"Ask Peters to pull a double shift. I think he'll be alright with it. He's been bugging me for overtime."

"And if he can't?"

"Ask him first. Tell him it's my request. If there's a problem, let me know." The two men glanced at one another as if there might be something more to say, but evidently there was not. Harkin shot a glance around the room. "Come' on guys, let's get going. The clock's ticking. People want to go home!"

Harkin left as abruptly as he had entered. *Problem solved.*

Although Drake hadn't achieved computer certification yet, he was damn close. *Close enough,* Harkin thought. The N.R.C. allowed for some flexibility in situations of problematic staffing. In such *rare* cases, a trainee could fill-in.

Though Harkin was reluctant to post Drake into the computer station, simply in fear of the repercussions that may follow—Drake being loathed by his co-workers and perceived as a subject of administrative favoritism, he had no choice. Jack's unforeseen absence put him in a bind. Perceptions would have to fall as they would. Still, seeing Drake's obscene grin upon his request didn't make matters any easier. *Arrogance is an unfortunate side effect of brilliance,* Harkin thought.

Drake gathered up his things and exited en route to Control Station Two.

Cameron, standing there like a cow needing a prod, looked back toward Grace's last name on the shift assignment.

"You heard him!" Sergeant Jacobs said.

"Aye aye, Sir!"

Snapping up his daypack, Cameron stuffed it in his wall locker, placed his lunch pail in the employee refrigerator, and headed for the door.

"Peters is waiting," Jacobs said impatiently. "And he's probably pissed."

Cameron shrugged. "Maybe not so much anymore, now that he'll be getting some overtime?"

"Get going!" Jacobs exhaled.

Cameron exited, down the hallway to the Armory where he would collect his utility gear and weapons.

# Chapter 8

The Armory was located in the rear corridor, not far from Control Station Two. Essentially nothing more than a cubbyhole in the wall, it consisted of a roll-up, steel, bay door and a countertop. Cameron likened it to an *armored hotdog stand*, whereby one could acquire an odd assortment of lethal weapons; hold the mustard, please.

Despite the small façade, in the rear was more than five-hundred square foot of storage space, housing the entire arsenal of the Mal Loma Nuclear Power Plant security force. Kept there was everything from the field utility belts, flashlights, radios, and batons, to the standard issue 9mm *Beretta* pistols, Mini-14 combat rifles, and a set of five 300 magnum Weatherby rifles—among the flattest shooting rifles in the world, along with their full compliment of sophisticated star scopes and infrared equipment. The thought was, they couldn't prevent a hill-top sniper, but maybe they could out-range them. Also there were canisters of pepper spray, mace defensive spray, gas masks, and a dozen *Stun-Master* 775,000 volt, stun guns; the latter of which had become a favorite tool for separating the non-violent protestors who occasionally locked arms across the entrance road at San Roque Gate. And, of course, there was enough ammunition to start a small war.

The *Ruger* Combat Mini-14 had become the Security Force's rifle of choice at Mal Loma after considerable debate. By some standards, it was considered an obsolete weapon. But its lethality, practicality, and reliability were never in question. Short and compact at just thirty-seven inches, lightweight at less than seven pounds, it was the ideal weapon for close-quarters combat, and with a 30-round, .223 caliber replaceable banana clip, it was not short on firepower. What won over the Mini-14 above the newer sophisticated weapons was its featured gas-operated, anti-recoil action. The rifle had absolutely no kick and could be fired without having to bring it to one's shoulder—a feature favored by the female officers.

The Mini-14s were kept in a long rack behind the counter, securely locked with a cable running through their trigger-guards.

Standing before Cameron was John Hunt, the lingering swing shift *'Armorer.'* It was an extra half hour of overtime with the responsibility of collecting, inspecting, and dispersing weapons from one shift to the next.

Cameron was handed a field utility belt, which he wrapped around his waist and buckled. Then came his handgun, retrieved from a back shelf. Hunt laid it on the countertop. Cameron picked it up and inspected it, pulling back the hammer, holding it out to one side, making sure the chamber was clear, then slapping in a clip and holstering it. He then made a radio call to Chris Peters, letting Peters know he was on his way out front. Peter's didn't seem too anxious now. Having driven around the Plant for an extra half hour, and having received word he'd be pulling a double-shift, he was in no hurry to reply.

On his way to the entrance lobby, Cameron made a pit stop in the employee restroom. Inside was Fred O'Neil, the affable, fiftysomething, father figure of the night-shift. Cameron joined him at the urinal, and before long a conversation commenced.

"You don't have to be the best dressed person at the party, just not the worst," Fred said.

"What?" Cameron asked, turning and looking at Fred.

"I heard Jack was a no-show tonight."

"Oh, yeah."

"Having a friend mess up worse than you can take the heat off."

"Oh, okay. Yeah, maybe you're right."

"That's what friends are for," Fred chuckled. Finishing up, he went to the sink to wash his hands. "By the way, Grace told me to say *Hi*."

"What?"

"Grace said to say *Hi*"

"She just said to say *Hi?*"

"Yeah. She said, tell you *Hi*."

Cameron paused, thoughtfully. He remembered they had agreed to meet, as usual, at the beginning of the shift. In his hurry to get to work and to avoid Harkin, he had forgotten all about it. It had become their nightly routine, after the draw of assignments, to meet, compare posts, and plan a possible rendezvous, if possible, sometime during the shift. If not possible, then at least they'd plan to meet during lunch. In the short time they had been acquainted they had met nearly every night; that is, so long as Cameron was not late.

"Did she say anything else?"

"Nothing," Fred replied. "That was it. But I saw her watching for you."

"Watching for me?"

"I think she was. She was standing in the lobby looking out the front windows, and she was looking at her watch. I think she was looking for you?" Fred looked over at Cameron. "She looked rather sad too, and when she was dispatched to her post her lips were all curled up."

*Shit!* Cameron was not sure he wanted to hear more.

"That's when she told me to tell you *Hi*."

"Hey Fred, can you do me a favor?"

"Of course."

"Give her a message when she comes in on her break?"

"Sure."

"Tell her I'm sorry I missed her, and I'll catch her at the end of the shift." Cameron knew she would understand that he had been assigned the mobile unit and therefore, could not meet on their lunch break.

"Sure thing," Fred replied.

"Thanks Fred."

"No problem."

Fred finished up and exited, saying; "Have fun out there. And try not to sleep too much," referring to the 'park and snooze' practice often employed by officers assigned the mobile units.

"Thanks," Cameron replied.

Cameron washed his hands, left the restroom, and as he headed for the Entrance Lobby, he thought of Grace. *Unforgivable,* was the word that came to his mind. *I should have at least called her.*

For better or for worse, it didn't matter, he thought. Their posts would be taking them in separate directions this night. Grace would spend the night wandering randomly through the power plant, while he patrolled the backroads of the property.

In the entrance lobby, Cameron looked out the large windows which overlooked the parking lot. He could imagine Grace standing there, waiting for him. As he went through the search train in reverse fashion, he pictured her looking out the window again, imagining it like a scene in a Hollywood movie; her hands pressed against the glass, anticipating him, beckoning him; the warm glow of her face, longing for him, wanting him; her thick amber hair flowing down.

She is a woman of unrivalled beauty, he thought, a woman pure of heart with eyes that radiated genuineness, and she *deserves better.*

As unpredictable as these things go, and as capricious as love can be, Cameron knew from the first time he'd seen Grace that she would become a major part of his life. It was one of those fleeting moments when you see someone in passing, at a train station or on a city street, and think it's someone you know, or someone you should know, but really you have never seen them before. Then you realize it might be that person you're supposed to spend the rest of your life with, and suddenly they're gone, and you live to regret it. It had happened on a sunny afternoon, driving home, passing the firearms range. Cameron heard the typical popping sound of gun fire, and when he looked up through the passenger-side window, he saw a line of cadets firing away at a row of silhouettes. At the near-end was a shapely young female, her full hair shining nearly red in the sunlight. He could not see her face but there was something attractive about her, and Cameron took note.

Three weeks later when she was presented to the night shift by Supervisor Harkin, Cameron instantly recalled the shapely young woman he had seen at the firearms range. But now he was seeing her for the first time up close and personal.

They were all gathered there in the briefing room at shift change when Harkin entered with this knockout gorgeous young woman.

Cameron was speechless.

"I'd like to introduce to you," Harkin announced, "…the newest member of the Midnight Shift, and recent graduate from the academy, Grace Baker."

Grace stepped in through the doorway with her long amber hair flowing down the lapels of her regal blue uniform and her almond-shaped green eyes flashing through the occupants in the room. Her face was bursting with personality. It seemed to Cameron, in that moment, he had found a long lost friend—one he'd been searching for all his life.

The attraction was reciprocal. Nearly simultaneous with Cameron's eyes locking on to hers, Grace's eyes latched onto his. Even though Cameron sat at the far side of the room among a dozen other security officers, somehow he gained her notice. There was something about his smile that likewise seemed familiar to Grace—a little shy but with an edge and boyish exuberance. Grace instantly felt something. She found herself smiling back at him, not knowing exactly why.

"She will be replacing Carl," Supervisor Harkin said. "Who will be moving on to the swing shift at the end of this week. We wish Carl good luck, and we welcome Grace."

The group applauded, and Grace blushed.

"Help her out and show her the ropes. And guys…" Harkin said, pausing to look around the room. "Go easy on her!"

In short order, the relationship bloomed, and with each passing night, their affection for one another grew in leaps. After a couple of weeks they were an inseparable duo. Grace made Cameron feel like a school kid again, in love for the first time, and Cameron provided Grace with constant amusement and a knowledgeable guide who could show her the *ins and outs* of 'nuclear security.' It could not have come at a better time for Cameron. Ready to quit, sick of a job that dragged him down, Grace provided him with newfound enthusiasm for the security work that paid his rent. He found himself once again wanting to appease the boss. Still, his impromptu nature sometimes got the best of him. Being tardy tonight was not a planned act of rebellion. It was part of his nature—an oversight, a slight diversion in his road toward renewal.

Cameron gazed out the large entrance lobby windows, and sighed.

*Sorry Gracie. I'll make it up to you, promise I will.*

The night was already turning into its typical succession of foul ups. But before the night was through, Cameron was determined to redeem himself to Grace, if no one else. He had too.

After getting through the search train he exited out the front doors to wait for Peters.

On the far end of the Security Building, Supervisor Harkin made a sudden return to the briefing room. Sergeant Jacobs, having finished the shift log, sat at the conference table reviewing a pile of vacation requests, arranging them in order of seniority and matching those with competing dates.

"We covered?" Harkin asked in his gruff voice.

Jacobs raised his head and looked at the shift assignment board. "For the moment."

Harkin, also glancing over the board, placed a hand to his chin.

"Gracie has Rover again?"

"Yeah."

"Twice in a row?"

"Yes, and three times this week."

Harkin looked uneasy. "Is that right?"

Jacobs nodded. "Yeah, three times this week. Luck of the draw."

Harkin frowned.

It was always a good thing for a rookie to be assigned to the '*Rover Patrol*' simply because it enabled them to familiarize themselves with the Plant. By design, it was an unaccounted-for post meant to roam haphazardly about the plant; the keycard of which was programmed with unrestricted access, except for areas of critical function. Grace having drawn the post on consecutive nights was merely her good fortune. Harkin's concern was with how it might look to the Regulatory Commission when they audited their shift records. And what the administrators might think when they learn that a *beautiful* rookie had somehow pulled the coveted assignment three times in one week.

"How long has she been out of the academy?"

"About a month," Jacobs said, and then paused. "Well, they had her on the day shift for a couple weeks before joining us. This will be her third week with us, first week solo."

"First week solo and three Rover posts?"

Jacobs shrugged. "She's lucky. Anyhow, it's good for her to see the plant at night. Things always look different at night."

"Yeah… Things always look different at night."

Once more Harkin glanced over the shift assignment board as if to weigh the night's allocation of assignments. Everything was covered. Things looked good. There was no need for him to feel uneasy, but he did.

"It's just another night boss," Jacobs said.

"Yeah, just another night." Harkin paused. "I'll be in my office if you need me," he said. "They've got me buried with the paperwork, as usual."

"Anything I can help with?"

"You've got your own paperwork, but thanks. Just keep an eye on them. Make sure there's no clowning around."

"I do that every night. It's a never ending job."

Harkin frowned again and headed back to his office.

Jacobs looked up at the shift assignment board and smiled. A full compliment of nightshift officers, minus one, was either on post or headed there. Despite a rough start, all was well.

He dropped his head back down to the stack of vacation requests and continued sorting through them.

# Chapter 9

Emil's unmistakable steel-grey eyes peered out through the pilothouse windshield as the Steel Monohull sliced steadily south through four-foot swells. He could vaguely make out the shore, a hazy white line of pounding surf below a grayish band of sandstone cliffs. Above the shoreline were the huge dark coastal mountains, the peaks of which were barely discernable from the sky.

The Pacific was rougher than Emil had expected, and with the hull nearly empty and the pilothouse riding high, he was feeling the full effect of it. Not that it bothered him much. He was no stranger to rough seas. As a young man he had seen his fair share of squalls. Long ago, on the Red Sea, he was among the crew of an Egyptian ferry which capsized when the captain failed to heed the weather warnings, drowning more than two-hundred of its passengers. The incident did not ruin his love for the sea. The unpredictability of it and danger associated with it, in fact, increased his admiration.

*But the sea was like a lake compared to this one*, he thought.

He gazed ahead at the whitecaps, appreciatively. He listened to the steady thumping of the swells against the bow. As any seaman knows, the ocean can have a lulling effect. It gives one time to reflect mentally. If one's mind was not free to ponder the issues at hand, after watching ocean swells for an hour it would be.

Emil was in the middle of one of these deep reflections when Ramzan abruptly entered the pilothouse.

"Is everything okay?"

"Many to kill," Emil said.

"Yes. Many to kill."

"Without causing alarm."

"Yes, without causing alarm." Ramzan paused thoughtfully. "Is there a problem?"

"No problem," Emil said. "We have rehearsed plenty. We are ready."

Ramzan nodded. "Our plan is god-given. The timing and sequence is what makes it work. It is always the timing; patience and preciseness of sequence."

"Yes, timing and sequence… and sureness of shot, and the American doing what he promised."

Ramzan's dark eyes studied Emil a long moment. "You have reservations about this one now?"

"None," Emil said, turning his eyes away.

*Funny,* he thought, *it was I who had to convince Ramzan.* "It is a good plan and everything will go well," he then spoke loudly.

"And we have our brothers with us," Ramzan reassured.

Emil paused.

"In spirit," Ramzan explained.

"Of course."

The ship was lifting and dropping and Ramzan grabbed hold of the handrail. "Is it always this rough?"

"Not always, but it is an ocean."

Still clinging on, Ramzan looked out the windshield. To the east the dark coastline moved slowly. There were many white-crowned waves separating them from the shore. Some of the waves had swirls of mist rising from them, looking like ghostly vapors.

"Yes, I think they are with us now," Ramzan said.

Emil gave Ramzan a curious gaze, wondering where those words had come from.

"Our brothers," Ramzan clarified.

"Yes, of course they are with us."

Ramzan continued watching the waves, specifically the ghostly vapors. He looked upon them as if they were spirits of dead *Jihadists*. He leaned forward and looked up through the windshield at the twinkling stars. "And we have a black night," he said, motioning up. "The *Great One* has provided us with a nice veil under which to do our work."

"Yes," Emil nodded.

The ship lifted again, violently and without warning this time, and as it came back down Ramzan felt a strange sensation. It was not a feeling he particularly liked. He had first recognized this feeling upon the boat's departure from the breakers at Port Piedras, but thought nothing of it. He had never been in a ship on an ocean before, so he was not privy to the havoc such motion could cause to one's equilibrium. He looked over at Emil, who seemed unaffected by the movement.

"I'll go below now, and prepare," Ramzan said, waiting for his stomach to settle.

Before departing he took one more glance out the windshield and saw some unusual movement on the foredeck. Tethered there was their Zodiac Mark III shore vessel—a high-speed inflatable nicknamed 'Grand Raid' by its manufacturer. As the big boat rocked back and forth, the inflatable rocked as well, seemingly off its mooring.

"Is it loose?" Ramzan asked.

Emil shrugged. "I thought I tightened it well?"

Ramzan gave a disgusted scowl and hurried out the pilot-house, down the ladder, intent on securing the water craft. As he crossed the fore-deck though, he felt the awful sensation again. The ship was swaying more fiercely now and with greater intensity and it compelled him to stop. He tried to hold steady, but his legs were wobbly beneath him. At one moment, standing there trying to gain his equilibrium, his head felt like it was being swashed back and forth in a washing machine. He paused until the swells lessened in height, then he hurried across the deck and secured the tether-line, pulling it down tightly on both sides and locking it in place. From inside the inflatable he took a waterproof duffle bag, cradled it in his arms, and made his way back across the fore-deck to the Captain's cabin.

Once inside, he set the bag on the table and unzipped it. From within, he withdrew two tightly-wrapped, bread-loaf sized bags. He removed the black plastic from the first, revealing within a rectangular package neatly wrapped in military-green wax paper. Stamped on its side were black numbers and "Block Demolition C-4". The contents of the second bag revealed an identical twin. He laid both packages carefully out on the table before him.

Despite not feeling well, Ramzan smiled. But feeling the way he was, it was best to prepare things now. He took from the duffle bag a cell phone with its back removed. It had a couple wires hanging freely from the rear. Proceeding cautiously, he centered the cell phone on the top of the first package and secured it using black electrical tape. He was careful not to cover the screen or keypad. He wrapped the tape around the top and bottom edge of the phone only. With eyes beaming, he removed the second package from its plastic bag. Then he aligned each package neatly, side by side.

They were unsophisticated as far as bombs go; each eight pounds of C-4 explosives, one with the face of a Nokia cell phone strapped across the front. The detonators—a simple wire with a blasting cap—were yet to be affixed. Although Ramzan preferred PE4 he had to settle on C-4 simply because PE4, the British military equivalent, was not easily obtainable in the United States. He had 'overpacked,' a common practice used to make sure there was enough explosives to perform the job at hand. Simultaneous detonation would be achieved using a simple connecting wire. The one cell phone would detonate each, simultaneously; the *SIM* card of which had been preprogrammed to the cell phone Ramzan kept in his pocket. It was a clever little trick Ramzan had learned in the oil fields of southern Iraq. They had lit more than thirty wells simultaneously with a single phone call. Theoretically, one could detonate a thousand bombs at once using the same technique.

Ramzan gazed at the two devices as one looks upon one's children.

*Tonight we will avenge the Innocents,* he grinned.

Ramzan had learned many things growing up in a war-battered country. The beauty of simplicity was one of them. Toting an AK-47 at the age of twelve, by the time he was sixteen, he was rigging IEDs and body-strapped explosive devices for suicide bombers heading off for destinations throughout Baghdad. He had lost his father to the government-sponsored militia. His two older brothers were likewise killed, and his younger sister raped and disfigured. He wanted likewise to be a martyr, but his wise teacher and mentor, a feared rebel leader, from whom he took his name after his father had died, had other plans for him. The value of *talent* in a war of attrition was a thousand times greater than that of a martyr, which in itself was great, but expendable. And Ramzan's talent was unique, and greatly desired in an age of underhanded warfare.

When fighting against a monster so large, Ramzan knew, one must use its strength against it, and use hit and run tactics, and strike with terror that shocks and demoralizes.

From a very young age, he showed craftiness, and frugalness. He had the unique ability to improvise, with less, using such items as mortar rounds, grenades, unearthed *Claymores,* and unspent rocket warheads. With the *Western* governments ratcheting up their 'War on Terror,' pooling together their resources and intelligence, creating international counterterrorism teams, having the advantage of satellite surveillance technology and drones, and smart bombs to strike from the sky, Ramzan had to prove to be as clever as they, if not more so. As soon as one method of detonation and concealment was uncovered, he'd find another. It had become a battle of wits and stealth, in which Ramzan seemed to consistently keep one step ahead. As they got smarter, he got smarter, and along the way he honed his skills.

The carnage seemed endless. It became a daily media event, to report worldwide, often with the aide of graphic video, the daily bombings by body count, associated with the doings of Ramzan. If not always an active participant, certainly he was a passive one by imparting his knowledge to others.

*But who had drawn first blood?* Ramzan always justified. *It was God's will and God's wrath that their blood be drawn too, and spilt upon their soil.*

Roadside bombs, vehicle bombs, package bombs, body bombs, and even false bombs to occupy the attention of the aggressors while the real ones went off behind their backs. Ramzan was personally responsible for deadly bombings in Turkey, Pakistan, Afghanistan, the former Yugoslavia, and Algiers, the later of which killed at least thirty people and ripped apart the facade off the prime minister's palace. It was all his handiwork. He developed a fine pride in his ability. He took a special interest in training teenagers in the deadly art of booby traps, and had spent time in Afghanistan and Pakistan educating the *new* brothers at rebel training camps.

Now, as Ramzan's eyes gazed down upon these two simple devices, there upon this foreign sea, he realized he was about to embark on his greatest of all feats.

And it was *so simple, yet so ingenious.*

A sudden movement of the boat caused his vision to blur. Holding on to the edge of the table, he looked up at the cabin ceiling. It seemed to elongate and twist before him. He was practically stationary, but everything was spinning. That strange gyration racked his insides again.

*Oh Almighty One!* he thought. *Keep me steady long enough to impart your will!*

The sea suddenly calmed. Ramzan inhaled deeply and his vision returned, so did the strength in his legs. He focused again on the two devices as they regained their form.

*This will make everything well*, he thought.

The sudden calmness between swells gave him the chance to smile again.

It seemed very little, just sixteen pounds in total. So often in the past it had taken one hundred times that amount to create havoc not equal in scale to one one-ten-thousandth of what this would produce.

Ramzan marveled at the genius of his plan.

There was no need to sneak an atomic bomb into the United States, nor to try to assemble one from many parts smuggled across many borders, which were now watched over like never before. There was no need to create clandestine laboratories to manufacture tons of nerve agent at the risk of being uncovered, nor to try and disburse it via a fleet of crop dusters or some other airborne method. The cleverness was in using one's enemy's own technology against him. Be it a jet airliner, an 18-wheeled gasoline truck, or best yet, a nuclear power plant.

It would be the ultimate *dirty bomb* Ramzan knew.

*To defeat an enemy so large, one must use what he gives you.*

But the brilliance of the plan went beyond having your enemy create its own dirty bomb for you, to be used against itself—although that was indeed clever enough. Targeting the cooling pipes of a nuclear reactor with a mere sixteen pounds of C4 would eventually drive the fission process into a crazed, unstoppable chain reaction resulting in a nuclear meltdown, from which would emerge deadly gamma rays of radiation with the potential of killing thousands—hundreds of thousands if properly dispersed.

It was the *Wind* that made the plan truly clever. The intentional use of the *Wind*—nature's natural force, one of unimaginable power and of broadest reach—to become the harbinger of death, carrying deadly gamma rays to inland cities.

*No crop dusters needed*, Ramzan thought.

Ramzan breathed in deeply again. The dizziness was tolerable now, especially with the hope of their soon-to-be executed mission. Months before, the plan had brought a smile to his face when first conceived high in the mountains near Fallujah, and it did so again now. Although there had been moments of great victory in his past, there had been moments of failure as well, and in those moments of failure, Ramzan had questioned whether his life's quest would ever really be realized—to destroy *Western* thought. Now these doubts seemed gone forever. He could hear the war cry of his teacher, the great rebel leader of their holy war:

*Strike frequently and with equal ferociousness, and with the faith of all of those who have died before you, the faith of all the martyrs who paved our way, and the faith of all the righteous before you, and the brotherhood will prevail. Persistence, and time, and faith, they are our allies against those scorned of mind and weak of spirit. The infidels will perish!*

It was he who coined the phrase; "Soon in your city, will be the battle."

Ramzan looked green when he returned to the pilothouse. Emil glanced over him and laughed. He pulled a small pack of tablets from his shirt pocket and handed them to Ramzan. "Take some of these."

"What are they?"

"Dramamine. It's for motion sickness."

Ramzan studied the packet suspiciously—the words were in English. It was the product of a *Western* pharmaceutical company, all of that which he despised and distrusted. He looked doubtful. But he took two tablets from their clear-plastic foil slots, popped them in his mouth, and swallowed them quickly.

"Our respite has been provided by our enemy?" he said suddenly.

Emil glanced over at him. "Yes it has," he laughed.

They both smiled together.

Then Ramzan's stomach turned again as the trawler lifted and sank into a deep trough, and each time the boat lifted and sank, the agony returned.

# Chapter 10

The inside of the Lighthouse Tavern looked like every other beach biker-bar along the California coast with a small wooden dance floor, a seating area for about thirty, two pool tables, a twenty-foot bar, and an old jukebox in the corner, blaring out rock-n-roll music. It was large enough to accommodate the usual suspects—a rough crowd of bikers and misfits serviced by a lone barmaid running between them with *margaritas* and beers. The place was a San Roque landmark—the lure was in its long, disreputable history. Having once served as an embarkation station for steamship passengers running up and down the California coast and a hangout for sailors during World War II, it had since digressed into a meeting place for biker clubs en route between San Francisco and L.A. and a hangout for local eccentrics and nonconformists. It was the type of place where you could still get killed over a pool game or stabbed by a biker type simply because you looked at him the wrong way.

At the bar sat a stranger; an unfamiliar face. He fit in well with the other patrons as he was a large man sporting a few days of unshaven beard and wore a t-shirt that revealed a muscular physique.

"Beer?" the bartender asked, wiping the counter clean before him.

"Tecate," the Stranger said.

The bartender popped the top off a bottle and set it on the counter. "Two-fifty."

The Stranger pulled a twenty-dollar bill from his wallet, placed it on the counter, and watched as the bartender took it to the cash register.

The wall behind the bar was littered with an odd assortment of posters, license plates, bumper stickers, and business cards of every kind. There were business cards from landscapers to divorce attorneys, and license plates from Maine to Hawaii. The centerpiece was an old, ornate mantle clock, carved with figures of a whaling vessel. The stranger compared the time on his wristwatch to that on the clock. They were almost identical.

It was early.

He swiveled around on his stool and surveyed the activity. Before him were two bikers, decked in black riding leathers, playing a game of pool. One of them, a big-chested burly man, was leaning into the table, resting his big belly fully on it. He drew back his cue and fired a long shot. A solid-yellow ball smacked soundly into the corner pocket. The other biker, likewise troublesome-looking with tattoos running down the length of his arms, stood on the far side of the table leaning on his cue stick, looking on.

The big man leaned in again and took another shot, sending another ball swiftly into a pocket.

The Stranger's eyes glimmered. He had a special affection for all things physical, especially those which required hand-eye coordination. Skill in boxing, sharp-shooting, high-speed auto racing, and billiards, were all traits he found admirable, particularly when done well.

As the time progressed and the effects of the beer settled in, he lost track of the pool game. Instead he found himself thinking of the tasks ahead. With it, came a mental accounting of how he had arrived here. Considerations, both past and present, slowly consumed his thoughts.

In the past five years he had seen a whirlwind of activity. Seemingly he had spent the last three years traveling alone from one Third World country to another. It was a requirement of his trade. Some considered it a benefit while others dreaded it. For him, it was simply a lifestyle, leaping from one shoddy hotel or military post to another. And despite the fact that he was now back in the United States, in California, drinking Mexican beer near a beach, a new job just moments away, a parade of faraway places marched through his mind.

*Sierra Leone* among them.

Seemingly ages ago with all the activity in between, in reality it had been less than two years. He had strangled a man there with his bare hands. It was not necessary, he knew, not worth the immense pleasure he found in it. A young, strong giant of a man, maybe twenty-five years old, after a tussle, he ended up with a grip on his neck and crushed his windpipe, holding him up until his legs went still. It was easy in an environment where death was so plentiful. Now, just the memory of it got the adrenaline pumping through his veins again.

But it was off-kilter and amateurish.

*A professional must separate pleasure from work,* he thought.

He had killed many. Nearly always it was a robotic act—a soldier, a guard, a consular—a non-human thing that had to be removed. Everyone he had killed needed to be killed. It was a job he had to do. But in Sierra Leone, he got carried away with himself. He killed someone who didn't matter.

He reflected further back on his illustrious career. Having spent two years in Afghanistan, and two summers in the Caucasus, fighting along side mountain guerrillas, and with urban hit-and-run teams, it seemed he was forever fighting Russians. Then there were months of work in Iraq and Syria, and Libya. At a time he thought the craft of the mercenary had nearly died in America, he had been offered this work stateside. It was the typical way of finding new work, networking from one job to another.

*History always has a place for a man of military training, skilled in the art of killing,* he thought. Nothing had changed in the modern world. Where there was money, talent, an absent of allegiances, one could find work.

From Bosnia to South America, Sierra Leone to Chechnya, he had participated in military coups, civil wars, armed overthrows, and religious fighting, all of which paid well. Although he found assignments through private enterprise were generally more lucrative than those politically funded, for him, it didn't matter. Either way. So long as the money was there, he had no politics. His pride was in his impartiality. A professional goes where the money is without concern for political affiliation, religion, or nationality. Killing was simply a military science, from which one could generate cash.

Having slipped in Sierra Leone was not satisfying, only pleasurable.

The sound of the ball slapping into another corner pocket brought his attention back to the pool table. The tall, lanky biker, having just sunk the eight ball, was now dancing with his pool stick and coming his way. His next shot was for the nine ball, there on the bar-side of the table where the Stranger sat. The biker eyed him as he approached. Then laying out for his shot, he drew back his cue stick carefully. As he did, the end of it came against the Stranger's knee.

"Excuse me," the Stranger said.

"Hey man, watch it!" the lanky biker cried out. Though it was purely accidental, the biker didn't see it that way.

"It was an accident," the Stranger said. He moved his knee to the side, giving the lanky biker space to make his shot.

The biker gave him a serious, hard look, and then resumed his shot.

Again the lanky biker leaned over, drew back his pool cue, and fired the shot, missing the pocket, barely.

The next thing the Stranger knew the biker was on top of him, standing over him, angrily, with his cue stick gripped tightly in his hand.

"What the *Hell*, Man!" the biker yelled.

"Pardon me," the stranger replied.

"You messed with my shot!"

He hadn't touched the cue stick this time, the Stranger knew. But he didn't want a fight. "Sorry." He gave an apologetic shrug, held his hands out open, and swiveled around in the chair with his back facing the biker.

The biker wasn't satisfied. He grabbed the Stranger's shoulder and spun him back around. "Hey man, I'm talking to you."

"Yes?"

"I said you messed with my shot."

"I don't think so."

For a moment, they just looked at each other. Neither said anything. The biker saw something in the Stranger's eyes—something wild and crazy. Instead of taking it further, he gave a quick shoulder feint as if he was going to punch the Stranger in the face. When the stranger didn't flinch, the biker just laughed.

The stranger considered the situation, seriously.

Standing before him, belligerent, half-drunk, and ready to fight, the biker appeared to be a twig in his eyes, one he could easily break in one hand, or smash with his beer bottle. The biker's big buddy stood tall at the end of the pool table, flexing his huge chest muscles, letting the Stranger know he was there.

There's that one too, the Stranger thought. A little more difficult perhaps, but once this first one is down, I'll have a cue stick in my hand, which I can snap in half and ram the sharp edge straight through that big damned chest of his.

He recalled, instantly, a childhood moment when he had shot a big breasted bird off a telephone wire with a BB gun. The bird stood above him, exposing his big barreling chest to the sights of his gun. With one simple pull of the trigger the bird dropped dead off the wire, falling to the ground like a sack of beans.

*It would be that easy*, he thought. *It would not take long.*

Then the stranger sighed, regretfully. His mantra for this evening came back to him. *Remember Sierra Leon.* He swiveled back on his chair, away from the biker, facing toward the bar.

"That's right. Just watch it," the biker said.

No reply was necessary. *No need,* the Stranger thought. He took a long sip from the bottle of beer, doing so brazenly with his backside exposed to the biker, and returned his gaze upon the old clock.

*No one will try anything,* he thought, regrettably.

# Chapter 11

Cameron leaned against the front wall of the Security Building, gazing up at the stars, waiting for Peters to arrive in Mobile One. He had time to reflect—reflect on his life, the career suicide he was committing, where he had been and where he was going. He was still thinking about being late, and what Harkin would do when he finally came around to it, which surely he would. He wasn't going to let it slide. He was just too preoccupied to deal with it now. But when he came around to it, it was going to be something bad, Cameron surmised—something beyond a write-up in his file; he already had three of those. It would be extended probation, a suspension, or worse yet, termination.

So much had gone into getting this job, so much went into his training, and getting qualified. It seemed like an awful waste. The twelve weeks of training flashed through his mind like a Rolodex. Courses ranged from bomb detection and nuclear physics, to radio operations, self-defense, first aid and CPR, and the powers of arrest. As part of the indoctrination process, every security officer was schooled in the fundamentals of nuclear power. Hours were spent in a classroom learning the difference between alpha, beta and gamma rays of radiation. Many hours were spent on the firearms range, getting qualified for State compliance, and in conducting mock terrorist attacks.

On that first day at the power plant, Cameron found himself being fitted for a uniform, photographed for an identification badge, assigned an employee locker number, submitting a DNA sampling, and had a hand-geometry scan, the latter of which was entered immediately into the security computer for the purpose of cross identification. Lastly he was provided his *keycard*. With it, access was granted, or denied, depending on his nightly function. The keycard system was the new wave in world security; its functionality being utilized at the Pentagon and security instillations around the world. What worked at the Holiday Inn worked with greater purpose and design at Mal Loma Nuclear Power Plant.

So many procedures to follow; so many trainings to be checked off.

And all for what? Cameron thought. A short-lived, boring job in which he was imminently in risk of losing?

And Jack! Where the *hell* are you Jack? You should have called me! Maybe then I wouldn't have been late?

Cameron chuckled now, thinking back about it. Jack and he were good friends, as good as friends could be. They had been hired together. They had come up the ranks together. They were in the same 'Armed Responder' training group. Together they had endured the same rigorous instruction and exercises; the four weeks of classroom study, competency tests, and state exams to secure their Guard's license, radio, and firearms permit. And together they had partnered during the 'so-called' contingency drills and 'war games' conducted both in daylight and night-time. They'll be good memories if nothing more, Cameron thought.

The bright headlights of Mobile One came barreling around the corner into the parking lot, blinding Cameron as the vehicle swung into its designated parking stall. Out leaped Chris Peters, who promptly handed over the Jeep's keys and logbook.

Despite Cameron's belated appearance, Peters did not offer any unpleasant words. "There's some elephant seals off the promontory at the bone yard," was all he said.

"Oh," replied Cameron. "I'll have to check them out."

And without further ado, Peters vanished into the Security Building.

It was a brief transaction, and Cameron was happy for it. He climbed into the driver's seat, tossed the clipboard to the passenger side, cranked-on the engine, and adjusted the heater.

As he waited for the compartment to warm up, he looked back at the warm glow emitting from the front windows of the Security Building, knowing he would not see it again until his midshift break. He leaned forward, resting his arms on the steering wheel, and gazed up through the windshield at the brilliant white of starlight.

*What'd ya know? Falling stars and nebulas over a nuclear power plant?*

He was in no hurry to be dispatched. He was enjoying the sauna-like heat that was filling the compartment.

# Chapter 12

The NRC's security requirements for nuclear power plants were among the strictest of all federal regulations. If anyone knew this well, Drake Fischer did, standing there patiently outside the heavily armored door to Control Station Two. In the eight short months Drake had worked at the power plant, he had digested two thousand pages of security procedures, including Title Ten of the Federal Energy Code and the subsequently developed ten-volume set of security and contingency-plan procedures for Mal Loma. He, of all the officers of the midnight shift, had truly taken the assigned reading to heart, and likewise, amassed the most comprehensive knowledge of the security system, maybe even more so than his supervisor, and the administrators. Even now, with his eyes fixed on the solid steel door waiting for it to open, Drake conducted a mental run-down of the manual sections which pertained to the procedures that lay ahead.

With the executive decision having been made that nuclear energy was to be a part of the Nation's future power source, public protection and prevention of terrorism had become the next top priority. The controversy of nuclear energy would not be swayed by an aptly placed bomb, nor would the country's political sentiment or foreign policy be influenced by an act of terrorism. "An energy source held hostage is without value," a Congressman had poignantly put it. "If it is to become a target for those who want to destroy our way of life, then what good is it?"

Among the slew of American targets found on surveillance videos confiscated in raids across the globe, nuclear power plants and storage facilities were at the top of the list. They were seen as fat, ripe, iconographic targets for terrorists interested in killing a lot of people. Consequently, the NRC, under congressional direction, added an entire chapter to the Federal Code of Regulations, dedicated specifically to beefing-up security at nuclear facilities. It was meant to do exactly what the Congressman had inversely intended—to keep the country's nuclear power plants safe from the hands of fanatics and ill-wishers.

Determined to follow-through in every detail, the executives at the Pacific Alliance Power Company set forth on an ambitious planning campaign; hiring professional 'anti-terror' consultants, scouring over volumes of regulations, and integrating the most cutting-edge technologies and tactics into their strategic design. No cost would be spared. The end result came in the form of a thick blue binder—known simply as '*The Security Plan.*'

The entire plan was built upon a single premise—the presence of an *Inside Man*. The exact wording, as spelt out in Title 10 of the Energy Code, required "safeguards be built within the security system" to protect against "an *internal* threat of an insider, including an employee in any position" from "acts of radiological sabotage;" radiological sabotage being defined as "deliberate acts directed against the plant which could directly or indirectly endanger the public health and safety by exposure to radiation."

The code went on to describe in sobering detail, what could be expected by energy companies when defending nuclear power plants from acts of terrorism:

"Safeguards and protection systems must shield against both internal and external threats, and a conspiracy between the two, by highly trained, dedicated, and capable individuals." Specifically "a determined, violent external assault, attack by stealth or deceptive actions, of several persons with the following attributes; well-trained, dedicated individuals, including military training and skills, with inside assistance from a knowledgeable individual, who may have detailed knowledge of nuclear power plants and security systems and who may act in a passive or aggressive role by providing information, facilitating entrance, disabling alarms and communication systems, and who may participate in a violent attack, or both; and which individuals possess hand-held automatic weapons, equipped with silencers and having long-range accuracy, and hand-carried equipment including incapacitating agents and explosives for use as tools of entry or for otherwise destroying the reactor, facility, transporter, or container integrity or features of the safeguards of the system."

For many corporate executives, sitting in their comfortable high-rise offices, the code descriptions came as alarming as they were problematic to enact. Some even balked on whether the effort of nuclear power was worth it. For the corporate financial officers, the security requirements translated into millions of additional dollars and reduced profits. Many of the regulations and hardware necessary to carry out the requirements had never been priced-out before, nor tested in the real world. But using the same calculators and spreadsheets, the bottom line remained the same; nuclear energy still afforded the best way to keep pace with the ever-increasing electricity demand of a consuming public, and to ensure tremendous profits, risk was required.

*The premise of an inside man* was the killer when it came to design and construction considerations. To protect a nuclear power plant from an internal threat, every person from top to bottom in a large organization had to be accounted for, including the Security Director, Plant Foreman, and even the top executives of the Pacific Alliance Power Company.

For the conceptual planners, the solution seemed simple. Access to every doorway to every vital area, those deemed crucial to public safety, would require *two* authorized persons, with authorized keycards. And following this logic, the issuance of any vital command from either of the two security computer control stations—two because one could compromise the Plant—would likewise require *two* concurring individuals.

Thus, painstakingly, the *Two Man Rule* was enacted.

It partially accounted for the reasoning behind the random assignment of posts, thought to make it impossible for a single 'insider' to plan ahead and know his post in advance, or the exact personnel configuration of any given shift. Likewise, the creation of a 'Rover' patrol, someone with a gun roaming the plant indiscriminately, would make it difficult for even the person with the highest authority to know where every defender was at any given time.

Every doorway in the power plant was governed by a computerized system, using the programmable keycards. Access to every door was pre-determined. Areas of vital function would require two such authorized individuals, each carrying authorized keycards with the corresponding PIN numbers.

By these measures, it was believed the security of the Plant was without compromise. The threat of an *inside man* had been conveniently dashed via automation and the *two man rule*.

The rest of the security was a matter of practicality. Physical-barrier protection, not unlike the fortresses of old, formed the front-line defense. Beyond a 'perimeter fence,' which by code had to be no less than ten-feet tall, topped with razor-wire, and equipped with micro-wave motion detectors, was a sophisticated system of intrusion alarms. State-of-the-art technology monitored every doorway, hatchway and passageway throughout the plant. *'Smart'* alarms, capable of identifying system malfunctions and fixing them, recorded intrusions of all types, by location and time. The buildings themselves were constructed of huge, thick walls of concrete and steel, and equipped with six-tumbler cylinder locks. All *'vital areas'*—areas containing critical equipment the failure of which could spell disaster for the operation—were housed in vault-like rooms, protected by tripling the thickness of both concrete and steel, and by using stainless-steel and vacuum-tight doors.

And, of course, if all else failed, there was a security force of *'Armed Responders'*—a fancy name given to foot patrol officers by the NRC—laying in wait, armed and ready. Though deadly force was authorized, *'interdiction'*—the act of placing one's body between an intruder and the power plant—was the administration's preferred method of intervention.

The heavily armored door to Control Station Two *clicked* unlocked. Drake looked up, pulled the heavy door open, and stepped in. The door closed behind him with a vacuum sound.

Inside, seated at the control console on an elevated platform, was John Haley, the swing shift Security Computer Operator, and standing over his shoulder was Supervisor Pierce, Harkin's swing shift counterpart. On the computer screen, the command request to open the door to Security Control Station Two, was still flashing 'APPROVED.' Lewis, far off in Control One, having reviewed Haley's routine request, had approved it seconds before.

# Chapter 13

Stepping into Control Two was a bit like walking into a Swiss bank vault. The suction sound of the door closing and the tumblers locking had a certain air about them, which oddly, reminded Drake of a movie he once saw where a convicted murderer was enclosed in the air-tight gas chamber at San Quentin.

Supervisor Pierce and Officer Haley turned back and looked at Drake.

"Hey Drake," Supervisor Pierce said.

Drake nodded a *hello*, but remained standing at the base of the door, two steps down from the security console.

Supervisor Pierce and Officer Haley continued with their shift-change procedure; designed to transfer the control of the security station from the hands of one shift operator to the next. Haley typed on the keyboard. Pierce watched from behind. The process, one that Drake knew well, involved the deletion of the swing-shift operator's access code and the creation of a new set of personal identifiers, specifically for the on-coming shift operator, Drake.

Drake felt smug watching it all. The complexity of the procedure, and the system itself, were all within the realm of things Drake felt worthy of—things of high technology and sophistication.

Supervisor Pierce turned and looked down at him. "Just a minute Drake."

Drake nodded.

The act of changing the access code took only five minutes, but was paramount to the overall security of the facility. The purpose was to ensure that the off-duty computer operator would not leave the Plant with a valid access code. It essentially prevented a rogue, off-duty-bound computer operator, or rogue supervisor for that matter, from subverting the two-man rule and disarming the entire power plant.

Haley stroke the keyboard again. Then Supervisor Pierce drew the *shift key* from a retractable chain on his hip. The *shift key*—a gold triangular-columned, laser-pocked key—was the supervisor's contribution to the procedure. He stretched it across the console, plugged it into a matching triangular hole, and turned it clockwise with a *CLICK*.

Immediately, a tiny indicator light on the console went from green to red. On the computer screen flashed the familiar words:

ENTER PASSWORD FOR PROTECTED COMMAND
OVERRIDE

Haley entered his password and the computer screen immediately flashed back:

PROTECTED COMMAND OVERRIDE
PROCEED WITH LEVEL ONE COMMANDS

Haley deleted his password and access PIN, all of while being watched by Supervisor Pierce. When Haley finished, he stood up, symbolically rubbed his hands together and flashed his palms outward toward Drake.

"She's all yours," he said.

Drake stepped up to the console as Haley took the position down near the door. Taking the console seat, Drake logged-in and confirmed his identity via a hand-geometry scan.

"Go ahead, Drake," Supervisor Pierce said, repositioning himself above Drake's shoulder.

The cursor light blinked, waiting.

Drake pushed his glasses further up the bridge of his nose. In the monitor, he could see his reflection, his wire-rimmed glasses catching the overhead light, and he could see the reflection of Pierce's face behind him.

"Go ahead," Supervisor Pierce repeated; his eyes fixed to the screen.

Drake typed-in the new password:

*Renegade*

As he hit the ENTER key, the screen instantly refreshed, requesting that Drake enter a PIN, which he did. Then he backed out of the windows to a blank screen. Pierce withdrew the triangular shift key, and the little red indicator light went back to green. The computer screen flashed back:

LEVEL TWO COMMANDS
SYSTEM INTEGRITY RESTORED

With a pat on Drake's shoulder, Supervisor Pierce simply said, "Have fun."

Drake nodded. "I'll try to."

Pierce stood up and arched his back, wincing. "God! You'd think there'd be a better way of doing this." He stood there for a moment stretching, waiting for the blood to flow back into his spine before he joined Haley at the door.

Drake, with his fingers still on the keyboard, reeled in a command and hit the ENTER key:

He waited for the door to open, as did Pierce and Haley, but nothing seemed to happen. Deep in the Auxiliary Building, Lewis Smith, sitting at the console of Control One, was chomping down on a cold hotdog. Instead of looking at the console screen, his eyes were focused outside the Plexiglas windows of Control One at the Plant's operational crewmen.

At only twenty-four, Lewis was probably the most computer savvy officer on the entire security force, a skill he credited to many long hours playing computer games as a child. He was a free-spirited throwback to the nineteen-sixties, wore John-Lennon-like spectacles, and had long, wavy, blonde hair that he kept neatly tied in a ponytail. The control room, which resembled the bridge of the Star Ship Enterprise, had several stations aligned before a ten-foot-tall switchboard of valves, gauges, blinking lights, knobs, and meters.

As Lewis watched the five-man crew, he stuck a handful of Doritos in his mouth. The crew, casually dressed in blue jeans, *Dockers*, polo-shirts and sport shoes, went about their business as they always did, preparing for the long shift ahead. Two of them were at their stations checking meters. Across the room two others held clipboards in their hands taking gauge readings from the switchboard. At his desk was Chief Engineer Stewart reviewing notes from his swing shift counterpart with a lollipop hanging from his mouth. Further down was the training room, where most of the training sessions for the security personnel had taken place. Another smaller room, the 'dressing room,' was at the rear. Here was kept the *KW-GARD* fabric—radiation protection suits, which resembled spacesuits.

Suddenly a voice on the intercom alerted Lewis. It was Drake. "Hey, are you awake up there?"

Lewis glanced down and saw the blinking cursor waiting. *Oh shit!*

Flashing on the screen was the familiar command prompt:

OPEN DOOR SB1 - CONTROL STATION TWO

Cramming the end of the hotdog into his mouth, he reached over and pressed the AUTHORIZE key.

Then he depressed the intercom button, and said: "Sorry about that!"

Back in Station Two, the heavily fortified door instantly *clicked* open.

Impatiently, Supervisor Pierce pushed through it, turned back, and said "Later" before stepping out.

Drake reciprocated with a monotone "Later," and watched as the two exited with a *clunk* as the door shut behind them.

*Finally!* Drake sighed.

He leaned back in the chair and glanced around the small room. It had been a week since he'd sat within the familiar surroundings. He felt happy to be immersed in it again.

In point of fact, the inside of Station Two was essentially a mini-fortress within a fortress, consisting of the most sophisticated surveillance tools and security controls. Above him flashed the eight surveillance screens featuring high-resolution imagery from throughout the Plant. Before him was the slanted security console and computer screen, above which was the large bullet-proof window that overlooked the entrance lobby—said to be capable of withstanding the impact of a hand-held bazooka. The entry door where Supervisor Pierce and Officer Haley had just departed was made of explosive-resistant, three-inch-thick solid steel. The room itself had been designed with an inner casing of rebar, steel, and concrete—basically a bunker.

Drake briefly checked the log book. There was nothing unusual. He glanced out the overlook at the activity in the entry lobby—all appeared anemically normal. Above the surveillance monitors flashed—some full-color, some black and white, some split-screen. Using the remote, he manipulated *screen one* and it began flipping through the cameras in a timed-sequence at five seconds intervals.

On the west-side, he saw Kelly Murphy marching along the perimeter fence in her assigned patrol zone one. To the north, Pryce Johnston walked diagonally across the blacktop toward the Turbine Building. On the east-side Carl Harrington, Patrol Officer Three, paced beneath the perimeter lights with his Mini-14 slung from his shoulder. In the Intake Cove, a circular-shaped half-ring of glistening lights, a buoy flashed a blue '*keep clear*' warning light beyond the rock jetty. Inside the Turbine Building, the plant's massive twin turbines spun at blinding speed, cranking out the millions of kilowatts of electricity every minute.

Two buildings away in Control One, Lewis smiled broadly as he watched Drake on his surveillance. Watching Drake watching others was amusing. Lewis stuffed a handful of Doritos into his mouth, gave himself time to chew, and then flipped on the intercom to Control Two.

"Big Brother is watching you," he spoke loudly into the speaker.

Drake's neck craned around to look up at the fixed screen. Lewis laughed and waved into the camera, knowing Drake could see him.

Drake grimaced. "How's it going Lewis?" he asked over the intercom speaker.

"Not bad," Lewis said, beginning to laugh again. Then he stuffed another handful of Doritos into his mouth. "Ready for another night of this boring shit?"

"Yep."

"Nothing interesting out there, is there?"

"Nothing."

Lewis closed the musician magazine he had laid out before him, and looked back up at the monitor. "So where's Garner tonight?"

"I have no idea."

"It's that little chili pepper he's got."

"Maybe."

"She's going to get him into big trouble if he doesn't watch it."

"They usually do."

"Well, anyhow, I wish him luck with it."

"Do you need something?" Drake's voice interrupted.

Lewis paused. "No, in fact I was going to ask you the same thing. I know it's a new experience for you going solo and all."

The intercom speaker stood silent.

"I'll be fine," Drake's voice came back.

"Well, if you need something, give me a ring," Lewis said. Lewis remembered the first few nights he was alone in the control station, so he was sympathetic with Drake's situation.

"I'm actually feeling quite comfortable," said Drake. "I'm ready to do this solo."

"Tonight's as good as any. Anyhow, if you need anything, I'm here. Just give me a ring."

"Thanks, I'll call you."

"Okay Buddy."

Back in Control Two, Drake took a deep breath. *Buddy?*

"That's a ten-four," he said.

"Over and out," Lewis said, clicking off the intercom.

Lewis leaned back in his chair, gazed up at Drake's image, and chuckled. Drake turned his back to him, facing the computer screen, and Lewis pulled back his camera, giving him a wider angle.

Drake looked confident there lounging now at the console with both hands locked behind his head. Beyond him the activity in the entrance lobby could be seen through the overlook. Lewis swiveled around in his chair and returned his gaze into the Control Room. The operators were further along with their shift preparations. Lewis smiled at Chief Engineer Stewart, who smiled back.

*All is well.*

In Control Two, Drake stood up above the console, crossed his arms, and gazed out the large bullet-proof Plexiglas windows. From his elevated position, the floor of the entrance lobby stretched out before him; from the rear corridor and badge counter, across the search train, to the front door. Jimmy Becker and Rae Anderson stood near the metal detector, conversing. The elder Fred O'Neil was at the badge counter, conducting an inventory of the badges of the swing shift officers. Across the lobby were the large front windows, through which could be seen the parking lot, sparely filled with employee vehicles illuminated beneath the lamp posts. Beyond that was only blackness. No more vehicles came down the access road.

Drake nodded. The shift had begun, uneventfully.

From the hall doorway on the left side of the room, Supervisor Harkin emerged. He walked directly across the floor toward the rear corridor meeting Haley and Supervisor Pierce half-way. Drake watched as Haley nodded a *goodbye* to Harkin and headed through the search train, processed through by Rae Anderson and Jimmy Becker.

Harkin and Pierce exchanged words and then Pierce reached down to the retractable chain on his hip, unclipped the shift key, and handed it to Harkin. Harkin clipped the key on to a retractable chain of his own, and tucked the key into his pocket.

*That's right, keep it safe,* Drake thought.

The two supervisors broke off and Pierce headed out through the search train, placing his briefcase on the conveyor belt. Harkin remained in the lobby momentarily with both hands on his hips as if taking inventory, and once he concluded all was in order, he turned and headed for his office.

The shift change was complete.

# Chapter 14

Inside the Turbine Building, down a long catwalk away from the droning turbines, the crackling sound of voices emitted from a solitary Motorola HT1000 handheld radio. It stood on its end on a barren space of concrete flooring beside a beautiful young woman with flowing amber hair. She sat with her legs straight out before her, her back resting against the wall, a can of *Coke* in her hand, and her Mini-14 rifle leaning against the wall beside her.

Listening intently, Grace Baker grinned as the radio started to speak. "Control One, come in. This is Taylor in Mobile One, awaiting dispatch."

She quickly sipped from her Coke, set it down, picked up the radio, and sharpened the tuning.

A second voice quickly replied: "Ten-Four, you're dispatched."

"En route to the Bone Yard," Cameron's voice said, coming in clearly now.

"That's a Roger."

Grace smiled broadly. Then she sighed and leaned back against the wall. *Mobile One*, she realized. It meant they could not meet tonight, unless by chance during their mid-shift break.

For a moment Grace stared at the radio. To have heard Cameron's voice was comforting, and reassuring. It meant he was okay, had made it to work after all, and was now somewhere not far from her. She picked up her Coke and drank from it again. She imagined Cameron behind the wheel of the Jeep Cherokee, driving out the parking lot of the Security Building to the Bone Yard. She knew this road, could picture it in her head, and him driving on it.

*He knows I heard him*, she thought, smiling. A consoling expression warmed her face.

She took another sip from her Coke, checked the time on her wristwatch, and sat quietly for awhile with her head tilted back against the concrete. As her eyes gazed blankly at the tall ceiling lights, and the cold, grey concert above her, she felt sadness sweeping through again. *They could not meet tonight.* She had been hoping to see him. She had many things to tell him. Now the chance seemed unlikely. Lunch breaks were staggered, to keep the fullest compliment of officers on post. The two Mobile Patrol units alternated their lunch breaks, so as to always leave one set of wheels pounding the backroads. So the odds of all the stars lining up in a way that their lunch breaks would coincide were not good.

A minute passed in silence before her eyes suddenly brightened. A mischievous grin came to her face. She glanced skyward, and then at her watch.

It was 10:50 p.m.

*There is time*, she thought.

Springing to her feet, Grace downed the last gulp from her can of Coke, gathered up her things, holstered her radio, and slung her Mini-14 over her shoulder. Like the winged-god *Hermes*, she flew down the catwalk and disappeared down a long, side corridor. Moments later, she burst through a door onto the main floor of the turbine room, pausing only to gain her bearings. Having entered at the northernmost end, she got a grand view down the length of the building.

Grace bolted down the central corridor, south, following the most direct route to Containment One via the Auxiliary Building. The gaping interior of the main turbine room, as large as any sports arena, was said to be capable of housing two Boeing Airbuses, wings-spread, end-to-end. Above, large, shiny stainless-steel pipes stretched across sixty-foot of ceiling. Beneath, through the steel-grated flooring, she rushed over the cavernous subterranean levels—a multi-leveled, myriad of steel catwalks and polished pipes.

With her rifle bouncing on her shoulder, she ran past rows of equipment, switchboxes, and generators, and as she approached the turbines, the humming sound became deafening. Each turbine stood seventy feet in diameter and was half-encased in an iron shell. They stood back-to-back on the central floor—mirrored-images of one another—spinning at a speed of more than two hundred revolutions per second; each cranking out more than two-million kilowatts of electricity, every minute, every hour, every day.

She stopped in the center between the two turbines. Glancing left, then straight ahead, she located the doorway to the Auxiliary Building. She ran for it, at the same time distancing herself from the ferocious sound of the turbines.

Reaching the door, she checked her wristwatch. It was 10:55 p.m.

*There's still time!*

Quickly pulling out her keycard, lining it up with the thin slot on the reader box, she slid it in. Grace had become very adept at flipping out her keycard, nearly always positioned upright, inserting it instantly into the card-reader, and speed-keying-in her access code, using her ambidextrous fingers. She kept it clipped to her lapel for easy access.

*Come on!*

Mounted above was a security camera, into which Grace smiled and waved.

*Clink!* The door unlocked.

Grace burst onto the second level of the Auxiliary Building, giggling now. She negotiated her way through a maze of a half-a-dozen hallways and doorways using her keycard to access each one. They were all non-vital 'level two' areas, so the *two-man rule* did not apply.

In nearly every corridor there were high-mounted security cameras, into which Grace smiled and waved. At every door-way evacuation wobblers stood silent as they had been since the plant's inception, except during emergency testing. The interior of the Auxiliary Building had been left unfinished; the walls were shear, grey concrete, as was the floor, and there were pipes and fire lines running exposed along the ceilings and floor-boards.

Grace reached another doorway, accessed her way through, and came into the Generator Room, a long hallway separated by large side-compartments, each housing one of six huge diesel generators.

Panting now, she slowed to a brisk walk.

The generators stood dormant behind huge steel-meshed bay doors as she passed. Their purpose—only to be used as an emergency back-up power supply for the cooling pumps should the main power supply ever fail. Glancing in at one, Grace had an ominous feeling. She recalled from her training days the automated lock-down feature. Built into the security apparatus was a self-activating defense system designed to foil sabotage attempts. In the event of an intrusion alarm, the bay doors would slam shut, the entire chamber would be sealed, and the room would be immediately flooded with liquid hydrogen spray, meant to freeze any bomb or incendiary device, as well as saboteurs—all with less than fifteen seconds warning.

Nearly breathless, Grace exited the far end of the Generator Room, entered the rear elevator corridor where the Auxiliary Building buttressed against the containment structures, stepped to the elevator door, pressed the button, and waited. It was now

10:58 p.m., and she was wondering if there was still enough time. The door opened, she hopped in, pressed the lift button, and ascended rapidly. She could feel herself breathing heavily as she stared up at the ceiling light.

The elevator stopped abruptly and the door slid open to a darkened sky. The sound of wind whisked in, and as Grace stepped out, the wind blew hard against her; her beautiful, long hair lifted straight back. Arching gloriously overhead, the night sky was filled with a myriad of diamond-like stars.

*Wow! So wonderful!*

She raised her chin into the wind and closed her eyes, taking it in for the moment. Then, realizing she was twenty-one stories above ground-level on a skinny catwalk, she quickly stepped forward and grabbed the handrail. Her pant legs flapped wildly in the wind.

The *Containment One* catwalk was a mere two-foot-wide strip of lattice-steel flooring, circumnavigating the top of the containment dome. It was more than two-hundred-and-ten feet above ground-level. The grated flooring, through which one could see straight down, was enough to give anyone vertigo. Some sixty yards away to the north was an identical catwalk around the top of *Containment Two.*

*No time to waste!* Grace thought, looking west. There, beyond the rail, was the vague, white outline of the coast, and just beyond, the dark, brooding Pacific. She hurried down the catwalk and positioned herself on the westernmost end of it, and looking straight down, saw a set of headlamps moving slowly north along the leeward side of the perimeter fence.

*Yes!*

It was Mobile One, she knew, and inside was Cameron.

Without a second to spare, at precisely 11:00 p.m., the radio on her hip began to speak.

"Control One to all posts. Control One to all posts," Lewis' voice said. "This is your 2300 hours Security Check."

Grace pulled the radio from its sheath and adjusted the volume. With her other hand, she took her flashlight from her utility belt.

Several stories below in Control One, Lewis paused, giving everyone time to ready themselves for the radio check. His chin hovered inches above the desk top microphone, which he oddly preferred to use for the radio checks over the headset. Before him was the Security Check log-sheet, a simple grid of posts listed on the left and hours in military-time across the top. Swallowing down the remainder of the chips and clearing his mouth, he readied his pen and began the security check; "Security One."

From the Briefing Room in the Security Building Sergeant Jacobs' voice replied: "Security One."

"Control Two," Lewis continued.

"Control Two," Drake's voice echoed back.

"San Roque Gate."

Marvin, seated high on his stool in the guard booth several miles away with an electric heater glowing at his feet, keyed the transmitter and replied; "San Roque Gate."

Back in Control One, Lewis continued, "Security Two."

"Security Two," came back Jimmy Becker's voice.

"Security Three."

"Security Three," Rae Anderson's silky voice confirmed.

And so on, and so on.

Out on the catwalk, Grace listened impatiently.

"Patrol One," Lewis continued down the sequence.

"Patrol One," Kelly Murphy replied from the blacktop far below.

Grace watched as Kelly responded and holstered her radio. Maneuvering around the catwalk, Grace did the same with Pryce Johnston, Carl Harrington, and Chris Peters, each responding respectively as their positions were called.

Coming back to the westside, Grace leaned far over the rail and watched as Cameron's Patrol Jeep drove slowly past.

*Now!* she thought.

Lewis' voice spoke. "Mobile One."

"Mobile One," Cameron's voice responded from within the patrol Jeep.

Grace smiled broadly.

As Lewis' drone-like cadence continued... "Mobile Two," and from afar, on the back roads of the property, Corley Harris, the officer assigned to Mobile Unit Two this night, replied, "Mobile Two," Grace held the flashlight ready, pointing it down at Cameron's vehicle.

"Rover One," Lewis' voice finally announced.

Just as he spoke it, Grace switched on her flashlight and keyed the radio transmitter. "Rover One here... here at Containment One," she replied, with the wind driving hard against her. Then she started switching the flashlight on and off, keeping it pointed at the Jeep.

In the Shift Supervisor's Office, Harkin glanced angrily at the radio in its desk charger. Immediately following Lewis' sign off, "That completes our 2300 security check," Harkin grabbed the radio and keyed the transmitter:

"Rover One. No locations! Just respond!" He paused, realizing he was being a bit harsh on a rookie. "Rover One, there's no need to give your location on a security check. Ever."

"Ten-Four," Grace's voice replied.

Having heard Grace's response in Mobile One, having heard it all; Grace's location disclosure and Harkin's admonishment, Cameron pulled along side the perimeter fence, slowed to a stop, stretched-out across the passenger seat, and looked up. High on top of Containment One was a light, flashing on and off.

*Crazy Grace!* Cameron smiled. He reciprocated by flashing the Jeep's headlamps on and off, twice.

Atop Containment One, wind-blown Grace, still gripping the rail, cried out triumphantly, "Yes!!"

*He saw me!*

Holding her radio and rifle-strap tight against her chest, pointing skyward with the flashlight in her other hand, she did a nifty little pirouette, spinning around so quickly she nearly fell down, but slid against the railing instead.

# Chapter 15

Aboard the trawler Ramzan lay stretched out on the bench in the Captain's cabin. He had spent the past half hour in this manner, nauseous and with head spinning, staring blankly at the ceiling. As the boat had carved its way steadily southward the wind picked-up and the swells had grown to six-feet. Consequently, the motion had become unbearable.

Curse this ocean, Ramzan thought. It is as wicked as its *western* governments. The governments that way lay my land and my people. He had plenty of time to think about it, lying there seasick on his back. But the sickness brought on by the sea did not compare to the sickening feeling he felt recalling the brutal acts of the *West*. In his mind, he saw the perambulating corpses, the ghastly death's heads of men and women. He saw a home which had been reduced to rubble in less than ten seconds. It was the accumulation of multiple atrocities, he thought, that brought him to a faraway ocean, to inflict enormous pain upon his enemy.

Someone had to take up the sword to defend the world against the lies and treachery of the Westerners, the infidels who shunned god's way, he thought. If not he, then who? Who then would vanquish the earth of their impurity?

It had been nothing but savagery. Raining down from the sky, from an enemy they could not see, who did not care about collateral damage, rockets that murdered, ripped, and dismembered women and children and goats alike. They were all hemmed in by it, in a small village high in the mountains. The cowards they fought would not show themselves. They were not men, not men who would stand to fight one other face to face. They were not willing to show their eyes to those they wished to kill.

*They were cowards.*

He remembered the sound of the rockets whistling and crackling through the morning sky, of children's screams and women crying. It was etched forever in his mind—a sound he would never forget. It was the sound of *hell*.

Those who survived were given the unenviable task of separating body parts, as best could be done, for delivery to kin for burial. In one place, the human remains were indistinguishable from an animal herd. It was a vision from an El Greco painting. The *West* had rained its *hell* down upon the *Innocent.* A peaceful village was no more.

This all happened when Ramzan was a teenager. And at the time, he did not understand English well. He was told by his elders how the westerners described the strike as a successful attack on a terrorist training camp. It was a village of women and children, he knew. What was more appalling was that so many people of the world believed in the deceit. It was like the entire world believed and trusted those who should not be trusted. He did not trust anything western, their aid packages, their humanitarian efforts, their U.N., and of course not their politics. To him, it was all trickery by godless nations. And he vowed to wage a lifetime of war against them.

But he envied their technology. To send a missile from far away and hit a target with absolute accuracy was remarkable. And there were valuable lessons to be learned by such technology, not that the brotherhood would ever possess these scientifically-advanced tools of war and engineering, but they would learn to turn the pointed edge of such tools back into the eyes of their creators.

*To use their strength against them,* Ramzan thought again now, lying in the Captain's cabin.

So it was that he and his brother Emil traveled now on this godforsaken ocean that had caused him to feel so ill; to bring enormous pain and destruction to his enemy. So many comrades in civil and military prisons throughout the world now held their breath, waiting on news of their success. The burden rested clearly on them. *Bloody retribution*, it was what Ramzan wanted most.

I cannot be sick now, he told himself.

He pulled himself to his feet, staggered out of the cabin, and hanging over the rail, forced a finger down his throat. The resulting involuntary convulsion returned to the sea that which he had eaten for the past two days.

From the pilothouse above, Emil looked down curiously.

"Dramamine doesn't work," he bellowed out. "If you don't keep it down."

Ramzan returned his finger deep down his throat several times making sure there was nothing more. Then he wobbled, weakly, across the deck, and climbed the ladder to the pilothouse. There he found no sympathy from Emil.

"Did you hear what I said?" Emil asked.

"What?"

"Dramamine doesn't work if you can't hold it down."

"No need for it now," Ramzan insisted. "After that, I'm feeling better."

Ramzan still looked as green as before. "You are funny guy, Ramzan," Emil said. "You can hang off the side of tall buildings with a pack of explosives tied to your back, but you get sick on a boat."

Ramzan shrugged. The two men glanced at one another, but nothing more was said. They looked out the pilothouse windshield at the dark sea.

For a good five minutes, silence prevailed. Then Emil checked the GPS device, a *Garmin* GPSMAP 4000 Series global positioning system. The high-tech device was oddly mounted on the dashboard amid antiquated controls and gauges. The twelve-inch, split-screen color display showed a coastal configuration moving on the left screen; and correlating sonar depths on the right.

As they passed over a reef, Emil watched curiously as the depth levels went shallow to less than fourteen meters. Then suddenly they dropped off to three-hundred meters.

"There are mountains below us," he said, bringing Ramzan's mind back into the pilothouse. "Mountains like home."

*Mountains under the sea?* Ramzan thought. "Mountains?"

"Yes mountains. And canyons too. You see this?" Emil pointed to the screen. He pressed a button on the control panel which turned the screen into a three-dimensional perspective of the ocean floor. Ramzan saw clearly the large rugged peaks and valleys beneath them.

Emil switched the image back to its original setting. Then he pointed to the other half of the screen which displayed the GPS map. A small blinking blue dot moved south along what was obviously the coastline.

"This is us." Further down on the coast was a stationary red dot. "And this is the power plant."

Ramzan eyes glimmered. "How much more time?"

"Less than an hour."

Ramzan smiled inwardly. "Those who defend the truth will be victorious. We, brothers of the truth, will be victorious."

"Yes, we brothers will be victorious," Emil said with a nod.

Turning back to the Garmin screen, Emil thought now of the test which lay ahead. He was happy to be along side Ramzan, despite his peculiarities. He was a celebrated warrior among many warriors. Though Emil might never be as deep-seeded in faith and fanaticism as Ramzan, he agreed with his principles. The *West* was an evil that had to be destroyed. He agreed with Ramzan's forthrightness, resolve, and obsession with prepared-ness. Only by strength and practice would they succeed. He was ready to give plenty, as was Ramzan, his life if necessary, to see their plan complete. With the notion of giving his life tonight, he had no issues.

# Chapter 16

As Mobile One bounced along the uneven dirt road out toward the bone yard, Cameron gazed silently out the front windshield. The roads around the power plant were not routinely maintained and were generally potted with plenty of ruts, especially now in late spring after the winter storms. And Cameron was feeling the brunt of it.

The power plant, a distant light in his rearview mirror, momentarily vanished from view as the Jeep dropped down along the coastal terrace; then it reappeared in the mirror—a bouncing reflection—as the Jeep rose back up another grade. On Cameron's left, white waves pounded the rocks some thirty-feet below. Ahead, the sky was black above the dark grayish-green land. Further on, a vague white sign slowly materialized.

As the Jeep lumbered in low-gear up a small incline, Cameron pulled in along side the sign and smiled.

It simply read:

> NORTH GATE – with an *arrow* pointing right
> BONE YARD – with an *arrow* pointing left

Cameron lifted the radio from its rack and keyed the transmitter. "Mobile One here."

"Go Mobile One," Lewis' voice came back.

"At the crossroads and heading for the bone yard."

"That's a *Roger*," Lewis replied.

As Cameron placed the radio back in its rack, Harkin's voice came from it, sounding a bit annoyed. "Mobile One. Come in."

Cameron brought the transceiver back to his mouth. "Mobile One here."

"I want you to go check the north gate," said Harkin's voice.

Cameron looked at the sign, focusing in on the right-pointing arrow. "Yes Sir. That's a ten-four."

"And please report back when you arrive," Harkin's said, firmly.

"Will do. That's a ten-four too."

"Ten-four, over and out," Harkin said.

Cameron placed the radio back in its rack. "Whatever you want, boss."

Without regret or fear of retribution, Cameron turned the wheel *left* instead of *right* and preceded toward the Bone Yard, completely disregarding Harkin's orders.

Still lamenting over missing Grace, his mood was not one of servitude.

*North Gate?* he thought. *Not tonight Harkin. There'll be no harm in spending a little rest and relaxation among the reeds.* Besides, the way things were going tonight he'd just as soon stay away. It would keep him out of trouble.

The Jeep followed the road left, its headlamps bouncing over the bumpy terrain until disappearing over a rise.

Minutes later, Cameron found himself peering out the windshield at another familiar sign:

BONE YARD–ARCHAEOLOGICAL SITE–KEEP OUT

Beyond it was a starlit field of blowing reeds.

He slipped the Jeep into park, pulled up the parking brake, and for a moment just sat there reflecting on his failure to follow his Supervisor's orders. *No harm done, boss. It's just better we avoid one another tonight.*

Across the field of blowing reeds, the starlight reflected like silvery sequins off waving shore-grass. At the very end of the slope, where the land dropped abruptly, the glitter blended into reflecting waves, and then into twinkling stars.

Cameron checked the time on his wristwatch. It was a quarter after eleven.

With the engine still idling to keep the heater going, he sat there looking out at the dancing reeds. And after a few minutes in silence, the reeds spoke to him, as he knew they would. This was the place, he thought. It was *his* place.

The *Bone Yard* was the affectionate name given to an ancient Indian burial site. There, high on a wind-blown, half-acre knoll of tall shore grass, the Chumash had ceremoniously interred their dead for several centuries, along with their keepsakes and treasures from life. Artifacts of jewelry made of seashells and abalone, beaded breast-plates, colorfully woven *bulrush* baskets, and small disk-shaped beads of *Olivella* shell—a form of money. A millennium had passed since the first band of Chumash Indians settled here, but the place remained sacred and protected via treaties signed long before the notion of a nuclear power plant had ever come forth. In fact, some items unearthed there in the early days of construction had to be carefully re-interred.

Cameron had first heard about the Bone Yard in a training seminar. A brief half-day session about the environmental and historical relevance of the area, touched briefly upon the Chumash occupation and the "archeologically sensitive" areas around the power plant. The instructor spoke mostly about the difficulties the archeological sites had posed during the construction process. By Federal Court decree, a descendant of Chumash ancestry had to be present on site throughout the grading process, partly to ensure no 'archeological sensitive areas' were disturbed, and also to guarantee if new areas were discovered, they would not simply be mowed over by bulldozers. The wage for this individual was to be no less than one-hundred dollars per hour.

Noting that the area had long since been abandoned by the Chumash, the instructor hurried on to the next subject, going into a long, drawn-out dissertation about the power plant's environmentally 'friendly' practices. Nothing more was said, aside from a few ghost jokes which were redundantly recited by the security personnel and plant operators, that is, until Cameron's first Mobile Patrol assignment.

Training day one, shift one, Harkin had tossed him a set of keys and said, "Go familiarize yourself with the backroads."

"Anywhere in particular?" Cameron asked.

"No, just get lost."

Taking the keyring handed to him, Cameron looked it over carefully. It had about twenty keys on it.

"There's a key for about every gate, except the one that goes into the State Park," Harkin said "The Bone Yard's an interesting place. You may want to go check it out. But be careful."

"Careful?"

Harkin let out one of his deep-bellied laughs. "Yeah, be careful of ghosts!"

"What?"

Harkin's eyes twinkled. "It's an old Indian burial ground. They say you can see the ghosts out there sometimes dancing in the reeds."

That first time out, on a sunny afternoon, Cameron parked the Jeep on the bluff above the water and took a stroll through the field of reeds. Really, it was disappointing at first. There was nothing distinguishing about it. A person would never know it was a burial ground except for the warning sign. Kicking into the soil, Cameron found nothing but a few small pieces of abalone shell. That was it—nothing more. Having the entire day though, he decided to stay for a while. The knoll top offered sweeping views of the Pacific. Behind him, the tall coastal mountains were emerald green and brush-stroked in yellow mustard flowers. He kicked back in the grass and enjoyed the California sun and ocean breeze. Seagulls streaked across the sky as misty swirls of spray lifted off the wave-crests. The breeze whispered through the tall shore grass. All seemed bliss. That's when it happened. A strong wind blew through the tall reeds, rattling them in a way that made them sound like wind chimes. He looked around, but as quickly as the wind had come, it died down. He stayed longer. Then it happened again. This time the chimes were louder and lasted longer, and he could swear the grass was alive and speaking to him. Or was it the spirits of dead Indians beneath speaking to him through the rustling reeds?

When he finally returned to the Security Building at the end of the shift, Harkin asked him how things had gone.

"Oh, it was a great day," Cameron said, avoiding the fact that he spent it in entirety at one location. "I found quite a few back roads. Went up a few canyons full of sycamore trees. It was great."

Harkin smiled. "See any ghosts in the Bone Yard?"

"Not many," Cameron said.

The following day Cameron took it on himself to do some historical research. He went to the local University library, grabbed the first three books he found on Chumash Indians, and began paging through them. Randomly, in opening the first text, he found an introductory preface:

'The Chumash were among the first peoples to inhabit North America, first settling in central California about 13,000 years ago. At one time or another, more than 20,000 Chumash lived along the California coastline…'

*What happened to them all?* Cameron wondered.

The prehistoric data was sketchy, but the historic information seemed to plainly spell out a lifestyle that was in tune with Nature and had remained constant for many centuries. The Chumash were a maritime culture, he learned, using long wooden canoes called *tomols* for fishing and traveling between the different villages along the Pacific coast, and between the Channel Islands. They were primarily a hunter-gatherer tribe. Though they killed to eat, they didn't waste any part of any animal. Nor did they pull a plant from the earth they didn't eat, or discard fish wastefully that they had taken from the sea. They believed that man's greed and desire for supremacy would eventually lead to his downfall.

Cameron liked this. He felt akin to it. It was something he could identify with. He read on. In the myths and legends section, he read about a spotted woodpecker caught in a deluge, rescued only by a warm wind blown upon him by his uncle, the Sun God, and surviving, he went on to become the creator of all life.

*A spotted woodpecker rescued on a breath of wind? Going on to become the creator of all life?* Cameron thought. Any people believing in such simplicity, and believing that dolphins were their sea-dwelling brothers, were all right by him.

Cameron was charmed by the Chumash. Yet he could not help but chuckle at the paradox. Over time, the opposite ends of two distinctly different worlds had collided.

*These poor folks would roll over in their graves if they knew a nuclear power plant now sat where they once laid their heads!* he thought.

For people to live in harmony with nature over eons of time, leaving the land as pure and as untouched as the day they had arrived, was unimaginable in a modern world of warfare, rampant development, and nuclear power plants. In the days of the Chumash, the Santa Ana winds were a harbinger of good things, bringing warm seas, good fishing, and festive celebrations. Now it had become the potential harbinger of death in a nuclear disaster.

The next day when Cameron returned to the power plant, he stopped along the access road, parked his car along the bluff, and climbed down to a secluded beach. He collected an assortment of abalone shells. He found shells ranging in size from tiny to nearly seven inches across. He assembled them into a nifty little set in which one fit perfectly into another. He kept the shells concealed in his work locker for two weeks until the next time he had a chance to walk among the reeds in the Bone Yard. Then, he scattered them there in the tall grass.

Cameron returned to the Bone Yard many times since, doing so in strict violation of company policy and federal regulation. Several treaties and State conservation rules protecting the sanctity of sacred sites forbid trespassing there, even by security personnel. Though security was to provide surveillance of the area, they were not to enter it.

But Cameron didn't care. His fondness for the place kept bringing him back. Each time he'd walked among the reeds, sometimes finding little pieces of abalone or hand-carved shells, causing him to ponder curiously of the people who once passed. But most often, he preferred to simply lie on his back in the tall shore grass and gaze up at the sunny sky, or night stars, and listen to the wind whistle through the reeds, making the sound of wind chimes.

Cameron turned off the ignition, clicked off the lights, and watched the sky fill with stars as the night blackened.

# Chapter 17

Peering down at the power plant from the mountaintop, the Driver nodded his head contently. He was amazed at his good fortune. What cross-current winds had blown up earlier seemed to have dissipated and become steady now, shoreward. And the view from the top was better than expected; a nearly straight-on, unobstructed angle, remarkably clear and well-lit.

*Too good!*

Finishing off another cigarette, he flicked the butt into the grass.

Behind him, already laid out on the damp grass, was an eight-by-ten black, plastic tarp. The corners of the tarp were held down by stones. Still, the ends flapped in the wind. Beyond the tarp, the Dodge truck remained parked precariously, tilted to one side, on the eastern down-slope.

The Driver returned to the truck. From the cab he took a black duffle bag. He brought the bag to the tarp, set it down, and extracted from it an oblong box. Using a small pen light held in his mouth, he flipped open the latches and slowly lifted the cover. Within were the neatly assembled pieces of a .50 caliber *M-107* Barrett Sniper Rifle; each carefully tucked away in pre-cut spaces of three-inch-thick foam.

The Driver's eyes gazed at the assembly appreciatively. The rifle's stock was made of lightweight polymer, with a grip-handle, and had a specially designed recoil pad meant to reduce the powerful kick of the weapon. The barrel and dual-chamber muzzle brake combination was made of a thick, solid chunk of well-honed steel. It was the longest piece in the case. The firing mechanism was nothing more than a simple trigger attachment. Also in the case was a V-shaped, quick-release bipod—just a pair of eight-inch-long legs with spiked feet, four detachable fully loaded 10-round magazines; and an odd-looking, custom-made cylinder-shaped device, which would serve as a noise suppressor.

Using an assembly progression he had followed many times, with penlight in mouth, he quickly clicked the pieces together, and in less than two minutes the rifle took form. A three-lug bolt locked the barrel firmly to the synthetic stock. The completed weapon, with its silencer extending from the end of the barrel and its railed, ribbed ventilation system, looked sinister. From a separate black bag, he removed an AN/PVS-10 Sniper Scope; designed for all weather, day or night shooting, and equipped with infrared and light intensification electro-optics—considered by many, the most advanced sniper scope ever fielded. He attached the scope to the top of the gun and made a couple quick adjustments using a small screwdriver.

Rising to his feet, he held his prize proudly in his hands. Flipping the weapon from side to side, he examined it carefully. The weight of the weapon was a hefty thirty pounds. He ran his hand down the length of the barrel, and reaching the end he twisted the silencer tight. Then he brought the stock firmly to his shoulder, and holding the rifle straight out before him, swung the barrel from side to side scanning the mountainside below through the powerful scope. Finally, he settled in on the power plant.

*Better than Vintorez.*

There, walking along the inside of the perimeter fence was a stick figure of a person. He tracked the figure for a few seconds until the firing mechanism involuntarily sounded with a *click!*

He smiled. No longer was he the driver of a Dodge truck—now he was a *sniper* with a lethal weapon capable of killing at great distances and with enough rounds to start a small war.

The M-107 had a range of two-thousand yards, and as such, was often used in a counter sniper role. Snipers using smaller caliber weapons, generally limited to one-thousand meters or less, and their counterparts, were often waylaid by the long-range M-107.

The Sniper had once been on the wrong end of an M-107, holding a *Dragunov* Russian-made sniper rifle in his hand. The *Dragunov* was plenty lethal. He had successfully used it to kill opposing snipers at ranges approaching fifteen-hundred meters. But in that instance, his squad of five precision snipers quickly found themselves disadvantaged and out-classed by a single enemy. It was simple mathematics. The range of the *Dragunov* could not match the M-107. The opposing sniper simply dropped back five-hundred meters and started killing again until nearly every man in the team was dead. If not for an unintentional dip of his head to pick up a dropped clip, the Sniper would have also been killed. From that day forward, he vowed never to be on the wrong end of an M-107 again.

Standing against an unusually strong gust of wind, with the dark Pacific sprawling out below him, the Sniper peered down at the stick figures patrolling the perimeter fence. Again, mockingly, he pulled the trigger and smiled. He held the ultimate weapon. No one below was going to outclass him, or out-distance him. That much, he was sure.

He set the rifle on the tarp, perched on its two-legged stand, took a seat in the grass, and crossed his legs. He lit another cigarette and waited. And as he waited, he studied the patrol patterns of the stick figures below, and took note of the wind direction and velocity, occasionally blowing out a mouthful of smoke and watching which direction it would go.

# Chapter 18

Drake sat mesmerized at the console in Station Two, looking up at the surveillance screens. He had achieved his goal of being seated, alone, among the most advanced security equipment in a power plant generating energy in a fashion even DaVinci could not have fathomed. Locked in on *camera one* was the reactor-core-housing in Containment One. Before him was the image of a multi-tiered step-pyramid with spaghetti-like pipes wrapping around it. The image, of course, showed no evidence of the dramatic process deep within. But within, Drake knew, a magnificent process was in fact taking place—one of splitting atoms and nuclear fission. Deep within the reactor core, a honeycomb of zirconium fuel rods encased in ten-inch-thick steel, subatomic particles called *neutrons* slammed into uranium atoms, splitting them, which in turned released more neutrons which split again, causing a nuclear chain reaction. The process generated enormous heat, more that six-hundred degrees Fahrenheit, which created steam, which turned the turbines, which generated electricity, which was routed over the mountaintops to inland cities via tall electrical towers.

The view out the large Plexiglas windows depicted quite a different scene. *A lack of intelligence or anything else ingenious,* Drake thought. *Complete folly.*

Standing idly in the entrance lobby were Fred O'Neil, Rae Anderson, and Jimmy Becker, conversing, trying to pass time. Drake lifted his glasses, cleaned them, and put them back on.

*A fortress is only as strong as those defending its walls,* he thought.

As difficult at times as it was for Drake to stomach how oblivious his fellow workers were of the fundamentals of nuclear physics, it was their ineptitude as security officers that really got him. They could not follow the simplest of security regulations. It seemed they were content to go about their duties halfheartedly, only interested in getting paid. They were content with boredom.

*Perfect boredom, as typical as it gets for security work.*

It was the very nature of security work that created an atmosphere of lethargy which served contrary to its purpose. How can one stay in a constant state of alert when the job itself lulls oneself into deep slumber? Boredom spawns complacency, Drake had often thought, and complacency spawns dereliction of duty, which was certainly the case at Mal Loma Nuclear Power Plant. It takes a non-ambitious mind to make a good security guard, Drake had surmised early on. An intelligent mind resents the lack of stimulation. Any man who can march over the same piece of blacktop again and again and be content with it had to be lazy. Truly, one had to be dumb-witted to do so. Likewise, any man with any sense of imagination or ingenuity would eventually feel trapped in such dreariness.

*The strongest of giants is defenseless when sleeping,* Drake thought now looking out the bullet-proof glass across the lobby.

Rae Anderson, Jimmy Becker and Fred remained huddled near the badge counter, debating the virtues of cable versus DSL. The various search and contraband detection machines lay idle. The *ready* light blinked on the Ionscan. There had been no activity since shift change, nor was there expected to be. It was the midnight shift at a nuclear power plant. No one came or left. There were just twelve security guards, a sergeant, a shift supervisor protecting a nuclear facility; and five crewmen, quietly going about their job that produced electricity for millions of Californians.

Drake clicked-on monitor *four*. There on the screen was Chris Peters marching drone-like beneath the bright flood lamps. *Good boy.* Using the wireless controller, he brought up the next camera in sequence. There Kelly Murphy held herself against a strong shoreward wind along the ocean-side of the perimeter fence. *At least she tries,* Drake thought.

Drake began haphazardly clicking through different camera locations. It was one benefit of being a security control operator. If things got dreadfully boring, which they inevitably did, one could always turn to the flat-screens for entertainment. He flipped to the Intake Cove. The bay lights illuminated the man-made breaker. Beyond the cove was the dark ocean. Beneath the waves, thousands of gallons of cold ocean water were being sucked up gapping intake pipes, the pull so strong it caused sixty-foot-long strands of kelp to drag shoreward toward the yawning intake port.

Less than a quarter of a mile away was the Discharge Bay, bubbling white with foam; beneath which roared a torrent of reactor-cooked water spouting out the ends of two seven-foot pipes. The entire cooling loop, from intake cove to reactor, took less than three minutes.

Back to the Intake Cove, Drake angled the camera up. Taking off his glasses, he looked steadily into the image. There was a shipping corridor offshore, running from San Diego to Seattle. Sometimes one could see the lights of passing ships, but tonight there were none. During daylight, sea lions could be seen lounging on a large rock beyond the cove—aptly named 'Sea Lion Rock.' But it was completely black now. Drake zoomed-in. The screen merely dissolved into fuzzy blackness. He clicked on the digital infrared feature and then saw some fat green images lying on the rocks. He smiled.

Sergeant Jacobs suddenly entered the security lobby from the rear corridor, drawing Drake's attention back to the overlook. Jacobs walked past Rae Anderson, Jimmy Becker and Fred without even stopping to say *hello* and disappeared through the doorway which led to Supervisor Harkin's office.

Drake raised a brow. *Something's up?*

Every night, though, Jacobs made trips back and forth between the Briefing Room and the Supervisor's Office. And Harkin as well; made trips to the lobby and trips to see Jacobs. *Probably nothing,* Drake then thought.

Back to the cameras, he switched to the Control Room, and for a while he watched the Plant operators. With their shift-readings having been logged and gauges set, they had each taken their respective workstations, in which they would pass most of the night away. The power plant pretty much ran itself. Their job was merely to monitor; to be there if something went wrong, but nothing ever did go wrong.

Overall, the power plant was diabolically quiet, as usual.

# Chapter 19

Among the many tasks dumped on the Night Shift Supervisor, the compiling of paperwork from the Day and Swing Shifts, checking logs for accuracy, and processing security clearances for visitors, were among the ones Harkin detested most. Because the day shift supervisors were generally inundated with daylight-related activities—escorting dignitaries and heeling to the whims of the Security Director—the night supervisor was inevitably left with the bulk of paperwork. Though Harkin funneled some of the work to Sergeant Jacobs, the bulk of it remained his responsibility, needing his signature or review.

Tonight, the pile was predictably larger than normal with the Security Director having just returned from his weekend off. Over time, Harkin had become fairly proficient at sifting through it in a methodical fashion. His mode of operation was to sort the pile, separating the papers into three stacks according to priority, tossing the meaningless stuff aside, and commencing work on the pile of highest urgency first. Always the stack on top consisted of the urgent memos from the Security Director, or employment and procedural circulars that needed routing to the troops.

Not all was bad though. Included in the nightly tasks was the reviewing of intelligence bulletins from the Justice Department and the Department of Homeland Security. Those related to terrorism or sabotage were flagged as high priority and evaluated for possible impact on Plant security operations. Also, there was the reviewing of manufacturers' literature and brochures on new weapons and security devices. In a world of heightened security concerns, it was an endless battle keeping current with the latest technology. As quickly as new contraband detectors, surveillance devices, and alarm systems hit the market, they became obsolete. Just as new state-of-the-art weapons came out, out-powering and out-distancing their predecessors, their performance had to be measured against what was used and available at the Plant. The Security Director wanted nothing but the best for his security squad, or at least to know of its existence, assuming the opposition could possibly have it. Manufacturers often pointed out the deficiencies of new security devices or weapons in competitive brands or the obsolescence of preceding devices, which also pointed out these weaknesses to terrorists.

Harkin, a former law enforcement commander, found the subject matter particularly fascinating.

But first, there was the mundane.

Harkin looked incredulous, staring at the huge mound of papers when Sergeant entered his office.

"Kelly just came off post," Jacobs said flatly.

Harkin's usual cynical frown came to his face. "What?"

"She's leaving. It's her kid again."

"Crap! What post does she have?"

"Patrol One," Jacobs replied.

"Damn."

It was not a post Harkin could leave vacant—not a designated patrol loop. He immediately began searching through the papers on his desk, again for the officer phone log. Finding the log, paging through it, he could feel his blood pressure rising. He told himself to relax. It had become a habit with Kelly Murphy, coming to work, clocking in so she'd receive a day's credit toward benefits, and leaving promptly thereafter, especially if assigned a cold night of foot patrol. Always it was something to do with her four-year old son, an illness or childcare issue of some kind.

Harkin's eyes, running down the list of security personnel, finally locked on to a familiar name; "Stevens. Try calling Stevens," he said.

Jacobs was doubtful. "It's a little late, don't you think?"

"He's been asking for more hours."

"And if I have no luck? Should I go down the list?"

Jacobs was experienced enough in these matters to know that the midnight shift was the most difficult of all shifts to cover when unexpected vacancies arose. Dayshift officers were generally sleeping and those 'on call' simply left their phones off the hook, or unanswered.

Before Harkin could reply, the radio on his desk started chattering and then it spoke. The voice coming through was Cameron's.

"Mobile One to Control One. Mobile One to Control One."

The two men exchanged glances. They had like minds and were thinking in like ways.

"Cameron was late again?" Harkin asked.

"Yes."

"How late?"

"Twenty minutes."

"We don't need two mobile units," Harkin said, knowing the code, which only required one. It was only Mal Loma's Security Director, wanting to double up on everything related to security, that they had two units.

"Yes," Jacobs replied, seeming to know where Harkin was going.

"Who' in Mobile Two?"

"Corley."

The radio started crackling again. It was Lewis responding to Cameron. "Control One here."

"Mobile One at North Gate," Cameron said, lying.

"Ten-Four," Lewis' voice said.

"That's all," Cameron said. "Over and out."

Harkin stared at the radio waiting to see if there'd be anymore, and when there was none, he said, "If you can't reach Stevens, call in Cameron. Put him in Patrol One, and let Corley know he's out there alone. But try Stevens first!"

"Okay." It was a reasonable solution, Jacobs thought.

As Jacobs started to leave, Harkin stopped him. "Wait. What did Kelly say when she was leaving?"

"She said she's sorry."

"Sorry?"

"Yeah, she said she's sorry. And something about her child being so important in her life, and how appreciative she was working for someone who understood."

"Swell. I'll bet they didn't think of nuclear power plants when they passed the Family Leave Law."

Jacobs made a quick exodus back to the Briefing Room.

Harkin tossed the phone log back on top of the pile of papers. Then, looking over the papers, he thought: *Better get to it.*

# Chapter 20

Cameron stared at the *No Trespassing* sign in front of the Bone Yard through the driver side window of Mobile One. The starlight barely revealed the Great Seal of California in the lower right corner. In the other corner was another emblem representing CEQA—*California Environmental Quality Act*—the agency responsible for the preservation and conservation of cultural and historical sites in California.

Where Cameron had parked, there at the road's end on top of a small rise above the field, there was a commanding view of the terrace and ocean beyond. Outside the windshield were the harmoniously waving tops of ten-thousand blowing reeds. Glimmering off the ocean's surface were the lights of a thousand stars. Cameron was immersed in it, feeling the tranquility of it, when the radio started crackling with Supervisor Harkin's irritated voice.

"Mobile One, Mobile One, this is Supervisor Harkin. Come in."

Cameron hesitated before lifting the radio transceiver. "Ten-Four."

"I want to see you in my office on your lunch break."

*Shit!* Cameron keyed the radio. "Ten-Four."

"And don't forget to log in your time at North Gate!"

Cameron looked out the window at the *Bone Yard* sign. "That's a Roger."

*So much for indebtedness*, he thought.

He picked up the logbook and scribbled in '*North Gate*' with the time. Then he tossed the logbook on the passenger seat and opened the car door.

As Cameron stepped out of the vehicle a falling star streaked across the western sky. He wondered if Grace might have seen it too. He was a little superstitious about things like that, as if there was a special significance if two people saw a falling star simultaneously from different locations.

The trail from the road's end to the ocean's edge was well-used and easy to follow, but Cameron preferred a deer path which cut diagonally through the grass of the Bone Yard. Reaching the cliff's edge, he looked for the elephant seals Peters had mentioned, but Cameron saw only crashing waves and craggy rock formations.

Cameron shrugged.

The Bone Yard was uniquely situated on a V-shaped promontory. On either side cliffs fell thirty feet to crashing waves. From the top of the bluff, in daylight, one could see south along the jutting sandstone cliffs, all the way to the promontory at Point San Miguel. Northward the view offered equally sweeping vistas, and even greater distances, beyond the tidelands several miles to the huge sandspit which provided the safe harbor at Port Piedras.

By now, Cameron's eyes had fully adjusted to the starlight and he recognized the familiar landmarks. Behind him and to the south, from beyond a rise, was the glow of the power plant. Far to the north a faint haze of lights marked the two coastal cities en route to San Francisco—Port Piedras and Chute's Landing. The dark Pacific surged straight ahead with a few, vague whitecaps flashing in the distance. There were no ship-lights on the horizon.

With the wind whistling through the reeds behind him, Cameron turned and walked through the tall grass. Before taking a seat, he checked the time on his watch. Then he shrugged, realizing time didn't matter. *I've got all night,* he thought. He laid back, stretched out in the grass, and gazed up into the heavens. Arcturus and the Big Dipper were straight above him. A hazy white band marked the path of the Milky Way. He could smell the earthy air, taste it even, and smell the marine layer, and he listened, quietly, as the wind blew through the reeds.

He found himself thinking about the Chumash Indians again. Beneath him, nonetheless, lay interred the bones of the ancients. But he was not afraid. Quite the opposite. He felt among friends. As he lay there listening to the rippling wind, with the aurora borealis flaming coldly overhead and the ground seemingly warm beneath him, Cameron closed his eyes and let the pressures of his day fade away.

# Chapter 21

Inside the Briefing Room Sergeant Jacobs held the phone pressed to his ear. Having dialed Stevens' number, having waited as it rang on the other end, he already knew the answer. There would be no answer. Holding the transceiver down, he tried another number, Stevens' cell number—still nothing. He looked up at the wall clock. It was half past eleven.

Three rooms away, Supervisor Harkin set a neatly-trimmed stack of papers at the edge of his desk, while leaving the larger mess of papers in the center. He picked up the phone and pressed Jacobs' extension.

Jacobs hurried voice answered. "Jacobs here."

"Were you able to reach Stevens?"

"Nope."

"Better go ahead and call Cameron in," Harkin paused. "Wait! First call Corley. Let him grab his lunch from the fridge. Let him know he'll be out there alone and he'll need to have his lunch on the road."

"Okay, got it covered," Jacobs said.

Harkin set the phone back in its stand and glanced up at the wall clock. They were more than an hour into the shift and still not settled in for the long night ahead.

In the Turbine Building, Grace was trying to find useful ways to pass her time and to keep her mind off Cameron. Bored rigid after only fifty minutes on shift, she had marched aimlessly back through the corridors to the turbine room without purpose. She was trying to gain a working knowledge of the Plant's floorplan, but couldn't get her heart into it. Still dismayed about missing Cameron at the shift change, she had spent nearly every moment since thinking about the two of them, and she felt empty now. Although her little escapade atop the catwalk was pleasing, it didn't fulfill her strong desire to see Cameron, to be with him, to talk to him—to touch him. The pent passions of the day would have to go unrequited.

*He will be mine,* she concluded. *I will not let him go.*

Grace had a plan, one she hoped to spring on Cameron tonight. But with a meeting not seemingly in the cards, she'd have to find another time, a time when it would be right. The plan was simple. She would move in, or he would move in with her. It was the only way, and she was ready for it. His apartment was smaller and not as nice, but it was in San Roque, such a beautiful place nestled along the seaside and so much closer to work. Santa DiRosa was a larger city, at least with a couple of movie theaters, but the thought of cozy evenings walking on the beach in San Roque, watching sunsets together, was very appealing. It didn't matter, Grace thought, either way. There would also be the benefits; saving money on rent and utilities for one. They would be able to save for *their* future. Being able to ride to work together would likewise save on gas. Her mind was set. It was just a matter of how and when? Should it be planned or spontaneous? Maybe it would be best to be spontaneous—just to show up on his porch with bags packed?

*I think he'd be pleasantly surprised.*

She had spent all her life trying to attain a feeling, and Cameron had given it to her in an instant. She tried to identify exactly what it was about him that attracted her so. *Many things,* she concluded. He was handsome, at least in her eyes, and he had a wonderful way of looking at her, a glimmer that told her she was something special. He knew exactly what she was thinking all the time, without asking, could sense her feelings, and always seemed to make her laugh. And there was that carefree attitude about life he possessed, his boy-like behaviors, and that wild and crazy streak inside of him; all of which Grace found very appealing. Cameron found charm in simple things and could laugh at humanity. He was different from any other guy Grace had met.

Mostly, it was that *something* she couldn't explain. There was something deep inside Cameron that just made her want to hug him endlessly and which caused a great warmth to well up every time she stood near him, or just thought of him.

*He will be mine.* Grace smiled broadly.

She looked up at the tall ceiling in the Turbine Room, and then out across the long floor. She could imagine the expression he would have on his face when she'd tell him she was moving in, especially if it were off the cuff. She would show up. He would swing the door open to see her standing there on his porch with a couple suitcases in her hand. At first he'd be surprised, maybe bewildered, but he would quickly disguise his surprise and delight and pretend it was expected and long overdue.

"What took you so long?" she thought he'd likely say with a big smile on his face.

"I was waiting for you to help me pack," she would reply.

*It would be so good!* Grace thought. *Every morning we could have coffee together, and we'd ride to work together. And best of all, I'd make sure he gets to work on time!*

*But we would have to hide it,* she knew.

Romances among the security guards were frowned upon by the administration, especially between couples on the same shift. Too often, the strong appeal of *love* between officers had caused a dereliction of duty. Tender passions inevitably came between one's sense of responsibility and loyalty to the job, and one's duty to perform it. Besides, Harkin would never stand for it. His mantra had always been; 'there'll be no chinks in my armor.' He'd certainly not allow the impregnable security of Mal Loma Nuclear Power Plant to be compromised by a couple of love-birds. One's infatuation with another would have to find another place, another time, to grow. If discovered, Grace knew, their relationship would promptly result in a forced transfer of one of them to another shift.

*It doesn't matter,* were the words that kept coming back to Grace. She would volunteer for a transfer right now, if necessary, although would prefer to remain Cameron's '*sourire complice*' —secret lovers stealing away time together unbeknownst to the attentive eyes of the administrators.

Grace gazed up into the cavernous ceiling of the Turbine Room. It rose more than sixty feet to an arching roof-top. She felt small and insignificant. I am in a fortress, she thought. She recalled the lyrics of a song:.

*Within a castle keep I'll hide my love for you.*

Pulling a little field-map from her pocket, Grace plotted her position. The map, a compact, laminated, two-sided blueprint of the alarm zones within the Plant, had been distributed during training. It served as a quick reference guide, especially for new security officers, at least until the Plant and all its alarm zones had became embedded in their minds. There were more than seven-hundred and sixty alarm zones in the Plant, so realistically; even the most experienced officers had to reference the map occasionally. It was a handy little tool; meant to facilitate compliance with the stringent NRC regulation of having to respond to any power plant alarm zone within ninety seconds.

Grace looked up at the tall generator housing. Stencil-painted on the side of it in big blue letters was: GENERATOR 546

Looking down at the map, she put her index finger on the exact spot.

"Alarm zone two-eighteen," she said.

She raised her head and continued walking. Bobbing her head from the fold-out to various objects within the Turbine Room, she continued along, familiarizing herself with the range of equipment and machinery. "It is imperative," the instructors had barked to all the cadets during training, "that one creates a mental map of the entire power plant." Knowing the terrain was of vital importance.

Despite the semblance of duty, Grace was still feeling melancholy. Through it all, though, Cameron's smiling face kept entering her mind, as if to calm her, but only caused her longing for him to grow.

# Chapter 22

*It must be a dream. What else could it be?*

Out on the coastal terrace, lying with eyes shut, those were Cameron's thoughts. He was somewhere in that place between awakeness and sleep and found himself strangely floating above blue oceans swells, traveling shoreward through white fog.

The fog broke to reveal a shoreline of crashing surf, white sandstone cliffs, and sweeping coastal terraces of tall shore grass. Beyond that, the shoreline gave way to green mountains towering against a blue sky.

Of course, Cameron knew these mountains, having driven through them on mobile patrols and having taken time to study them in bright afternoon sunlight. Once he drove the mobile unit adventurously high on a ridge, nearly to the top. In the summertime, when inland temperatures rose and scorched the earth, the cool, marine layer kept these mountains temperate and green. Often he had found himself wanting to forego his patrol duties and climb into their shaded canyons. They were mountains that beckoned, warm and majestic.

As his dream continued, so did he, shoreward, and he felt a strange sensation of weightlessness. It was the wind that was propelling him, he thought. In fact, wisps of wind swirled all around him. He expected to see a colorful parasail spread above his head, but there was none. He was loftier than a feather. He was like the seagulls he had often seen, using the updraft along the cliff's edge to stay afloat.

Below, ocean swells surged into long rolling mounds of bluish-green water. White curls trailed off their tops as they drove shoreward. Ahead, the shore grass rippled closer, like a huge blanket of green silk, inviting him as warm bedcovers invite on a cold night. In his half-awake mind, he remembered this restful place, though he did not recall it with full mental consciousness. He remembered lying on his back there with a blue sky arched above him. He remembered pelicans flying overhead in a 'V' formation. And he remembered the cool ocean breeze blowing like wind chimes through the tall shore grass. It was a good place, his mind told him.

That is, until he reached the shore.

As sudden as the wind had taken him, he was standing, perilously, at the edge of the bluff. And he saw an Indian boy running across the field. Though it should have been a good image, it was a bothersome image. As dreams often go, he felt racked with the unexplainable. Where and when he had seen this boy before, he did not know. And when the boy was gone, he heard muffled voices. And the voices seemed to be coming from beneath him. *Yes*, he thought, the sound was definitely coming from below. Or was it the tall reeds? And as he tried to discern the sounds, they rose into a chant, in a dialect he could not recognize. Then it happened.

As he turned his head to the wind, and brought his eyes back, an ominous apparition stood before him. There, mounted on a black stallion, in full-feathered headdress and with lance in his hand, was a near-naked Indian Warrior. His face, lined deeply with age, was painted over in traditional colors of war paint; red, yellow, white and black. The horse had huge, muscular flanks and shiny, black fur that glistened in the sunlight. It stood restless, pawing the earth. Together, man and animal seemed as one—some kind of mythical creature from the past.

The horse craned its huge neck around to one side, allowing the warrior to direct his menacing gaze upon Cameron. The tip of his lance shone brightly in the morning light.

With a sudden jerk, the horse reared, aggressively. Cameron stumbled back, nearly falling off the cliff's edge. He turned and looked down. Thirty feet below waves crashed upon rocks. Above him, the horse reared again, pawing its hoofs forcefully in the air.

*It's not a dream*, Cameron thought.

As the horse advanced, snorting, prancing, his knees kicking high against its shiny chest, the chanting returned, louder. And as it reached a crescendo, the radio on Cameron's side spoke.

Cameron sprung upright from the tall grass as one does from a bad dream and exhaled forcibly. As his senses came back to him, he realized the sound coming from his side was the familiar voice of Sergeant Jacobs.

"Security Control calling Mobile Two," Sergeant Jacobs' voice repeated.

"Mobile Two here," Corley's voice responded.

"Please report to the security building, A.S.A.P.," Jacobs said from the radio.

"Ten-four."

Still rattled from the dream, Cameron turned and scanned the reeds behind him. There was nothing but rippling shore-grass.

*That was weird. A warrior apparition on a horse?*

For a moment his eyes remained riveted on the blowing reeds. *Too many nights spent sitting in a graveyard I guess.*

Almost as eerie as the dream was the sudden realization that he was sitting above the bones of dead Indians. So many times he had cheerfully sat there in the reeds among his *Chumash friends*, peaceful and happy. Now he felt uneasy. Suddenly it had become what it truly is—a *graveyard,* the resting place of the dead.

In the distance was the glow of the illuminated power plant; the twin, white, Trojan-helmet-like containment domes stood out in the blackness. Looking back across the field, he saw the silhouette of Mobile One, backlit by the northern skyline.

Suddenly the radio beckoned: "Security Control calling Mobile One… come in." It was Sergeant Jacobs' again. "Security Control to Mobile One… Come in."

*Crap!*

Cameron fumbled with his utility belt, trying to get the radio out of its sheath and up to his mouth. Then, exhaling first, he keyed the transmitter. "Mobile One here."

"Ten-Nineteen Mobile One. We need you to return to the Security Building."

*Ten-Nineteen?* Cameron looked at his wristwatch. It was only 11:50 p.m. and they're calling me back? He purposely kept his finger off the transceiver trying to digest the information. His mind raced through a number of scenarios, none of them good. *Did they find out about his detour to the Bone Yard?* No, not likely. It was Harkin then, coming around to his senses and ready to dish out the retribution due him.

"What's up?" Cameron asked.

"We need you to fill a foot patrol post," came back Sergeant Jacob's voice.

Cameron glanced skyward. *A foot patrol post?* It took a moment to register, like the slowly gathering swell of an ocean wave, and then when it peaked, he realized the blessed meaning. A bright light filled his eyes. *Maybe I'll be seeing Grace tonight after all?*

"Ten-four," Cameron replied, smiling broadly now.

"Ten-four, over and out," Jacobs said, ending the transmission.

Cameron could hardly put his radio back in its sheath while simultaneously running for the Jeep. Once inside, he cranked on the engine, stomped the gas pedal, and swung around in a spinning U-turn nearly hitting the Bone Yard's *No Trespassing* sign. Straightening the wheel, he powered down the dirt road back toward the power plant, several hundred yards away.

Now it fully registered. It wasn't the executioner's call after all. Someone left post early. Probably Kelly, he thought. She was always going home early because of her infant son. Cameron was as aware of her motherly demands as was Harkin.

The situation could not have served Cameron better. It was a patrol post, which meant he'd be somewhere within the perimeter fence near Grace. In lieu of the guillotine, he was being granted a reprieve.

Ahead, through the windshield, were the approaching lights of the power plant. Somewhere within, Grace had undoubtedly heard the transmissions. But she was unaware of which post Cameron knew he'd be assigned.

*I have to let her know,* he thought, *somehow. It will make our rendezvous easier, and faster. But how to do it without alerting the entire security force?* He grabbed the Jeep's radio transceiver from its rack.

"Mobile One to Security Control," he spoke into the transceiver. "Mobile One to Security Control. Come in."

"Security Control here," Jacobs' voice came back.

"I've been reassigned to foot patrol?" Cameron asked.

"Yes, that's what I said! You've been assigned to foot patrol—Patrol One."

Cameron glanced up at the approaching Turbine Building.

"Patrol One?"

"Yes, Patrol One."

Cameron took his finger off the transmitter. *"Thank you Jacobs!"*

"Okay, thank you," Cameron replied.

*Grace had to hear that.*

Several hundred yards away, Grace walked alone through the Turbine Building in a '*dead-zone*'—one of many places where radio reception was either poor or completely lacking; an unavoidable consequence in the construction of a power plant built of thick walls, concrete and steel. She was still referencing landmarks on her little fold-out map when she heard an indistinguishable crackling noise emitting from her side. She pulled her radio from its sheath, tuned it in, and when she couldn't get a clear signal; she hurried forward trying to find a spot with better reception.

Back in Mobile One, Cameron keyed the transmitter; "Coming home, Mobile One, over and out."

"That's a ten-four, over and out," Jacobs' voice replied.

Then suddenly, the radio spoke again. It was Grace. "Ten-four Mobile One," she said. There was a brief pause and then she added, enthusiastically; "from the Turbine Building, *West.*"

In Mobile One, Cameron cringed. *Shit! What are you thinking?*

Harkin's irritated voice immediately followed, "Knock it off! This frequency is for security use only! No locations! No personal communications!"

"Ten-four," Grace's snickering voice replied.

Cameron smiled and pressed down on the accelerator, barreling down the dirt road back toward the lights of the Security Building. Inside the Turbine Building, Grace hurried across the central floor toward the west wall hoping to get a glimpse of Mobile One's headlamps through the tall, seaward windows.

*Wishing does not make a dream come true,* she thought, *purity of heart is what makes it real.*

Reaching the windows, looking through, she saw a shimmering pair of headlamps bouncing and dashing across the coastal terrace in her direction.

# Chapter 23

From offshore, the power plant glowed ominously. Across the western face of the Turbine Building, the twenty-four uniformly spaced vertical windows radiated like roman candles. But from a distance of ten miles, Grace's silhouette in the window could not be seen, nor the windows themselves. In fact, the entire power plant appeared only as a pale glow in the darkness to Ramzan and Emil.

"That is it?" Ramzan asked.

"Yes, that is it," Emil said, pointing to the light. "That light it is the power plant."

Emil checked the Garmin screen and confirmed. The positioning and distance to their longitude and latitude was undeniable. Then he checked his watch and backed off on the throttle.

"What are you doing" Ramzan asked.

"We're early," he said.

"It is good."

"Yes."

"How are you feeling?" Emil asked.

Ramzan still looked pale. His forehead was sweaty and his eyes had a distant look to them. And though he tried to shrug it off, he appeared to have difficulty focusing on Emil when he replied: "Better, but not perfect. I will be much better when we are on land."

"Of course. We will be on land in an hour. Maybe you should go and rest?"

Ramzan gave another one of those displeased expressions.

"I have some readings to check," Emil continued.

"Okay."

Ramzan climbed down the ladder and disappeared into the Captain's cabin.

Not more than five minutes later, Emil saw Ramzan back out on the forward deck. He had something under his arm, and as Emil watched, Ramzan rolled out a prayer rug on to the wet, lifting deck, and kneeled on it.

It was an odd sight, to say the least, on a swaying deck above a foreign sea, to see a sea-sick worshiper paying homage beneath a California sky speckled with *western* stars. Prayer was compulsory before battle, Emil knew, but they had already done so in the morning, together. But it did not surprise Emil, seeing Ramzan at it again. His devotion was fanatical. Once Ramzan had even paid homage in a sandstorm. And it seemed, in addition to his keen faith, Ramzan had inner demons, which Emil knew existed but did not know why or from where they came. While all soldiers of the brotherhood had faith and commitment to jihad, Ramzan had faith and commitment and a jihad raging within.

Emil looked at the Garmin and got a GPS reading.

"Mecca is that way," Emil shouted down from the pilothouse, pointing off the starboard bow.

Ramzan, with forehead flat to the deck, raised his head up and looked.

"That way," Emil shouted, again pointing.

Ramzan looked in the direction he pointed. "Okay, thank you Brother!"

Ramzan repositioned the prayer rug, trying to face into the proper direction. In his disorientation, he was actually facing it northeast.

"No! That way!" Emil shouted.

Ramzan looked up again. Then he positioned the rug properly and continued with his prayer.

"I would join you," Emil shouted down, feeling unworthy. "But I must drive this ship."

Ramzan did not reply.

Emil watched until Ramzan finished. Then he watched Ramzan roll up his rug, place it carefully in a small pack, place his neatly folded koofi cap and Qur'an on top of it, and return to the cabin.

# Chapter 24

On the mountaintop, the Sniper knelt in the tall wind-blown grass, leaning against a particularly steady breeze. In his hand was a pair of compact Night Owl binoculars. Far below in the northeast quadrant was a speck of a man, no larger than a pinhead, marching north along the perimeter fence. The Sniper waited for the wind to die down. Then he lifted the binoculars to his face and, adjusting the dials on the light intensifier, the greenish image grew brighter. Another adjustment on a top dial increased the sharpness and clarity. There, clearly as if under daylight or stadium lights, Carl Harrington patrolled the interior of the back fence.

The Sniper dropped the binoculars back to his knee. His trained eyes flickered contently.

The fence was high enough to cause a slight obstruction, especially when Harrington walked close along the inside of it. Also, the Fuel Handling Building would be problematic. It spanned the central length of the eastern fence, blocking the view of a sizeable portion of asphalt between the fence and the power plant itself. Each time Harrington went behind the building, he was completely out of view. But each time he reemerged, he'd be on the same route north, clear and bright beneath the illuminated flood lamps.

Turning his attention south, the Sniper studied Chris Peters' route, which he knew would be a little more challenging. The southern end of the Fuel Handling Building protruded into *Patrol Zone Four*, shadowing it for a considerable distance. Only when Peters changed his route toward the rear of Containment One would he emerge from beyond the building. Since that was unlikely and unpredictable, the Sniper would have to take him on the southern end. But to the south, at the place he would always come clear, there were dark shadows created by the building, and also there was the problem of the Security Building. The trajectory was aligned in such a way that a miss would ricochet off the asphalt and career directly into the rear of the Security Building.

The Sniper watched Peters repeated his route several times. Finally, he detected a sweet spot between the shadows and the rear of the Security Building. It was a place where Peters came clear every time, albeit for only three steps; a step out of the shadow and two steps before he aligned with the Security Building. The Sniper timed the route—*seventy-three seconds.* He timed it again—*seventy-two seconds!*

*Nothing like the soldier efficiency,* the Sniper thought, amazed at the consistency of Peters' pace, *to make my job easier.*

Behind him, waiting on the tarp, was the M-107 rifle. He set down the binoculars, got up, lifted the M-107 into his arms, and planted it at the mountain's edge. It was set there just beyond the edge of the tarp. He adjusted the two legs of the bipod, securing the legs in the grass, and then laid lengthwise behind the rifle. He swung the barrel westward, settling in on Carl Harrington in the northeast corner of the perimeter fence. Holding steady on him, he tracked him, waiting for him to make his turn into the open spot.

*Come on. Come on, a little more, a little more, right... now!*

*Click!* The weapon dry-fired.

Looking above the scope, the Sniper smiled as the speck that was Harrington walked harmlessly away. He took a ten-round magazine from his pocket and slapped it into the base of the gun, making sure it was locked in place. He wrapped his arm around the stock again, pulling it snugly into his armpit and against his chest, and looked through the scope once more. Once more it lined up nicely. Carl Harrington appeared close and vulnerable. Content, the Sniper pushed up with his arms, rocked back on his knees, and stood up. He let the weapon sit there, its barrel tilting lazily up. A glance at the illuminated hands of his military wristwatch told him there was *no hurry*.

The wind had remained steady from the northwest, rushing through the grass and flapping the edge of the tarp. Taking a seat at the edge of the tarp beside the rifle, he let his legs hang out over the grass. He inhaled deeply, taking in the marine scent. Then he took a sandwich from the duffle bag, unwrapped the saran-wrap and tossed it in the grass, and began munching.

The beaming white stars made him recall the *white nights* of northern Europe. Staring at the vague line which marked the horizon, he could almost feel the curvature of the earth. There at the lower edge of the world, he thought, where it sloped down to the other side, a new day was dawning.

His mind flashed to the *Church of the Assumption Cathedral*, a place far north on the opposite side of the globe. It was a cultural and religious shrine of national importance and pride, wherein the lives of two men had been changed forever in a single flash of a rifle muzzle.

He shook off the image and turned to his side and watched the wind blowing through the grass over the rounded mountain top. The grass rippled and fluctuated in harmonious thrusts. The M-107 rested behind him, barrel up, pointing skyward. *You're ready and so am I.*

Facing forward again, he munched on his sandwich. Relaxing his thoughts, he gazed back out at the horizon. Without realizing it, his mind flashed back to the Cathedral again. This time he found himself looking through the cross-hairs of a scope.

A man stood with an obvious bomb strapped to his chest, holding a detonator chord high above his head. He recognized the face of this man. It was the face of Kamir, a friend and military comrade. Kamir had come up through the ranks with him, both having been selected to a specialized military force as young men. They had done and seen plenty together, through years of training and specialized assignments in foreign lands. They had crossed rivers together, climbed mountains, and killed together.

Kamir was missing his leg, he knew, though one would not know that by looking at this man in the Cathedral, as he had a prosthesis hidden beneath his military pants. He was without one leg nonetheless, having lost it in one of many military campaigns. Kamir, once a strong man of absolute confidence and physical fitness, was perched on his prosthesis with a bomb strapped to his chest, vowing to destroy the old cathedral and its sacred relics. *How did it come to this?*

The Colonel had summoned him, along with a group of others specialists, for what reason the Sniper did not initially know. Now looking through the scope and seeing Kamir in the cross-hairs, he knew exactly why. They had become the best in their field, trained to kill at great distances. How to control one's breathing, to steady one's arms, to feel one's heart beat and co-incide it with a squeeze of a trigger; it was an art in which he and Kamir had equally excelled, and had mastered together, above all others in an elite military squad.

But then there was the casualty; the incident that cost Kamir his leg. And the military showed their true colors, callously handling the matter. Their once prized possession was cast aside. The military hospital did its part, but Kamir was immediately dispatched from the squad, rendered useless to them, and after convalescing, sent out into a world where he had no means of making a living; eventually reduced to a dishwasher in a shoddy back-street café.

As he looked at Kamir's face, he knew exactly what Kamir knew and thought. Kamir knew every place in and around the cathedral and which would provide the best tactically position for a clear shot. He knew which angle would be taken and why. He knew it would have to be a head shot. He knew that a ricochet could kill one in the crowd of patrons, and therefore, knew the type of bullet that would be used; one with a soft, flattening head. And most of all, Kamir knew who would be behind the rifle.

Kamir turned and looked directly into the scope. *It is me brother.*

The Sniper timed his breathing, carefully, placed the crosshairs at the precise spot where the temple meets the hairline, and squeezed the trigger.

His eyes refocused on the dark horizon. Beside him, the piece of saran-wrap he had tossed in the grass lifted in a breeze and sailed skyward into the night. It disappeared over Miguelleto Canyon.

# Chapter 25

From the railed-rooftop of the Auxiliary Building, Grace anxiously watched the rear doors of the Security Building. She had rushed up the stairs from the Turbine Room and positioned herself on the southernmost end of the observation deck. She had not seen the headlights of Cameron's patrol Jeep pull into the front parking lot, as she had arrived at her roof-top perch too late. But now, below, eighty-five-yards away, she watched the glow of light from behind the double-pane glass.

And it was not long before she was rewarded, as a shadow came across the glass. Then Cameron emerged.

Grace smiled broadly and pulled her radio from its sheath.

Having reentered the Security Building through the search train, having turned the vehicle keys over to Fred, having reported to Sergeant Jacobs, having been issued his 'armed responder' gear, Cameron was now equipped with a Mini-14 rifle slung from his shoulders and a complete field utility belt, carrying four twenty-round banana clips of the .223 caliber ammunition.

Grace keyed her radio transceiver, "Rover One to Control One."

Watching below, she saw Cameron stop dead in his tracks, and look down at the radio on his side.

"Control One here," Lewis' affable voice replied.

"Ten-twenty turbine building two, north," Grace spoke into her radio.

"Ten-four," Lewis's voice echoed back.

"Over and out."

"Over and out."

On the blacktop below, Cameron looked up. He could not see Grace from where he stood, only the tall, brown steel siding of the Turbine Building towering above him. But he understood the message. It was the place they would meet. And he dashed for it, reaching the Turbine Building door in less than ten seconds, fumbling with his keycard, finally sliding it in the cardreader, and punching in his security code.

Above, Grace smiled. *He got it!*

Then it dawned on her that she had just telegraphed her location at *'turbine building two north'* when truly she was atop the southern end of the Auxiliary Building, five levels up, a good ten-minute sprint from the actual spot!

Grace sprang to the nearest stairwell. Concentrating on the steps, she tried to skip two at a time, nearly tripping, and on more than one occasion she had to lunge for the rail and hold on until she could regain her balance. Each time followed by a deep breath and a continued downward flight. The staircase was open-mesh, steel-grated, giving a harrowing view of the blacktop forty feet below. But Grace was not afraid. She was on a mission.

Cameron meanwhile, dashed across the main floor of the Turbine Building, past the loud sound of the spinning turbines, to the center of the huge room. He scanned in all directions but could not see Grace anywhere. Then he climbed the two-rung guardrail which encircled Turbine Number Two. Perched on top, he looked out over the tops of equipment and machinery. But beneath the bowed, six-story ceiling, across the entire floor, he saw no one.

*Where are you?*

Dropping back down, he ran to the north end, thinking he might find her there.

In the interim, Grace had dashed down the entire length of the exterior staircase, entered the Auxiliary Building through an exterior door, went down a short hall, accessed another doorway, and raced down yet another stairwell. All the while her heart was thumping and her face was beaming.

For better or for worse, tonight was going to be *their* night, she thought. *It was meant to be.* Luck had clearly called them. In addition to informing Cameron that she'd be moving in, she was going to spring a surprise on him, something so unique, and strangely romantic, even she could not believe she had imagined it. They had suffered through too many nightshifts and days apart. They had endured sneaking around and concealing their true feelings, avoiding the condemnation of others and the wrath of Supervisor Harkin. And Cameron had, at times, risked it all to be with her. Their relationship had progressed long enough, she thought. *It's time to take it to a higher level!*

Grace dashed across the last steel foot-bridge, down a short set of steel stairs, key-punched her way through another door, and accessed the Turbine Room. Then, with a big smile, she raced down another long catwalk of steel-lattice-flooring toward the center of the main floor.

From thirty yards away, Cameron saw her. Like a moment from a Hollywood movie, they dashed for one another, colliding in an embrace, and they kissed, passionately, for a full minute. Then Cameron lifted Grace off her feet and whirled her in a half circle.

Finally breaking to exhale, Grace gave a delightful, "Together at last!"

Cameron nodded. "I thought we'd never be together tonight."

"Some things are meant to be!" Grace proclaimed. "The planets have fallen in line just for us!"

Cameron gave a funny look. "Maybe," then he kissed her again.

For a moment they just stood there, intertwined, holding each other and kissing like long lost lovers, though, truth was, they had seen each other less than twenty-four hours before. Love causes time to elongate, as it did for them. Hours turn to days, weeks to months, or years even, when two are separated, and for Grace, it felt like more than a year had past since they'd last kissed. Now Cameron felt so good in her arms she didn't want to let go.

Cameron, on the other hand, was already thinking about his post—that cold section of asphalt and perimeter fence he must go and guard. The lines on his forehead showed it.

"What's wrong?" Grace asked.

"Nothing, I'm fine." Cameron said. He did not want to spoil the moment. "I'm here with you!"

Grace suddenly remembered, and paused and tilted her head. "Where were you?" The tone of her voice was playfully serious.

"Late as usual. What can I say? Sometimes it just happens. Sorry."

Grace continued her serious gaze; then she smiled and hugged him. "Don't worry about it. You're here with me now. We're here together!"

Cameron smiled and returned the hug.

"Grace, you're as crazy as me."

"Maybe."

Cameron glanced around to make sure they were not under the scrutiny of any surveillance camera. There were none.

"We can't go on meeting this way," Grace said, half-jokingly.

"No kidding." Cameron paused. "I've only got about ten minutes. If I don't get out to my post, Drake and Lewis will be looking for me."

Grace furled her lower lip making a sad face.

"Sorry, I can't afford getting into any more trouble. Harkin's got me on his blacklist, though it's not like I really give a damn. I don't give a damn. But I should give a damn. You make me want to give a damn."

Graced smiled. "Well then, I'm glad you give a damn."

Amidst the humming of the turbines came the sound of voices. Cameron instinctively ducked down, as did Grace

"Did you hear that?" Cameron asked. Grace's eyes said *yes*. Cameron put his hand on her shoulder as to keep her from moving. The two of them remained frozen, continuing to listen, and above the sound of the droning turbines came the unmistakably sound of voices.

"Who is it?" Grace asked, quietly.

"Engineers probably."

"Should we leave?"

Cameron held a finger to her lips. "Don't move," he whispered.

Cameron lifted his head and looked west across the main floor. Two white hardhats were coming their way. He ducked back down.

"Shit!" Cameron said.

"What?"

"They're coming this way!"

"Let's go!"

Cameron poked his head up again.

"No. It'll look too suspicious." He paused thoughtfully. "Follow me."

Cameron stepped out from behind the voltage boxes, pulling Grace with him, directly into the line of sight of the two oncoming engineers. They had evidently heard them too, as they had stopped whatever it was they were doing and had turned their heads their way. Realizing now it was Chief Engineer Stewart and George Cullman, one of the night operators, Cameron sighed.

"Act unconcerned," Cameron said in a low voice.

It was routine for engineers to be wandering about the plant, taking readings, checking equipment, and so forth. There was no reason to be alarmed by it, Cameron knew. And Chief Stewart, of all the engineers, was a particularly affable and easygoing one.

"And here we have the turbines pumping out a couple thousand megawatts of electricity to millions of Californians, everyday!" Cameron spoke loudly, directing Grace's attention to the turbine housing.

"Really?" Grace said, pretending to be astonished.

Cameron nodded a friendly *hello* to Chief Engineer Stewart and to Operator Cullman. "Isn't that right, Chief Stewart?"

Chief Engineer Stewart took the lollipop from his mouth. "That's right, Cameron."

"This is Grace Baker. She's new on the night shift. I'm giving her a night tour."

Chief Stewart and Cullman exchanged doubtful glances.

"Hi Grace," Chief Stewart said, nodding a friendly *hello*.

"Hello," Grace replied.

Cameron looked surprised. "You know each other?"

"I met Ms. Baker in the Plant Overview class," Chief Stewart explained.

"Yes, of course."

Chief Stewart turned toward Grace. "I remember you had the great question about accelerating the thermal process by increasing the mix of neutrons with other fissionable isotopes."

"It was an absolutely amazing lecture," Grace replied.

*Fissionable isotopes?* Cameron looked at Grace. "You didn't tell me you knew about nuclear physics?"

"I don't. I just really enjoyed the class," Grace said.

"She was a great student," Stewart said. "Very smart."

"Thank you," Grace politely came back.

"So how are things going tonight?" Cameron asked, trying to move the conversation along.

"Fine thanks. Same old thing, just taking some turbine readings," Stewart said. "And you two?"

"Same here, just doing the night tour thing." Cameron paused, thinking whether it sounded plausible or not. "Well, you guys have fun with those readings now."

"And you two have fun with that night tour thing," Stewart said, with a little smirk. He tipped his hard hat.

Cameron and Grace looked at one another and simultaneously started to walk forward.

"Have a good one," Cameron said.

"You too, have a good one," Chief Stewart replied.

"Bye."

Moving fast now, Cameron and Grace turned at the first possible corner and ducked down beyond some large transformers. They both began to laugh and had to cover their mouths with their hands. Cameron pulled his keycard from his pocket.

"Let's get out of here," he said.

They hurried to the nearest door, keeping low. Cameron opened it. But before Grace could step through, he swung his jacket wide onto the floor before her. Puzzled at first, Grace stared down at the jacket. Cameron then made a knightly gesture, rolling his hand out forward.

"This way Madam Grace," he said, with a very bad English accent.

*Ah!* Grace returned a dainty smile, held out her hand. "Thank you kind Prince," she replied, in nearly perfect King's English.

Cameron took her hand, and passing through, swooped up his jacket from behind. As the door swung safely shut behind them, they both burst out laughing, loudly now.

"An escorted tour?" Grace cackled. "Where did you come up with that?"

"It seemed plausible enough."

"Do you think they bought it?"

"I doubt it."

"I doubt it too."

"Well, maybe…" Cameron said. "But I don' think it matters. Stewart's cool. He's not the type to report something like this."

"Yeah, I think you're right."

"Well, unfortunately, nevertheless, I'd better get out there. Duty calls."

"Do you really need to go so soon?"

"Those guys are going to be looking for me on the monitors and when they don't see me, they're liable to report me." He was referring to Drake and Lewis.

"You think so soon?"

"Drake's in Station Two tonight and you know how he is." He looked at Grace. "Well, maybe you don't know how he is. He's a real bean counter."

"Well, if you must go…"

"I think I must."

"Too bad," Grace said. "I had a surprise for you." She said it with a sexy little smile.

"A surprise?"

"Oh, nothing really."

"What do you mean nothing? What kind of surprise?"

"It can wait." Her smile was now mischievously sexy.

*Oh, shit,* Cameron was thinking. "Well, maybe another twenty minutes or so wouldn't hurt."

Grace's lovely green eyes shined back. "Are you sure? I don't want you getting in trouble."

"I'm not sure, but I'm not worried about it."

"You really think those guys will turn you in?'

"Yes, especially Drake."

"He's really that way?"

"Positive. But what more can they do to me? Fire me?" *A handsome reminder,* Cameron thought as those last words left his lips. He made a mocking frown. *A handsome reminder of the fine fix I'm in!*

"Yes," Grace replied bluntly. Grace didn't know Cameron's entire employment history, how spotty it truly was, or the recent mess he had gotten into with Harkin, otherwise she would have insisted that he go to his post now. Besides, it wasn't their first time. They had eloped off post together before and nothing became of it.

"Really Grace, I think I'll be fine," Cameron said now, insisting all would be okay. "Besides, being here with you now is what I want. I want to spend the whole night with you."

The sexy grin returned to Grace's face. "If you insist."

"I do."

Grace took Cameron's hand. "In that case, it's my turn to be your tour guide."

"What?" Cameron chuckled.

"I want to show you something." Grace's eyes were twinkling.

"Oh? I thought you said you had a surprise?"

"I do. But first I want to show you something."

The way the night was going, Cameron was ready for something different. He was ready to follow Grace in whatever direction she wanted to lead him, despite the cost; albeit there was a preference to keep out of the sight of the surveillance cameras. Standing in the cold night air next to a cyclone fence was no option compared with being with Grace.

*Being with the one you love—isn't it the sweetest wine of life?* he thought, looking at Grace now. *No, it's sweeter than wine!*

Begging him on with the mischievous little grin, Grace tugged his hand. "Follow me?"

"Sure, why not?"

With Grace leading and Cameron in tow, together they dashed away down the corridor, Grace laughing playfully as Cameron tried to stay with her. She did not look back.

Meanwhile, he was thinking, *why of all nights, did I have to put myself under Harkin's watchful eye tonight?*

# Chapter 26

"It's been a while since the harbor's seen the likes of them," the bartender in the Lighthouse Tavern said abruptly.

The Stranger looked up at him. He had been studying the old ornate clock behind the counter. He'd become a bit fascinated with it. It was indeed an antique, he thought, probably nineteenth century. It had a large, gilt bronze base, elaborately detailed hands, and a schooner carved intricately upon its face.

"The ship," the bartender said, dragging his dishrag across the bar-top in front of him.

With a glance back at the clock, the Stranger said nothing.

*Time to leave*, he thought. It was approaching midnight.

The bartender went about his business, collecting some empty bottles from the counter and tossing them into the trash.

The Stranger took a final swig from his beer bottle and swiveled around in his chair. At the nearby pool table, the lanky biker he encountered earlier straightened tall. So did his bigger friend. The Stranger rose slowly to his feet. He stood easily three inches taller than the pitted-faced lanky biker, and outweighed him by at least thirty pounds, but gave an inch and twenty pounds to the large biker. The Stranger walked past them both, quietly, without further confrontation, and exited the pub.

Out front, the old neon sign—*The Lighthouse Tavern*—flashed its emulating beam across the sidewalk. The Stranger looked up at it for a moment, and then walked quietly down the sidewalk to his 1980's Cadillac. He unlocked the door and climbed in. Adjusting the rearview mirror he checked if anyone was behind him, and seeing no one, he then reached down under the seat and hoisted up an oversized revolver. It was the classic Colt *Python* 357 Magnum, which, despite its fame in movie theaters and pulp detective novels, was an archaic weapon. It lacked the fast-reload clip common in the newer automatic models, and was tremendously bulky, not easy to conceal. With a six round cylinder, it gave up at least a half a dozen rounds to the automatic models. But for the Stranger, it was the weapon of choice. He wrapped his big hand around the oversized black grip and looked over its distinctly long ribbed-ventilated barrel. Its smooth trigger-pull and firepower, for him, was something never to be questioned.

He checked the cylinder; six rounds—*full.* Then he laid the gun on the seat beside him.

For a moment he sat there with the window down, feeling the fresh, crisp ocean air blow in against his face. The strobe of the neon sign reflected off the hood of his car, sometimes flashing in colorful hues. He looked over at the entrance to the pub. It was as if he was expecting to see the lanky biker burst out with a gun in his hand, but he knew he would not. He had wisely let him save face. After a minute, the Stranger straightened, checked the rearview mirror again, wedged the Colt Python snugly between the seat and his thigh, and cranked on the engine.

*Good to go back to work*, he thought.

The Cadillac backed out from its parking spot, sputtered down Front Street to the sound of a tapping valve, and turned onto the Coast Road. Following a string of street lights, it headed on toward Port San Miguel.

Fifteen minutes later, the Cadillac pulled off the road onto a dark shoulder between two street lamps. He turned the engine and headlamps off. Staying inside, he peered out the front windshield at the rounding beam of the lighthouse at end of Point San Miguel. He marveled at its consistency, and for a moment was hypnotized by it. Then coming back to the area in the foreground, he studied the Port locality. He saw only one person, two hundred yards away, beneath a lamppost. The individual was at the public boat launch, apparently securing a boat to a trailer. There was no other movement or activity at the port. To his immediate right was the glow of another light coming from behind an earthen embankment, beyond which he knew were the highly-luminescent flood lights of San Roque Gate—the power plant's main entrance. He could not see the guard booth directly, but *it was there, all right.* He had seen it in daylight several times, studied it on maps, and knew it lay just thirty meters up the approach road.

All was quiet.

He checked his wristwatch. Still nearly two hours to burn. He lounged back in the seat, lowering himself the best he could and trying to get comfortable. Patience was a necessity, he thought, a necessity of the trade; one he had learned to respect and follow. He eased his head back against the head-rest and waited.

The light beam continued to come around, sweeping its long reach across the ocean, onto the land, and flashing its light into the passenger compartment of the Cadillac. He timed it with his chronographer. It made a complete revolution every six seconds; ten in a minute.

*Preciseness...* it was another thing the Stranger appreciated.

In a profession of killing—preciseness of timing meant everything. It meant the difference of losing a limb or two, or losing one's life. It's what separated the amateur from the professional.

He closed his eyes to the recurring flash of the light-beam, counting out its revolutions in his head, every six seconds.

# Chapter 27

*It is time, Brother.*

Emil stared through a windshield sprayed with sea water. A mile away was an empire of lights; the two white containment domes encircled by a ring of fiery flood lamps. He marveled at the hugeness of it, and how well lit it was. Its proximity to the cliffs made it seem too easy, like a low-hanging peach ripe for the taking.

Emil checked the sonar. The depth told him they were above a reef now. The depth had gone from over one hundred meters to less than thirty in less than five minutes. He continued forward, watching the depth finder, and, reaching a sweet spot, he dropped the throttle to a slow idle and the trawler eased back in the water. From beyond the stern came a large wake rolling past and disappearing into the dark swells beyond the bow. The cessation of forward movement was followed by a slow, side-by-side rocking motion. Emil reversed the gear box, easing back on it to steady the boat.

For the past forty minutes they had chased the distant lights, seemingly never drawing nearer. Then suddenly they were upon them. They had taken advantage of the time, alternately going below and slipping into black pants and long-sleeve black pullovers. Ramzan had spent most of the time trying to shake-off his sea-sickness, staying flat on his back in the Captain's cabin.

He came up for air occasionally, but just as quickly, he returned to his roost below. By virtue of his sickness, he had plenty of time to mentally rehearse, staring up at a blank ceiling.

The distance was good, Emil thought as he studied the configuration of lights just southeast of them. They were far enough to be out of sight and sound of the power plant, but close enough to make their shoreward trip swift and safe. They had not come completely parallel with the Plant, but stayed a distance north. Though the Plant was still fifteen-hundred meters away, the shore was less than four-hundred. From the port side, he could hear the distant sound of waves pounding the shore, and he could see the white sandstone cliffs, seemingly taller and close now. With the ship's engines still idling, Emil turned the wheel slightly seaward pointing the bow of the vessel into the approaching swells. Then, checking the sonar once more, he confirmed a depth of *Twenty-three meters.*

He depressed the anchor's auto-release and listened as the chain dropped from the forward hull, further, further, further, stopping finally as it hit bottom. The trawler drifted briefly before the anchor caught. Reversing the engines, Emil retracted the anchor chain and locked it in place. Then he shut off the engines.

From a case on his belt, he took a compact pair of binoculars, similar to the ones the Sniper used. He brought the binoculars up to his face, adjusted the eye width, and sharpened the focus. Though his line of sight was angled from the north, by using the built-in infrared illuminator, he was able to gain a brilliant view of the perimeter fence, the Turbine Building, and the upper portion of the Auxiliary Building beyond. He could see the row of vertical windows across the face of the Turbine Building. They glowed brilliantly like evenly-spaced slits of gold. He could nearly see into them, except the angle did not permit it. The rear windows of the Security Building glowed equally as bright, but the distance was too great to discern anything within. Following carefully from the Security Building north across the many lights of the Turbine and Auxiliary Buildings, up and past each of the huge containment domes, he finally angled up to the dark outline of the coastal mountains which were barely discernable from the dark sky. He located the tallest mountaintop, the one in the center where the Sniper now waited, but he could not make out anything from this distance.

He dropped back down to the power plant, scanning it once more, then to the flashing blue beacon in the Intake Cove. All seemed conspicuously quiet. Then to the north, the coastline gave way to the semi-circular Discharge Bay, about two hundred meters from the Plant. It was marked by a surface of white foam. Further north was a small cove tucked in between two protruding points of sandstone cliffs. A small beach in between was protected from the open sea by a group of off-shore rocks. Just south in the direction of the power plant was a huge cliff, jutting out into the ocean like the prow of a battleship.

*Perfect*, Emil thought. It provided ideal cover from the power plant, and the protective off-shore rocks would serve as a breaker, making their beach landing all that much easier. He promptly re-sheathed the binoculars.

Just then, Ramzan joined him in the pilothouse, still looking green. His legs were wobbling and his face looked placid.

"You okay?" Emil asked.

Ramzan nodded. "I'll be better when my feet touch the earth again."

Emil gave him a head to toe glance over. What he saw worried him. "There it is," he said, pointing to the Plant.

Ramzan's eyes fixed on the glowing power plant. "That is it?"

"Yes."

"It looks too small."

"It will look bigger when you're standing beneath it." Emil turned his attention north. "And there's where we will land," he said, pointing to the cove.

Ramzan glanced at the cove, but his eyes quickly went blurry. He hung on to the rail.

"I'll have you on shore quickly," Emil said.

With that, Ramzan opened his eyes, opened them with some life back in them, and he returned his gaze to the power plant. In the dark world of night, the power plant looked like a neon sign.

"May my burial shroud be dark so no enemy can find me so easily," he said, and he grinned in a sickly fashion.

Emil acknowledged by nodding his head. "Get your things ready," he said. "I'm going to take one last GPS reading. Then I'll join you."

Ramzan did not respond. He simply exited the pilothouse.

Emil clicked on the *Garmin* global-positioning unit. His mind was still on Ramzan, and when he looked down at him crossing the deck, he saw him wobbling unsurely. "I'll have you on the beach quickly," he shouted out the door. "You'll have time to sit and wait... and to feel well."

From out the door of the pilothouse, down the ladder, there was no reply.

The *Garmin* screen glowed green with their latitudinal and longitudinal numbers. Emil scribbled the coordinates on a small piece of paper. Then he took a reading of the landing cove, and of the power plant, and triangulated the distance from the cove to the power plant using a nifty little feature on the Garmin unit. The digital read-out flashed out in blue letters:

*Seven-hundred and twenty-six meters.*

Plenty good, Emil thought. Nearly a half a mile—far enough from the Plant yet close enough to lug two heavy packs through grass and ice-plant. He tucked the paper in his pocket.

In the darkness, the two men prepared to launch the Zodiac on the leeward side. Double-checking their gear, making sure it properly secured in their waterproof swathes along the inner wall of the beach craft, they tethered the craft to the power wrench and hoisted it up. Once the nose cleared the rail, they pushed the craft out over the water. Emil reversed the winch and the craft dropped slowly into the swells.

A faint light illuminated from the leeward window of the pilothouse. Glancing up at it, Emil realized he had left the Garmin unit on. "I'll be right back," he said.

Ramzan nodded and held steady, grasping the rail.

Returning to the pilothouse, Emil clicked off the *Garmin* unit and waited for his pupils to dilate. Looking out across the surging swells, he focused on the power plant once more. Strangely, it looked like an offshore oil platform. *Odd,* Emil thought, because it had been another target they'd considered. The oil platforms out in the Santa Barbara Channel seemed ripe for exploding and would have effectively demonstrated the vulnerability of America's oil reserves. But they had dismissed the plan in favor of an attack which would cause massive casualties. The destruction of oil platforms, as tempting as they seemed, did not contain a sufficient element of terror. Not enough lives would have been lost.

Emil descended the ladder, joined Ramzan at the rail, and from the pouch on his hip, withdrew the Night-Owl binoculars. Scanning the coastline once more, he followed along the vague white surf below the sandstone cliffs until again he found the cove where they'd make their landing. Lifting his face above the binoculars, he viewed the cove with his naked eye. *There,* he thought, eyeing the protruding cliff just south, which provided his landmark. He locked the image in his mind and sheathed the binoculars.

"Look at it," Emil said to Ramzan, referring to the magnificently illuminated power plant. It glowed warmly in the midst of darkness. "It is close enough to touch."

Ramzan tried to look out across the swells, but his vision blurred again, and twisted into odd contortions. He looked straight down into the water, hoping it would make him feel better, but the bobbing craft only made him feel oozier. The boat was perpendicular to the land and the shoreward swells rocked it like a cockleshell.

"Get me to the shore," he said. "It's time to avenge the Innocent."

*Then I will show this monster my worth.*

He tried looking up again, only to find himself having to avert his eyes.

Emil pulled the tether line tight so that the Zodiac came flush against the hull of the big trawler. Then he motioned with his hand to Ramzan, *go! Go!*

The two men descended into the bobbing Zodiac, their automatic assault rifles slung on their shoulders. Small wakes splashed against the hull of the ship and into the Zodiac as they settled into the craft. Emil unhooked the ties and shoved off. Then he flipped open the fuel hatch and opened the valves wide. Cranking-on the dual Evinrude engines, he turned the rudder and throttled shoreward.

# Chapter 28

Drake sat in his throne-like chair overlooking the entrance lobby of the Security Building. He compared the time on his wristwatch with that on the lobby wall clock. The wall clock read: 11:53 p.m. His wristwatch read the same, *nearly to the second.* And the digital clock in the corner of the computer screen was likewise identical.

Despite Drake's apparent satisfaction with the flawless synchronicity of clocks, he found himself restless. He looked up at the perforated ceiling tiles and then turned his attention to the rotating surveillance screens. Like before, he picked up the wireless remote and started scrolling through the cameras, beginning with the patrol zones around the perimeter fence. Shooting through them in a descending sequence, he started with *Patrol Four* and counted down to *Patrol One.* As each zone flashed up on the screen, the image appeared nearly identical—the respective officer, with rifle slung from his shoulder, dutifully patrolling a lonely section of fence. That is, until he reached *zone one*—Cameron's abandoned post.

Drake leaned in with brow arched. He manipulated the camera, widening the lens to its peripheral limits and scanning back and forth along the fence. He could see the little weather station beyond the fence—it's tubular directional flag flying horizontal on the flagpole—and he could clearly see down the length of blacktop to the distant figure of Pryce Johnston.

But where's Cameron?

*A head break,* Drake theorized.

It was early yet. Cameron's absence could be due to any number of things. Jacobs might have asked him to run a task. He may have run the shift log up to Lewis; a procedural function which was not always facilitated faithfully. It could have been a restroom call. Or Cameron may have just taken a lackadaisical route to his post.

He'll show up eventually, Drake thought.

Moving on, Drake scanned the Intake Cove again, angling the camera up toward the dark sea. Beyond the flashing-blue buoy the screen dissolved into blackness. He clicked on the infrared feature, but the lens picked up no hint of light.

He flipped the screen to San Roque Gate. The camera there, mounted high on a pole twenty yards back from the gate, faced directly out across the kiosk and down the approach road. The view of the guard booth was marginal at best, but, through the rear window, he could see Marvin seated inside, apparently eating something. Drake tilted the camera up, and viewed the lights of Port San Miguel and the bay beyond.

*Nothing interesting.*

He began scanning through other cameras quickly; the full-color, high-definition images flashed by in scroll sequence, one scene to the next. Drake was mesmerized by it; the same old images, replications of still-life, nothing different and nothing unexpected.

Until a flash streaked by in the Auxiliary Building.

Drake sat upright in his chair. The image had gone by so quickly he didn't get a clear view of it, but what it appeared to be was something that shouldn't be—two people running down a hallway together, quickly, and bizarrely, and it looked like they were laughing, and... *holding hands?*

Drake quickly flipped-back in sequence searching for the image. *It was camera thirty-four,* he thought. Finally finding the camera, the image crossed the screen again, this time with clarity. To Drake's shock, and dismay, he saw Cameron and Grace running together down a long corridor. *And yes*—they were holding hands, and smiling and grinning, looking like two mischievous high-school kids evading the truant officer.

*What the...?*

Drake followed them from one camera to the next. They reached a doorway. Cameron pulled out his keycard and began accessing their way through. Grace looked up and waved into the camera.

Drake lifted his glasses and frowned. *Idiots!* Tapping his fingers on the counter, he considered calling Harkin. A glance at the clock and he thought otherwise. *Umm, I think not yet.*

He pulled out a notepad and logged the time and location. Then he tossed the notepad on the counter. He swirled around in his chair, considering the implications of Cameron and Grace's misconduct. What effect would it have on the nightly functions? None for now, he thought. If anything, it would only delay the inevitable, and further solidify Cameron's fate with Harkin. I'll give him twenty minutes, Drake commented mentally. I'll give him enough time and a rope to hang himself.

A couple buildings away in the Auxiliary Building, Cameron and Grace exited a long hallway and entered the Generator Room. Running the length of it, still holding hands and laughing, they came out the door on the far side, and stumbled into the rear elevator corridor nearly falling to the floor, having to use one other's body as a crutch to hold each other up.

"Grace!" Cameron laughed, completely out of breath. "Where are you taking me?"

"Shhhhh! Close your eyes!" Grace ordered.

Grace looked at Cameron, making sure his eyes were closed. Then she took his hand and led him across the corridor to the Containment One Elevator.

"No peeking!" she commanded.

They waited for the elevator door to open, and she pulled Cameron inside.

"I know where you're taking me," Cameron said, as he felt the elevator ascend rapidly

"Shhhhh! Be quiet… And keep your eyes closed!"

They were both breathing hard. Grace looked at Cameron. Somehow, standing there beneath the small ceiling light with his eyes squeezed shut, he looked very boyish. She smiled and laughed at him.

"What?"

"Nothing. Keep your eyes closed!"

Cameron could hear himself breathing, as well as Grace's breathing, and she was breathing excitedly, and it made him want to lean forward with his lips and try to find hers. Which he did, but she leaned away from him, giggling. Whatever this game was of hers, wherever it was she was taking them, Cameron was ready and willing to go along cheerfully.

The elevator door opened to a rush of cold air. From behind, reaching up with her hands, Grace covered Cameron's eyes.

"Go forward," she commanded, pushing her thigh gently against the back of his leg.

Cameron stepped forward, with Grace nudging him ahead, and out the elevator door they went into the cold air.

"Put your hands out front," she ordered.

He reached out with his hands, and Grace, carefully, escorted him across the narrow catwalk and placed his hands securely upon the rail.

Cameron felt like a blind man being led to a healer, or more so, like a convicted convict being led to clemency, or at least he hoped it was some form of clemency from Harkins wrath. If he were to end up in Grace's arms, then clemency it would be, as well as healing, healing of all which was going wrong in his life.

Keeping his eyes shut as instructed, he felt the wind flailing against him, blowing his hair straight back. He gripped tightly to the rail.

Grace checked his hands to be sure they were gripping tightly. Then she let go and shouted, against the wailing wind; "Okay. Open your eyes!"

Cameron opened his eyes to a celestial feast. Above him a thousand brilliant stars arched across the Californian sky. The Milky Way portrayed its hazy glow in glorious fashion, in a way he had seen it only from the bone yard. Of course he had seen it many times, but not like this, not so brilliantly and at Grace's side.

"Whoa! It's great!" he exclaimed.

"Come here. Come here." Grace had already walked a quarter of the way around the circular catwalk to the western side. She was leaning far over the rail and pointing down at a walking speck. It was Pryce Johnston. "Do you think he can see us?" she laughed.

Cameron looked down and saw only a tiny stick-of-a-shadow moving across the blacktop. "I hope not."

"And there," Grace said, pointing to the speck to the northeast which was Carl Harrington.

Cameron looked down and saw Harrington as well.

They both lifted their eyes, straight out to the dark Pacific. The rolling ocean seemed to stretch-on to the very cusp of the starlit horizon. Below and all around them, completely encircling them, was the ring of perimeter lights; evenly-spaced, high-intensity flood-lamps. Far to the south was a glow outlining the mountaintops, beyond which was San Roque.

Cameron was amazed. "Wow, isn't that something!"

As long as he had worked at the power plant, he had never been to the top of the containment structure at night. It certainly provided a new perspective, one of wonderment and awe.

As the wind drove against them, they stood there together, closely, clinging to the rail and enjoying the spectacular view. Grace playfully pushed her hip against Cameron's.

"Do you like it?"

Cameron returned the hip movement. "Of course I like it! I love it!"

"Have you been here before?"

"Never at night, and never with such a gorgeous escort."

Grace smiled. "I want to take you everywhere."

Cameron looked at Grace. "I want to go with you everywhere, Grace."

For a minute, they both looked out at the ocean, enjoying the night wind. The huge, curving wall of the Containment Structure sloped off below them. The catwalk, affixed to the concrete by bolts and plates, extended on narrow metal struts, was precarious at best.

"Look at us!" Grace spoke. "It's like we're flying!"

One-hundred and sixty feet below, on the fourth level of the Auxiliary Building, Lewis sat at the console in Control One looking up at the wall clock. The second hand was approaching 12:00 midnight. He positioned the desk microphone beneath his chin. Then, with eyes following the second hand, he depressed the transmitter as it reached twelve o'clock.

"Control One to all posts. Control One to all posts. This is your 2400 Security Check."

Pausing for all the officers to ready themselves for the security check, Lewis then began the roll-call in the same monotone cadence, but with the same affable voice, as he had done an hour before.

"Security One."

"Security One," Sergeant Jacobs' voice responded from the Briefing Room.

"Control Two," Lewis continued… and so on.

In Control Two, Drake flashed through the surveillance monitors, following each officer as they responded to the security check, keeping one post ahead of the count. When Lewis reached Patrol One, Cameron's abandoned Post; Drake already had the monitor fixed on the unoccupied section of the perimeter fence.

"Patrol One here," Cameron's voice replied.

Drake frowned. *Bullshit!* Rising to his feet, he panned the camera wide to double check. As he expected, Cameron was nowhere to be seen; not even far off en route to his post.

Catching up with the count, following down as each officer replied in sequence, Drake listened inquisitively as the Rover, the last post to be called, was summoned.

"Rover One," Grace's voice immediately echoed back.

In the background, Drake could hear the faint sound of laughter. *Bullshit!* He frowned again. *And she's a liar too!*

His curiosity intensified. He began searching through the cameras trying to find where they had gone. He had last seen them on the turbine level of the Auxiliary Building, but he could not find them there now or anywhere in the vicinity.

Well, we'll see how long this lasts, he thought.

In the Security Building, Harkin sat at his desk listening in on the security check. Having completed the bulk of the paperwork, his boots were propped up on the desk, and he was reading an intelligence briefing on the resurgence of 'Black Talon' ammunition, now available only on the black market. It was interesting for him to know that this very lethal slug, which expanded on impact into razor-sharp talons that cut through flesh and bone, and which was once only used by law enforcement, was now only in the hands of thugs and terrorists. Prior to this article, he had reviewed an interesting piece about new

GPS technology. Testing had been completed on an innovative, miniaturized GPS device that can fit under a firefighter's oxygen tanks so that, unlike the firemen of 9/11, they could be tracked in a burning building. Harkin thought it was a nifty idea, but in the world of nuclear security where rover positions were conversely designed *NOT TO BE* found, he dismissed its application to their operation.

When Grace answered, he also heard what sounded like giggling which caused his mind to redirect. But it could have been any number of background noises, he thought, equipment or the wind for that matter. Everything was fine. Everyone was answering in sequence. It was the same old thing, just a different night.

As Lewis's voice signed off; "That completes your 2400 Security Check," Drake was still madly perusing a montage of surveillance monitors, trying to locate Cameron and Grace. Scrolling from one camera to another, he searched the familiar *'hide-outs'* —those places at the outer edge of camera surveillance ability commonly used for 'naps' or a fast hand of solitaire—but they were no where to be seen. He returned to the hallway where he had seen them earlier—empty. He scanned the corridors on the first, second, third, and fourth levels of the Auxiliary Building, but found nothing. He felt himself becoming a little nervous about it. He huffed, leaned far back in his chair, and stared at the monitors, attentively.

Nestled snuggly together high on the catwalk atop Containment One, Cameron and Grace now sat with their feet dangling off the edge, taking in the breeze and feeling the cold marine air against their faces. Where they were, Cameron knew, there were no surveillance cameras. Beneath them, the huge white, curving rotunda of the containment structure dropped off into the vague white outline of the coast.

"You see that?" Cameron asked, pointing to a dark rise along the coastal terrace. Grace strained her eyes to make out the hump of land which stood above the otherwise flat, curving contour of the coastline.

"That's the Bone Yard," he said.

"Bone Yard?"

"You haven't heard about it?"

"Umm, yes, maybe I have. What about it?"

"Nothing really. It's an old Indian burial ground."

Grace did a double-take. "Oh, I have heard about it. I just didn't know where it was."

"Chumash Indians," Cameron said. "It's one thing I can say about them... they knew how to pick great places to plant their bones. I mean million-dollar, California, ocean-view property."

Grace smiled.

"Anyhow, I was there tonight, just before getting the call from Jacobs to come in."

"Oh, yeah?"

"Yeah. It's a place I like to hang out." He paused. "I fell asleep."

"What? You didn't!" Grace gasped.

"I did," he admitted. Then he realized how it must have sounded and he thought, *should I have told her that?* Well, it's too late now. He looked over at the dark hump of land. "Anyhow, when Jacobs called me, I was out there with my eyes shut when this strange dream came back to me."

"What strange dream?"

"I told you about it." He glanced over at Grace.

"You did?"

"Yeah, last week. About the Indian on the horse?"

"Okay, I remember you mentioning something about that."

"Anyhow, I am laying there in the grass and oddly enough, that dream comes back to me. It's like I'm there, on the grassy terrace, enjoying nature, and this Indian Warrior comes up behind me on his horse."

"Weird."

"And then the horse starts rearing itself and pawing its hoofs at me. And the warrior gives me this mean, belligerent look. It was like he was trying to warn me or tell me something."

"Strange it would happen in an Indian graveyard." Grace tilted her head. "Well, maybe not so strange?"

"And even after I opened my eyes, I could swear I heard something in the reeds."

Grace looked disturbed. "What was it?"

"Nothing," Cameron shrugged. "Just the wind."

Nearly as he said it, the wind gusted against them and Grace cuddled in close to Cameron. "Like that?"

"Yeah, just like this!"

"Maybe it was one of those Indians coming out from the grave?" Grace said, jokingly. She made herself look like a ghost, crouching down with hands up, and she let out a shrilling, "Woooooo!"

Cameron didn't seem amused. "Really Grace?"

"Sorry. Maybe it's some kind of subconscious message? Maybe you're an Indian Warrior from a previous life, and it's your spiritual vision coming back to you in your present life? Maybe you'll come sweep me away on your horse?"

Cameron looked at her. "Do you believe in all that shit?"

"Ghosts and heroes?"

"Ghosts."

"I don't mind ghosts, as long as they're good ghosts... as long as it's your ghost, coming for me on horseback."

"Ghosts don't normally ride around on a horse. They usually just drift, a few feet off the ground." Cameron said it in jest.

"Well then, you'll have to promise to remain drifting faithfully at my side."

Cameron pushed her away playfully. "Well, I wish I could say it was a good dream, but it wasn't. It was a bit disturbing actually, haunting in some ways."

"I'm sorry."

"Here I am in this place I consider my sanctuary among all places. Among all this, this..."

"Modern technology?" Grace interrupted.

"Bullshit," Cameron finished, "and that damn dream comes back to me."

Grace looked serious. "Maybe you should have it interpreted?"

Cameron looked doubtful. "You believe in that?"

"Partly," Grace shrugged. "I had a friend who had her dreams interpreted and the symbolism was amazing, and helpful."

"Well, I don't really believe in that crap. Besides, what the hell's the symbolism of an Indian ghost on a horse?"

"I don't know. But it's likely related to something that's on your mind. There are correlations between what's going on in a person's life and what they dream about, you know. I'm not saying dreams foretell the future or anything like that. Just that they can be a good barometer of what's going on in your life, and where you need to go." Grace gently wrapped her knuckles playfully against Cameron's head. "And what's going on in there."

"What's going on up there? I don't remember watching any Westerns lately?" Cameron said, teasingly.

"What?"

"Never mind."

"My grandmother use to get premonitions," Grace said. "She said they came from dreams."

"Well, it did seem like he was trying to tell me something," Cameron said, referring to the Indian warrior.

"Maybe it means I was right in the first place? That you are destined to be a hero of some type, and you will steal me away on a horse?"

Cameron laughed. "That'll be all right by me—the part about stealing you away on a horse." And as the last word left his lips, Cameron leaned in and kissed Grace on her cheek. She immediately rolled her cheek around so that their mouths met completely and they could take full advantage of it. They kissed for a minute, breaking away to the silence of the wind, and kissed again. Then they sat quietly gazing into the star corridors.

Grace thought of how perfect it was, to be there in this special spot with Cameron.

Cameron, on the other hand, was thinking about what Grace said—about premonitions. *Why does everyone have to put meaning to dreams?* It meant nothing, the dream, except that he needed more sleep and to put his troubles aside. He glanced back over at the dark hump of land which was the Bone Yard. *All is okay.*

"You like that spot?" Grace asked. She caught him looking off with a puzzled expression on his face.

"Yeah, I like it. It's my refuge from the sea of life."

He wanted to tell her more, but didn't think it was the time or place. Nor did he know where to begin. It seemed all too complicated to try and explain between gusts of wind, his mystical connection with the Chumash Indians. That was for sure one thing he'd need time to explain—how he felt every time he sat among the reeds in the Bone Yard. Those trouble-free tribal people of the past, those land-dwelling brothers of the dolphins who simplified life through tales of spotted woodpeckers, who had found a place in his heart and mind, and soul; how their presence radiated from the earth and the reeds. In the short time he had known Grace he hadn't found the time to delve so deeply into personal thoughts and passions, especially those related to the Chumash Indians and their bones. Nor was now the time, he reaffirmed.

"It's almost as good as being in your arms," he said, lightheartedly.

"Wow! I'm flattered, I think!"

"Well, it's not like I'm comparing you to Indian bones or anything like that."

She pushed at his shoulder. "You'd better not be!"

"I'm saying you're beautiful, and I love you, and I can find heaven in your arms."

"That's sweet."

"I want to take you there sometime."

"To the Bone Yard?"

"Yes, to the Bone Yard."

"You can take me anywhere, anytime," Grace replied with adoring eyes.

A sudden gust of wind slammed against them, causing them both to hold tightly to each other and to the rail, and Grace began to laugh again.

"Wow! So windy! It's great!"

"It's too bad we can't harness it for energy, instead of this." Cameron reached down and wrapped his knuckles against the thick concrete of the containment dome beneath them.

"Yeah!" Grace's replied.

The wind swirled up an alluring whiff of her perfume that filled Cameron's nostrils and made him realize how close they were, and how much closer he wanted to be.

"What perfume is that?"

"It's Chanel *Chance*."

"I like it."

"So do I."

Cameron snuggled in closer and began kissing Grace again. The wind was again the bringer of life, Cameron thought, through the dispensing of a designer fragrance. Like the wind had blown life back into the *Spotted Woodpecker* from the old Indian tale, it was bringing life back into Cameron's veins now. He inhaled deeply, savoring the aroma, and they remained attached at the mouth for some time

"Have you ever had sex on top of a nuclear reactor?" Grace suddenly broke away and said.

"What?"

"That's my surprise. I want to make love with you on top of a nuclear reactor."

"Here?"

"Yes! "We'll be the first in the history of the world to do it."

Cameron looked down at the narrow catwalk. Besides it being barely wide enough to walk along, it had no railing along the bottom section. And there was the wind too, gusty wind.

"I don't think it's safe, or possible."

"Sure it is." She started up, she began to position herself as if to show Cameron how it was possible, how they could lay on the catwalk, but Cameron gently pulled her back.

"Are you refusing me?" she asked playfully.

"Not at all." Cameron said, looking into Grace's eyes. They were smiling eyes, more sexy than ever. "I know a better place."

"Really?"

"Absolutely."

"Okay! Let's go!"

"First one more kiss," he said, and Grace leaned into Cameron, giving him a better angle to kiss her deeply, which he did.

# Chapter 29

From offshore, Cameron and Grace appeared as mere specks on the catwalk, dwarfed by the huge white containment domes. Even if someone knew where to look, they would have been hard to find, especially from a speeding boat crashing through the surf.

Emil had timed the wave perfectly. Waiting, waiting, waiting, then as the new swell surged up before them, he gunned the dual *Evinrude* engines and the Zodiac lurched forward and rode the wave all the way into the sandy cove.

As the Zodiac skidded up on the beach, Emil quickly tilted the engines forward, and leaping from the craft as it was still moving, used its forward momentum to assist him in dragging it up the sand. Ramzan was still onboard, white-knuckled and hanging onto the gunwales. He remained onboard until they reached the rocks. Then, he too leaped out and helped Emil pull the watercraft all the way into the dark shadows at the base of the sandstone cliffs.

Ramzan's head was still spinning. He planted his feet firmly in the sand and looked out at the ferocious waves. Though he could still feel himself swaying, he was thankful to be back on solid ground.

"May God reward you," he said to Emil.

"For what?"

"For delivering me back to land, though it is the land of our enemy."

Emil chuckled.

Leaning their rifles against the rocks, they proceeded immediately to unload their gear. As Emil had thought, everything about the cove was perfect. It was small, protected from the surf, and out of sight, and definitely out of sound, of the power plant. A person would literally have to walk right up to the cliff's edge and look straight down to see them. Even then, it would be difficult as long as they stayed tight to the base of the cliff in the dark shadows, as they were now.

Emil checked the time on his wristwatch. They were still well ahead of schedule.

*Some time to wait and watch,* he thought. He looked over at Ramzan. *And time for this one to be well and ready.*

Just as he thought it, Ramzan said, "I can feel my legs again."

"And your head, and your stomach, how are they?"

"My head feels better already. The cold air is good." He looked around. The sound of waves were crashing all around them. "And my stomach... there's nothing left in it to worry about."

They organized their items, laying them out on a sheet of plastic which they put down on the wet, sea-packed sand. Having already conducted a mini inventory aboard the trawler, now the task was simply to re-organize and re-pack, specifically into their respective backpacks. Each would take one of the eight-pound bombs, and in addition there was a pair of bolt cutters, two rolls of duct tape, over forty ammunition clips, enough for a mini-war, and a fifty-foot scaling rope, which Emil would carry.

Ramzan was smiling again, finally. The exhilaration of this long-awaited event, being back on land, brought life pumping through his veins again. The sea-sickness had nearly left him as swiftly as it had come on. With his feet back beneath him, he could focus on the tasks ahead. And focus is what he did. He carefully took the bread-loaf sized packages of C-4 and situated one in his pack, keeping it centered and cushioned between some pieces of styrofoam he had brought along. He handed the other one to Emil.

"Here, use this." He tossed two spare pieces of styrofoam to Emil, who seemed to be having difficulty deciding exactly how to pack the explosive.

"Don't worry, it will not go off," Ramzan said, "unless you sneeze."

Emil returned a worried look.

Ramzan began to laugh. "Just put the styrofoam around it so it doesn't get smashed."

Emil carefully wrapped the explosives in a t-shirt and placed it at the very top of his pack, surrounded by the styrofoam.

Into the outer pouches of his pack, Ramzan tucked the ammunition clips, counting them out as he set each one in place, all twenty of them.

*Enough for a small war,* he thought, smiling. *Enough to kill many.*

He had longed for killing. He had wanted so much to spill the blood of Americans, and to do it on their own soil as they had spilled the blood of his people and his ancestors. Too often, he thought, the battles were fought on their land, far removed from the American conscious and from their media's deceitful eye. To bring this war to them; to the *land of the Westerners,* was more than pleasing, Ramzan thought. It was prophetic.

With his pack loaded, Ramzan zipped open the rear flap and removed a piece of paper. Unfolding it, he held it in the faint light just outside the shadows. It revealed a detailed diagram of the Plant, with notes in Arabic scribbled in its borders. A blue, felt-pen line traced the path they would take from the ocean-side of the perimeter fence to a doorway at the southernmost end of the Turbine Building. Another path drawn in red denoted their return route. Where the two lines met on the far south side of the Auxiliary Building, was marked boldly by two simple *red X's*—the target points.

*Here we will bring down this monster,* Ramzan thought.

Like cutting the throat of a massive goat, the precious cooling water would spill out onto the blacktop as blood would run. And what pleasure it would be watching this goat die; in a self-destructing, unstoppable process that he and Emil would initiate. And from its last breath would come radiation, a plague of colossal proportion which the goat itself created; airborne and ready for distribution.

Above was a steady shoreward wind. *A beautiful wind,* Ramzan thought, glancing skyward at it. Months of planning were finally coming to fruition. Every moment spent hiding out in dingy hotel rooms; hearing the lies told about *western* intervention, about bombings of militia which were bombings of villages; and the fallacies spread about his government and faith without chance for rebuttal, was about to find retribution. All of those who had suffered and who had died would now be avenged. It was their time.

Best of all, Ramzan knew, their path lay open. One can always rely on the greedy and the faithless to betray their own, he thought.

*Bring forth thy vile tongue, Goat,* Ramzan recited in his head, *and we shall cut it out. Bring forth thy killing hand, and we shall cut it off. Spill thy blood now! In your belly lie the seeds of your own destruction.*

The two men lifted their packs, strapped them to their shoulders, adjusted the straps, balancing out the weight evenly, and with their automatic rifles slung from their shoulders, began to climb.

It was a good ten-minute scramble to the top, having to carefully pick their way up an earthen embankment strewn with rocks and ice plant, but Ramzan was possessed by unusual strength. He climbed zealously. His legs were definitely

178

grounded again, feeling the earth, and in short time he was breathing down Emil's neck.

"No need to rush," Emil said. "We have plenty of time."

But Emil's words had no effect on slowing Ramzan down. He passed Emil along the side of a hazardous crevice, a cliff's edge at his side, without regard for his safety.

When they reached the top, a welcomed wind hit them. Though it swept coldly through their veins, Ramzan felt the warmth of it.

Flattening themselves against the cliff's rim, Ramzan's eyes were blazing. "Praise be to God! Praise be to you, Brother!" He looked back at the ocean. The swirling, ghost-like mists wisped off the swells. *It was joyful evidence,* Ramzan believed. *The spirits of the fallen are with us!* "Praise be to all our brothers. We have a favorable wind!"

Emil looked at him oddly.

The wind came from across the seas, Ramzan believed, from their homeland afar, from where the blood of his brothers had seeped into the Islamic earth and had risen like ghost spirits. So long they had rested—the spirits of the dead—waiting for their time, and now they traveled across this foreign sea, enduring the seasickness as he had endured, to this distant land to avenge decades of crime. None of those who had fallen had fallen in vain. Such were the thoughts running through Ramzan's head.

The weight was now on their shoulders. So long as they did their jobs properly, tonight would find fulfillment. The fallen—who now manifested themselves in this vigorous wind, would now themselves be whole. Once they cracked open the belly of the goat; the wind would sweep through its entrails and bring havoc and destruction to the inland cities, east and south of them. The forces of the earth are stronger than the evils of the infidels, Ramzan thought, and these forces were converging tonight; here in this spot on the westernmost edge of the earth, to avenge the wicked.

The vitality of the wind—*it was proof,* Ramzan thought, that the earth-spirits were with them.

"Death to those who have killed the innocent," Ramzan mumbled out loud as they marched through the shore-grass along the cliff's edge. "Now we kill their innocent."

Emil, listening in on Ramzan's self-directed rant, only looked over at him. Ramzan's eyes looked crazed. "Are you well?" Emil asked.

"Very well," Ramzan replied.

When they reached the rise in the terrace, Emil paused. With a prudent arm, he held Ramzan back. Lifting his head above the edge of the bluff, he scanned the surface beyond. Ahead of them, at a distance of less than four hundred meters, was the brightly-lit power plant. He saw no one and heard nothing, but he felt his heart pounding and heard the wind whispering through the tall shore grass.

"We wait here," he said.

Ramzan acknowledged with a nod.

They laid low in the grass, packs flat against their shoulders; the glow of the power plant just beyond them. They were still breathing heavily from their scramble up the cliffs and along the bluff.

Ramzan looked back at the sea.

*I will not fail you,* he thought, as if speaking to the wispy swirls of mist blown from the wave-tops. *I will not fail the brotherhood. I will not fail the memory of all the generations who worked to make this moment possible. I thank you for giving me this blessed burden.*

Emil heard Ramzan mumbling again, but queried no further. He could see the dark resolve in Ramzan's eyes and knew it was a special moment for him. A true believer, Emil thought, a mosque's dove. His was only one path; to follow God's way, to follow Jihad's way. Their moment was upon them, in truth, and Emil was happy to have this devoted one by his side.

"It's good," Emil's deep voice grunted.

Then they both went silent, completely silent, and stayed low, hidden in the tall reeds which blew like velvet above their heads.

# Chapter 30

"I think we have an officer off post." Drake spoke calmly into the interoffice intercom. He was on 'line one,' the line which connected directly to Supervisor Harkin's office.

The real-time image on the surveillance screen above him displayed the forty-foot section of the perimeter fence of Patrol Zone One, void of any signs of a human presence. The small weather station beyond the fence stood partially lit and partially shadowed beneath the perimeter flood-lamps. The windsock above blew nearly horizontal in the wind.

"Who?" Harkin's irritated voice came back.

"Taylor," Drake replied.

In speaking that name, Drake knew he had just summoned Harkin's most dark and unforgiving side.

"Are you sure?"

"Pretty sure. I'm looking right at Zone One right now. He's not there. No one's there. I saw him and Grace earlier, running through the Auxiliary Building... together."

Drake could hear Harkin draw in a seething breath.

"He was running with Grace?"

"Yes, with Grace."

There was a long pause while Harkin digested the information, then his voice returned on the intercom speaker, firm and resolute. "Hold on a minute, I'll be right there."

In less than two minutes a *buzz* came from the fortified entry door. Drake looked up at the surveillance screen to confirm it was Harkin. He saw Harkin standing there impatiently just outside the door to Control Two. Drake typed in the computer command to unlock the door, which Lewis promptly approved, and the door *clicked* open. Harkin leaped up the two steps and joined Drake at the console, taking a position just above his shoulder. With set of eyes both fixed to the surveillance monitor, Drake sequenced down through the four patrol zones: Zone Four, Zone Three, and Zone Two, each showing the corresponding officer dutifully patrolling their respective section of perimeter fence.

"Now look at this," Drake said.

The monitor flashed to Zone One, Cameron's abandoned post—there portrayed the forty feet of vacant fence line. Harkin reached over Drake's shoulder and manipulated the joystick, reversing the zoom and panning the camera to its peripheral limits. Then he switched to a different camera, which provided a reverse view of the area from further back. He zoomed in and scanned left to right. Leaning in, he took a long, hard look. *No one!*

Harkin grunted. "When did you see him with Grace?"

"I don't know exactly when, but it was sometime before the 2400 security check." Drake's eyes flashed to the notepad he had tossed on the counter earlier. It was face down. "Like I said, I saw him running with Grace. They were running through the Auxiliary Building, turbine level."

"What time?" Harkin glanced back at the monitor.

"It was about twenty minutes ago. I searched for them. Couldn't find them. I didn't notify you immediately because I thought they were on an errand of some kind."

"No errand," Harkin grunted. "And now?"

"I searched for them again, before and just after my call to you." Drake shook his head. "I couldn't find them. I searched nearly every camera, both interior and exterior, but I couldn't find them anywhere. They must be somewhere in a dead zone."

Harkin inhaled deeply.

At ground level in the Auxiliary Building, the elevator door of Containment One swung open and Cameron and Grace tumbled out, drunk with laughter.

"You are so crazy, Grace!" Cameron cried out.

"So complimentary!" Grace sarcastically replied.

Cameron stared into her green eyes wanting to kiss her again, but instead found his mind racing through an assortment of ingenious thoughts. During their training, in the process of 'plant familiarization,' Jack and he had discovered nearly every blind spot in the surveillance system. Now he had one in particular in mind. And thinking of it brought a big grin to Cameron's face.

"What?" Grace asked, with a twinkling gaze.

"Follow me," was all he said.

Cameron took her hand and led her away, dashing across the rear corridor, accessing through the door on the opposite end, heading down the long hallway, and disappearing into yet another passageway.

Moments later they emerged through another door, still laughing. It opened into a spacious corridor where the Auxiliary Building adjoined the Containment. At the far end, was a short stairwell that led up into Containment Two. They ran to it. Stopping at the bottom, they stared up the steep steps, then at one another.

Above them was the massive entrance door to the containment dome, an imposing fortress-like gate meant to keep the structure sealed like a vault. On either side were the universal warning symbols for *radiation*; a circle with three equally-spaced black triangles against a yellow background. Just above the door was another sign which read simply:

WARNING: RADIOACTIVE AREA

Cameron turned back and glanced over his shoulder. They were alone. He looked up at the surveillance camera wondering if they'd been seen, but realizing he didn't care.

"Do you know what this is?" he asked.

"Yes, of course."

Cameron leaped up the steps, pulling Grace with him. Still breathing hard after their long jog across the Auxiliary Building, he pulled his keycard from his pants pocket and placed it in the cardreader.

"Come'on," he said impatiently. "Take out your card."

"We're going in?"

"Yeah, why not?"

Grace hesitated. "It's Level One," she said, pausing first to study the warning signs.

"Yeah, I know," Cameron said, nonchalantly.

Grace looked doubtful. It seemed more than danger-ous—going into an encased room with a nuclear reactor. It seemed foolish. Though she had been inside before on a train-ing tour with Chief Stewart and class, it was during refueling—a time when the reactor is inactive. Besides, it was a restricted area, invoking the *two-man-rule*, requiring two authorized people. That alone might alert the control operators.

"Cameron, it's Level One," she said.

"There's two of us, isn't there?" Cameron replied brightly.

"Yeah, but… isn't it dangerous?"

"Nah," Cameron replied.

Grace let out a nervous laugh as she gazed up at the Radiation Warning symbol above the door.

"Come on," Cameron insisted. "All this concrete is just in case of leaks—in case someone tries to blow it up or drive a commer-cial airplane into it."

"That's comforting."

"It's absolutely safe inside. The engineers go in there all the time."

Grace seemed to recall from her training that it was basically safe inside, so long as one did not go within the reactor core housing.

Cameron entered his pin number on the cardreader pad and waited for it to respond.

"What about Harkin?" Grace asked.

"What about him?"

"Are we going to get in trouble?"

"You're the *Rover*, Grace. You can go anywhere you want."

"I mean you?"

"What about me?" He turned and looked into Grace's eyes. "I don't care what Harkin does. Tonight I just want to be with you."

Just then their radios started crackling in unison. The reception near containment was marginal at best, but the gruff voice was unmistakable. It was Harkin. The coincidence of having just spoken his name when his voice came on the radio was a bit startling. Cameron and Grace exchanged surprised expressions.

Reaching down, Cameron raised the volume on his radio.

"This is Supervisor Harkin calling Patrol One," Harkin's voice said, sounding angry. "Come in! Harkin calling Patrol One. Come in!"

Cameron unsheathed his radio and brought it to his mouth. "Patrol One here."

"What's your ten-twenty?"

Cameron paused, scanning his immediate surroundings. "I'm center-west Turbine Building," he said. "Some raccoons got into the perimeter fence and I'm going to escort them out."

Grace started giggling, but quickly covered her mouth.

There was a pause.

"Where are you?" Harkin's voice came back.

"Westside center of the Turbine Building. I'm standing against the wall."

Back in Station Two, Drake flashed through the surveillance cameras on the westside of the Turbine Building. Harkin stood over his shoulder watching too, weighing the information Cameron had just provided.

Drake reversed the pan on camera forty-three and forty-four, straining each camera to their peripheral limits, but was unable to pull in the central wall of the westside.

"It's a blind spot," he said flatly, which he knew.

Harkin reached over and tried himself, panning the two cameras, but neither seemed to be able to reach the exact center. He stared at the screen.

*Swell.* He grunted and placed both hands on his hips. "They can build a sophisticated security system, but they can't figure out how to overlap two cameras."

Drake looked up at him but said nothing.

"How many are there?" Harkin asked Cameron.

"Two."

"Two?"

"Yes, two of them. A mother and a child, I think."

Here was another pause.

It happened before, raccoons getting into the perimeter fence without tripping the alarm system. But somehow, it didn't seem plausible coming from Cameron.

Harkin gave a doubting expression.

"Escort the animals back outside the perimeter fence," he said. "Then I need you back on your post A.S.A.P."

Drake looked up at Harkin, shocked. "You believe that? He was with Grace earlier!"

"Is Grace with you?" Harkin asked into the transmitter.

"Yes, she's helping me with the raccoons," Cameron replied.

Grace began to giggle again and had to turn away so as to redirect her mouth from the radio.

"And the animals are already on their way out," Cameron added.

This time the pause was even longer. Harkin's imagination was conjuring up a slue of unsettling possibilities—the least appealing of which was that Cameron was corrupting his rookie officer. But the *raccoon story*, as farfetched as it sounded, was believable. In the past six months there had been at least three such incidents, along with another animal-related fiasco when a pelican landed within the protected area, tripped the microwave detector, and had to be chased by three officers before it flew off.

"See how they got in and put it in your report."

"That's an affirmative," Cameron's voice replied.

Harkin's eyes remained riveted to the screen. "And I want to see you, in my office, at your mid-shift break. You were supposed to see me when you came in from patrol!"

"That's another affirmative," Cameron's voice came back.

"Ten-four, over and out," Harkin said.

"Ten-four," Cameron signed off.

Harkin did a double-take of the surveillance screens.

"Did you really buy that?" Drake asked.

"It's possible."

"I think they're up to something," Drake said.

"Maybe," Harkin said, but he said it as if he didn't care. "I'll deal with Cameron later." He looked around the control room. "Everything else going okay?"

"Fine," Drake said.

"You know that Lewis will help you out if you run into any snags."

"Yeah, we already talked."

"Good."

At the entrance to Containment Two, Cameron holstered his radio with a boyish smirk. "Let's face it. I can hardly get into more trouble than I'm already in."

Grace burst out laughing. "I'm absolutely amazed! You pulled that off without batting an eye!" Then she looked worried. "You wouldn't snow me like that, would you?

"Never."

They looked at one another in one of those moments, as humans do, knowing the other's thoughts and emotions, and realizing such, they burst out laughing again together. Then Grace turned serious. "Can they fire you?"

"Probably," he shrugged.

"Don't worry," Grace said. "I'll pay our rent until you find a better job."

Cameron's eyes lit up. "Our rent?"

Grace smiled and nodded. "Yes, *our* rent!"

Turning their attention back to the huge, imposing door, Cameron looked at Grace again. "You said you wanted to make love on top of a reactor?"

"Yes."

"Let's go?"

Without wavering this time, Grace pulled her keycard from her lapel, held it ready, and when the little red indicator light on the card-reader went yellow and the digital letters flashed, *Enter Second Authorized Card,* she inserted her keycard and entered her pin code. The indicator light instantly turned *green* to the sound of an unlocking door.

Once more exchanging glances, they then pulled the heavy door open and entered the containment dome, passing first through the four-foot gap in the concrete walls, then through a second eight-inch-thick steel door.

# Chapter 31

Drake was beside himself. He couldn't believe Harkin got sucked in by Cameron's fairytale. Yet he did, and he seemed to be content with it.

Drake flashed through the overhead surveillance monitors searching for Cameron and Grace. He searched the Turbine Building, the Auxiliary Building, and the outer grounds. Marvin was dutifully seated in the guard booth at San Roque Gate. The other patrol officers continued their drone-like marches across the blacktop.

He pulled the keyboard close to his chest, tapped the ENTER key, and watched as the screen instantly refreshed. The cursor waited, blinking for a moment. Then he typed-in the command:

LOCATE PATROL ONE

Instantly appearing on the screen was a detailed floorplan of the power plant, and through it, a *red line* tracing Cameron's movement through the plant, beginning at the Security Building, and ending with a blinking red DOT over Containment Two.

Drake stared at the image. He knew the program could show which doors had been accessed by Cameron's keycard, in what sequence. It could not, however, give an exact location, with absolute certainty, because some areas had only entry keypads, not exit keypads. But, without a subsequent entry, it could be reasonably assumed a person would be at their last location.

He clicked the mouse to *minimize* the window, bringing back the blinking cursor, and with fingers still hovering over the keyboard, he typed in a second command:

LOCATE ROVER ONE

As before, a new screen instantly flashed up—the same detailed floorplan of the power plant, but this time showing Grace's path, a much longer red line weaving, crisscrossing, and overlapping through many buildings and floors, but also ending at the same blinking red DOT, centered in Containment Two.

He backed to the previous screen. Cameron's locate-map appeared with the blinking red dot on Containment Two. Then back to Grace's locate-map, showing the same blinking red dot in the same place. Superimposing both maps, the lines looked like two intricately woven spaghetti trails which, eventually, came together in the same exact place—Containment Two.

Drake leaned in. *What? What would they be doing in there?*

Of all nights, tonight these two decide to elope? Drake felt the anger welling up inside. Incompetence, he knew, was something he had little tolerance for, but blatant incompetence, wanton incompetence—well that was a whole nother story. That was deliberate insubordination. Drake stared at the computer screen, angry as hell.

# Chapter 32

Stepping inside the massive dome rotunda of Containment Two was like stepping into a mini-version of the U.S. Capitol Building, but not so mini. Rising above, two-hundred and fifteen feet to its apex, were thick walls of reinforced steel-rebar and concrete, sectioned off by three separate rings of wall-mounted lights; illuminating the entire inner dome. In the center, rising from the main floor, was the reactor core housing; a five-story step-pyramid with a mass of spaghetti woven stainless-steel cooling pipes. The floor, though concrete, seemed to have been polished or lacquered. It reflected everything above in mirror-like images.

Cameron and Grace looked up at the heavy double-door as it closed behind them with a *clonk!*

Grace was awed. "Wow!"

A soft humming noise resonated from the housing core. A higher-pitched sound came from the huge shiny pipes that trailed away from the core and followed along the curving walls until disappearing through them. Every sound reverberated off the walls in echo-like fashion.

"You've been in here before?" Cameron asked.

Grace looked up and listened as his voice sounded off the inner walls.

"Yes, with Chief Stewart's class."

"That's right," Cameron nodded.

"But never while it was running," she replied. "They were refueling at the time."

"Take it in for a moment."

They both stood open-jawed. Then, exchanging glances, they started to chuckle. And soon, Grace's sexy smile returned.

"Follow me?" Cameron asked.

Grace nodded.

Taking Grace by the hand, Cameron escorted her across the polished floor to a stainless-steel ladder leading up the side of the reactor core housing. She followed in tandem, curiously gazing at the various gauges and machinery. It was all so amazing to her—she couldn't keep her eyes off the tangled assembly of silvery pipes webbing in and out of the core housing. The noise coming from them seemed to have a soothing quality to it. Up close, it sounded like a million hummingbirds.

As Cameron continued up the ladder, Grace stopped. "Where are we going?"

"To a place out of the watchful eyes of the surveillance cameras." He reached down from the third rung and offered a hand.

Grace looked giddy. "Okay!" She took his hand.

They ascended a series of three short ladders and a stairway, and traversed a foot-bridge, finally arriving at the top of the reactor core. There was a steel observation deck with handrails all around it. The platform was about twelve-feet by twelve-feet and the floor was constructed of steel lattice-work which permitted a filtered view down below.

"Do you know what you are standing on?" Cameron asked.

"A nuclear reactor?"

Cameron nodded his head affirmatively. "Millions of megawatts of energy, lighting thousands of homes all across California—whole cities actually."

Grace seemed mesmerized. "Wow! Just think… So many homes out there, so many people cozy in their beds with their night-lights on, watching the *Tonight Show*. And here we are standing on the source of it all."

Cameron nodded. "Yep."

"I can't believe we are having this conversation on top of a nuclear reactor."

The floor beneath Grace's feet was softly vibrating. *So amazing!*

She gazed around the vast chamber, considering the complexity of the operation. It was one thing to learn about the inner-workings of a nuclear reactor in a classroom, quite another to actually feel one humming under your feet. She looked at Cameron, glad he had brought her to this place. It was *he* who brought her to a higher level of existence. He had succeeded in impressing her, dazzling her with this wonder of the modern world. *With him, only with him,* she thought. She leaned into him and looked directly up into his eyes.

"So, you've never made love on top of a nuclear reactor before, have you?"

"Never," Cameron said. But he knew he was about to. He knew, above all things, he wanted to be with Grace. With her green almond-shaped eyes now begging him on, any consequences for this indulgence would have to wait. If he ended up getting fired, it wouldn't matter. When he was an old man on his death bed, it would be this experience he would remember, and he would recall it with a big smile and a warm heart.

"And you?" he asked.

"Not yet."

She started kissing him, pecking at his neck, and worked her way up to his chin and cheek. Then she started unbuttoning his shirt and kissing his lips. Cameron reciprocated, pulling Grace close to him, kissing her deeply, and unbuttoning her shirt as well.

Not far off, deep in the heart of the Auxiliary Building, Lewis sat at the console of Control One preparing to commence the

0100 security check. For him, the night was passing quickly and uneventfully. He had completed the initial alarm system testing sequence, succeeded in getting through three separate articles in *Musicians Magazine*, and finished off two bags of chips. He planned to start the second and final alarm testing sequence after the security check.

Dropping his chin to the desk microphone, he fixed his eyes on the wall clock above the console and watched as the second hand approached 1:00 a.m., counting down mentally.

"Control One to all posts," he announced. "Control One to all posts. This is the 0100 Security Check." He waited ten seconds and then jumped right into it, "Security One."

"Security One," Sergeant Jacobs' voice echoed back.

"Control Two."

"Control Two," Drake came back.

"San Roque Gate."

"San Roque Gate," Marvin repeated.

Back in Containment Two, on top of the reactor housing, on top of the observation platform, Cameron and Grace's radios lay side-by-side still sheathed in their respective utility belts, each resonating Lewis' voice in an unusual falsetto that echoed softly off the lofty interior walls of the rotunda. Cameron and Grace lay prone just inches away on a cushion made of their clothes. What remained of their garments not beneath them, were strewn across the steel-lattice flooring where they had been hastily deposited. Their rifles leaned idle together against the corner guardrail.

"Security Four," Lewis' voice continued.

"Security Four," Fred's voice echoed back.

Cameron pressed his lips deep into Grace's, and Grace obliged him, returning with her full lips reaching up into his.

Finally, vaguely, Lewis' voice recited Cameron's call-sign. "Patrol One."

"He's calling you," Grace whispered.

"Patrol One," Lewis' voiced repeated.

"I don't care," Cameron whispered back.

Reaching down, Cameron fumbled for his radio. Finding it, he switched off the volume.

From Grace's radio, Lewis' voiced continued counting down the sequence until reaching the end of the security check—Grace's call-sign. "Rover one."

"He's calling you," Cameron said.

"I don't care," Grace replied. In a replicating action, she reached down, searched for the volume knob on her radio, and switched it off.

"They'll find us a week later," she paused, again breathing heavily under a volley of kisses, "Two skeletons copulating on top of a nuclear reactor."

Grace closed her eyes, as did Cameron, and they kissed feverishly. Everything outside the concrete walls of containment seemed inconsequential to them. As much as the world continued to spin and the reactor beneath them continued to split atoms, they were oblivious to it. Nothing mattered. No one cared, especially them.

# Chapter 33

*Goddamned fools!* was Drake's thought.

He flashed through the overhead surveillance monitors frantically trying to find the cameras in Containment Two. When he did, he saw nothing. Although there were cameras in the containment structures, none of them revealed the top of the observation platform, as Cameron had known.

Drake was mortified. Not that it was unprecedented. Officers occasionally missed their security checks, sometimes having untimely stepped into radio 'dead zones,' or wandered off for a head break at an inopportune time, or sometimes officers simply goofed off—yes, they did that. But on Drake's first solo shift in Control Two? He dropped back in his chair, settling in on the monitors overhead. Two screens directly above; one fixed on the reactor core housing in Containment Two; the other remained fixed on Patrol Zone One—the southwest perimeter fence, Cameron's abandoned post. Suddenly the intercom light came on. It was *line one.*

"Call them in," Harkin's voice said. He said it matter-of-factly, as if he knew it was something he would have to do before the night was done.

"All right," Drake said. "I'll do that right now."

He flipped on the radio transceiver. "Control Two calling Patrol One," he spoke calmly into the headset. "What's you ten-twenty?" He paused, waiting for an answer. There was none. "Control Two to Patrol One. Please report to the Security Building." Again he waited, but there was no reply.

Drake looked at the wall clock. It was 1:06 a.m.

Then he called Grace. "Control Two to Rover, what's your ten-twenty?" He repeated the call, three times.

No reply.

In the Supervisor's Office, Harkin stared at the radio on his desk with an expression of disgust.

"Damn it! What was I thinking?" *Raccoons? I should have known better than to believe that cockamamie story.* He immediately depressed the intercom button to line two, the Briefing Room.

"Jacobs are you in there?"

"Yeah, I'm here boss."

"Did you hear that?"

"Yes, I did."

"Sounds like we have a couple renegades out there."

"Sounds like it."

"Come on down here."

"Okay, I'll be right there."

Seconds later, Sergeant Jacobs entered Harkin's office.

"The two of them are undoubtedly up to some kind of shenanigans," Harkin said. "Most likely conjured up by Cameron."

"Yeah, that'd be my guess."

"Well, go out there and find them."

"Alrighty."

"I guess we'll have to transfer one of them to another shift."

"That'd be my recommendation."

Sergeant Jacobs turned and took a step for the door.

"Wait," Harkin said. "Let me try them."

Harkin inhaled deeply. Then, taking the radio from its charger, he keyed the transmitter. "Harkin to Patrol One. Ten-twenty? Harkin to Patrol One. Ten-twenty?"

As expected, there was no response.

He repeated; "Harkin calling Patrol One. Come in." Then he tried Grace. "Harkin to Rover One. Ten-twenty?"

Again, there was no response.

Harkin looked at Jacobs. "What the Hell's going on out there?"

Jacobs could only shrug.

Setting the radio back in its charger stand, Harkin inadvertently depressed the transmitter as he retorted the expletive, "Idiot!" unknowingly sending it out over the radio waves.

"Go find them!" Harkin commanded.

Jacobs paused. "I'm going to take a head break first, if that's okay?"

"Sure, why not."

# Chapter 34

*He's an Idiot all right!* Drake thought, staring at the silent radio speaker in Control Two.

Above, the surveillance screen locked-in on *Zone One* displayed the human-less unguarded section of perimeter fence that was Cameron's post. The only thing moving out there was the tubular windsock, blowing wildly beyond the perimeter fence.

Drake nervously tapped the countertop. Being the type of person who liked having everything in place, he was on edge. *Everything was not in place.* And it unnerved him.

He checked the wall clock. It was 1:08 am.

*What to do about them?*

He tapped the mouse, refreshing the computer screen. The locate map was still there. Cameron and Grace, evidently, had not moved from the containment structure.

Drake pondered the image for a moment. Then he clicked on camera *one,* revealing Lewis seated in Control One. Lewis looked occupied, hunched over with his eyes glued to the screen. He was still busy running the second of the two alarm testing sequences, keying codes into the computer, advancing from one alarm zone to another. After a minute, Drake flipped on the intercom.

"Hey Lewis, what do you think about this shit?" Drake watched as Lewis reached over and switched on the intercom transceiver.

"Hi Drake," Lewis replied. "Don't know what they're thinking. It's not like Harkin isn't going to make toast out of them once he catches up with them."

"He will catch up with them," Drake replied

"I don't think Cameron gives a damn anymore."

"Perhaps, but he shouldn't be taking Grace with him."

"No, he shouldn't." Lewis paused and then said, "They'll surface soon enough."

"Maybe." Drake watched Lewis on the surveillance screen.

"But I guess it's not their first time." Lewis' voice continued.

"It should be their last." Drake paused. "I saw them earlier, running through the Auxiliary Building holding hands."

"Really?"

"Yes."

Lewis chuckled. "Harkin going to roast them, all right."

"Harkin knows about it," Drake said, although he realized he didn't mention the part about them holding hands.

"You have to hand it to him, Cameron has a way of charming the ladies, and Harkin," Lewis said. "Chasing raccoons!"

Drake wasn't amused. Lewis' lack of concern was as frustrating as the incident itself. "Well," I guess it's okay to be off post nowadays?"

"Umm," Lewis' voice returned. "It's Harkin's call." Another pause. "He must be having a geriatric moment."

"Must be." Drake paused.

Through the lobby overlook window, Drake saw Sergeant Jacobs step out from the hallway which led to Harkin's office, walk briskly across the lobby, and disappear into the rear corridor.

"Something's up," Drake said to Lewis. "I just saw Jacobs come out from Harkin's office and he didn't look happy."

"He's going to go get them," Lewis said.

"Yes, I think so." With that, Drake abruptly concluded the conversation. "Over and out." He switched his attention to camera *seven* locked-in on San Roque Gate. Marvin's statue-like image remained seated in the guard booth. The approach road was empty, beyond which was only the reflective sheen of ocean.

The wall clock now read: 1:12 a.m.

*Okay then*, Drake thought. *The night must move along.*

He impulsively peeked over his shoulder. Behind him was the electronic eye which belonged to surveillance camera *two*. It was aimed directly at him. He checked the image of Lewis once more. Lewis remained occupied with the alarm testing sequence. His timing could not have been more perfect, Drake thought. He positioned himself with his back fully to the camera. Then, from his shirt lapel, he unclipped his keycard, set it down on the countertop, and from his wallet slid out a second keycard. He laid the second card down beside the first. For a second he just looked at the two cards together, seated side-by-side. Then he snapped up the first card, lined it up with the thin slit in the cardreader, slid it in, and entered his pin code.

The screen immediately flashed back the familiar instructions:

INSERT SECOND KEYCARD
for
SINGLE LEVEL ONE COMMAND OVERRIDE

A trite little smile lifted the corners of Drake's mouth.

Drake followed the instructions succinctly, first extracting his keycard, lining up the second keycard with the thin slit, inserting it all the way into the cardreader, and watching as the screen flashed back:

ENTER SECOND SECURITY CODE
for

# SINGLE LEVEL ONE COMMAND OVERRIDE

He shot another discerning glance back at the electronic eye behind him. Even if Lewis was looking now, the camera angle was blocked by his back, and Drake knew it. Feeling unwatched and unbridled, he extracted a small piece of paper, also from his wallet, unfolded it, and set it down before him. It bore a handwritten pass code.

Drake eyed the paper inquisitively. *How could he have known?* The pass code simply read:

MeetMe@2

Drake entered the security code into the keyboard. The computer screen instantly flashed back:

SECURITY LEVEL ONE COMMAND OVERRIDE
*Proceed with single command entry.*

Below the message the cursor blinked, waiting for his fingers. He stretched them across the keyboard and typed:

DISABLE SURVEILLANCE CAMERAS 3, 4 & 7

Before striking the ENTER key, Drake paused, leaving his right finger resting on it. He watched the second hand on the wall clock as it proceeded with its downward sweep, counting down the seconds; five seconds short of 1:15 a.m. Then, as it reached its mark, he pressed down his finger.

*So much for the two man rule,* he commented to himself mentally.

# Chapter 35

Outside San Roque Gate, the bright beacon from the Point San Miguel lighthouse swept through the old Cadillac briefly illuminating the interior and revealing the Stranger slouched low in the car seat. He squinted into the light. He had been biding his time, thinking about Maasai warriors—the African tribe famous for their ability to rise from the deepest sleep to a state of total battle readiness in a matter of seconds. He had studied war-like tribes and had become fascinated in the various ritualistic preparations leading up to battle. The Maasai were without ritual. It is what he liked about them. There was no bullshit.

*Battle ready always,* he thought. *The way a warrior should be.*

And now, he knew, it was his moment of readiness.

He waited for the lighthouse beam to swing around again. Then he hauled up the huge Colt revolver, clicked-off the safety, and wedged it back between his thigh and the seat. He checked the rearview mirror. There was no one, and no headlights. Switching-on the ignition, he turned the wheel and came back onto the Coast Road, and then turned into the entrance road, heading toward the front gate.

In Control Two, Drake summoned Lewis on the intercom.

"I have a camera out," Drake said.

Lewis, having just finished up the alarm testing sequence, looked up at the surveillance monitors.

"Camera seven," said Drake.

Lewis found the camera, and sure enough, the screen was BLANK. It was the post-mounted camera at San Roque Gate, he knew. He used the wireless remote and tried to manually retrieve the image, without success.

"Whoa!" was his explicit into the intercom. "Yeah, it's out for me too."

Clicking through various other images, Lewis found two more surveillance cameras inexplicitly BLANK; cameras *three* and *four*, that covered the entrance lobby of the Security Building.

"I must be seeing things," he said to Drake.

"What?"

"Cameras three and four are out as well."

There was a pause, Drake was giving it time, then he replied, "Yeah, they're out down here too."

In the three years Lewis had been working as a security computer operator, he'd never seen three cameras out at once. There was always the occasional malfunction of a camera or two, but never three at once.

"Should we try re-booting?" Drake asked. It was the protocol, Drake knew.

"Yes, of course. I'll handle it," Lewis replied.

"Okay," Drake said. "Thank you. I'm not sure I'd know how to do that."

"No worries. I've got it."

At San Roque Gate, the Cadillac was already up at the kiosk. Marvin exited the guard booth and approached the vehicle with rifle slung from his shoulder.

"How can I help you?" Marvin asked, standing just outside the driver's window.

"I'm looking for the Lighthouse Tavern," the Stranger said. His right arm, hidden from Marvin's view, was flush against his side and his right hand was gripping the Colt revolver tightly.

"Oh, that's back in San Roque." Marvin looked over the roof of the Cadillac and pointed east. "This here is a nuclear power plant."

"A nuclear power plant?"

Marvin turned and pointed up at the huge sign—MAL LOMA NUCLEAR POWER PLANT. It glowed bright with light and was surrounded by all its warning and no trespassing admonitions. As Marvin turned, the Stranger pulled the Colt up from his side, across his body, and rested the barrel above the window. Before Marvin could turn back around, the Stranger pulled the trigger twice.

The sound was deafening; the white powder flashes bright. The weapon was so large and packed such a kick, only a man of the Stranger's size and strength could have fired the shots one-handed from that position. Even so, the barrel kicked so high on the first shot the Stranger had to pull down the barrel in order to properly place the second shot.

Marvin lay dead, sprawled out on his back on the pavement with two red bullet holes in the chest of his regal-blue shirt.

Stepping from the Cadillac, the Stranger quickly stripped Marvin of his jacket and his utility belt. He then dragged the body by the legs back around to the trunk of the vehicle. Seemingly effortlessly, he lifted and rolled the body into the trunk, somewhat in the manner of a discarded carpet, and slammed the trunk closed.

He returned to the driver's seat, backed out the short driveway using the rearview mirror, and swung the Cadillac in a broad u-turn across the Coast Road to a wide spot on the harbor side. There was an embankment there along the shoulder of the road, built up above the surf, which served as an RV parking area during the summer months. Now it was conveniently vacant. He dropped the vehicle into park and turned off the engine.

The familiar aroma of gunpowder permeated the front seat. The Stranger looked down at his big Colt revolver. It lay on the seat beside him with the barrel still smoldering. He latched his huge hand around it, stepped out of the vehicle, and scanned the surrounding area. He looked both east and west. The port and harbor were dark, sparsely lit by a couple lamp posts in the main parking lot. The bait shops and wharf beyond were likewise dark, aside from a few security lights. The fog horn bellowed from the end of the jetty, though there was no fog. To the east were the distant lights of San Roque. The rounding beam of the lighthouse passed, and for a split second, the beach illuminated like daylight, revealing only the softly breaking waves. It was what he expected. It was twenty past one in the morning. It was a mid-week night in the off season. There was nobody out and about. The area was void of any life.

From the rear seat of the Cadillac the Stranger snatched a black duffle bag, slung it over his shoulder, and hurried back up the approach road to the guard booth. Inside, wasting no time, he dumped the bag on the small countertop, zipped it open, and began removing its contents. On top was a compact *Uzi* submachine gun with eight magazine clips. He slapped a clip in the Uzi, drew back the cocking mechanism, and set it on the countertop. Next he took out a neatly pressed and folded regal-blue guard uniform—the standard issue for security officers at Mal Loma. Glancing down the approach road, he quickly stripped off his clothes and fitted himself into the uniform. The uniform bore the same shoulder patch with the spinning atoms emblem and the words ’*Nuclear Security.*’ He strapped Marvin's utility belt around his waist, finding he had to adjust it out several rings, and lastly he straightened his shirt lapel and put on the tie.

Looking down, he saw Marvin's uniform jacket, which he had brought with him from the Cadillac. He picked it up and held it out before him. It became quickly apparent that he wasn't going to fit into it. The arm sockets were simply too small to accommodate his huge arms. As he held it there, he noticed the two bullet holes through the back. He matter-of-factly placed two fingers through the holes so that they came out the other side. The inside was blood-soaked and the blood got on his fingers. He wiped them clean on the jacket and tossed the jacket to the floor.

Checking out his reflection in the glass window, he adjusted his tie.

On the floor a small heater glowed bright with electric embers.

In less than ten minutes, the switch was complete. The Stranger now sat on the high stool, his attire in place, and his Uzi in plain view on the counter ledge. He took the Uzi and set it below, down and out of sight. He leaned its short barrel against the wall in the corner by the door. On the ledge next to him was Marvin's thermos. Lifting it, he found it to be still half full and warm. Groaning contently, he poured himself a cup into the plastic thermos cup.

From his position inside the guard booth, he had a clear view straight out the thirty-meter approach road. Although he couldn't see the Cadillac, parked off to his left, nor Port San Miguel, blocked by a large earth embankment on his right, he could see out across the Coast Road into the bay and starlit sea, and there gleaming off the surface, every six seconds, was the faint flicker of the rounding lighthouse beam.

The Stranger propped his foot up against the door jam and peered out the square window. Sipping on the coffee, he thought again about the Maasai, the battle-ready warriors of the Serengeti. There was a time in East Africa when he had come across a large lump on a road. The object, nearly three feet long and two feet high, was indistinguishable at first. When he stopped to check it, he found it to be the bloodied head of a giraffe. It was typical of the Maasai, after a successful hunt, to flaunt their kill. They had purposely left it in the middle of the road for all to see. Meanwhile, back in the village, a celebratory feast took place.

Although Marvin's body was now buried in the trunk of his Cadillac, the Stranger knew by morning, with the help of the news media, it would be publicized for all to see.

*It is just,* he thought. *For a warrior to display his kill.*

He took another sip from his coffee, contently.

In Station Two, Drake lowered his glasses and looked up at the clock. It was now 1:25. He eased back in his chair, staring at the blank monitor that would have featured camera *seven*—San Roque Gate, feeling no emotion. He clicked off the screen. Then he switched on the intercom.

"How's it going?" he asked Lewis through the intercom.

"Nothing yet," Lewis' voice replied.

"Did you re-boot?"

"Yeah, but no luck."

"Is there anything I can do?" Drake asked, all the while keeping an eye on Lewis' image. "Do we need to notify Harkin?"

"Give me fifteen minutes," Lewis' voiced replied. "I think I can fix this."

"Okay," Drake said.

In Control One, Lewis glanced at the overhead surveillance screens. On the one monitor that featured Control Two, he could only see the back of Drake's head. He swiveled around in his chair to the nearby bookshelf. From it, he pulled the computer operator's manual and quickly began paging through it. His finger ran down the 'table of contents,' and flipping to page eighty-six, he found what he sought: *Protocol for Camera Malfunction.*

# Chapter 36

Far below the mountaintop, the headlamps of Mobile Two bounced along a steep portion of road nearly three-quarters of a mile away from the Plant. Through the pair of *Night-Owl* binoculars, the greenish-colored-image revealed a shadow of a driver within, angling away at first, and then coming back nearly parallel. The Jeep dropped into a gully and momentarily disappeared. It was a place in the road where it snaked in and out of the western flanks of the coastal peak before completing its loop back to the power plant.

The Sniper set the binoculars on the tarp, dropped his cheek flat against the rifle stock, clicked 'on' the star-scope, and braced himself, waiting for the Jeep to reemerge. His legs were stretched out behind him, positioned a little more than shoulder-width apart. The weight of the stock, pivoted on the bi-pod, balanced perfectly in his arms. The trajectory was flawless—thirteen-hundred feet at a forty-five degree downslope with only the wind between the muzzle and the target.

Through the scope, the Sniper saw a glow pulsating from beyond the canyon rim. Then two down-facing beams of light suddenly emerged, moving parallel at first, turning, and tilting, and finally coming around to provide a nearly dead-on shot into the cab. In the cross-hairs, through the windshield, came the hazy silhouette of the driver—Corley Harris.

The Sniper relaxed his muscles, inhaled, and then exhaled slowly, squeezing the trigger. The rifle bucked violently, unexpectedly, the barrel kicking skyward more than six inches. A noise coughed out, almost perfectly muffled by the silencing device. Far below, the bullet smashed through the windshield striking the driver squarely in the chest, immediately followed by a second blast tracking nearly the same trajectory as the first.

The Sniper lifted his eyes above the scope and watched as the vehicle, dwarfed in size without the aid of the scope's powerful magnification, veered left, then right, and then plunged off a short embankment down into a ravine. The lights of the Jeep suddenly went off.

*Nice,* the Sniper thought.

He had not expected to douse the headlamps and conceal the entire vehicle in a ravine with two quick blasts.

He quickly turned his attention back to the power plant. There in the northeast corner of the perimeter fence, coming out beneath the flood lights, was the speck of a figure, Carl Harrington.

He checked the time on his military watch. *Not yet.* He repositioned the rifle, facing down at Harrington, but he did not get behind it. Instead, he lifted the night vision binoculars from the tarp and placed them to his face. He adjusted the image until the greenish-shaped figure came into focus. The guard, as expected, was exactly on schedule.

For two minutes, the Sniper just lay there spying down on the stick-figure like an owl upon a field mouse. Harrington continued on his southerly march and disappeared behind the Fuel Handling Building. Moments later he reappeared under the bright flood lights, exactly as anticipated, heading back toward the northeastern fence.

The Sniper then quickly turned south and looked for Chris Peters in *Patrol Zone Four*. Peters was in the exact position he should be—in the one sweet spot between the southern end of the Fuel Handling Building and the northern end of the Security Building.

*Like clockwork*, the Sniper thought.

*But not yet, not yet.*

He dropped the binoculars to his knee and looked straight out at the Pacific.

*Time to exhale*, he thought.

It seemed odd that he'd find this moment, of all moments, to take in the beauty of the night, but he did. Long ago he had learned how to calm his mind—how to remove all anxious thoughts and concerns. With the onshore winds gusting through his light-brown hair and rippling against his dark shirt, he pondered the beauty before him without worry. It was revitalizing, as was the breath he took deep into his lungs. It was all he needed, he knew—a burst of cool ocean air trekking through his body and the feeling of fresh wind blowing against his face before the next series of shots.

# Chapter 37

"Harkin has requested some papers," Drake said to Lewis over the intercom. "He wants the log sheet from last night, and a few other items. And while I'm down there, I'm going to let him know about the camera problems."

Lewis hesitated. He wanted more time to fix the problem. He preferred not to dump on his supervisor something he felt capable of repairing. But if Drake was going to see Harkin now, he might as well tell him about the cameras.

"All right," Lewis said, and as he did, he acknowledged Drake's command prompt, requesting to open DOOR SB1, exiting from Control Station Two

"I'll be back in fifteen," Drake said.

"Toodaloo."

Drake dropped down from the console and exited the door. Lewis flipped his main monitor to camera *five,* the Rear Corridor of the Security Building. He was shocked to see that it, too, was now blank. He checked the other cameras. *Three* and *four* were still out, but somehow he had gotten back the transmission from camera *seven*—San Roque Gate. There sat a lone silhouette in the guard booth, presumably Marvin.

Gain one, lose one, Lewis thought. That's weird.

If Lewis could see Drake, he would have seen him standing poised outside the gray metal door to Station Two. Now Drake had his handgun drawn, raised and ready. The time had come. In fact, there was no time left. Drake listened to footsteps approaching from down the hallway. He drew back the hammer on his pistol.

Twenty steps away, Sergeant Jacobs, having exited the employee restroom en route to the rear double-pane exit doors to go search for Cameron and Grace, now rounded the corner down the hallway and came into direct view of Drake. He froze. Unsettling as it was to see Drake outside of Station Two, it was even more unsettling to see a fellow officer, wearing the same blue uniform, standing before him with a handgun pointed directly at his chest. Even for the trained veteran he was, it was a disabling sight.

Drake didn't hesitate. Two rapid shots fired out from the muzzle of his Berretta, striking Jacobs cleanly in the chest and sending him whirling, arms flailing, backward to the floor. Following through, Drake quickly walked up and stepped along side Jacobs, positioned his pistol ready to fire an additional shot, but saw there was no need.

The gunshots rang out loudly in the entrance lobby. The head's of Fred O'Neil, Rae Anderson, and Jimmy Becker's craned in unison to the opening from the rear corridor as Drake emerged walking calmly but briskly with his handgun low at his side. He had a flat expression on his face as he approached Fred, who stood closest to him.

"What was that?" Fred's voice sounded rattled.

In a movement that seemed nonchalant, Drake raise his gun and placed the gun-barrel at Fred's chest. He fired one shot as he strolled pass, striking him squarely. As Fred crumbled to the floor, Drake swung the barrel toward Becker. Now Drake squared himself, legs shoulder-width apart, in a full, two-handed stance.

Naturally, Becker went for his gun. But it was already too late. Drake fired twice *BAM! BAM!* And Becker flew backward to the floor.

Rae Anderson barely having time to digest what was going on, instinctively dropped behind the nearest desk when she saw Drake's gun flashed in her direction. She looked down at her holster and drew her gun. Holding it out before her, she realized her hands were trembling. In fact she was shaking all over. A quick peek around the desk revealed that, where Drake had been standing, he was no more. On her knees, she pivoted, crawled around, reversing her position, and looked the other way. *Still nothing.* Just as she did that, there was a sound from behind her. She turned and looked. There was Drake, standing just where she had been. Somehow he had flanked her in some kind of ghost maneuver and now stood above her with his gun angled down. Swinging her pistol around, it was too late. Drake squeezed the trigger, firing two quick shots into her back, execution style.

It all happened so quickly, it seemed surreal. In less than forty seconds, four security officers lay dead beneath the florescent lights with the smell of gunpowder still fresh in the air.

Down the hallway, Harkin had heard the gunshots, immediately recognized them as such, and sprang from his desk with his *Glock* already out and extended. He thought better than to shout out to his officers. There were too many shots for it to have been an accidental discharge. Though he was not certain, it seemed to him that the shots fired came from a 9mm Berretta—the standard issue firearm at Mal Loma. He slowly, and cautiously, angled down the hallway toward the entrance lobby.

Beyond Drake waited, patiently, concentrating on his breathing so to ensure it was without sound. He had predetermined the sequence in which he had killed the officers, in exact order. Fred first because he was closest; Becker next because he was the best shot; and Rae Anderson last because Rae would panic and give him time to reposition. Jacobs had come too easily—an unexpected gift.

Harkin on the other hand, would not be so easy, Drake knew. A combat-ready veteran, known for his coolness under fire and sureness of shot, he would be a challenge worthy of Drake's skills.

From inside the hallway, Harkin approached, pistol held high and ready. The doorway-opening loomed just ahead. He listened, but heard nothing. Then, reaching the opening, he poked the barrel of his handgun into the spacious lobby, keeping his body shielded behind the wall. Peeking in quickly, what he saw was a cool and calm Drake walking toward him, gun down and relaxed at his side.

"They got them!" Drake announced.

At the sight of Drake, Harkin's gun barrel locked in on Drake's chest. His eyes flashed over at the bodies of Fred and Jimmy Becker—Rae was not in his line of sight. Clearly something awful had happened. They were down, apparently shot, blood was visual on both of them.

A dozen scenarios flashed through Harkin's head. In that millisecond of thought his eyes left Drake, and in doing so he gave Drake the slight edge he needed. Drake's pistol flashed up from his side, locked onto the small portion of Harkin's chest exposed from behind the door jam, and fired twice in typical two-burst fashion.

*BAM! BAM!*

The first bullet caught Harkin's right shoulder, the impact of which pushed him further into Drake's line of fire, allowing the second shot to hit him dead-center. Two more shots followed, sending Harkin, all six-foot-two of him, crumbling to the floor.

Without skipping a beat Drake stepped forward and kicked Harkin's Glock from his wilting hand. Keeping his pistol aimed at his chest, he reached down and pulled the *shift key* from Harkin's pants pocket. The key was still attached to its retractable leash so Drake had to unclipped it from the belt-loop. Then he promptly tucked it into his pants pocket. After checking Harkin for vital signs, he returned to the entrance lobby.

Drake seemed completely unruffled as he walked back to Control Two. His mind was free of the tasks he had just completed and focused on the tasks ahead. As he stepped past Fred laying face down on the floor, Fred moaned and Drake fired another shot into his back. Drake released the empty clip to the floor and slapped a full one in, all in stride. As he passed, he glanced over at the keys to Mobile One hanging on the wall behind the badge counter. It hung right beside the huge ring of keys to the many back-country gates.

*How convenient,* Drake thought. *One less officer to account for.*

In the rear corridor, a pool of blood had formed under Sergeant Jacobs' body. Drake grabbed Jacobs by the legs, whirled him around, and dragged him into the hallway, over the blood, doing so in such a way that it wiped most of the blood clean from the tile. Before leaving Jacobs' side, he glanced down at his face.

"So much for the heightened state of alert," Drake muttered.

Back in the corridor, Drake stood for a moment without emotion, thinking if there was anything he had missed. Having just killed five people in a time span of less than two minutes, everything seemed perfectly on schedule. There had been no unforeseen element. The first sizeable body-count had been added without incident, and Drake showed no wear from it. His composure was uncanny. Every red hair on his head remained in place, his uniform still tightly creased, and his shoes shining brightly beneath the fluorescent lights. In fact he looked as if he had just stepped out of an actor's fitting room. He straightened his lapel, turned, and headed to the heavy metal door of Station Two.

# Chapter 38

With the surveillance screens strategically disabled, Drake's bloody rampage had gone unseen by Lewis in Control One. Completely oblivious to what had taken place, Lewis reviewed the protocol manual awaiting Drake's return. He was anxious to hear what Harkin had to say about the malfunctioning cameras. In the few minutes that passed he had tried several options to retrieve the video signals, but nothing seemed to work. A second re-boot of the entire camera system had likewise failed. The flat-screens above him remained blank. Drake's quickness to notify Harkin of the camera dilemma, which at first seemed self-serving, now seemed proper. In the interim, Lewis had discovered a third camera out; camera *six*—the Briefing Room.

A buzzer sounded from the console signaling that Drake had returned to the doorway of Control Two. Although camera *five* was still disabled, Lewis knew it was Drake the moment Drake slid his keycard into the cardreader. His name, identifying information, and photo-ID-badge flashed up on Lewis' console, along with the familiar command request:

OPEN DOOR SB1

Lewis placed the cursor over the *approve* option, hit the ENTER key, and watched on the surveillance screen as Drake came back into frame inside Control Two. Drake climbed into the console, reached over and flipped on the intercom.

"Hey, I'm back," Drake's voice announced, calmly.

"I can see that," Lewis replied. "So what words of wisdom did Harkin have?"

Lewis watched as Drake tapped the mouse, bringing his computer screen back to life.

"Yeah, I spoke to Harkin," Drake's voice said, nonchalantly. "Jacobs is calling in a technician as we speak. Meanwhile, he wants you to do a run down of every camera, from top to bottom, including checking the zoom and wide-angle capabilities on cameras fourteen to twenty-four."

"I already did that," Lewis said.

"Really?"

"Camera five and six are also out up here. You still have all your screens?"

"Hold on a minute." Drake simulated a run-through of the suspected cameras, swiveled around in his chair, and looked directly into the eye of the camera lens. "No problem here. I've got them all. Harkin wants you to run a continual check on all the cameras until the technician arrives in case others go out."

"That makes sense," Lewis said.

"Is there something I can help you with?"

"No, I think I've got it. Besides you're the only eyes of the Plant right now."

Drake grinned. "Nothing else for me to do but sit here and watch the monitors until the technician arrives."

"That's a ten-four," Lewis said.

Drake glanced out the large lobby overlook windows. The entrance lobby looked like a war zone with dead bodies scattered across the floor beneath the bright fluorescent lights. All was eerily quiet. The green readiness light pulsated from the Ionscan detection machine.

Lewis pulled the keyboard close to his chest and ordered up a screening montage of all the security cameras. Then he leaned back in his chair and looked up at monitor one. It immediately began sequencing through the surveillance cameras, all one-hundred and thirty-seven of them.

*Such a devoted worker,* Drake thought, watching Lewis on his screen in Control Two. He waited for Lewis to be totally focused on the rotation. Then he pulled the gold *Shift-Key* from his pocket, aligned it with the triangular keyhole, slid it in until the shaft completely disappeared, and turned it with a *click.* The small indicator light on the console went from green to red. The computer screen immediately refreshed with the familiar prompt:

ENTER PASSWORD FOR PROTECTED COMMAND
OVERRIDE

The cursor blinked, waiting. Drake's wire-rimmed spectacles glared conspicuously off the computer screen as he stared at it. Considering how many months had gone into the planning it seemed somewhat anti-climatic. Yet, a pivotal moment it was. He typed in his password. Then he hit the ENTER key, the screen flashed back:

PROTECTED COMMAND OVERRIDE
PROCEED WITH LEVEL ONE COMMANDS

*Presto!* Drake's face lit up.

The consequences of his actions were indisputable. That simply, the entire security computer system had fallen into his hands.

Drake lounged back in the chair and locked his hands behind his head. He glanced up again at the wall clock. Only one minute had passed.

*All according to schedule.*

He looked up at the surveillance screen. Lewis was still mindfully watching the rolling montage of images, while throwing an occasional glance down at the camera manual open before him.

# Chapter 39

Inside the Containment Dome Cameron and Grace sat, half-dressed, with their legs dangling freely from the top of the reactor-core-housing platform. Their pants were on but their shirts were unbuttoned and open, and their shoes were still lying on the lattice flooring behind them.

"For three nights in a row we were heroes," Cameron said, laughing about it. "Harkin couldn't figure out how we were doing it. He commended us for our 'uncanny tactics.' He told the class we were 'clairvoyants.' He said, 'we were heroes, and what was most important was that we had found a way. Defeating terrorism, defending the Plant, sometimes has no method.'

"What he didn't know was that Jack and I had found a way of getting above the training room, just above his podium, by climbing through some ventilation ducts. While he was laying down the attack plans for the night's exercise, we'd be above him, lying on the ceiling boards, listening in."

"Really!" Grace said.

"Yep. Our egos grew larger by the minute," Cameron said. "The accolades were ridiculous."

Grace laughed. "You guys are lucky you got to have war games. Our class wasn't large enough, so they're going to combine us with the next cadet class this summer."

"You'll love it. It's lots of fun. They basically divide the class up; half terrorists, half defenders of the Plant. Then they send you out, and you basically mess around all night, playing war."

"I'm jealous."

"Your time will come."

"No. I meant jealous of you and Jack's success."

"Well, let me finish the story… So here we were getting all these hoorahs, feeling like our chests would burst. But what we didn't know was that someone was jealous and divulged our secret to Harkin. Evidently, we told the wrong person and this person leaked our modus operandi to Harkin, who devised a trap for us.

"So on this fourth night, Harkin divides the class up again—half to be the terrorist group, or the saboteurs as it was, and the other half to be the security force. He sends us 'good guys' out while he keeps the' bad guys' back and lays out the evening's attack plans. And here, Jack and I were right above him, I mean right over his head, listening in on it all!"

"That's funny," Grace said.

" 'Tonight we will have an approach from the sea,' Harkin said." Cameron was trying to imitate Harkin's deep voice. "'There is an area along the west perimeter fence, just north of the weather station. From there, we will simulate a rush attack. Ten of you will *blitzkrieg* the Control Room, while two remain outside the fence to guard the escape route. You must first take out Patrol Officer One, Zone One, on the southwest side. Then quickly reach the Turbine Building door.'

"We should have known something was up, because Harkin kept glancing up at the ceiling.

"'Seeing their fallen Officer on the surveillance monitors,' Harkin said, 'the others will come running so you'll have to make it fast. Once you reach the southwest Turbine doorway, you'll blow the door lock, a simulation of that of course…'

"The class was laughing.

"'Then rush the Control Room. Two will remain at the door-way while the remaining eight rush.'

"Kelly raised her hand with a pre-scripted question. Yeah, the whole class was in on it. Harkin acted surprised, and called on her.

" 'There's a lot of blacktop between the perimeter fence and the Turbine Building.'" Cameron raised his voice, trying to sound feminine, to mimic Kelly's voice. "'And it will take a minute or two to blow the lock. What if there are rover patrols in the area?

"'Great question,' Harkin replied.

"At the front of the training room they had this big diagram of the Plant; with an aerial view. Harkin took a pointer and identified the area in question on the map.

"'It's more than fifty yards of open blacktop,' he said. 'You're not concerned with anyone seeing you, because they have already seen you on their surveillance monitors. What you are concerned with is what has been pointed out… the possibility of a Rover already being in the area and subverting your rush. You will first have to scan the area. Really, there's no strategically sound place to hide…' Harkin took the pointer and stuck the tip of it in a place directly in the middle of the open area between the power plant and perimeter fence. 'Except, right here' he said. 'There's a contractor's out-house, a honey hut, portapottie, you know what I mean.'

"The class started laughing again.

So did Grace.

" 'Right there,' Harkin said, and when he did, he kind of paused and glanced up at us. Like I said, we should have known." Cameron made his voice deep like Harkin's again. "'It is the only possible place a Rover could hide without being seen by the group,' Harkin said. He made issue of it, keeping the pointer there. 'If a Rover is anywhere else, he or she will be seen, and there is ten of you and one of them. It's unlikely one of the security team will be sitting on the toilet with an impending terrorist attack.' The class started laughing again. 'Unless you believe in what people say about security guards.' More laughter cried out from the class. "But of course not here at Mal Loma Nuclear Power Plant. Not us."

"He's a good trainer," Grace said of Harkin, chuckling.

"Yeah, he is…and so he goes on, 'So in conclusion,' he said. 'I really don't expect any of the Rover Patrol officers to be in the area, except the ones you can see and kill. The key to your success as a Terrorist group tonight, is *rush* and surprise.'

"From above the podium, lying on our bellies looking down at the top of Harkin's head, Jack and I had already formulated our plan. All we had to do, of course, was get into that outhouse without being seen, before they could assemble at the perimeter fence. Then we were certain victory would be ours again for the fourth night in a row, or so we thought.

"So Jack and I hustle out to that outhouse and went in. And we waited, and waited, like for fifty minutes. Occasionally we'd peek out the door. We had to leave it cracked open.… It smelled really bad in there. I mean picture it, here we were, cramped together in this four-by-four box filled with chemicals and human refuge!"

"How gross!" Grace cried.

"But we knew it was temporary and despite the awful conditions, we held tight and kept optimistic. Truth is, we were anticipating another night of heroism.

"I figured it would be best to let them pass, and get them when theirs backs were turned to us, so I whispered that to Jack and he agreed.

"So we're in there waiting and we hear this rustling noise. Then suddenly, the entire outhouse started rocking back and forth, and before we knew it, or could do anything about it, the entire outhouse went over, to the ground, door-side down. We were pinned inside. The chemicals and human sewage spilled forward, covering both of us, completely. The smell was unbearable, but worse, the chemicals consumed what oxygen was inside and we nearly choked to death and our eyes were burning.

"My God!" Grace cried out. She said it loud enough to where it echoed off the containment's inner walls. For a second, they both looked up to where the echo had sounded.

"From outside came this thunderous pounding," Cameron went on. "Basically it was ten security officers with night-sticks wailing on the sides of the outhouse. Finally we hear this familiar deep voice; 'Okay, that's enough. Let them out. It was Harkin.

"The debriefing that night was one to remember. Everybody gathered in the training room. They had Jack and I sitting in the far back. I mean, we were covered in chemicals and smelled like shit. I remember some of the officers scooting their chairs as far forward as they could, so they were all tight at the front of the room."

Grace was laughing so hard her beautiful eyes creased into thin slits with her pupils barely visible. She covered her mouth with both hands.

"Harkin took to the podium. 'When fighting terrorism, there are no rules,' he said. 'Use every resource, every angle, any method. If you don't, they will. Despite all the contingency plans in the world, sometimes you just have to fly by the seat of your pants. What Cameron and Jack did was commendable. What they did wrong was trusting someone they shouldn't have.' "

Both Cameron and Grace laughed together. They laughed so hard, the sound of it was reverberating off the rotunda like an echo chamber.

"We trusted in someone we shouldn't have," Cameron repeated, and then they both burst out laughing again.

After a solid minute of laughter, Grace went quiet, as did Cameron. Her brow furrowed in her cute little way.

"How interesting? Defeated by one of your own. Did you ever find out who turned you in?"

"No. We only had some guesses as to who it was, but never actually knew."

# Chapter 40

The Sniper lay flat in the wind-blown grass, his body now full-length behind the M-107 rifle. Below, Carl Harrington walked across an illuminated section of blacktop in the northeast corner of the plant, looking very much like a toy soldier through the crosshairs of the star-scope. In a surreal way, the light intensifier gave him a near animated appearance.

Tracking him steadily as he proceeded along the perimeter fence, the Sniper averted his eyes for a second to glance at his wristwatch.

The time on his watch told him it was time to proceed. *It's killing time*, he thought.

He dropped his eye back to the scope and began concentrating on his breathing. Years of training had taught him the value of breathing rhythmically, so as to be able to time a shot; and also, the value of dehumanizing a target, making it simply a thing that needed to be removed—not a human being with a life and history. The way Harrington now appeared in the star-scope, he did not look human. He appeared video-game-like; a human image, but not a human. The Church of the Assumption and Kamir had taught him differently. As much as his training had taken him to a higher level of indifference when it came to killing, that which he saw now—the image in his crosshairs, was indeed a man with a life and history as was the man in the Jeep he had killed minutes before. A shadow in a crosshair, but a *man* nevertheless. They were soldiers like he, trained to carry and bear arms; trained to kill; prepared to take a life and to lose one.

*There's honor in a soldier's death.*

Harrington disappeared behind the Fuel Handling Building, soon to reemerge. The sniper watched and waited.

More than twelve-hundred feet below, Lewis' eyes remained riveted on the overhead surveillance monitor as it continued auto-paging through the camera sequence; once completing a loop, continuing with another, and another. When it reached cameras eighty-six and eighty-seven, he found them to be blank now too. Just like the other malfunctioning cameras, the screen images from these two featured nothing but black with fuzzy gray lines running through them.

*A wild night for cameras,* he thought.

He knew them to be the cameras that covered the eastern side of the perimeter fence. They were both pole-mounted cameras, designed to overlap and cover the entire rear portion of the Plant.

He flipped on the intercom.

"Hey Drake," he said, still eyeing the overhead monitor. "I found two more cameras out… eighty-six and eighty-seven."

"Hold on a minute," Drake's voice replied. "Umm, I've got them. Not a problem here."

In Control Two, Drake looked up at the wall clock and watched the second-hand pass 1:40 a.m. "It's a good thing you found them. I saw the technician come in through San Roque Gate several minutes ago. He should be arriving anytime."

Lewis brought up camera *seven*—San Roque Gate. The kiosk at the gate was empty, the toll-bar down, and the lone figure, again, presumably Marvin, remained seated inside the guard booth. The pole-mounted camera facing south didn't afford a view up the access road. There was no way for Marvin to check for the tail-lamps of the technician's car.

"Must have missed him," Lewis said. "I'll keep monitoring the cameras and see if I find anymore."

"Great, Lewis," Drake's voice replied, cheerfully. "That's a ten-four."

Less than half a minute later, the intercom in Station Two started crackling again. Lewis' surprised voice broke through, saying; "Hey, I just got *six* back."

"That's a start," Drake returned into the speaker with a grin. *The Lord giveth, the Lord taketh away.*

Looking up, Drake glanced at the same surveillance image from camera *six*. There he saw the rear corridor of the Security Building empty, just as he had left it minutes ago. But as he was about to avert his eyes, he saw something—something on the floor. He leaned in and raised his glasses.

*Shit!*

He had left a smudge of blood showing on the tile. It was barely distinguishable, however, on the far end of the corridor. Nothing to be alarmed about, Drake thought.

"Did you do something on your end?" Lewis' voice asked.

"What?"

"Did you do anything on your end that may have inadvertently recovered the camera?"

"No, I'm just sitting here watching the security lobby," Drake said. He continued manipulating the keyboard.

"Well, obviously we've got a problem of some type," Lewis said. "It's a good thing Jacobs called in a technician."

"Yes. You'd better get back to the cameras and see if there's anymore in or out before he arrives."

"They're a still a rolling," Lewis said.

Drake looked up at Lewis on the monitor. As before, Lewis appeared conveniently busy.

*It's all a matter of sequence,* Drake thought. *Sequence according to schedule.*

Then a glance at the wall clock, *well, almost.*

In truth, time was becoming a critical factor. In fact, time had almost run out. And lingering still were the two renegade love birds, Cameron and Grace.

He positioned the keyboard at the very edge of the counter-top, rolled his chair in closer, and began to type. His fingers reeled off the same command sequence he had processed ear-lier—the one he used to locate Cameron and Grace, but this time he combined the process:

LOCATE PATROL ONE & ROVER ONE

Once again, instantly striking the ENTER key, appearing on the screen was a detailed floorplan of the power plant, upon which were the same two red lines crisscrossing and overlapping, eventually coming together in the same exact place—Containment Two.

Drake did a double-take. *What? They're still in there? What are they doing in there?*

He dropped back in his chair, trying to digest the information.

Far above on the mountaintop, the barrel of the M-107 held steady above the blowing reeds as Carl Harrington suddenly re-emerged from behind the Fuel Handling Building, directly into the Sniper's crosshairs. Waiting for him to reach his northern apex, where he would stop and pivot, the Sniper held his finger lightly on the trigger.

Then he silenced his mind and slowly began to draw back his finger; and the trigger mechanism descended.

As the fully illuminated image of Carl Harrington planted a foot, pivoted, and turned facing south, the rifle kicked violently. The muffled discharge, shot like a burst of hot air, resonated from the hilltop. As the rifle kicked skyward, the Sniper momen-tarily lost the image. But just as quickly as he lost it, the image reappeared and he saw Harrington down on the pavement.

Without haste, the Sniper swung the rifle south, repositioned himself, and locked a bead on the speck that was Chris Peters. The timing was crucial. And as anticipated, Peters was completing the southernmost end of his loop with his back facing north. As Peters slowed, turned, and stepped forward into the one clear spot just beyond the roofline of the Fuel Handling Building, the Sniper repeated to himself, "There's honor in a soldier's death."

In another quick, violent jolt, the barrel of the M-107 kicked skyward; coughing out its muffled discharge. At the same moment, the speck below, which had just turned north, staggered briefly, and dropped to the asphalt.

The Sniper's eyes gleamed with satisfaction.

Five seconds before, a missed shot would have careened into the Security Building. Five seconds later Peters would have been concealed behind the roof-line of the Fuel Handling Building. Neither mattered now. He was dead, along with Harrington.

In Control Two, Drake had watched it all on the monitors. Zooming in now on Section Four, he perused Chris Peters' sprawled body. He lay flat on the pavement half in the shadow of the Fuel Handling Building and half exposed to the tall flood lamp near the perimeter fence. Switching to camera *eighty-six*, he saw Harrington, jumbled in an awkward position on his side, almost resembling a sleeping fetus. Magnifying the zoom, Drake could see blood glistening. It was forming a small pool that came out from beneath Harrington's body.

*A .50 caliber leaves plenty margin for error,* Drake thought.

He keyed the radio transmitter.

"Control Two calling Patrol Two—copy. Control Two calling Patrol Two—copy."

"Patrol Two here," Pryce Johnston replied from the seaward side of the Plant.

"We're having some camera problems tonight," Drake said. "Please report to Zone Three. There's a control box located there that appears to be the culprit. Sergeant Jacobs will be escorting a technician out to you."

"Ten-four," Pryce replied.

"Over and out," Drake said.

"Over and out."

Drake flipped off the transmitter switch.

Out on the wind-blown side of the power plant, Pryce Johnston marched briskly northeast, the barrel of his Mini-14 glistening beneath the perimeter lights. He passed the radio tower and cut diagonally across the blacktop, the most direct line toward the northeast corner of the Turbine Building. He was a bit puzzled by the fact that he had been summoned to Carl Harrington's zone. The question bubbling in his mind: Why wasn't Harrington handling something that was occurring in his own patrol zone? Best he could surmise was it had something to do with the Fuel Handling Building. There were NRC regulations meant to safeguard nuclear fuel storage facilities. There were staffing ratios that must be met and maintained at all times. It must have had something to do with that, Pryce concluded.

Pryce rounded the northwest corner of the Turbine Building and came into plain view of what appeared to be a lump some fifty yards away near the far end of the perimeter fence. He could not tell what it was at first, but as he got nearer it began to take form. And as he got within thirty meters, it became apparent—it was a human figure. Harrington was down on the ground for some unknown reason.

In one of those surreal moments when one looks at something, sees it, can't believe it nor understand it, and questions one's own senses, Pryce balked. *Is it some kind of a joke? Is he playing, sleeping, or hurt?*

Pryce broke into a run. He simultaneously pulled his Motorola from his utility belt. Ten yards away he saw the blood pool. Upon reaching Harrington he confirmed it was in fact blood and that his fellow officer had been gravely wounded somehow. He instinctively pulled his rifle from his shoulder and pointed it warily into the darkness beyond the perimeter fence. Then, with his left hand he fumbled for his radio.

On the mountaintop, the Sniper lay flat on the tarp taking careful aim at the image. Bright now within the star-scope, he watched as the human figure took the radio from its hip, snapped it up along his side, and lifted it to its face. Then the M-107 rifle suddenly kicked, coughing out the same muffled noise and the speck fell, slumping over the body it had just discovered.

# Chapter 41

Drake smiled and clicked off the monitor. Having witnessed the killing on the overhead screen, he felt an obscene sense of fulfillment having personally drawn Pryce to section *three*.

In thirty short minutes, the once impregnable security system of Mal Loma Nuclear Power Plant had been practically, if not completely, laid to ruins. Ten of fourteen security personnel were dead, the protected *Level One* commands had been overridden, the two man rule had been laid asunder, and the eyes of the entire security surveillance system removed from the view of the one man who could stop the impending disaster—Lewis. Such a brilliantly orchestrated plan would have made even the most notorious criminal masterminds envious.

But Drake was feeling no elation. He was a bit worried actually, if worry was an emotion Drake felt. It was a quarter to two. In less than fifteen minutes, Lewis would commence the 0200 security check—*a security check among a dozen dead security officers!* Also he knew, both the Coast Guard and National Guard remained only a radio call away and Cameron and Grace remained somewhere in the Plant unaccounted for, each armed and dangerous with radios by which to make an outside call. Additionally there was the operational crew. At a moment's notice they could drop the control rods and shut down the reactor; thereby averting a nuclear disaster

Drake adjusted the keyboard in front of him. He started reeling off more commands. As expected, not long into it the intercom began to speak.

"Drake, I just lost all my cameras," Lewis' concerned voice said.

Point of fact—all eight monitors in Control One went simultaneously blank. Gazing up at them, Lewis was wondering if his mind was seeing things.

Drake's voice conveyed an appropriate surprised tone. "What?"

"No kidding. All of them just went blank."

"Hold on a minute." Drake kept Lewis waiting twenty seconds before he came back. "Modern technology, eh? No worries, I still have all my cameras. Also, the technician has arrived."

"Yes, I heard that," Lewis said, having heard Pryce's radio summons to the northeast quadrant. "The technician thinks it has something to do with the switch box in Zone Three?"

"That's what he said." Drake was still working the keyboard.

In Control One, Lewis' gut instinct was to check the security camera in the northeast quadrant, but the moment he did, he realized he couldn't—*all the screens were blank.*

"Seems to be some kind of a cable line or routing problem," Drake's voice broke.

Lewis looked out the bullet-proof windows into the Control Room. All seemed drearily normal. The operators were all in their designated positions, placidly passing the night away. Lewis grabbed a spiral-bound binder from the bookshelf near him. The heading on the vertical spine read, '*Surveillance Systems.*' He laid the binder on the countertop and paged to the table of contents. Using his finger to run down the various subject headings, he stopped at the one entitled *Routing Schematics.* The page he turned to revealed various diagrams and schematics of communications and surveillance systems.

"They think it's some kind of a routing problem?" he replied into the intercom.

"That's what they're thinking."

Lewis paused. "Okay. Let me know if there's something I can do from here."

"I'm sure they'll call you if they need you," Drake said.

"That's a ten-four," Lewis said. "Over and out."

"Okay buddy," Drake said. "Over and out."

The speaker went silent.

Lewis looked up at his blank screens. It was bizarre to see so many hazy lines. And it was frustrating too. As much as he wanted to watch the progress in Zone Three, he could not. It was funny, he thought. One survives months on end with nothing happening. Then, the boredom of every night is suddenly answered by a compendium of oddities; with little that one could do about it except sit and wait.

In Control Two, Drake was not sure how much longer he could keep up the charade. He stared at the keyboard. It didn't matter he surmised. He looked up at the wall clock. Now it was ten 'til two. *Time to move on.* It was time to finish it, to finish him.

He hit the ESC key, refreshing the screen back to blue. He stared at the onscreen prompt:

PROCEED WITH LEVEL ONE COMMANDS.

He immediately began typing:

DISABLE ALARM ZONES 1-765

He hit the ENTER key, and the screen flashed back:

ALARM ZONES 1-765 DISABLED

Inwardly, he felt a sense of triumph—like chipping away at a castle wall for decades then throwing one last stone and seeing it crumble before one's eyes. But the feeling was fleeting.

He tapped the ESC key again, refreshing the screen back to "PROCEED WITH LEVEL ONE COMMANDS," the cursor waiting once more.

His fingers typed on the keyboard:

UNLOCK DOOR ZONES 1-325

Drake paused before hitting the ENTER key. He let his finger hover above the keyboard momentarily. Then, using his pinky, he tapped down.

From where he sat he heard the heavily armored door of Control Two, just below him, *click* unlocked. Likewise simultaneously, throughout the power plant, a soft '*clunk*' resonated as every doorway, every hatch, and every possible access portal indiscriminate of its vitality or function, unlocked.

Drake grinned shrewdly. *There go the keys to the kingdom...*

He reopened the window of his early search for Cameron and Grace's location, refreshed it, and it revealed no change. According to the computer, they had not moved.

"We'll see about that," he muttered to himself.

He stood up, quickly, pulled his 9mm from his holster, and checked the ammunition clip—it was full. A matter of habit he thought, realizing he had just slapped in a fresh clip when he returned from the lobby. It's always good to be robotic about things like that.

He descended the two steps to the doorway, stood there for a second, and then gently pushed on it with his fingertips. *Presto!* The disarmed, heavily-fortified, gray-metal door, earlier likened to a Swiss bank vault, swung open freely on its hinges.

Drake smiled as he stepped through.

At the rear, double-glass doors which entered into the *'protected zone,'* Drake likewise pushed out, unobstructed, and strode briskly across the blacktop. When he reached the entrance door of the Turbine Building; *Voila!*—the door pulled open without resistance.

# Chapter 42

A breeze swept up off the ocean, rippling the tall shore grass all along the coastal terrace. There, where the white sandstone bluffs fell to crashing waves, above the hidden cove, two heads emerged from the dancing reeds.

Lifting his eyes from the glowing hands of his military watch, Emil looked at Ramzan. "We go now, Brother."

Ramzan nodded an affirmative; his eyes burning with readiness. He motioned Emil to lead, which Emil did.

Beneath the weight of their heavy packs, they ran along the edge of the rocky cliffs, following south toward the illuminated power plant. Staying low, backlit only by the shimmering lights, they moved as cat-like creatures, skirting along the very lip of the terrace. Through the Bone Yard they jogged, not even knowing of its existence, past the white foam of the discharge bay, briefly looking down at it, and finally came to a place in the reeds just west of the power plant.

"This is good," Emil huffed, indicating they had come far enough.

Settling low in the grass, they took a moment to catch their breaths and take it in. Before them, the plant stood brilliantly large, fully illuminated, just beyond the perimeter fence.

"It is bigger than I thought," Ramzan said, taking in the enormity of it. *So it will fall that much farther.*

Emil pulled the binoculars from the sheath on his hip and scanned the perimeter.

Straight before them was an open field of maybe seventy-five yards, separating them from the perimeter fence. Dead-centered beyond the fence was the elongated Turbine Building. From their position on the west, they could plainly see the doorways, one on either side of the Turbine Building, either one of which could be their port of entry. To the southeast beyond the weather station, was the rear end of the Security Building. There were no signs of activity from the light within. To the north the blacktop was barren and void of movement.

"The others have done well," Emil commented.

Ramzan grinned with delight.

The crossing to the perimeter fence would be open, through an exposed field, but it was the most direct route and from the looks of things, it didn't appear they'd encounter any resistance, nor would it matter. Glancing skyward, Emil smiled. The darkness was complete. Even if they encountered one of the remaining guards, there were plenty shadows in which to conceal themselves.

With a nod of Emil's head, and a concurring nod from Ramzan, they took off running, Emil leading the way and Ramzan trailing closely behind. Their packs flapped softly as they hurried across the field. Twice Ramzan looked back expecting to see someone, thinking perhaps the ghostly swirls of sea-mist had followed them on land; only to realize it was the wind.

Reaching the fence in less than twenty seconds, they peeled off their backpacks. Emil pulled out a compact pair of bolt cutters and immediately commenced clipping links from the bottom of the fence.

"Quickly," Ramzan said. He was breathing deeply now, impatiently watching the Turbine Building.

*Click, click, click, click…* and in less than a minute, Emil cut a three-foot, vertical line in the fence. He tossed the bolt-cutters onto the ground and pulled the slice wide, stretching the chain-links on either side. Ramzan slid their packs through, and then went through himself, down on one knee. Emil handed Ramzan their automatic rifles. Then Emil slithered through like a big python. On the other side they quickly re-donned their backpacks and dashed across the blacktop to the nearest doorway on the Turbine Building.

Again Ramzan felt a surge of wind rush up against his back. He turned and looked seaward with eyes ablaze. The wind seemed to be rustling violently through the reeds at the cliff's edge. *Patience Brothers,* he thought. *We are almost there.*

# Chapter 43

Nearly simultaneous with Emil and Ramzan's crossing, Drake walked, with a confident stride, down the length of the turbine room floor into the Auxiliary Building, and toward the rear corridor. His path was completely uninhibited. Every doorway lay unlocked before him. There were no wandering *armed responders* to confront him. Even Drake felt odd about it. No need for keycards or pin codes. Simply pull the handle and he was in.

Despite Drake's cool composure, his mental clock was ticking. *Time* was of the essence, he knew. Lewis would commence the security check at exactly 0200—*only a few minutes away.*

Yet despite the time constraints, Drake passed the forward stairwell that led most directly to the Control Room, and instead headed for the entrance door to Containment Two. *A brief detour* was his plan. Sure of himself, sure that he could do it quickly, he was determined to resolve the evening's principal distraction first. Cameron and Grace were to be liquidated; simply entombed in the Containment Dome with a quick pull of a locking-lever. His timing had been impeccable thus far. He had no reason to believe anything would change in that regard. And the thought of it was particularly pleasing, *to kill the two love birds in one stroke!* It caused him to smile even now.

By all accounts, Cameron and Grace should have been dead already. The knowledge of this spurred Drake's resolve to finish it now. It was only by their insubordination and carelessness that they had escaped the bullets of the hilltop sniper, and Drake knew it.

Four floors above in Control One, Lewis had completed a schematic review of the entire power plant's surveillance systems. He thought it odd that the camera problem was specific only to Control One. He had crawled beneath the console, tracing a conduit of cables from the rear of each surveillance monitor to a place where they all merged into one large bundle of wiring. Then, returning to the manual, he found specifically what he was looking for: The Control Box in *Zone Three* did in fact seem to serve as a router for the surveillance cameras coming into Control One, and Control One only.

Drake had anticipated it before it even happened. He knew Lewis would eventually pull the schematic binder and check for himself, and so Drake had purposely researched the camera schematics ahead of time and concocted a plausible cause for camera failure specific to Control One.

Lewis, curious for a progress report, grabbed the desktop microphone and keyed the transmitter.

"Control One calling Patrol Two; Control One calling Patrol Two, come in." He paused, waiting for Pryce Johnson to respond.

Of course the radio speaker remained silent.

Down near the entrance to Containment Two, Drake froze in his tracks.

*What the…? Crap!*

He promptly pivoted, turned back toward the rear stairwell, and listening again as Lewis's voice repeated the call, began to move his legs faster.

Taking a direct path across the central floor, Drake tried to remain unflustered. But when he reached the doorway on the opposite side and found it locked, he about panicked. It was inexplicable. The door should have been unlocked. *Must be some kind of oddball malfunction?* he thought. He yanked on the door but it would not open. With the system completely disabled, there was no logic to it. And what it meant was that he would have to go all the way back across the central floor and through the adjacent hallway to the westside corridor to the forward stairwell. It was the only other way up to the fourth-floor Control Room where Lewis was now trying to contact a dead officer, and would soon commence the 0200 security check.

Drake shoved on the door hard, but it wouldn't budge. A glance at his watch told him he had less than three minutes. The *bravado* which rallied him on earlier had now completely dissipated.

He broke into a run.

Above in Control One, Lewis stared at the silent speaker. Having repeated the call for a third and fourth time to no avail, he was without explanation. He looked out the large Plexiglas windows at Chief Stewart, who smiled back nonchalantly. The other crewmen were likewise calm, ordinary, and going about their nightly business. In fact, for them, the night was progressing with mind-numbing normality. The myriad of blinking lights on the operational switchboard were ostensibly normal. Apparently, nothing was amiss.

Better talk to Sergeant Jacobs, was Lewis' thought. Have to find out what's going on. He reached for the intercom button and was ready to depress it when he saw it was nearly 2:00 a.m. The second hand on the wall clock had already rounded twelve o'clock and was on its downward loop with less than a minute to spare.

He glanced out the huge window again into the Control Room. Chief Stewart smiled back again. Lewis forced out a half-smile in return. The call to Jacobs would have to wait. He positioned the desktop microphone beneath his chin, and readied himself for the 0200 security check.

Drake, meanwhile, reached the fourth level of the forward stairwell, completely breathless. Glancing at his wristwatch, he grimaced to see it was right at 2:00 a.m. His unexpected detour around the backside of the Auxiliary Building had taken more time than he expected. As he exited the stairwell and came down the short hallway toward the Control Room door, the radio on his side began to speak.

"Control One to all posts," Lewis' voice announced. "Control One to all posts. This is your 0200 Security Check." As usual, Lewis paused, giving the officers a moment to ready themselves for the roll-call. Then he dove into it; "Security One."

Drake drew his pistol. Ahead of him was the door to the Control Room, which had on it, centered chin-high, a two-way window, through which he could see the crewmen inside. Keeping his stride, he reached out his left palm, pushed through the door, and entered the Control Room. He did not break his stride. He continued briskly across the Control Room floor.

Shocked, the crewmen all turned with stunned expressions on their faces. It was unusual enough to see Drake burst into the control room, seemingly through an unlocked door, but with a gun drawn made it even more bizarre.

Drake nodded a friendly *hello* as he strolled past.

Ahead of him now were the large Plexiglas windows of Control One, through which Drake could see Lewis' back. Lewis, hunched over at the console with the desktop microphone at his chin, was waiting, and waiting, and waiting, for the reply which would never come.

"Control One calling Security One," Lewis again called, and as he did, it echoed from the radio at Drake's side.

In Control One, the sound of his own voice behind him caused Lewis to stop and crane his head around. What he saw was a flash, Drake passing the window with gun still low at his side. Then he was at the door. By the time Lewis swiveled around in his chair, Drake was pushing through it with gun raised.

And he didn't hesitate. With the same coldness he had displayed earlier, and at nearly point-blank distance, Drake pulled the trigger, twice.

*Bam! Bam!*

Lewis, hit squarely in his chest, reeled backward in the chair, and then slumped forward dead. Drake glanced over the console. The spiral bound schematic binder was still out and open on the countertop. He snapped the Mini-14 rifle from the wall rack and immediately returned to the Control Room.

All five crewmen stood mortified, and speechless, not knowing if they should run, fight, or even believe what they had just seen. There wasn't much more they could do. Though it was one on five, the one had a Mini-14 in his hand. Before they could fully comprehend the events unfolding, Emil and Ramzan burst through the Control Room door behind them, likewise wielding assault rifles.

Chief Engineer Stewart was so shocked he staggered backwards, tripped over a file box, and fell to the floor. Just as quickly, he sprang back up and stood there with his legs quivering.

For a brief moment, no words were spoken, nor did anyone move. It was as though a giant pall fell upon the room.

"Glad you could make it," Drake finally said.

"We stopped to collect seashells," Emil shrugged.

Drake frowned.

At gunpoint, the crewmen were promptly corralled against the nearest wall. Having just witnessed Drake's cold-blooded murder of Lewis and seeing these two foreigners brandishing their automatic rifles, both with faces ready to kill, they complied without resistance. Drake, the one and only left to defend them, had obviously gone bad.

"No need to do anything rash," Chief Engineer Stewart said.

"Shut up and get against the wall," was Drake's reply.

"Everything good?" Emil asked Drake.

"Perfect," Drake replied.

Emil's deep voice sounded comically baritone against Drake's higher-toned, refined speech.

"Just need to follow the plan," Drake said.

"Which one's the boss?" Ramzan asked, who had remained silent until now.

"That one," Drake said, pointing to Chief Engineer Stewart, who hesitantly raised his right hand.

"You make this thing work?"

"No."

"You don't make it work?" Ramzan insisted, not believing.

"No, we just monitor it."

Ramzan glared back at Emil. "A liar like the rest of them."

"It doesn't matter," Drake said. "Let's get on with this."

"I am not talking to you," Ramzan said, looking at Drake a bit crazed.

"He is right," Emil said. "Let's get on with it."

But there was no reasoning with Ramzan. He had waited too long for this moment. The battle had finally been taken to the enemy.

"You make this thing work?" he asked again to Chief Stewart.

"Okay, I guess you can call it that. We make this thing work."

"You make nice bomb for us," Ramzan said. "Do you know that?"

Chief Stewart looked forward, comprehending his meaning.

"We will kill many with it," Ramzan said. "Did you know that?"

Stewart just stood there, quaking in his white overcoat.

Drake, on the other hand, was conscious of the time. It was nearly 2:10 a.m. There was plenty of work ahead of them and there was still Cameron and Grace hiding in the Plant; a small tidbit he purposely neglected to mention to Ramzan and Emil.

"Take care of them," Drake said, coldly, referring to the crewmen, directing his attention toward Emil only. "I have some unattended business to take care of. All else goes exactly as planned."

"Everything is okay?" Emil asked.

"Everything's fine."

The two men looked at each other for a moment, Emil waiting as if there was something more Drake needed to say, but apparently there was nothing more. Drake holstered his pistol, slung the Mini-14 on his shoulder, and swiftly exited the Control Room. Emil and Ramzan herded the crewmen into the Training Room. The crewmen gathered fearfully against the furthest wall. With gun barrels raised, Emil and Ramzan stood in the doorway for a moment. Emil looked on solicitously, as if debating in his mind exactly what to do with them. He checked the locking mechanism on the door. In addition to the automated lock, it was equipped with a dead-bolt.

"No need to kill them," he said in Arabic. "They can die in here, by their own hand."

Ramzan was taken back by the suggestion. Too long had he waited to shed some *western* blood. He leveled his rifle barrel at the cowering crewmen, and in a short, ten second burst, pulled the trigger. All five crewmen tumbled to the floor in a dead heap.

"No need to worry about the lock now," Ramzan said, flipping off the light and pulling the door shut.

# Chapter 44

The radio stood SILENT. Standing on its end on the lattice platform flooring above the reactor core housing, it had suddenly, and inexplicitly, ceased at the very commencement of the security check.

Cameron and Grace stared at one another with equally puzzled expressions.

"Is that normal?" Grace asked.

"Definitely not," Cameron said, flatly.

For Lewis to start a security check promptly, and abruptly stop it, practically in mid-sentence, was highly unusual. In the eight months Cameron had been working there, it had never happened.

"It is very weird," Cameron added.

Lifting the radio from the floor, he checked the volume and frequency controls. All looked okay. Clicking it on and off and listening into the speaker, he found it to be fully functional.

*Very weird.*

"Is it because we're in here?" Grace asked, referring to the fact that they were within the three-foot-thick concrete walls of the containment dome.

"Maybe, but its odd how we were getting a transmission and then it suddenly just stopped. I've been in here before when I could get nothing, and other times when I received calls crystal clear. Sometimes it just depends on where you're at. In this case, it's strange that we were getting a signal perfectly and then lost it completely."

"What do you think we should do?" Grace asked.

"Get out of here."

"Should we try calling first?"

Cameron hesitated. It wasn't a bad idea. For a moment they just looked at each other. Cameron was considering the deep trouble he was already in having missed the last radio check and having failed to return to post as ordered. By now, he thought, they must know the 'raccoon' incident was bullshit. Still, he was concocting another excuse. And Grace was beginning to feel a similar neglectful sentiment.

"We'd better get going," Cameron said.

Grace nodded.

They quickly slipped on their shoes, strapped on their utility belts, gathered up their Mini-14s, and headed down the ladder.

As they climbed down to the main floor, buttoning their shirts and tucking them in neatly, Cameron felt a sudden and inexplicable sense of urgency. It was too damned odd the way the security check abruptly ended. As they approached the huge nine-foot door, he fumbled to retrieve his keycard from his pants pocket, but Grace already had hers out and slid it into the cardreader.

Curiously, there was no red or green indicator light showing. She pulled the card out, angled it in again, horizontally, and again there was nothing, not even the yellow light requesting she re-insert the card.

They glanced at one another.

"I'll try my card," Cameron said.

Grace nodded.

He took his card and slid it all the way into the cardreader. But just as before, there was no green indicator light, no yellow light, and no red light—no message at all.

*What?* Okay now, this is getting really weird. "Something's up."

The fascinated expression on Cameron's face caused Grace concern. "Do you think they're trying to pull something on us?" she asked. "I mean like they did to you and Jack during your training war games?"

Cameron shook his head. "Not likely. I think something's wrong."

As Cameron stared at the cardreader, his curiosity intensified. He stepped in and took hold of the door handle, and looking up at the towering slab of metal above him, he gave it a tug.

Surprisingly, the door sprung opened effortlessly, sliding easily on its ball-bearing rollers.

"What the heck?"

Cameron inspected the locking mechanism, found it incapable of staying in a locked position, stepped back, and forced out a calm smile.

"What's going on?" Grace asked.

"That's not suppose to happen," Cameron said.

"I didn't think so," Grace replied.

For what seemed like several seconds, Cameron and Grace were unable to tear their stunned gazes away from the door. Before them, oddly open was what resembled the yawning hatch-way of a World War II bunker. Cameron, searching his mind for a plausible explanation, could not find one. "Maybe they're running some kind of a security test?" he said. *Not likely* was his self-imposed answer. They would have announced it at the shift briefing. "It could be a single, isolated malfunctioning cardreader or glitch in the locking mechanism." But of all places, on a containment door? "We'd better get to an area of good radio reception and call it in. Harkin's going to want to know about this."

As Cameron pulled the door wider, giving them enough room to pass, he was thinking that this could be his salvation; having discovered this critical anomaly in the system may bring him some praise and forgiveness from Harkin. Then he realized it was all too coincidental. For both the security check to suddenly stop mid-sentence and then to find the Containment door malfunctioning and unlocked, was beyond accidental. It was eerie, and foreboding. The second door was no different; a dead cardreader and malfunctioning door in unlocked position. Cameron pulled it open to a rush of cool air. He took Grace's hand while pulling out his Motorola handset from his hip sheath.

"Down this way," he said, leading Grace to a place he knew to have good radio reception.

Grace followed closely behind, taking two steps at a time trying to keep pace with Cameron's fast walk.

"Maybe Harkin will cut us some slack for finding this?" Cameron said.

Grace looked at him but did not answer.

Reaching an area closer to the Turbine Building, Cameron already had his Motorola at his face. Just as he keyed the transmitter, a noise came from down the corridor. It was the sound of a door opening.

Drake emerged from a stairwell. There was no look of surprise on Drake's face. In fact he looked completely calm, normal, unflustered, though he was breathing heavily and had a gun at his side.

"The doors are malfunctioning," Drake announced, bearing his disarming smile.

Cameron gave an expression of relief. "Uh, yeah, we..." he sputtered out. Of Cameron's many faults, one was his excessive good nature, and this time it nearly did him in.

Drake's gun rose before Cameron could finish the sentence; it rose in a calm and purposeful fashion, pointing directly at Cameron's chest. So sudden was it, and so unexpected, that Cameron could do nothing more than react on instinct. He sprung into a nearby stairwell, pulling Grace down with him. Just as he did, Drake pistol cracked off two shots. The bullets careened off the wall just behind where their heads had just been, taking chunks of concrete with them.

Cameron quickly returned three rapid shots, causing Drake to take defensive action. Then he backed further down the stairwell, taking several steps. Grace, who had already gone down several steps, drew her gun too. Looking down at her, Cameron motioned her to descend even further, which she did promptly, all the way to the bottom.

Cameron listened for approaching footsteps, but could only hear his own heart beating, and Grace, below, breathing heavily. He kept his Beretta poised in a two-handed grip, still high enough to sneak a peak above the rail, but then he continued to descend, back-stepping his way while keeping his pistol leveled at the top of the stairs. As he descended, he noticed his Motorola lying on the step below. He reached down, picked it up, clicked-off the volume, and carefully sheathed it with his free hand.

The stairwell was situated in such a way that provided perfect cover. Though its depth was only eight feet, it sloped at a right angle to Drake's position and was surrounded by concrete and steel. There was no way out, or in, other than through the big door behind them.

Cameron looked above. The sign over the door read:

CONDENSER ROOM
Approved Personnel Only

There were a variety of warning signs and notations, announcing the room's vital functions. Breathing hard, Cameron pulled his keycard from his pants pocket.

"Take out your card," he whispered.

Grace looked at him, grabbed the huge, lever door-handle, pulled it down, and pulled the door opened. She shrugged her shoulders. Cameron gave a shrug in return. It's all he could do.

Above, Drake was cursing himself for not having waited one second longer. Then, the two of them would have cleared the handrail of the stairwell with no chance to escape. In his eagerness to finish them, he had lost his one advantage—*the element of surprise*—which this night, until now, he had employed brilliantly.

He approached the stairwell cautiously, watching the top edge for the slightest movement, ready to blast it. He was half-expecting to see Cameron's head pop up, or the tip of his Beretta rise from beneath the concrete wall attempting to steal another shot. But instead he heard only the clunking sound of the heavy metal door closing.

Drake rounded the top of the stairs, pointing his weapon down the stairwell to find it empty.

He looked up at the sign above the door, as Cameron had done, and chuckled.

*How convenient...*

The Condenser Room, like the containment, housed vital equipment, and liked all vital areas, it was constructed as a bunker for the defense of its vital function—a virtual vault of concrete and steel with only one way in, and one way out. And the doorway, also likened to the entry door of the Containment Domes, only smaller, was fortified and vacuumed sealed.

Drake proceeded down the stairs, keeping a careful aim on the huge, steel door. On the wall next to the door was a steel box, with a glass front like a fire alarm box. Drake broke the glass with the butt of his pistol, snapped off a plastic tie, and pulled the lever down with a *clunk!* It was the emergency 'manual' locking mechanism, meant to be used when all else fails.

Stepping back, he looked up at the door. *Rest in peace.*

The Condenser Room, he knew, had just become a second tomb. Since the first tomb did not work out, that being the containment dome, this one would serve just as well, Drake thought. Upon conclusion of the night's events, he knew, Cameron and Grace would be impaled by a million deadly gamma rays, if not first roasted in scalding steam.

*Love's an irony*, Drake mused.

Drake hurried back up the stairs toward the Control Room. He couldn't help but laugh, and his laugh was a sadistic one. As much as there had been variations in the night's plan, he had been equally blessed with counter-balancing fortune—the last of which was the two love birds making it easy for him. He leaped up two steps at a time, cheerfully, feeling almost like a school boy heading to the prom. Or maybe more like a school boy heading to the screening of a favorite movie he had long awaited seeing.

# Chapter 45

For Cameron and Grace, the last sixty seconds had been nothing more than a blur. And now, like two stunned jackrabbits having been chased by a rabid dog, they suddenly found themselves back in a burrow-like structure, dazed and disbelieving. They stood back now from the large door with guns raised and ready.

"I never did like that guy," Cameron said.

Grace wasn't amused. She was shaking. Her chest was heaving. She thought her heart might thump out at any second.

"He was grinning," she said. "Did you see that?"

Cameron did not reply. He was thinking about the sound he had just heard—the *clonking* sound made when Drake had dropped the locking mechanism.

"Did you hear that?" he asked.

Grace nodded.

"Watch the door," Cameron said.

Grace stepped further back, raised her gun, and pointed it squarely at the door.

Cameron pulled his Motorola from his hip, keyed the transmitter, and spoke loudly into it. "Patrol One to Control One; Patrol One to Control One."

Cameron turned as his words echoed off interior walls. The hollowness of the sound made it ever more apparent where he was. They were within the vault-like construction of the Condenser Room.

"Patrol One to Control One, come in."

There was no answer.

Cameron repeated the call, and after a few more tries, he tried Sergeant Jacobs with the same negative results.

Cameron checked the door. The cardreader was dead, just like the one in Containment One. There were no indicator lights or messages upon it. Holstering his radio, Cameron repositioned himself along side Grace, leveled his Berretta at the doorway, and motioned her forward.

"When I say go, try to slide the door open."

Grace nodded.

With a bead at the very edge of the door, Cameron motioned Grace to *go*. Grace pulled on the door, but it would not budge. She tugged harder, still nothing. Cameron came along side her, and using their combined strength they could not make it move a millimeter.

"Bastard locked us in," Cameron said, bluntly. The dread in his eyes revealed to Grace the seriousness of their situation.

"How?"

"There's some kind of manual locking mechanism for emergencies. That's what that fire-box by the door is."

"It's not right."

"No kidding."

Cameron yanked on the door again, using all his body weight, knowing, however, the effort was in vain. "He's locked us in all right."

Cameron gave a weary, satirical sigh. He turned and glanced around the large room. Grace looked around too. Like the containment structure, there were wall-mounted lights leading up to the top of a lofty copula. In the center was a huge stainless-steel vessel, most of which was submerged below the floor-level, but large enough to put a couple greyhound buses in. Like an iceberg, only a portion of it showed, and what did show, had large metallic pipes coming and going from it; pipes which emitted a high-pitched humming sound, generated from the steam and water rushing through them. The sound echoed off the interior walls of the large room.

"What is it?" Grace asked.

"It's the condenser. It's where the steam is dissipated and the water is cooled before sending it back into the ocean."

Grace recalled learning about the condenser and its function in her classroom training.

"I think that's the only door," Cameron said.

"Is there another way out?" Grace asked.

"I don't think so. This place was made to keep intruders out and vital equipment in. In the event of an emergency, it's supposed to lock down. It's airtight."

"Maybe down on another level?"

Cameron didn't look optimistic. This night's turning into a real nightmare, he thought.

"Any ideas?" Grace asked.

"None," he paused.

Trying to gather his thoughts, trying to recall all information he had learned about the condenser and the room in which it was housed, Cameron scanned the interior. It all looked as solid as bedrock. Above there was nothing that looked like a hatchway. Several levels below, however, could offer the possibility of a passage-way out.

"Maybe there's another way out on another level," he said, "but I just can't imagine it. I think this place is airtight."

"Well, we can't just stand here."

"Over there," Cameron then said, pointing to a stairwell which led to the subterranean levels.

They hurried across the floor and began descending rapidly.

"What do you think is going on?" Grace asked, following Cameron down the open staircase.

"Whatever it is, it's not good," Cameron replied, gravely. It was the best he could offer.

Five minutes later, they found themselves three floors down. Having crisscrossed several stairwells and traveled laterally between a web of stainless steel pipes, they had come to a dead-end. Now backtracking, they traversed a catwalk beneath the condenser housing. There they found another metal ladder leading down to yet another level. All the time they were silent, their minds trying to digest the gravity of their situation, and trying to conjure up a way out.

Cameron was first to speak. "I'll make this up to you."

Grace stopped and looked at him. "What are you talking about?"

"It's one thing that I screwed-up," Cameron said, breathing heavily. "But taking you with me? And all that stuff on top of the reactor?"

"That was my idea," Grace said, trying to keep up. "Remember? Besides, I have no regrets."

"None?"

"None."

Graced grabbed at Cameron's shirt, stopping him. He turned around facing her. "Do you?" she asked.

"Of course not," Cameron said.

He started forward again, following along some scaffolding. They went under some pipes, had to duck their heads several times while holding on to the overhead scaffolding, and came out near the far side of the room.

"Have you ever heard the story about the young Prince on his way to his coronation?" Grace asked.

Cameron looked back. "No. What happened?"

"He stopped to watch the sunset."

"And he missed his coronation?"

"Yes, but he saw the most magnificent sunset of his life! Magnificent colors of purple, orange, and lavender. It was a rare, unique eclipse that caused it to be so brilliant, something that happens only once in every one hundred years."

"So what's the point?"

"Was it worth it?"

"No!"

"In this case it was… because he became King two days later. But the point is, he missed his coronation. But instead, for all his life, until his dying days, he had the most magnificent image of a sunset in his head, one that gave him strength and caused him to smile. He never saw another like it."

"Not all stories end so perfectly," Cameron said, as he climbed down some pipes to another level. He turned and held out a helping hand to Grace. "Let's say your story is true, but he lost his chance to be King, forever. Was it still worth it?"

"There are moments in life that power, and money, and all the fortunes in the world can't buy. And there are things in life, people and feeling… one cannot replace and must cherish above all."

"How did we get on this conversation anyway?"

"We're trapped in the Condenser Room."

"Oh, yeah." Cameron turned and looked back at Grace. "Did you just make that up?"

Grace did not answer.

Cameron continued forward, silently, thinking about what Grace just said. It made him recall how he had fallen in love with her. Sure she was beautiful, but she was also down to earth and had a simplicity about her, like the simplicity of the Chumash Indians, and there is great beauty in simplicity, he thought. It was that inner beauty again, radiating outward. In Grace he found love from the heart, not the mind. A person who so completely appreciated simple things was someone he could be with forever. And he was feeling very guilty now, having placed her in danger by his utter stupidity. It was his carefree, happy-go-lucky nature that had gotten them into this mess, not to mention his dereliction of duty. And it would have to be his cleverness that would get them out of it. The fortress he'd been hired to defend had fallen into the hands of a madman it seems, and he was partially, if not completely, to blame for it.

He recalled a time when he and Grace had eloped from their posts and found a quiet place to sit in the Fuel Handling Building. They sat on a catwalk above the pools of boric acid, wherein were submerged dozens and dozens of unspent fuel rods. They were having a good time together, battering back and forth in a getting-to-know-one-another type conversation, when they saw an ant, walking along the rail. Suddenly the ant slipped, and teetered, hanging on, but before Grace could reach out and help it, it tumbled into one of the pools of boric acid.

"It's always sad to see a beautiful thing die," Grace had said, "whether it's a gorgeous flower, a slender blade of grass… or an ant."

Cameron looked on inquisitively. He could not see the ant in the pool, but knew its fate.

"Saddest of all is when love dies," Grace said. "But love never really dies, does it?" she added, correcting herself.

Thinking back on that moment now, and that statement, Cameron was even more enamored with Grace. *I will make it up to you, Grace,* he said inwardly.

A noise sounded from one of the upper levels. They both glanced up.

"What was that?" Grace asked.

"Don't know." Cameron said. "I don't think it's anything. I think it's just the equipment."

Ahead, the scaffolding led through a dimly lit corridor. Cameron strained to look through it.

"There's a light," he said.

Grace looked and saw the faint light too, some twenty meters away.

"Can I lead?" Grace asked.

Cameron nodded. "Okay."

Cameron followed, watching Grace carefully, thinking again how much he cared for her and how badly he felt about getting her into this fix.

"Everything okay back there?" Grace asked.

"As good as it could be under the circumstances. Just trying to keep up."

Grace smiled.

At the end of the corridor, they found nothing. There was no light. It was just a reflection off a stainless steel tube. They turned around and Grace led them down another level. They followed along another narrow foot bridge, finally coming to another dead-end. The scaffolding simply ended into a concrete wall. Below them was impassible steel-mesh. On either side were concrete walls and steel grating. There was no way out.

"It's going to be okay," Cameron said, not believing it.

Grace let out a nervous laugh. "Yes, of course it will."

"Let's go back up to the second level," Cameron said. "I saw something up there that looked like a hatchway. It's worth checking out."

Grace nodded and they began to climb.

En route, Cameron flogged himself with negative thoughts. His culpability for this predicament seemed paramount and his remorse about it was growing larger by the minute. *If I would have taken my job seriously; if I'd listened to Harkin orders; if I had gone to my post when I should have, and stayed there. You plan and prepare, you train and submit, and then when war really arrives, you're goofing off.*

So many nights Cameron had trudged repetitious on patrol. So many times he had shirked his duty to lay among the reeds in the Bone Yard, or to steal a moment with Grace. Now, suddenly, there was an enemy among them, one of their own nonetheless, and he could do nothing about it. The heroic visions of a horse-backed warrior, lost Indians tribes, buried bones, and wind chiming through the reeds did nothing for him now. Nothing else mattered other than getting Grace to safety, and to do, whatever possible, to defend the power plant from obvious destruction.

# Chapter 46

Beneath their heavy packs, Emil and Ramzan labored up a steel ladder along the outer shell of the Auxiliary Building. They switched from one ladder to another, having to toggle over forty-feet of open air. Reaching out from one rung to another, Emil went first, gripping tightly to the cold metal bars, toggling over, and continuing his climb. Ramzan followed, like a cat, with little effort. He was in his element now, and his veins were pumping with adrenalin. They reached a rooftop, ascended another ten feet to another rooftop, and stopped there to get their bearings. Ramzan pulled out the small hand-folded diagram and pointed west to a configuration of pipes and transformer poles. He turned and looked up the south wall of the Auxiliary Building.

"Yes, it is there," he said, pointing back westward.

Stashing the diagram back into his pocket, he led the way now, angling along a ledge which passed precariously beneath several high-voltage lines.

The night was black, though the surrounding grounds were well-lit, and there was a crisp, cold shoreward wind, which made Ramzan smile with each blowing gust.

"It is beautiful," Ramzan said loudly as they climbed.

"What?"

"The wind," Ramzan repeated in between gusts.

"Yes, of course!"

"I have always liked the wind—the desert wind. How it blows through the palm trees in the evenings before sunset. It is beautiful. It will serve us well tonight, no?"

"Yes, very well," Emil replied.

The reference to the wind's velocity urged them on. It was a favorable omen. In Ramzan's mind, it was evidence of God's will.

Further along, they began hearing the high-pitched sound of pump-driven water rushing through pipes. Higher and further and the sound grew louder. Finally reaching the source, Ramzan stopped to check the diagram again.

"This is it," he said.

Just above them was a huge, curving, seven-foot-diameter pipe, singing out a continuous high-pitched note similar in tone to that of the spinning turbines, just not quite as loud. It was a section of the *primary loop*—the main cooling system for the reactor core; one of only two places in which the pipes protruded from the building's walls.

*A colossal error,* Ramzan thought, in terms of construction design.

Best of all, it would provide, with a little help of high explosives, a portal through which radioactive contaminants could escape from the containment structure. The very design of the containment structures was to prevent such a release; yet the architects left open this possibility, and with the assistance of a little C-4, Ramzan intended to exploit it.

They stripped off their packs, laid them on the ledge, and from each withdrew the bread-loaf sized packages of C-4. Emil held out a small pen-light as Ramzan removed the plastic wrapping, letting it fly off into the wind. He pushed in the blasting caps, sinking the activators an inch into the clay-like substance. He attached the wires from the blasting caps to the face of a Nokia cell-phone and secured the phone to one of the C-4 bundles with a strand of duct tape.

With a boost from Emil, Ramzan scaled up to the topside of one of the huge, seven-foot cooling pipes. Emil handed up the first explosive, gingerly. Ramzan positioned it on the outer side of the pipe, and secured it with several straps of duct tape.

The second device was handed up, just as cautiously, and Ramzan took it and walked carefully along the top of the pipe, pacing out ten meters. There he began strapping the device to the bottom curve of another pipe above him. He had to stretch to do it, using one hand to hold the bomb flat against the stainless steel, while strapping it with the other. Once it was stationary, he secured it with several additional strands of tape. He stretched a small, black wire from the second bundle to the first, and connected the wire, holding his hand against the wall to brace himself.

Ramzan stepped back, as far back as safely possible, and carefully inspected his work. He was very pleased with the positioning. There, on the outward up-curve of the pipe, the explosion would facilitate the greatest loss of water in the shortest amount of time. The distance between the two devices was ideal, far enough so that the combined blast would sever two sections of pipe; yet close enough for the blasts to be simultaneous. He had witnessed, in times past, a minute discretion in timing to cause a second explosion to be snuffed-out by the first.

Leaning out to the very edge, he tried to broaden his view.

*The crafty American was right,* he thought. Not far beyond, the huge cooling pipes curved into the wall of concrete. Once blown, they would serve nicely as ventilation-ducts for the gamma rays to escape.

Ramzan looked down at Emil.

"We're good?" Emil asked.

Ramzan nodded. "Very good."

With a press of a small button, Ramzan turned on the Nokia cell phone. The digital display instantly lit up to the accompaniment of a brief musical tune. He waited for the screen to pass through the typical welcome displays and reach the option menu. Then, he tapped the bomb softly with his hand as if to wish it *good luck*, and hurried back to the place in which he had scaled the pipe.

Emil had already gathered their things, discarding that which they no longer needed, and waited for Ramzan. Ramzan planted a solid foot on the overhead crossing beam and reached down with the other foot. Emil helped him find a footing. Once back on the ledge, Emil handed Ramzan his assault rifle.

"It's in the hands of the *Great One* now," Ramzan said, his eyes aglow.

Emil looked up nervously at the bombs, and acknowledged with a double-fisted shake.

"Let's go!" he said.

They scrambled down the outer wall of the Auxiliary Building, like two spiders, following the same route they had come up. Two minutes later, they hit the blacktop, running, and a short time thereafter they rounded the southern end of the Turbine Buildings. One last sprint, across the fifty-yards of open blacktop, and they arrived at the vertical hole in the chain-link fence. With a deep breath Emil went through first. Ramzan, kneeling, looked back at the power plant. He checked the time on his watch—several minutes had already elapsed since their departure from the Auxiliary Building. When Emil was ready, Ramzan scooted through.

Hurrying back across the long field of grass, they reached the cliff's edge and concealed themselves in the reeds. It was the same place they had waited an hour earlier. The Plant showed no sign of change—desolated and absent of any signs of life. The Security Building was likewise lifeless, though light glowed from its rear windows.

Ramzan flipped open the cell phone from his pocket and looked at its illuminated face, waiting for it to come on. The digital time display read 2:45 a.m. He lifted his eyes toward Emil. Emil looked at the glowing hands on his watch. It said the same—about a quarter to three.

"Close enough," Emil said.

Ramzan opened the 'recent calls' menu, scrolled down to a number, and pressed a finger down on the redial button. The cell phone immediately dialed, sounding out each number, and upon reaching the last one, a brief tone sounded, followed by a huge explosion from the power plant that echoed like the double-crack of a cannon.

*CAROOOM! CAROOOM!*

The twin, thud-like concussions reverberated across the coastal terrace and up the canyon to the east. From the top of the Turbine Building, a group of nesting seagulls scattered frightfully into the night sky. On the mountaintop, the Sniper watched the flash through his high-powered scope.

Ramzan's fiery eyes flickered with wild satisfaction. Almost immediately, steam-funnels rushed skyward through the flood lights, quickly forming a white cloud in the sky. It was evidence that the bombs had been aptly placed.

Ramzan and Emil exchanged congratulatory smiles. Then Ramzan tucked the cell phone into his pocket, and together they hurried away along the bluff's edge, back toward the cove where the *Zodiac* waited.

# Chapter 47

Upstairs in Control One, having just returned moments before, Drake heard the blasts—*CAROOOM! CAROOOM!*—and grinned. He watched now on the overhead screen as thousands of gallons of water gushed out from gaping holes and cascaded down the outer framework of the Auxiliary Building. The water, still driven by the powerful pumps at a rate of more than three-hundred gallons per second, quickly flooded the blacktop below. Above, bellows of steam rushed skyward.

Beside him, Lewis' body remained slumped forward in his chair. Drake grabbed Lewis' collar, pulled it forward, and let the body fall to the floor. Taking the seat for himself, he swiveled around to the computer keyboard and tapped in some more commands, further recovering the surveillance system. Then he paged through various exterior cameras until he found another, on the southeastern side of the Auxiliary Building, which gave a better view. There, in high-definition imagery, were the huge cooling pipes from another angle, revealing the damage from the eastside of the building.

Drake turned and looked into the Control Room.

*What had they done with the crew?*

He got up and entered the U-shaped command center. On the floor was the lollipop which had fallen from Chief Engineer Stewart's pocket during the siege. Drake picked it up, unwrapped it, and stuck it in his mouth. Behind the desks and file cabinets he saw nothing. The dressing room was likewise empty. Across the room, the lights and meters on the Plant's huge operational switchboard were coming alive. The blasts registered immediately, activating the automated warning lights and alarm buzzers. Chief Stewart's desk, scattered with papers, was as he had left it. There was no sign of blood anywhere.

*Where?*

Drake looked up at the small window on the door to the training room. *There!* He walked over and eased open the door. Inside was a bloody pile, heaped together, the five-man operational crew. Among the arms and legs, Drake made out the body of Chief Engineer Stewart. He tilted his head thoughtfully, so as to better see his face. There had been a mutual reverence between the two; some kind of shared intellectual admiration. But Drake wasn't feeling it now. He pulled the door shut, drew the lollipop from his mouth, and tossed it on the ground.

Back at the operational switchboard, Drake scanned the various meters and gauges. Upon detonation, the seismometer had jumped more than five centimeters, scratching out a large, uneven peak on the recording paper. The temperature gauges were already reflecting an unusual warming in the reactor core, but the heat was still far from the crucial point needed to cause a meltdown.

*First things first,* Drake thought. He disabled the emergency shut-down mechanism, an automated feature which served to take preemptive action in the event of an anomaly. He also disabled the area-wide, siren system, meant to alert local citizens of the impending catastrophe. Then he came back to the meters. Sitting side-by-side front-and-center were two eight-inch-diameter glass enclosures, above which were the corresponding reactor denotations: *Reactor One* on the left, and *Reactor Two* on the right. The face of each had a clock-like dial, starting at eight o'clock and running clockwise down to six o'clock, along which were black numbers in increasing increments of fifty-degrees Fahrenheit. At three o'clock on the dial was a *red zone*—indicating seven-hundred degrees Fahrenheit. The meters' downward limit was one-thousand degrees.

Now the needles on both gauges stood steady at about six-hundred degrees. With the fuel-melting-point being five-thousand degrees Fahrenheit, this might take awhile, Drake thought.

He took note of the time and the reading, returned to Control One, and sat in the console chair.

# Chapter 48

Cameron and Grace heard the explosion too, muffled blasts from deep within the subterranean levels of Condenser Room.

"What's that?" Grace asked nervously.

"I don't know, but it didn't sound good," Cameron replied.

Then they heard, vaguely, what sounded like down-pouring water, coming down the outer shell of the building.

"What's that?" Grace asked again.

"I think we have a problem," Cameron replied.

Two levels above on the main floor, the emergency warning system suddenly activated. Four swirling red lights positioned high in the ceiling of the grand concrete room, flashed to the sound of screeching sirens. The radiation evacuation lights anchored above the huge entry-door kicked on too, blinking on-and-off in colors of yellow and red.

Cameron, listening to it, looked at Grace and said, "We definitely have a problem."

He could tell Grace was frightened. *And for good reason,* he thought.

"We've got to get out of here," he said.

His voice sounded troubled now. There was a quiver in it Grace had never heard, and it caused her increasing alarm.

He motioned toward the ascending stairwell. Without hesitation, he jumped to it, and Grace followed, and they hurried up toward the main floor. Reaching ground level, they found the top of the large room alive with all the warning lights and screaming sirens. They ran to the door and tried pulling on it again, to no avail. Cameron shoved his shoulder into it, hard, but it refused to budge. By the time they turned around, there was steam rising from the large pipes on the condenser housing.

Grace looked up at the cloud forming above. "Is it radioactive?"

Cameron was asking himself the same question. His mind flashed back to his training days. There were three water loops, he recalled, one of which was radioactive, two of which were not. It seemed to him the two loops that went through the condenser were not.

"I don't think so. I think its harmless water vapors."

But as he gazed up at the expanding cloud, he was thinking further along, as he was trained to do. If some kind of anomaly had occurred in the adjacent Containment, it was just a matter of time before it would be radioactive in here.

"I think the steam is safe for now," Cameron's said. "But eventually it will be radioactive."

"How much time do we have?" Grace asked.

"Not much. We have to find a way out."

"But how?"

Cameron hadn't the slightest idea.

He scanned the huge interior of the Condenser Room. As before, he saw nothing that looked like a possible exit. His cleverness and creativity were things he could always rely on, but now when he needed them the most, they were failing him. His lack of resourcefulness in this time of need made him think of his heralded hero figure—*Bugs Bunny*. Even he couldn't find a way out of this mess, he thought.

One thing was for sure, it was getting hot already.

"The steam will keep rising," he then said. His eyes settled back on the descending stairwell from which they'd come up. "Which means we need to go back down."

Grace was thinking the same thing.

Feeling a surge of panic, Cameron took Grace's hand and they dashed to the stairwell beneath the swirling warning lights. As they began to descend, Cameron remembered something Chief Engineer Stewart had once said; words which seemed very ironic now, and sometimes when past words become ironic twists, they get repeated out loud, and abruptly, which is what Cameron now did.

"Radiation is a good thing," he spit out.

"What?" Grace asked.

"It's what Chief Stewart said once in his lecture. Can you imagine that?"

"No."

"Well, I don't think Chief Stewart ever imagined this."

"No, I don't think he did."

Cameron further recalled his training sessions in nuclear radiology; how Chief Engineer Stewart had described, in graphic detail, the potency of the gamma rays, stating how a relatively small dose "broke down" the immune system and altered a person's DNA, causing death in a relatively short period of time. How it can penetrate twelve-inch-thick walls of concrete and go through two-inches of lead. The thought of it made Cameron's legs move faster, taking two steps at a time.

"Can it get in here," Grace asked, referring to the radiation.

"Yes, it can get in here!"

Though they descended, the temperature still seemed to be rising. Above, the sirens echoed off the interior walls.

Two levels down, they once again came along the large stainless steel cooling pipes. Cameron looked up at them, as though seeing them in a different light.

"I have an idea," he announced.

He climbed up on some scaffolding and began tapping on the pipes and listening for sounds of rushing water. Twice he pressed his ear against the pipes, listening to see if he could distinguish between the sound of rushing water and rushing steam.

"What?" Grace asked.

"There are three cooling systems," he said, "the Primary, Secondary, and Tertiary. One's clean, one full of pressurized steam, and one is radioactive. We need to find the clean one."

"Okay," Grace had a puzzled expression. "Why?"

"It may be possible to get out of here, if we can find the right one."

He reached down, offered his hand to help pull her up.

Grace wasn't sure exactly what Cameron had in mind. She had taken the same 'Overview' course from Chief Engineer Stewart, explaining the basic functioning of the primary, secondary, and tertiary cooling loops, but couldn't fathom Cameron's wild plan. Nobody could. But she believed in Cameron. She felt fortunate to be with him. She could not imagine enduring the night's events alone, or with anyone else. Of all people, Cameron was the one she trusted, and if he believed he found a way out, she was in.

She extended her hand, and Cameron helped pull her up on top of the scaffolding.

It was now unbearably hot and humid. Both of their shirts were drenched in perspiration. Together they climbed higher, on top of the cooling pipes.

# Chapter 49

Drake sat smugly at the console in Control One, proudly watching the overhead surveillance monitors as the water continued spewing from the blown pipes, indifferent to the fact that Lewis lay dead at his feet.

Above all things, Drake detested unfinished business. It was contrary to his nature. He was prepared to wait it out, as long as it might take, to risk hazard to body and health beyond reason, anything necessary to ensure a melt-down was imminent. His madness knew no caution. Nothing else mattered now, only that he would win. And win, he would. There was nothing anybody could do to stop it.

He checked the image from camera *seven*, the pole-mounted camera at San Roque Gate. His cohort sat idle in the booth, as he was assigned to do until 5:00 a.m. Beyond the entrance gate and approach road, and the view out into the harbor, all appeared quiet. There was no activity.

Drake waited, patiently, calmly, occasionally checking the monitors. He spent some time checking the cameras in the containment structures; the entire rotunda in Containment Two was filled with white steam. He found himself having to lean in and look above his glasses in order to make out anything. Still, he could barely see the housing core. It was completely fogged white. Outside, white steam was funneling up through the exterior floodlights and above the containment domes, and it was slanting east, pushed in that direction by the wind.

After twenty minutes, the two waterfalls spewing down the side of the Auxiliary Building had considerably dwindled in size. They were now just two small streams of water. Below, the deep pool of water stretched halfway across the blacktop to the Fuel Handling Building. Zooming in, Drake inspected the damaged cooling pipes. Two ragged orifices of twisted and bent metal, each seven-foot in diameter, showed the destructive evidence of C4. From the upper portion of each crevice bellowed out steam.

Behind him, the Control Room switchboard was lit up like a Christmas tree; many red and yellow warning lights flashed and the alarm buzzers cried out in competing falsettos. Drake left Control One to go watch the slow digression on the various meters and gauges. He stood triumphantly before the indicator lights. The temperature in each reactor core was rising slowly. Each meter now stood at eight-hundred degrees Fahrenheit.

*Coming along just fine*, he thought.

It could take several hours, he knew, before the peak temperature would be reached. But eventually the overheating process would escalate; then it would spiral out of control; the heat feeding on itself jumping in leaps and bounds.

Drake checked the wind velocity gauge. It read *15 mph SE.*

Twenty mph is what they had anticipated, and had hoped for, but with occasional gusts spiking at twenty-eight mph, and with the wall clock now reading *3:45 a.m.*, there was plenty of time before sunrise.

# Chapter 50

"This is it," Cameron said. He stood on top of one of the huge cooling pipes. "It will take us right out to the ocean," he added candidly.

Grace looked shocked. "You're kidding, right?"

"No. I'm not." Cameron tapped, and listened, and tried to gauge the temperature of the pipe. The warmth of the steel and the sound emitting from it made him feel more confident. There was a three-foot diameter circular access hatch on top of it, with a locking wheel, like something you'd expect to find in a submarine. He dropped to his knees, placed both hands firmly on it, and started to pull on the wheel.

"Are you sure?" Grace asked, still trying to digest his plan.

"No," Cameron replied. "But I think so."

The question was a good one, Cameron knew. Opening the wrong hatch now would be their last act on earth. The six-hundred-degree, radiation-contaminated water of the primary loop would kill them instantly. Likewise would be true for the secondary loop, consisting of pressurized steam.

"Come on, help me," Cameron said.

Grace joined him, kneeling opposite him on top of the large pipe. She also locked her hands on to the wheel. Together they looked at one another. Their eyes each searched for a light of approval that wasn't there.

"What if we're wrong?" Grace asked.

"Then it won't matter," Cameron replied. "And if we don't try, it won't matter either."

Then Grace nodded her head, *yes.*

With all their might they pulled, breaking the wheel free. Spinning the hatch open, they lifted it, slowly, and looked inside. About a quarter of the way down was a river of greenish-colored water rushing past.

"This is it!" Cameron said.

"How can you tell?"

"Look," he motioned into the hatch. "See the color? Smell that? It's salt water! It's ocean water!"

They both looked down and breathed in the smell, and it seemed very obvious now that it was in fact ocean water—their nostrils immediately filled with the scent of brine, salt, and sea-weed.

Cameron reached in and stuck his fingertips into the rushing water.

"It's warm, but not too hot."

Grace exhaled with a sigh of relief. Then she looked at Cameron cautiously. "Are you sure it will work?"

"No," was Cameron's candid reply. "I'm not sure at all. But it's our only chance."

Cameron glanced skyward. Though they could not see clearly through the mesh to the top floor, what they did see was now thick in steam. Also, the radiation wobblers continued flashing and screaming from above. One thing was certain, time was running out.

"There are bars across the intake ports," Cameron said, "but there are no bars or gates at the Discharge Bay. At least I don't think so. I was down there once and don't recall seeing any. And when you think about it, it makes sense. There's no need for it. The pressure of the out-going water keeps everything clear."

Grace stared down into the rushing, deep-green water. "I trust you."

Cameron leaned way over into the hatch and reached down, touching the water again.

"It's not bad at all."

"Good."

"Can you swim?" Cameron asked.

"Of course."

"It's good that one of us can."

*What?* "You mean you can't swim?" Grace looked shocked.

"Don't worry," Cameron said. "I can do a pretty damn good dog-paddle."

Grace didn't seem amused. "We'll go together then."

Cameron nodded. "Feet first."

With no time to debate further, they both stripped off their utility belts and set them aside on an adjoining platform. Cameron looked at his Beretta, still holstered, wondering if it could survive the cascading journey through water—wondering if they would survive. If they did get through, he'd need it, he knew. He pulled the pistol from its holster, tucked it in his pants, and looked down at it. It looked incredibly clumsy and loose.

Grace shook her head. "It's going to fall out."

Cameron tried to secure it better, but no matter how he tried, it didn't seem to be secure enough.

"I think you're right," he said.

Truth was, he was going to need both hands if he was going to have any chance of surviving the ride, and surviving the ocean. Also, there was no telling if the path would be clear. If the weapon snagged on something it could fire, and he couldn't risk wearing the utility belt as it could likewise snag and bogged them down.

He laid the pistol on top of his utility belt. Below, their Mini-14s remained leaning against a rail—likewise impossible, and dangerous, to carry along; although his primordial instincts told him they would need them.

He looked at Grace affectionately. "Are you ready my love?"

"Yes."

"Here we go."

Cameron began to lower himself into the pipe, thinking exactly how best to do this.

"We're going to have to do this fast. When I say *go!* Grab hold of me, wrap your arms and legs around me, and don't let go!"

Grace nodded. "Okay."

Down Cameron went, back first, holding the edges with his fingers and keeping his feet pressed against the opposite rim so he would not fall completely in. It was an awkward position to say the least, and he knew he could not hold it for long. As he went further down, the rushing water started splashing against his backside.

"Wow, it's really warm," he remarked.

"Really?"

"Really! Okay, Grace, come on."

Grace immediately began to position herself above Cameron. When she was stretched out from rim to rim with only arms and legs keeping her aloft, she looked down at Cameron. "Ready?"

Cameron nodded. "Ready. GO!"

Grace dropped in, simultaneously wrapping her arms and legs around Cameron, and the weight of her body coming against Cameron broke his grip free. They immediately sank deeply into the water and were swept away, feet first down a torrid of rapids.

In a position resembling a love embrace, locked together in one another's arms with barely enough space to grab a breath—two intertwined twigs in a raging river—they careened down the pipe, rapidly gaining momentum. In less than forty seconds, they plunged two-hundred-and-fifty feet vertically through eight-hundred yards of pipe, banking off several turns before finally hitting deep ocean water. Oddly, through it all, Cameron felt like a child again at a theme park. They dropped so abruptly it felt like they had left their stomachs back on the launching platform.

When they hit the Discharge Bay, the force of it tore them apart.

Grace rose first, kicking hard above the foaming waves. She couldn't see Cameron anywhere. Paddling left, paddling right, she shouted out his name, but there was no reply.

Cameron had been taken by the fierce undertow, twisting and tumbling, fifty yards out, nearly to the reef, and when he finally surfaced, popping his head from the foam some thirty yards beyond Grace, he was gasping desperately for air.

"Cameron!" Grace cried, seeing the dark outline of a head beyond the bubbling surface.

Cameron turned shoreward and saw Grace, backlit by the glow of the power plant. They paddled hard for one another, Grace with full, graceful strokes, Cameron in a frantic dogpaddle. Meeting near dead-center of the Discharge Bay, Grace immediately embraced Cameron and kissed him.

"Grace! Crazy Grace!" Cameron cried, his lungs still searching for air. His shouts were barely audible above the crashing waves. All around them was turbulent, bubbling water.

"We did it! We did it!" Grace cried back.

As much as they wished they had time to celebrate, the urgency was to get ashore. They began swimming for the seawall. Moments later, they pulled themselves out of the water, exhausted and breathless, and collapsed on the rocks. Soaking wet and panting, Cameron's arms felt like lead weights. He laid flat on his back, seemingly unable to move them. Grace likewise, drained and weary, lay back on her hands with her chest heaving, trying desperately to get air back into her lungs. Her long, wet hair was flat against her head and hanging down behind her.

"Was that a ride, or what?" Grace spurted out.

Cameron didn't reply. Instead, he rolled over, pulled her in close, and kissed her. She reciprocated, and for a moment they just held one another, awkwardly, breathing heavily, trying to revel in the fact they had survived.

The enormity of the situation broke them apart, however. Cameron sat up, as did Grace. Their minds became two rivers of converging thought. Everything that had just happened in the last forty minutes flashed through their respective minds. Above lay a power plant under siege, about to be converted into some kind of weapon of mass destruction. A fellow blue-shirted officer had taken shots at them with the intent to kill, and they had narrowly escaped an entombed death only by virtue of their death-defying plunge down the discharge pipes. Neither knew the extent of the siege, nor that all their fellow workers were dead. But they knew something terrible was happening, and that they had to do something to stop it.

"We have to get back up top," Cameron said.

"I know," Grace replied.

"We're going to need guns."

"But how?"

"Maybe in the Security Building?"

From where they were, below the cliffs, they could not see the power plant.

"We must to do something," Cameron said.

"Let's go," Grace nodded.

Struggling to their feet, they both looked up at the edge of the white sandstone cliff above them. The glow of the power plant radiated from beyond the hilltop. As exhausted as they were, and as emotionally drained, they had no choice but to keep moving. Time was of the essence. They scrambled together, climbing up the steep rock and ice-plant embankment. Twice Cameron reached down and pulled Grace up.

At the top, they huddled low in the grass, shivering wet. What they saw before them caused silence and solemnity; from the wounded power plant, huge plumes of white clouds bellowed ominously skyward. From the side of the Auxiliary Building, geyser-like fountains of steam shot out at forty-five degree angles.

"They blew the cooling pipes," Cameron said, flatly. He paused and then added, "They're trying to melt-down the reactors."

"A nuclear meltdown?" Grace gasped. She knew what that was, if not by training, through media, television, and movies. Even after the wild ride down the cooling pipe, she didn't expect this—something more horrifying. The thought of it made a chill run through her body.

Scanning the perimeter fence and buildings beyond, they saw no one. The patrol post in the northwest quadrant where Pryce Johnson should have been was unmanned. The back windows of the Security Building were lit, but lifeless. And though they expected to see someone responding to the obvious disaster, there was no one. The front parking lot was likewise void of activity; though the many officers' vehicles remained in their assigned slots. The access road beyond was dark—there were no lights either coming or going. The Plant was essentially a ghost town, unmanned and unguarded.

"I can't see anyone. Can you?" Cameron asked.

"No one," Grace replied.

The unsettling notion began sinking in... *we're alone.*

Cameron rolled over on his side and gazed blankly up into the heavens. His thoughts were running wild. *He couldn't have killed them all?* he thought of Drake. The answer seemed clear. *There must be others.*

Turning back toward the Plant, Cameron studied the funneling clouds. The primary cooling loop had obviously been blown. If nothing was done soon, by this time tomorrow Mal Loma was going to be 'Radiation City.' What they must do, what they had to do, seemed obvious now.

"We have to get back into the Plant," Cameron said abruptly.

"Yes, I know," Grace replied.

"*I* have to get back into the Plant," Cameron corrected.

Grace looked over at him.

"There's a way of shutting down the reactors," he went on, not giving her a chance to reply. "There's an emergency shut-off in the Control Room; a lever that lowers the control rods into the reactor."

Grace recalled Chief Stewart's sermon about the odd-looking handles in the Control Room—the *control rod levers*. She nodded her head.

"If I can get to that switch, perhaps we can avert an all-out disaster," Cameron said.

"If *we* can get to the switch," Grace said.

Cameron turned and looked at Grace. "You need to get back to the Security Building and call for help."

"I'm not going without you."

"Grace, somebody has to warn the people. Think about all the cities out there."

Cameron suddenly realized the huge air-raid-like, civil defense warning sirens were not wailing, which by now should have been. Though he could hear the faint cries of the localized alarms from within the plant, there was not the distinct dual-tone cry of the regional sirens.

"Grace, someone has to activate the alarm system!"

Grace too, then realized the absence of the civil defense sirens. A vivid scene of helpless, unknowing and unprepared local citizens rushed through her mind.

"Besides," Cameron added. "I don't know what I'll find in there. If the reactors can't be shut down..."

"What if there are others in the plant with guns?" Grace asked.

*There have to be others*, Cameron thought.

"We'll fight them together," Grace added.

"There's no time to debate," Cameron said. "For all we know, the plant could be melting down already. Someone has to activate the warning system. Someone has to notify the Coast Guard, and I mean now. We both can't do it."

Unusual noises were coming from the power plant. Lifting their heads, they both looked out at the smoldering ruins. It now resembled a torpedoed ocean-liner. The white smoke which rose into the sky was forming a colossal, funnel-shaped cloud, drifting slowly eastward.

"Is it safe in there?" Grace asked.

"Not for long," Cameron said. He had in fact concluded it was not safe. By the look of things, the plant was already loaded with deadly gamma rays and returning there now was nothing short of a suicidal mission.

"Come on, Grace."

Grace hesitated, but the urgency of the situation seemed catastrophic now, and she knew there was no time to waste.

"Okay, I'll go. But don't try anything stupid." She paused. "And if things look really bad, you promise you'll get out?"

"Okay."

"You promise me?"

"Yes."

Cameron turned his gaze to the Security Building. The rear windows, aglow with fluorescent light, revealed no activity within.

"In the Security Building there's a main radio line," he said. "You need to get to it and call someone, anyone—the police, the sheriff, the Coast Guard… the National Guard."

"Will 9-1-1 work?" Grace asked.

Cameron felt a bit stupid; *why didn't I think of that?* "Yeah, that should work. Try the phone first; then the radio. If all the communication lines are out, you'll have to get in Mobile One and drive out to San Roque Gate. Listen to me, you'll have to get in the Jeep and drive out to the gate, understand?" As he repeated these words, he realized he wanted Grace to get out, regardless.

Grace listened intently, but said nothing.

"It's important," Cameron said. "Thousands of lives may depend on it. Including mine," he added.

Grace looked worried, and again didn't reply, and Cameron took her by the shoulders and stared deeply into her eyes. "Okay?"

"Okay."

"And don't trust anyone, Grace! Uniform or not," Cameron added. "Especially Drake."

"No kidding."

They watched the plant in silence for a moment.

"Remember, you promised to be safe and do nothing foolish?" Grace said.

"Just get help, Grace. I'll be fine."

"Kiss me then."

Cameron leaned in and kissed her, and when Grace tried to return the favor with more vigor, Cameron gently pushed her away.

"Go Grace!"

Reluctantly, Grace stood up and looked out at the power plant. The Security Building was south of them by four-hundred yards. The lights still glowing from the rear door and windows seemed normal and inviting, but Grace knew it was not likely the case. Everything had changed from a few hours before; from being in Cameron's loving embrace, to a life and death struggle.

"Go Grace!" Cameron shouted.

"Be safe my love."

"Go Grace! Drive fast, and don't look back!"

As Grace began to run, she stopped and glanced back. Cameron frowned and motioned with his arm for her to go, waving it forcefully in the direction of the Security Building. Staying low, Grace ran off, south along the bluff's edge, ironically following the same path Emil and Ramzan had taken thirty minutes before on their return to their Zodiac.

As Cameron watched Grace fade into the reeds, he felt impending doom. The wind had picked up, blowing the funnel cloud further east. Though it was likely harmless steam for now, it would not be that way for long. The distant sirens sounded louder and were now accompanied by a groaning sound coming from within the plant. It seemed, in a very short time, conditions had worsened.

Cameron took a deep breath. He looked to the north. The *Bone Yard* rippled silvery beneath the starlight; the tall shore-grass wafted back-and-forth in a mesmerizing way. There was a presence there, he felt. The fierce warrior in his dream had in fact been a revelation, he thought. It was a cerebral premonition of things to come. He was a spiritual messenger from the past come to foretell Cameron's future.

*Now I must be the warrior*, Cameron said to himself, saying it in the same way a soldier would call out a battle cry in the midst of war.

Instinctively, he reached for the Beretta at his side, but it was not there—it remained back in the Condenser Room resting on his utility belt, along with Grace's and their Mini-14 rifles.

*Crap!*

He glanced once more at the Bone Yard. The long hours lounging in the tall shore grass, his mystical connection with the Indians of the past, even getting this job at a nuclear power plant, all seemed too prophetic now.

Time to amend for wrongdoing, he thought. It was his moral awakening time; time to make things right and prove himself to Grace, and to himself. Upon that he was resolved.

He sprang to his feet and ran directly east toward the perimeter fence. The one-hundred yards of open field flashed by in seconds. Upon reaching the cyclone fence in full stride, he leaped halfway up it, clinging to the links. Above him however, were the impenetrable rows of overturned razor-wire. Glancing around, his eyes followed the fence line. To his surprise he saw something, not more than ten feet away. It was the hole Emil and Ramzan had cut through the fence. He didn't have time to wonder about it; how it got there, other than to know it had gotten there for the wrong reasons. He dropped to his feet, ran over to it, pulled the chain-link wide, and scooted through. Sprinting the remaining distance across the blacktop to the west doorway of the Turbine Building, he made the crossing in less than ten seconds. Reaching the door, he fumbled for his keycard, but quickly realized he didn't need it—the indicator light off. Pulling on the handle, the door swung open effortlessly, unlocked.

*Bastard disarmed the entire Plant!*

Cameron did not know what lay ahead, only that he would be in for the fight of his life.

Amid flashing warning lights and wailing sirens, he bolted across the Turbine Room floor, pausing only briefly to catch his breath, passed the huge turbines, still droning away, went between a row of switchboxes, his lungs burning now, and headed straight toward the generator room, the quickest path to the forward stairwell. It was the surest and fastest way to the Control Room.

Grace looked back as she hurried across the field to the Security Building. The towering Containment Structure was bleeding heavily the steam which shot from its severed pipes. Her mind could not help but consider the structures. Every security officer knew the purpose of the containment domes. But as many times as she had glanced up at the two magnificent monuments, she had never recognized them for that purpose. She admired them only for their architectural design. Now she saw them as nothing more than thick egg-shells, with equal fragility, supposedly meant to keep radioactive terror from destroying the land, but now failing to do so.

*It's funny,* she thought. *Sometimes it's difficult to see things right under you.*

She had always felt lucky to live on the central coast of California. Of all the places in the world she had been, it was the place she loved most. Now she felt like she had been sleeping next to a time-bomb waiting to go off.

How could a morning that started out so bright produce such a dark night?

# Chapter 51

Grace entered the rear door of the Security Building cold and wet, and shaking. She immediately noticed the blood smear on the tile floor. Following it, she found Sergeant Jacobs' body, dragged feet first into the hallway where Drake had left him.

She gasped.

Clearly he was dead. There was nothing she could do for him now.

She began speaking to herself, calmly. *You MUST keep steady.*

She reached for Sergeant Jacobs' Beretta, still holstered at his side, retrieved it, and checked the clip, quietly as possible. It was full. Then she slowly pulled back the hammer and clicked-off the safety. Counting her steps forward, she headed for the lobby. Glancing down the hallway, she saw no movement. Listening, she heard nothing. Looking at the tile in front of her, she realized she was trembling.

*Steady!*

A weary undertow pulled at her as Grace approached the large opening to the Entrance Lobby. She was as much afraid for herself as what she might find inside.

*It is too quiet,* she knew.

Though she sensed death, the thought of Cameron stayed with her. The rest of the crew too; Rae Anderson, Jimmy Becker, and Fred O'Neil, their faces, alive and smiling, flashed through her mind. If they needed help, she wanted to help them, and the thought of it kept driving her forward. Got to be strong and resolute, she told herself.

Carefully coming around the corner, she slowly breached it and froze.

Staring blankly forward into the sizable room, at first she couldn't see what lay directly before her. Then, that which would be her worst nightmare, suddenly appeared at her feet. Fred lay bloody just a couple feet away. Jimmy Becker not far beyond and Rae Anderson stretched out partially exposed beyond a desk.

Nothing could have prepared Grace for what she saw. All the training in the world can't desensitize a pure heart to the sight of human carnage; especially when it is that of familiar faces, friends and colleagues. Not even many months embedded in a war zone can prepare a person for that.

Grace collapsed against the wall, breathless. *They're all dead.*

An unknown amount of time passed before Grace realized she was seated against the wall, sobbing. Her mind had wandered. She was trying to shake the image.

*I have to move,* she told herself. *I can't just sit here.*

Rising to her feet, she saw the bloody scene again. Closing her eyes, hoping it would go away, she opened them again to the same carnage. Additionally, from the doorway on the far left, she saw a pair of legs extended in tan Dockers and cowboy boots. *Supervisor Harkin had fallen too!*

*Whoever kills so blatantly, would not hesitate to kill again,* she thought. She realized that the *killer* could still be nearby with a gun

She steadied her feet and pointed the pistol straight out before her. She panned the barrel across the room, trying to hold it still in her shaking hands.

*Whoever kills so blatantly should die himself,* she added to her thoughts.

She bravely stepped forward, scanning the room from end to end, but saw no one.

In a trancelike state, Grace went from body to body, checking for signs of life, but found none. It was difficult enough to see Fred and Jimmy Becker, both of whom she'd gotten to know and like in her short time on the night-shift. Finding Rae, however, brought tears to her eyes. Rae had become a close friend in the few short weeks they had gotten to know one another. They had shared common experiences, and womanly talk. They had even gone out twice together in the first week, had some drinks in a club in San Roque. Now Rae appeared like a sleeping doll; gracefully poised with eyes closed and curled hair along the side of her face; her knees tucked up against her chest. She was not bloodied like the others. The two bullet wounds in her back had somehow missed vital arteries.

Grace checked for a pulse—there was none. She ran a caressing hand down the length of Rae's arm, then up to her face, brushing the hair from her eyes. Grace felt numb.

Rising to her feet, Grace realized just how surreal the moment was. Here she was, standing in the center of the lobby, pistol straight out before her, all alone among dead friends.

*Have to call for help,* her mind insisted.

Looking toward the hall doorway where Harkin had fallen, she thought of the emergency phone line on Harkin's desk. She hurried that way, carefully side-stepping over Harkin's body and looking down as she passed. Sprawled out awkwardly with his chin crimped tightly down against his chest, his white shirt was full of blood. Clearly, shot to death.

*Sorry, there is nothing I can do for you,* she thought.

Coming down the hallway, Grace raised her gun. *The Killer could be there.*

Grace found herself trembling again. She could feel and hear her heart beating. *Hold steady! Please hold steady!* Still wet from her plunge into the Discharge Bay, she realized her pants were making a swashing noise, trailing water on the floor behind her. She pulled up her pant-legs with her free hand, trying to silence them.

Upon reaching the door, she turned the corner into Harkin's empty office with her pistol aimed and ready. Sitting idly on the desk was the phone. Harkin's papers remained neatly stacked along the front edge, and his chair was swiveled around facing the door, as he had left it in a hurry.

Grace grabbed the phone and pressed the receiver, only to find it was dead. She tapped it, clicked it on and off, still nothing. There was no dial tone. *Cameron was right,* she thought. *Someone severed the phone lines.*

Grace tried not to go into pieces as she set the phone down. "Be calm, Grace," she muttered to herself. Taking Harkin's Motorola from its charging rack, she fumbled with the dials, searching for an outside frequency. Then she keyed the transmitter, and not taking time to compose herself, she screamed into it: "This is Mal Loma Nuclear Power Plant. We need help! Come in please!"

She paused briefly, waiting; then she repeated the call: "This is Mal Loma Nuclear Power Plant. We need help! Please help us!" Still there was no answer.

*What's the distress code?* Her eyes frantically searched among the papers on Harkin's desk. Though drilled in her head, in her panicked state she couldn't remember the single-digit code. There on the top of the pile was the small pink radio-code booklet, and there in bold letters near the top of the booklet was the distress code—CODE 3, 998. She brought the radio back up to her mouth and screamed "CODE 3, 998!" into the transceiver.

In Control One, Drake sprung to attention. He had been lounging, quietly, watching the chaos in the Control Room, and watching the steam-venting action on the surveillance screens when he heard Grace's voice on the radio. He immediately grabbed the wireless remote and began clicking on it, trying to locate Grace's position. But before he flipped through three cameras, Grace's voice came again, louder and clearer.

"This is an emergency. CODE THREE, 998. Hello, we need help! Mal Loma Nuclear Power Plant… at least five dead. 9-1-1! 9-1-1!"

*Five dead? Crap! She's in the Security Building!*

He switched to camera *three*, and then camera *four*, but the two cameras mounted in the entrance lobby revealed only the ghostly images of the bodies which lay there beneath the fluorescence lights; exactly how he had left it two hours ago. There were no cameras in the supervisor's office.

*She has to be there*, Drake thought.

Not wanting to waste time, Drake rushed out into to the Control Room. Still trying to think ahead, he propped a chair against the doorknob on the main entrance door. He figured if anyone tried to rush the Control Room, this would be the way they would come. As he came back past the switchboard, he stole a glance at the temperature gauges. Both were pegged at about nine-hundred-and-fifty degrees.

Drake exited the rear, seldom-used door, rushing down the back stairwell in a near panic. It was a more round about way of reaching the main floor of the Turbine Building, but Drake was convinced it would get him there just as quickly.

Back in the Security Building, Grace stood impatiently with the radio in her hand. She had tried calling again, and again, with no reply. She fiddled with the radio dials, searching through the frequencies, thinking she may have better luck on a different line. She tried again.

"This is Mal Loma Nuclear Power Plant. Please reply! We need assistance NOW!"

There was no answer.

"Damn it!"

*No time to wait!*

Grace dropped the radio on the desk and rushed back into the entrance lobby. At the badge counter, still in the lock-box were the keys to Mobile One. She grabbed them and headed directly for the front doors, pausing there only to look back briefly at her fallen friends.

"I should have been there with you," she said, ruefully.

Behind the Plexiglas windows of Station Two there was no silhouette of Officer Drake Fischer. Grace looked into the windows as if her eyes were going to bore a hole through them. *You Bastard!*

As she dashed out into the parking lot, she thought she might be dreaming again. But it had all really happened. Her friends were really dead, the power plant was really under siege and about to be lit-up like a Roman candle. More importantly, within that bellowing monstrosity was Cameron, trying to make his way to the Control Room and do something to stop it.

*I must hurry!* Grace thought. *I must get help NOW! I must help you, Cameron!*

Somewhere off Point Honda, in the communications room of U. S. Coast Guard Cutter 174, the communications officer sat with headphones on and with an odd expression on his face. He lifted the headphone from one ear and turned back to the Second Officer, standing right behind him.

"Did you hear that?"

"Yeah."

There was a moment of silence, as if they were expecting to hear more, and when no further transmissions came through, the Second Officer said, "Try to reach them again. I'll go alert the Captain."

The Second Officer promptly left, down a narrow hallway en route to the bridge.

Quickly adjusting the small mouthpiece—nothing more than a thin microphone at the end of a wire, the officer commenced his reply. "This is United States Coast Guard Cutter 174, come in. This is United States Coast Guard Cutter 174, come in."

Back in Harkin's Office, the radio sat on the desk resonating the communications officer's transmission loud and clear, but Grace was already gone.

# Chapter 52

Drake made it down to the security building in record time. Now with his deadly pistol raised and ready, he stalked in through the rear corridor. He was on high-alert, listening for the slightest of sounds, but he heard nothing. Stepping past the radiation victim carrier, he glanced down the hallway at Sergeant Jacobs' dead body. It remained exactly where he had left it, neatly deposited lengthwise, feet first.

He looked again.

*Wait...* the weapon holster was unsnapped and empty.

*She's got his gun!*

Drake approached the large opening to the entrance lobby warily, first stealing a couple quick glances into the spacious room before poking his gun-barrel in. Apparently it was empty. Stepping out into the opening, he stood brazenly with his feet shoulder-width apart, scanning the room behind the barrel of his Berretta.

*No one.* He moved forward.

Passing Fred O'Neil, he admired his handiwork. Moving on, he took notice—the others had been likewise killed with artistry.

A noise came from the hallway beyond Harkin's body. Drake's attention was instantly drawn to it, as was his gun.

He heard *voices*, or a voice.

Side-stepping over Harkin's body, he stalked down the hall-way. Now he realized the voice did not belong to Grace. It was a male voice. And bursting into the room, Drake's gun-barrel fell upon the source, ready to blast it. There lay the Motorola radio on the desk, crackling out another transmission from the Coast Guard ship:

"This is United States Coast Guard Cutter 174, come in. This is United States Coast Guard Cutter 174, please come in."

Drake eased his finger off the trigger, reached over, and clicked-off the radio. As he did so, he heard another sound—that of a *Jeep* accelerating away up the access road. He hurried back into the entrance lobby and looked out the large windows just in time to see a pair of tail-lights disappear over the first hill.

*Damn it!*

Rushing back across the entrance lobby, he pushed through the heavy metal door to Control Two and went to the console. Looking out the Plexiglas, he could see the distant tail-lamps fading away over yet another hill. With a concerned glance at the wall clock, he set his handgun down on the countertop, grabbed the desk microphone, and switched it on. He keyed the frequency to the front gate.

"There's a bird flying your way," he spoke, matter-of-factly.

The surveillance monitor above was still locked-in on camera *seven*—San Roque Gate. Drake watched as the Stranger stepped out of the guard booth, looked up at the camera, and waved. Then the Stranger walked out into the middle of the road and positioned himself there, in front of the kiosk, and raised his Uzi submachine gun.

In Mobile One, Grace had heard Drake's transmission. She responded by stumping her foot further down on the gas pedal. Coming to a corner, the wheels of the Jeep started to squeal. She straightened it out and accelerated down a long straight away. She was blazing down the narrow roadway at a speed unsafe under any conditions. In the dark of night and fraught with horror, it was even more perilous. Coming on another curve, she nearly ran off a cliff into the ocean. *What are you doing?* She corrected the wheel and slowed a bit, and tried to concentrate on keeping the vehicle on the road.

Drake remained marginally confident in Station Two. On the screen remained the image of the Stranger at San Roque Gate standing dead-center in the access road with his Uzi raised and ready.

"Okay Grace, let me see you get past that!"

But in the same moment he thought said it his face went blank. If Grace had gotten out, then likely Cameron did too. And if Cameron had gotten out, *where in the Hell was he?*

Drake quickly switched to monitor two and began scrolling through the cameras. The Control Room was still empty—the chair still propped against the door. The third level hallway in the Auxiliary Building was likewise empty except for the flashing evacuation lights. Paging through the cameras one-by-one he realized it was going to take too long to do this manually. He flipped on the five remaining monitors, put each into auto-scroll mode, and let them run at a different interval. Now, with all one-hundred-and-thirty-seven surveillance cameras scrolling separately on seven different overhead flat-screens, he stood back and watched.

It didn't take long. A sudden movement on monitor *five* and Drake, with a click, froze the screen. Using the remote, he flipped back to the proper camera. There in the Auxiliary Building on level one, was Cameron, dashing past a set of transformers. Drake followed on the next camera, and as Cameron headed toward the forward stairwell and disappeared off-screen, Drake recoiled in disbelief.

"Shit! He's heading for the Control Room!"

Drake promptly snapped up his Beretta, leaped down the two steps to the door, pushed through, and flew out the rear access doors toward the power plant.

It was comical, Drake thought. Of all the people who could ruin such a well-conceived plan… Cameron? It was one of those flawed inconsistencies of life, how luck and circumstance could play a role in the outcome of fate.

Seconds later Drake was flying through the Turbine Building, en route to the rear stairwell. He was glad now he had propped the door with the chair. In fact he was applauding himself for it. Cameron was going up the wrong stairwell. He was not going to be able to get into the Control Room. Realizing that now, Drake slowed to a brisk walk. It gave him time to think. He needed time to think. He needed to consider the sequence of events to follow; if he could disable the radio system; how to lock the control rod lever in an upright position; and how he would kill Cameron. But Drake's mind was wandering, and wondering; how Cameron and Grace manage to get out of the Condenser Room? It was nothing short of a Houdini trick, he thought. As far as he knew, there was no conceivable way out. Yet somehow they had gotten out. It made him think of luck again; the randomness of it, and the inequity of it. And as much as he wanted to know how the two escaped, he realized he'd probably never know as he'd have to kill Cameron before asking. It would have to go down as one of those great mysteries in life.

# Chapter 53

At San Roque Gate, the Stranger stood waiting with his Uzi locked and loaded. As he watched for the first sign of Grace's headlights coming down the access road, he noticed a flickering of light on the hillside to his east. The shadows there on the grassy slopes pulsated. When he turned back to look, it happened again—a flickering of lights, and he saw what it was. It was the harbor lights going on and off. Across the open bay, far on the distant shore, he saw the same thing—faint lights flickering on and off.

*It's happening,* he thought.

Inside Mobile One, as Grace sped down the winding access road, coming closer to San Roque Gate, she witnessed it too. The glow of light from San Roque outlining the mountain tops to her south, flickered on and off. She squinted out the windshield into the darkness, wondering what it was, and as she did, the light-glow flickered again. Then, suddenly, it went out completely.

*Oh my God!*

In the Turbine Building, the release of pressure and steam from the Primary Loop had in fact caused the huge turbines to grind down to a slow, agonizing crawl. The generators were no longer providing the motion necessary to produce electricity. The Martian-like power towers which spanned from one hilltop to the next crackled with the sound of electricity, and then went silent. The power plant was dying. For better or for worse, its ability to produce electricity had come to an end.

Following the path of her headlamps, Grace's mind raced. She was still tormented by what she saw in the Security Building. Nearly every moment since leaving the parking lot she had spent trying to free it from her mind; trying to keep focused. She prayed it was some kind of bizarre dream, but assured herself it was not. They were all dead. Someone had killed them all, and they wanted to kill more—many more evidently.

*Can an hour get any darker?* she asked herself. *Yes, it can get so dark that there isn't any light at all, and never will be again.*

Cameron was never far from her thoughts. She imagined him alone in the power plant, her faithful soldier, doing what he could to rescue the beleaguered plant. She imagined the path he would be taking now, to the Control Room, one that she knew well; through the turbine room, across the generator room, and then to the forward stairwell. She prayed it would be free and clear of danger—of Drake and his counterparts, of harmful radiation, but she was not too optimistic.

*He'll make it, won't he?* Her eyebrows crinkled deeply. *He has to!*

She recalled the moment earlier that night when they had walked from the containment structure and she had seen Drake approaching, smiling, and then lifting his gun quickly. Cameron's quick reactions had saved their lives. He possessed the qualities needed to survive such an ordeal, she thought, the ability to win over evil.

*But Drake! That pathological, wire-rimmed murderer!* Grace felt her stomach churning at the thought of his arrogant face. *And God knows how many friends he has with him?*

*I've gotta get help, now!*

Grace went hard on the gas pedal. Negotiating her way through the last winding section of road with screeching tires, she then came out onto another straight-away, punched it, and the V-8 engine purred as the Jeep powered ahead over eighty miles per hour.

The hills to the south remained dark. San Roque, as well as the other coastal cities, was completely blacked-out. The entire central coast was dark. Aside from her headlights, and the starlight, the only external light she could see was the faint glow of the power plant in her rearview mirror. It remained lit for now, powered by the emergency generators.

A few last sharp turns and the road straightened once more. Grace leaned forward into the windshield. Far ahead were the approaching lights of the guard booth at San Roque Gate. Grace gunned it.

Before the toll-bar at the kiosk, the brawny Stranger stood brazenly in the middle of the road, his Uzi submachinegun up and ready. The gun was still slung from his shoulder tucked securely beneath his massive right arm, tight against his side with the barrel barely extending beyond his massive chest. His left hand held the upper part of the barrel down, in a way to keep it from rising on discharge. It was aimed up the access road at the approaching headlights of Mobile One.

Grace could see him ahead. Not sure at first who it was, she quickly surmised it was not Marvin. The guy was too damn big for one, and his stance was threatening; and it gave the appearance that he wanted to stop her. Also Grace had heard Drake's radio message; an obvious signal to an awaiting cohort.

As the Jeep rapidly closed distance, Grace could tell by the size of the figure it was definitely not Marvin. And she could see now, that he held something in his hand, pointed directly at her!

Suddenly, the Uzi opened fire.

*Rat-Tat-Tat-Tat-Tat!!*

The grill of the patrol Jeep burst apart; the lower plastic bumper shredding into many pieces, as did the left headlamp assembly. Bullets also cracked across the hood and up across windshield, just as Grace ducked. Keeping her head low, she tried to sneak a peek to maintain her bearing. But as she did, the bark of the Uzi sung out again, and she heard the pinging sounds of bullets racking the front end of the Jeep, and cracking through the windshield.

In her mind she saw only one thing, someone trying to keep her from getting the help Cameron needed.

*You can't stop me! I won't let you stop me!*

Her foot floored the gas pedal. The needle on the RPM meter spiked as the engine roared ahead.

"Die you Dirty Bastard!" Grace screamed, to the sound of the rapidly accelerating Jeep.

There was a brief chorus of Uzi bursts; then *BANG!* the Jeep hit the Stranger squarely. A thud and crunch of breaking bones sounded as he careened off the hood and flew behind the Jeep, tumbling lifelessly to the road. Instantaneously with the impact, the Jeep crashed through the toll-gate sending splinters of wood arching skyward.

Grace lifted her head and slammed the brakes just in time to avert running the Jeep into the bay. The Jeep skidded sideways across the Coast Road, straightened, and then accelerated east. Grace looked back. She could not see the Stranger laid-out on the road, but she knew she had done him considerable damage. She went further down on the pedal, heading swiftly down the Coast Road toward San Roque.

# Chapter 54

Cameron's path to the Control Room had been marred by various obstacles; and he had yet to reach the blocked doorway. Passing through the Generator Room via what he believed to be the quickest route to the forward stairwell, he rounded a corner directly into a flashing warning sign: *DO NOT ENTER - RADIATION CONTAMINATION*. He wisely chose to find an alternate route. Further down he heard the power plant moaning loudly like a sinking ship, the sound of twisting metal and crunching beams, which caused him to back-track again. Finally reaching the fourth-level, breathless, he rushed across the foyer, grabbed and turned the knob on the Control Room door, and pushed, but it wouldn't budge. Peering in through the small viewing window, he couldn't see it was propped shut. He tried to look down, but the angle did not give him a view. He tried ramming the door, driving his shoulder hard into it, but it still refused to budge.

Through the window, he saw mayhem among the gauges and meters on the switchboard, each now responding to unprecedented readings of pressure and heat. Less than twenty feet away were the control-rod levers—the levers which could avert an all-out nuclear disaster. They seemed so close but so far. Across the room, his eyes fell on the rear access door. Cameron remembered using this door during training sessions, but it was not a viable option now. To reach it meant dropping all the way back down four levels, down to the area of flashing contamination lights; then, crossing over to the other side of the building, and re-ascending the rear stairwell.

*Too much time, even if it were possible.*

A voice suddenly called from above.

Cameron glanced skyward.

It was Drake summoning over the PA system, accessing it via the broadcast feature on his Motorola hand-held.

"Hey Cameron," his voice said. "It's too late. There's no stopping it. This baby's going down, and so are you."

*Great!* Cameron thought.

Time seemed to freeze, morphing into a slow-motion dream. The panicked cries of the switchboard alarms swept through Cameron as his mind desperately searched for alternatives. Not only would the door on the other side take too long, but he'd likely encounter Drake en route, and Drake had a gun and he did not. He looked around to see if there was something he could use to ram the door, but there was nothing. *There had to be another way?*

As is usually the case in moments like these, the revelation hit him suddenly, out of the blue. His eyes flashed skyward to the ceiling panels.

*Of course, the ventilation ducts!*

He recalled the ventilation system by which he and Jack had gained access above the Training Room nearly eight months ago; there where they had listened in on Harkin's training plans during the contingency drills and war games.

Cameron dashed down the hallway, kicked out the tin cover panel to the access closet and ducking down into the central ventilation shaft, climbed vertically. Shimming his way up above the ceiling, he went horizontally through a square tunnel barely large enough to get his shoulders through. Reaching the spot above the training room podium where the vent screen was located, he punched it out with his elbow and dropped to the floor, landing on all fours. Rising to his feet, he was greeted with the shocking view of the dead crewmen piled against the far wall.

*Bastard!*

Cameron could do nothing for them, he knew. The only thing he could do now was try to prevent more death. He bolted out the door into the Control Room. He did so to the screaming sounds of evacuation wobblers and flashing lights. As he rushed past the Plexiglas windows of Control One, he saw Lewis lying dead on the floor. *A gun!* he thought. He pushed in through the door, checked his pulse, and fumbled with his utility belt. He quickly strapped the belt, with its radio and assortment of ammunition clips, around his waist.

"Sorry, buddy."

Pulling the Beretta from its holster, he checked it—the clip was full. Slapping the clip back in, he cocked the weapon back, and dashed out to the switchboard.

The switchboard was a sight to behold. Lit up like a Time Square marquee, it displayed a colorful array of flashing lights and strobes, and ringing from the control panel was a chaotic cry of bells and buzzers. At first glance, Cameron was stunned by the panicked cries. The temperature meters were pegged now, all the way down, well over one-thousand degrees Fahrenheit. The built-in Geiger counters monitoring the radiation levels around each reactor core, were chattering in rapid vibrato. The seismograph needle was etching out a tall plateau of activity.

Above, the large viewing screen of Containment One was completely white—steam had entirely engulfed the interior dome.

Cameron's eyes turned urgently left. There stood the control-rod levers; slanted slightly forward on the control panel at the precise angle they had been set several hours earlier by the operational crew. The throttle-like grips were positioned side-by-side and fixed at the same latitude. Beside them were the simplified instructions: UP ARROW to withdraw; DOWN-ARROW to lower.

*DOWN!* Cameron thought, immediately.

Cameron leaped to the levers, and just as he grabbed them, a sudden noise came from behind. He turned in time to see Drake coming through that rear doorway with his gun in hand, raising it and aiming it directly at him.

Drake, having flown up the rear stairwell with the same perfect timing he had efficiently maintained all night, popped through the door catching Cameron entirely off-guard. Cameron was awkwardly turned with his back toward him, having to look over his left shoulder just to see him. Though Drake was surprised to see that Cameron had somehow gotten into the Control Room, it didn't matter.

Drake fired instantly, in his usual two-shot burst.

*BAM! BAM!*

In the millisecond that elapsed, Cameron found himself dazed on the floor. The first bullet had ripped into his shoulder, knocking him down. The second bullet dug a hole in the control panel just behind him. His body had reacted on instinct. Ducking down while simultaneously bringing up his handgun up from beneath his stomach, he had squeezed off two shots in Drake's direction without even knowing it, causing Drake to take cover and affording him the valuable seconds to drag himself behind a desk.

On the far side of the room, Drake was seething. *Again!* he had squandered his moment of surprise. It was twice now he had Cameron dead in his sights, and twice now let him live.

Drake mulled his situation from behind a tall file cabinet.

*Such a fool!*

He had hit pay dirt with the first shot, he knew, although was unsure of the exact damage he had caused. Cameron had gone down so quickly, it was hard to tell. Now he was wounded somewhere on the floor just beyond the crewmen desks. It was the only cover available in the center of the room, although Cameron could make a break for Control One and find cover behind the bullet-proof glass.

*What to do next?* Drake's eyes furtively searched for a plan. *Perhaps a flanking maneuver?* It had worked well on Rae Anderson.

He knew Cameron was as good as any marksman, and likewise as good at coming up with surprises of his own. He was exactly the kind of chess player Drake despised—the type any trained and disciplined player loathed because he never took the expected move.

*Do nothing,* Drake finally thought.

Time was on his side. The Plant was in meltdown mode, and there was nothing Cameron could do about it. Cameron was trapped behind a desk, Drake had a clear shot at the switchboard and control-rod levers, and Cameron could not reach them without getting a bullet in his back.

Drake grinned.

From the floor, wounded but not disabled, Cameron was thinking the same thing. He looked up at the switchboard behind him—the control-rod levers were still upright. He was hoping that maybe in that crazed moment before the gunfire, he had managed to drop them. But evidently, he hadn't.

He dragged himself further behind Chief Stewart's desk and reversed his position. Peeking around the backside of the desk, he still couldn't see Drake.

He considered a rush for the control rod levers, preceded by a hail of bullets in Drake's direction, but realized he was in no condition to make such a leap. The sharp pain is his shoulder told him so. He looked down at his blood-splattered shirt. It was a bullet wound all right. With all the excitement, he wasn't sure if he'd been hit or grazed or just hurt himself hitting the floor.

In that moment of pause that always comes in a gun battle, and always seems to last forever but never does, both men regrouped. Drake checked his ammunition clip on reflex—he still had thirteen unspent rounds. Cameron inched further toward the corner of the desk.

"It's all come down to the two of us," Drake finally said from across the room. "You know that, don't you?"

Cameron didn't reply. His eyes were searching.

Drake peeked around the file cabinet. "Cameron," his voice continued with a cold chuckle. "You never impressed me as the kind of guy who would die for the company store." As Drake spoke, he continued maneuvering himself from behind one tall file cabinet to another, trying to reach a position where he could see Cameron. "As for me," he went on. "I'll die only for money."

*Bullshit!* Cameron thought. It was more than money Drake wanted. He had always been someone who looked beyond money, that much Cameron would give him. For Drake, it was the love of one's self that drove him. No different than the government operatives who sold secrets to the Russians during the cold war, Drake's prize was in the ability to out-wit; that inner need to prove one's superiority; to be the front-runner in a game where death was nobler than losing.

*I can't just sit here,* Cameron thought.

Cameron felt a bizarre numbness in his shoulder. Glancing down at it again, he saw the blood oozing through his shirt in rhythmic pulses. All around him were signs of urgency; the flashing evacuation lights, the warbling alarms, the control-rod levers still upright. Here he was with his life slowly draining from his shoulder and Drake just across the room waiting for any chance to finish him.

As he lay there trying to keep his mind from fading, his dream suddenly came back to him—the flash-vision of the Indian Warrior mounted on his horse, rearing above the blowing reeds with eyes boring down on him, arousing him to action.

*It is time to be the Warrior,* Cameron thought.

He glanced back at the control-rod levers. *So much for premonitions, this is fate.*

Cameron quickly formulated a plan. Inching forward to the very edge of the desk, he readied his pistol, grasping the handle tightly in one hand and holding a finger above his radio transmitter with the other. With a deep breath, he reached down for his Motorola and *keyed* the transmitter, twice.

Immediately, from across the room came the sound. *Buzz, Buzz.*

Drake's attention was instantly drawn to the sound emitting from his utility belt, and as he looked down at it, a blue flash rolled out across the tile floor before him. Glancing up, he saw it was Cameron, already fully extended behind his handgun.

For once this night, the two-shot blast of a Beretta came from a gun other than Drake's. *BAM! BAM!* Cameron squeezed off two shots. Drake reeled backward, falling awkwardly to the floor. His gun slid out of his hand and across the tile floor. He twitched for a second and then laid there motionless.

Cameron watched him for several seconds, warily keeping his gun aimed at him. When he was satisfied he was no longer breathing he dropped his head to the tile floor. The adrenaline rush was over. The moment of battle gave way to fatigue. Cameron closed his eyes and just lay there, seeing it all happen again—Drake turning, aiming, with eyes alight, then dropping suddenly to the double-crack of his pistol.

*It's over.*

Cameron laid there beneath the fluorescent ceiling lights until the crying distress sirens summoned him—bringing him back to place and time. He raised his head and looked around. The flashing-yellow strobe lights shot discothèque-like rays across the room and the alarm bells rung out belligerently.

*Have to get up.* He spoke to himself in absolutes. *Must get up! Have to get to the control-rod levers!*

He stood, wavering, feeling the blood drain from his head. He concentrated on keeping his balance, but everything around him seemed to be swaying. Drake, a blurry image on the floor, lay with his wire-rimmed glasses sideways across his face, his out-stretched hand unable to reach the gun that had killed so many. The overhead strobes seemed to be fading into slow motion. Even the bullet wound to his shoulder seemed to have lost its pinch. He looked down and saw blood spattered down the length of his thigh.

Behind him, the gauges and dials on the operational switch-board called out their urgency, struggling to maintain a semblance of order in a Picasso-like assortment of colorful lights.

He staggered toward the odd-looking set of handles, one step, two steps, then three and four, and reaching them, with an exhausted sigh, he dropped each one down until the handle could go no further. He hung there for a moment, resting his body weight on the levers.

Deep within the containment domes, the tethered control rods lowered instantly into the honeycombed fuel assemblies of each reactor core. The effect was immediate. Millions of sub-atomic particles, bouncing in an uncontrollable frenzy, were instantly absorbed and neutralized. Precisely as they were designed to do, the control-rods ended the fission process. Within moments, the steam searing out of the spaghetti-like pipes on the core housings began to subside.

Cameron lifted his head and looked over at the exit.

*If you want to live, if you want to see Grace again, you have to move, and move now!*

He staggered to the door, kicking the chair out that blocked it, stumbled down the hallway, and down the first set of steps in the forward stairwell, barely able to cling to the rail. The flashing warning lights were vivid reminders of his urgent situation. Although the reactors had been shut down, the damage they had sustained was unknown, and the amount of radiation leakage, if any, unmeasured. With Grace still on his mind, he drove forward, but the blistering vapors which filled the stairwell were suffocating. He told himself one thing and one thing only; he must get out of this steam-swamped matchbox and breathe clean, fresh ocean air again.

The good news was that he had made it this far. He had defeated Drake, had dropped the control rods, and had descended two levels. The bad news was that he was already feeling nauseous—an early symptom of *radiation poisoning*. In his mind he was hoping it was related to the gunshot wound and not the former. He had lost a lot of blood nonetheless, and nausea was likewise a symptom of trauma. *It had to be.*

# Chapter 55

It was 5:20 a.m.

Grace had made it to San Roque, only to find everything closed. Not being a municipality, it didn't have its own police department. The County Sheriff covered the area, and their nearest office was over the hill in the larger city of Santa DeRosa. Her cell phone and change was in her purse back in her locker at the power plant, so she couldn't even make a telephone call.

Feeling desperate, Grace had gone screaming at the doors of a couple apartments, but no one would answer. Wasting another ten minutes running through the bait shops on Front Street, she hoped to find an early fisherman, but there were none. She had already decided to make the additional twenty minute drive to the Sheriffs Office in Santa DeRosa when her vehicle radio began to speak.

From the moment Grace had hit the Coast Road, crashing through San Roque gate, she had made repeated distress calls on Mobile One's vehicle radio. She had tried switching frequencies, and tried the 'auto-search' feature that was supposed to lock onto the strongest signal, but had no luck in getting a reply. Now finally, someone was answering.

"Mobile One, Mobile One, this is the California Department of Forestry. We received a Code Three distress call from Mal Loma Nuclear Power Plant. Please confirm."

Before Grace could answer, the radio spoke again, a different voice. "Ten-Four, this is the Bonita County Fire Department. I received the same, Come in."

Grace grabbed the radio microphone from its rack with a shaking hand and screamed into it. "CODE THREE! Mal Loma Power Plant Under Siege! I repeat! The Power Plant is under siege! At least five people DEAD! Help!"

"Ten-four! We are mobilizing," the voice from the Department of Forestry came back, followed immediately by a similar message from the Bonita County Fire Department.

Already halfway en route to Santa DeRosa, Grace slammed on the brakes. Before sliding to a complete stop, she swung the wheel around, punched the accelerator, and the Jeep made a screeching fish-tail-turn back toward San Roque Gate and Port Miguel.

Within a minute, there were six different agencies locked into her frequency, simultaneously responding, each trying to get information from Grace.

"Ten-four" "What is your twenty?" "Exactly what happened?" "How many assailants are there?" "How do you know the Power Plant is under siege?"

Grace stared at the radio in disbelief. Then she keyed the transceiver and yelled back into the microphone: "Because they *BLEW* the *DAMN* thing up!"

There was a brief moment of radio silence as the various dispatchers digested her message, followed by a new voice, that of a woman, calm and sure: "This is Central Dispatch. All agencies please clear this frequency. Santa Clarita County Sheriffs Department will coordinate all communications and response. Stay tuned and contact Central Dispatch for all coordinating efforts." There was another pause, and then the calm female voice continued. "Fire and sheriff personnel are already responding. The National Guard has been mobilized, as well as the Coast Guard. Mobile One, what is your twenty?"

Grace looked out the window into the pre-dawn light, trying to get her bearings. She keyed the transceiver. "I'm on the Coast Road, somewhere between San Roque and Port Miguel. I'm en route back to the main entrance gate."

"We need you to return to San Roque," the dispatcher said. "Officers will meet you there for a debriefing."

"Sorry, I can't do that!"

"You need to be debriefed," the voice said.

*Bullshit!* Grace tossed the radio to the passenger-side floorboards.

"Mobile One, do you read me?" the dispatcher's voice came back, speaking from the floor.

Grace reached over and clicked off the radio while stomping further down on the accelerator. The Jeep's engine purred as the needle on the speedometer climbed steadily.

Outside, the dawn was coming fast, its crimson aura gathering offshore. But the road was still black, lit only in segmental portions by the street lamps.

Grace could think only of Cameron. Her heart was pounding, and she felt an overwhelming sense of anxiety inside. "I am with you, my love," she said, out loud. "Stay with me."

The dissolving veil of night seemed to evaporate even more quickly as she motored closer to the gate. Within minutes, Grace arrived, along with dawn's early light. A host of emergency vehicles had already gathered there with their lights flashing. There was a small crowd of policemen, a couple *HAZMAT* officials, some fishermen, and a lone news reporter who had the fortune of a sleepless night and had been tuned-in to the police scanner.

As Grace slowed, she saw an ambulance on the left shoulder. In the dim light, two policemen were pulling Marvin's body out of the trunk of the Cadillac.

Grace gasped. She didn't know who it was, of course. The sight of another familiar regal-blue uniform, laid out like dead, was shocking enough. She saw enough death for one night. Seeing another fallen co-worker only made her ill, and to think of Cameron, still alone in the power plant against unknown odds, nearly eight miles away.

Up at the guard booth, detectives were taking inventory of the carnage. They had already wrapped up the Stranger on the emergency stretcher kept available at the gate; his head covered in a blue wool blanket. They had removed him in haste to get a patrol car past and up the access road. An outline of where his body had fallen had been spray-painted on the asphalt.

The Lieutenant in charge was trying to make sense of it all. At first he thought the Stranger was the fallen guard assigned to the gate. But then he received the radio call from his men down at the Cadillac. *Two guards? Not likely.*

"Hey Lieutenant," called a finely dressed young detective from the grass on the shoulder of the access road. He stood ten yards away from the broken kiosk, holding the Stranger's Uzi up in one hand. "Check this out." The weapon was not a standard weapon used in the security at Mal Loma, he knew, nor was it the type of weapon commonly used by law enforcement anywhere in state. It was a weapon used by criminals, thugs, and terrorists.

Surrounding the gate were several police cars parked on the shoulder with engines running and ready. The officers were all eager to storm up the road to the power plant, to engage the enemy, but for now had orders to stay put. Still fresh in the young Lieutenant's mind were visions of cops and firemen storming up the stairwells of the Twin Towers. Sending troops into a wind-powered wave of ionizing gamma rays would only result in similar disaster; a pile of crashed police vehicles with blistered patrol officers inside. They were waiting for the Plant executives, the Security Director, the Sheriff himself, and the radiological experts from Hazmat with their radiation detection gear and Geiger counters. No one knew the extent of the damage, nor the hazards which lay ahead. Their protocol was to assume the worst—the entire area was radioactively contaminated. A perimeter needed to be established, both to keep out curious bystanders, and for establishing, via a ring of Geiger counters, any evidence of radiological particles in the wind. The one patrol car that was sent up the road had been done so on specific orders, to provide a *visual* only, and as soon as possible. The other officers were needed for now for the quarantine.

In the meantime the San Francisco office of the NRC had been notified, the local National Guard had dispatched four helicopters from their nearby base and executives of the Pacific Alliance Power Company were already on the tarmac at SFO climbing into a Lear jet. Offshore, the Coast Guard cutter which had received the tail-end of Grace's earlier unconfirmed distress call was now slicing its way through the morning swells around Point Honda in a direct route toward the power plant. They had issued an all-ships bulletin more than an hour ago—primarily for 'Information Only'—to stop any incoming and outgoing vessels within a twenty-mile radius of the power plant. They had since heard further confirmation with Grace's panicked transmissions to the Santa Clara Sheriff's dispatcher. Now, seeing the distant steam clouds, they knew it was the real thing and no hoax.

Grace inched forward in Mobile One, trying to part the crowd at the foot of the gate's main entrance.

*Come' on, come' on.*

She honked the horn, getting restless. Rolling down the window, she cried out, "Get out of the way! Please move! I have to get through!"

Through the windshield, she watched as the crowd slowly parted to a single, uniformed police officer, who stood with arms spread-eagle across the hood of her Jeep.

Grace leaned out the driver's window. "I have to get through!"

"Back up lady!" was the officer's reply.

He noticed the front of the vehicle was completely riddled with bullet holes and had cracks across the windshield. "Stop Lady! Pull the vehicle over there, now!" He pointed to an open space on the shoulder of the road.

"I work here! I have to get through!" Grace insisted.

The officer wasn't buying it.

Grace revved the engine and inched forward, trying to nudge the police officer out of her way, pushing him backwards.

"Hey! Hey! Lady, Stop!"

Determined beyond reason, Grace continued forward, defiantly, and just as the front end of the Jeep nosed passed the officer, she floored it and sped up toward the gate. The officer simultaneously slammed the palm of his hand down hard on the hood as she surged past, as if it would somehow get her attention, but Grace was so singled-minded she didn't really even notice him, or what he said or did.

As the Jeep went past, the officer recognized the colors and model, and saw the emblem on the side. He knew for sure now, it was one of the power plant's patrol Jeeps.

"Get back here!" the officer cried.

Grace didn't look back. She was a woman on a mission, with a singular, unrelenting focus. She was going back to the power plant, back to Cameron's side, at any cost. They'd have to shoot her to stop her.

The officer immediately keyed his radio transceiver with the thought of radioing ahead.

At the guard booth, the detectives turned their heads in astonishment as Grace flew past. The Jeep crunched over the wooden fragments of the toll barrier and accelerated up the access road.

The Lieutenant's radio signaled. It was the police officer down at the foot of the entrance road.

"A woman just went past in a power plant Jeep."

"No kidding," was the Lieutenant's reply.

# Chapter 56

Twenty miles north, four National Guard helicopters thundered down the coastline looking like a horde of mad dragonflies. There was no need for a GPS reading. Hugging the uneven contour of the coast, they were taking the most direct route toward the besieged power plant. Though the broad shoulder of the coastal mountains kept them from seeing what lay ahead, they could see smoke-clouds on the rise, had heard all the mornings' dispatches, and knew it had to be something serious to have pulled them from their beds so early.

Dawn's light revealed a vacant mountaintop where the Sniper had been. Nothing remained except some cigarette butts and the black tarp, which the wind gradually blew toward the eastern edge. A final gust sent it airborne and it soared down into the deep, sycamore-filled Miguelleto Canyon. The cove where Emil and Ramzan had beached their Zodiac sea-craft hours before was empty. The tide had come in and washed away their tracks from the sand. They had departed back north nearly three hours before, narrowly escaping the Coast Guard's "All-Ships" bulletin.

In the Entrance Lobby, golden slivers of light reached in through the front windows illuminating the bodies of Fred, Rae Anderson, Jimmy Becker and Supervisor Harkin. They lay eerily quiet where they had fallen. On the blacktop near the eastern side of the perimeter fence, long morning shadows stretched across the bodies of Harrington and Johnston, one lying on top of the other. Likewise was the scene in the southeast quadrant where Peters' fallen body was revealed in the early light.

From offshore, on the decks of the Coast Guard cutter, the early light revealed a crippled and smoldering power plant. Steam simmered from the blown pipes into the morning sky. The huge, Trojan-helmet-like containment domes were shadowed by the steam-clouds rising along their flanks, through which sunlight was beginning to brighten their rounded tops.

Cameron staggered through the open field between the perimeter fence and the cliff's edge above the Discharge Bay. Having made it out of the power plant and through the hole cut in the ocean-side of the fence, he gazed back at the white clouds bellowing up into the morning sky. The power plant loomed as a stark reminder of a night gone terribly bad.

Dazed and disoriented, he mumbled to himself. *Have to get home. Have to find my way back home.*

He had lost plenty of blood, but knew the shoulder wound was not fatal. *Sore and painful, but not fatal.* He had taken a moment to flex his left hand upon exiting the Turbine Building. It seemed to work fine. It was this other feeling inside that concerned him, this dreadful feeling, which seemed to be compounding by the second. His head was throbbing and he felt nauseous. Twice now he had stopped to throw up, but could not seem to muster up anything. Also, there was a ringing in the ears, and he found himself having to pause to remind himself where he was and what had happened, and what he must do now—to get as far away from the power plant as possible. Looking down, he noticed his arms were sunburned, but there had been no sun, and his face and neck were likewise feeling the effects of too much sun. *But it had been night?*

The grim reality settled in. He had been exposed to gamma rays, *and these were thermal burns, so it must have been a fairly strong dose too.* In the days and weeks that would follow, assuming he would survive even an hour, the amount of exposure, and type of exposure, would determine his fate. Thanks to Chief Stewart's informative lectures, Cameron knew the dreadful signs, and the fatal digression which would follow. What he saw and felt now, was not promising. But he wanted to stay optimistic. He had to stay optimistic.

Cameron stopped and pulled from his wallet a small clear receptacle containing three pills. They were potassium iodide (KI), 130 milligram tablets. He tried to read the instructions on the back:

| | | |
|---|---|---|
| Adults 18 Years and Older | …… | One Tablet |
| Pregnant or Nursing Women | …… | One Tablet |
| Adolescents 12-18 Year Old | …… | Half to One Tablet |
| Children 3-13 Year Old | …… | Half Tablet |
| Children 1 Mo. To 3 Year Old | …… | Quarter Tablet |

But he couldn't seem to focus, nor could he concentrate on the words. Holding the receptacle up to the morning light, he could barely make out the instructions: *Take KI ONLY after direction from state or local Public Health Official.*

*What?* He broke open the seal, tossed all the tablets in his mouth, crunched them down, and swallowed them.

Before him was the sea, a blurred blue horizon gaining color with the coming light. He tried to focus on it.

*It is to the right*, he thought. *Must continue to the right.*

With all the grim news bouncing in his head, and with what concentration he had left to muster, Cameron could think of only one thing—the Bone Yard; his safe haven, his place of peace, his refuge from the modern world. Struggling now, even to put one foot in front of the other, he turned back and glared into the bright morning light, trying to get his bearings.

Looking forward again, he turned his head north.

Ahead was the protruding knoll, where the terrace hung out over the Pacific, the place the Chumash had so cleverly chosen to bury their dead. *It is the place,* Cameron thought. *It is my home. I must go there, I must go now.* As determined as Drake had been to destroy life, as resolute as Ramzan had been in wanting to spill the blood of crusaders—of those he believed had spilt the blood of his innocents; and as stubborn as Grace was now, trying to reach her beloved Cameron, Cameron was equally determined to sit once more in the blowing reeds of the Bone Yard, gaze out at the Pacific, and listen to the wind.

# Chapter 57

Somewhere beyond the midway point between San Roque Gate and the power plant, the lone police car was blazing along the access road with sirens wailing and red lights flashing. Inside the driver, a uniformed officer, gazed steadily out the windshield. For the moment, his view of the plant was blocked by the buttressing mountainside, but he could see the tall smoke-clouds above.

Coming up over a final hill, the ominous sight of the power plant suddenly rose in his windshield.

*Whoa!*

He stomped the brake peddle, turned the wheel to the right, and pulled over on to the shoulder.

Before him, huge plumes of smoke bellowed skyward, rising into the stratosphere into what appeared to be a towering nebulous cloud, the upper portions of which was now lit golden by the rising sunlight which peeked above the eastern mountaintops. Leaning further into the windshield to the full view of it, he could see a violent torrent of steam twisting up from the tops of the two containment structures. In the distance was the vague sound of sirens and wobblers.

He fumbled for the radio.

A mile back, Grace was flying down the same access road at the speed of light. She had that grim feeling, when the past begins looking brighter than the future. Tears had formed in her eyes and as one now rolled down her cheek, she wiped it off with the back of her hand.

"I love you. I love you so much!" she mumbled.

Although the sun had not completely crested the eastern hills from where she was, it was providing plenty of light now, and she could see the plumes of smoke too rising in the distance. It was a disaster.

*A doomsday cloud*, she thought.

Grace stared up at the cloud full of dread. As she did, the Jeep's tires skidded precariously close to the bluff's edge, nearly leaping off into the crashing waves below. Correcting the wheel, she promptly pulled the Jeep back onto the pavement.

*Keep steady!*

Coming out on to a straight-a-way again, she accelerated directly toward the ominous cloud.

She envisioned Cameron's face. She saw his eyes looking into hers. *I am asking you to be safe. I am pleading for you to be safe. I am begging you!*

In her mind she started thinking about God. She was not an overtly religious person. She had been raised Catholic and had always kept her faith there in reserve, for when she needed it. She thought back about a time when she was a little girl and she prayed by her bedside for her pet terrier after the dog had been struck by a car. The poor animal lay limp, looking dead, and the veterinarian had given it no hope. But after some prayer, the dog miraculously came back to life. He went on to live a full life, many years romping in the sun. As an adult Grace hadn't relied much on prayer, but had always believed in it and knew it was there, saved up like time in a bottle in case she ever needed it.

Well, she needed it now. That one seemingly miracle in her youth—God's gift to a child—was on Grace's mind, and she was thinking if it worked then, it should work equally as well now.

"I'll be a good girl," she promised, muttering. "I'll give to charity. I'll visit my grandmother twice a week…"

Then she spoke in her mind as if Cameron were beside her. *I am coming my love. Soon I'll be at your side.*

Back up the access road, the patrolman had exited his car and now stood in the small space between the open car door and the vehicle itself with a radio in his hand, its extension cord coiling out from the vehicle. His jaw was still gaping. White smoke continued to roar and balloon out from the rear of the Auxiliary Building, in dramatic fashion, and the forces of nature seemed to have taken over. The wind-driven cloud was moving decidedly eastward.

He had just radioed-in his observations back to the main gate, and was waiting for further orders when the radio crackled with the Lieutenant's voice:

"There's a blue, Jeep Cherokee coming your way. Block the road and stop it!"

Suddenly, while the officer was still holding the radio in his hand, Mobile One came ripping over the hilltop and zoomed past him, heading down the final strip of access road toward the power plant. All the patrolman could do was give it a double take.

"Sorry. I think it just went past!" he said. "Do you want me to pursue?"

"Shit!" the Lieutenant's voice slipped. "No. Do not pursue! I repeat. Do not pursue!"

The four National Guard helicopters were now approaching the crippled power plant from the *north,* coming in low above the crashing waves and white sandstone cliffs. As they swept past the cove where the Zodiac had been, they crossed over the large, projecting brow of the marine terrace. Skimming low, narrowly above the carpeted earth, the downdraft from their rotors flattened a path through the shore grass.

As they breached the promontory the power plant emerged in full view in the cockpit of the lead helicopter. Shining in the morning sunlight were the magnificent domes of Mal Loma, and rising from the base of each were the large columns of twisting steam.

The pilot was awestruck.

"It's definitely been hit," he spoke loudly into his headset. "And by the looks of things, some kind of catastrophic anomaly has occurred. You'd better get *Hazmat* out here. And they'd better bring protection."

Looking back to observe his position in relation to the other helicopters, he spoke again into the headset, "Stay clear of the smoke, boys. It could be nasty stuff."

Three of the helicopters broke from the coast and stormed directly east toward the power plant, carving wind-blown corridors through the grass. The lead helicopter continued south, following the contour of the coastline. Ahead, the pilot saw something stumbling across the terrace. It was a small blue speck, apparently heading for the bluff's edge. As the pilot came in close, he dipped down and could see clearly it was a person in blue uniform. Swinging past, the pilot waved his hand up and down, but the person did not seem to acknowledge in any way.

Cameron glared up as the helicopter swept past, blinded momentarily by the morning sunlight which now fully crested the eastern mountaintop. He felt the powerful wind-gusts from its rotors pushing down on him, and then they seemed to vanish. He continued across the grass, groggily, staggering, stumbling, and finally collapsing in the tall reeds. Rolling over on his back, he laid there looking up through the grass into the morning sunlight. The rays seemed to come down as if heaven-sent, splintered and partially filtered by the huge steam cloud. There was the whistling of wind, which sounded appeasing as it sung through the reeds, and as he laid there listening to it, he let the wind ease his pummeled mind. He was absolutely exhausted.

The pain in his shoulder had gone completely numb. Despite the crippling effects of radiation exposure, the damage to his organs he knew it had caused, he was without pain. He lay there flat on his back smiling, letting the wind caress him; letting it dance through his dark-brown hair and toss it across his forehead. Above the sky changed colors. The rays of light seemed to contort into hues as if through a prism and the stratosphere beyond was gaining in its tint of blue.

Offshore, the U.S. Coast Guard Cutter sliced across the calm morning swells, coming within a mile of the power plant. The Captain stood on the bridge with his First Officer. Although they each held binoculars in their hands, there was no need for them now. The disaster was spelt out blatantly before them, as if in neon lights. Now they could see the four National Guard helicopters buzzing around the Plant. They watched as the one rogue copter swung around against the blinding sun, and came back toward the windswept promontory where Cameron lay.

Three miles back on the access road, a long, slow train of fire trucks, police cars, Hazmat vans, and emergency vehicles headed steadily, though cautiously, toward the power plant. The pre-stationed gamma ray detectors strategically positioned around the property's 'Protective Action Zone Three,' a six-mile radius surrounding the Plant, had not registered any unusual readings, but the visual provided by the patrolman, the National Guard, and the Coast Guard had given them reason for concern. Encountering armed terrorists would be one thing, coming against a wave of invisible gamma rays; quite another. Out front was the *Hazmat's* rad-detection vehicle with its built-in, sophisticated radiation sniffers and recording equipment. The slightest reading of an errant gamma particle would cause the entire entourage to halt and retreat.

Inland, across the green fields and oak-studded hillsides, and the canyons filled with sycamores, all along the Coast Highway and within the cities of San Roque, Port San Miguel, and

Santa DeRosa, the huge, fog-horn shaped sirens mounted on telephone poles began to bellow-out a slow, wailing cry reminiscent of World War II air-raid sirens. The Plant's early warning system had been manually set off by the local authorities.

Citizens throughout the Central Coast awoke looking skyward. Although they were accustomed to regularly-scheduled alarm testing, never before had they heard them so early, nor continue to wail past the normal duration of a test. The regional power outage had gone unnoticed by most until rising from bed and flipping on a light switch or trying to make a pot of coffee. *An alarm test coinciding with a blackout?* It was abnormal.

Inside Mobile One, Grace was in a state of panic. As she roared over the last hill down toward the Security Building still trying to hold back her tears, she struggled to gain a view through the windshield through watery eyes, having to wipe them frequently. Ahead she could see the helicopters buzzing around the containment domes. Being beneath it now, the vapor-cloud seemed even more colossal, reaching up into the heavens practically. In the parking lot out front were still the vehicles of her co-workers, including her car, and Cameron's little Honda sedan.

A hundred thoughts blasted through her mind, foremost of which was where to start looking. If Cameron had gotten out of the plant, he would have jumped into his car and high-tailed it out of there. *Surely he had gotten himself out of the plant. Right? But what if he had not?*

Grace was struck with the grim notion that he may still be inside, wounded and needing her help, or worse yet, trapped in some radiation-engulfed place where he could not get out and she could not gain access. With the number of hours that had passed, with a skilled-killer on the loose, and with the plant now looking like a radiation factory, her thoughts sank into the deepest cavern of self-doubt. Although she fought to deny it, there was the possibility that he had not survived the night at all. And if he did, he may have been mortally exposed. Further, she knew, she may have to brave radiation to rescue him.

She barreled downhill, watching the helicopters overhead. Her instinct was to rush to the Security Building and the power plant; to search every crack and cranny until she found him, regardless of the risk.

The one lone helicopter now hovered above the coastal terrace beyond the power plant to the north. At first sight of it, Grace felt angry. *What the hell is he doing? He should be searching the Plant for survivors, for Cameron!* Then she realized the helicopter was setting down.

A light came to her eyes. *The Bone Yard!*

It is the place Cameron would go, Grace thought, *his refuge among the modern!*

And as she continued to watch, she saw the helicopter descending upon the protruding knoll as if it had found something, or someone.

*Of course, the Bone Yard! It's where he is! It's where he'd go!*

She imagined Cameron sitting there, in the tall shore grass, above the crashing waves. She knew very well he loved this place, oddly there among the bones of the dead. As the helicopter lowered down, staying steady above the reeds, Grace watched it faithfully. Her eyes brightened with hope. It just remained hovering, a few meters above the reeds.

*Among the bones of dead Indians? It has to be Cameron, crazy Cameron!*

Still not certain but feeling increasingly optimistic, she floored the gas pedal, zipping straight past the parking lot and Security Building. The Jeep skidded along the access road that paralleled the perimeter fence, there between the power plant and the ocean, past the hole in the chain-link fence cut by Ramzan and Emil, and vaulted off the end of the pavement onto the dirt road, fish-tailing nearly out of control. Straightening the wheel, Grace came down again on the gas pedal, hard. The

Jeep bounced violently in a cloud of smoke at a recklessly high speed, sometimes going airborne above the dirt on toward the Bone Yard.

Overwhelmed with a multitude of emotions; *fear, regret, loss, hope, and love;* Grace kept nodding her head affirmatively, as if to convince herself it was true: Cameron had gotten out, he was okay, and that he was there lounging in the Bone Yard among his dead friends. Her deepest passions, fueled by that wild streak of his—that inner magic that he possessed, gave her promise. She was hoping now, praying, that somehow that craziness, that magic, had carried him through this dreadful night, and down to the cliffs above the Pacific.

The rogue helicopter treaded air above Cameron. He lay there just below it, looking nearly dead, stretched out in the flattened grass which shifted violently to the powerful downdraft of the copter's rotors. Just as its rails touched the grass, the helicopter suddenly lifted and swung away in a wide arch, circling back around toward the mountain's western slopes.

Cameron heard the sound of it, vaguely. Although it had been directly above him for a minute or so, thunderously, his senses barely recognized it to be a helicopter. Now the sound was gone. He struggled to lift his head to see where it had gone, but could not see above the tall, waving shore grass. He listened for the sound of the helicopter, but he could not hear it. He dropped his head back into the grass.

*I'll listen to the sound of the wind chiming instead*, he thought, as he had many times.

But as he lay there he realized he could hear nothing; nothing except a ringing tone in his ears.

*No chimes?* Cameron thought, disappointedly.

He lifted his head again, saw the reeds blowing above and all around him, but heard nothing. He dropped his head back down in the grass and saw his blood-stained shirt rippling from a breeze and felt a tousle through his hair, but again heard nothing.

*Where are you now, my Chumash friends?*

Dazed and disappointed, he glared silently into the blue morning sky as he felt the life fading from him. The crimson rays of paralleling lights flickered through the stratosphere.

The four helicopters buzzing around the smoldering power plant had been joined by a fifth. It was a Department of Homeland Security helicopter, flown up from Los Angeles carrying two nuclear engineers from the NRC. The engineers made an initial aerial assessment of the damage and had reported back to the authorities who had stepped-up the evacuation process. The billowing clouds of steam had subsided somewhat; it appeared, somehow, a complete meltdown had been averted. The containment domes remain apparently intact, doing the job they had been designed to accomplish; keeping the bulk of the gamma rays within. The highly-sensitive, hand-held Geiger counters at their feet in the cockpit bell, barely crackled. What radiation had been released seemed to have been harmlessly dispersed, and diluted, by the wind.

Back on the windswept knoll, the rogue helicopter returned, setting down, flattening the tall shore grass near Cameron. Strapped to its landing rail now was a radiation victim carrier, its clear oblong bell glistening in the morning sunlight.

As the helicopter set down, Mobile One flew up from the end of the dirt road and slid to a long stop in the grass. Out popped Grace running in stride, as if still with the momentum of the Jeep. She cut a direct path across the rotor-blown grass toward Cameron, who she now saw lying in the flattened grass, and upon reaching him, she slid to her knees and cradled him in her arms.

Cameron seemed lifeless. Looking down at him, glancing into his eyes, she hoped to see that familiar twinkle, but there was none; only vacant stares from glazed-over eyes.

Nor could Cameron see her, but only brightness of the morning sky, which blinded him.

"You can't die," she cried. "You won't die. I won't let you!"

Grace began crying; tears mingled with feelings of depression and love.

As Cameron lay limp in her arms, she felt helpless. He was still alive but breathing placidly. The radiation burns on his face and arms, which had turned a brighter red, testified to the fact he had been exposed to radiation; and his blood-soaked shirt made it known he had been wounded somehow. He had been through hell, Grace knew, and it had taken a toll.

Fading in and out of consciousness, Cameron scarcely knew where he was, what had happened, let alone that Grace was with him now. Although her arms were wrapped completely around him, he was completely oblivious of her presence.

Grace began rocking him back and forth nervously, pleading for him to stay awake. "Please stay awake, Cameron. You must stay awake." Then she looked skyward, remembering her prayer. "Please God, please."

As she continued to rock, she continued rambling, "I'll be with you always. I'll stay at your side. I'll never leave you…"

*Come back to me.*

From beyond the Plant, the sun shone brightly on the tall coastal mountaintop where the Sniper had been. The place where he had laid down killing many now rippled in blowing grass. Below, the waves crashed on the beach and the wind blew swirls of mist off their crests. Sweeping up over the cliff's edge, the wind blew Grace's long amber hair flattening it against her face, making it trail in long wispy curls behind her. She reached up and pulled it away from her face, then placed her arms back around Cameron, stroking her hand gently across his face and down his arm.

For Cameron, the wind came like a revitalizing breath. He felt himself in a caressing embrace, as if the reeds had wrapped around him like the arms of a loving mother, comforting him, taking him to another time, another dimension, and he thought, for a moment, he could faintly hear the reeds rattling again. *They're chiming*, he thought. He opened his eyes to the sound of it, and smiled. Then, as suddenly as the sound had come, it left, inland, blowing up the steep face of the coastal mountains and shouting through the dark sycamore canyons beyond.

The End

Lightning Source UK Ltd.
Milton Keynes UK
UKHW031241111120
373211UK00003B/428